D⸏⸏⸏⸏⸏⸏ ⸏⸏⸏ Eyes romance
⸏⸏⸏ning in June 2000

DAUGHTER OF IRELAND
by Sonja Massie

Jove titles by Lisa Hendrix

TO MARRY AN IRISH ROGUE
RAZZLE DAZZLE

To Marry
An Irish Rogue

Lisa Hendrix

JOVE BOOKS, NEW YORK

This is a work of fiction. Names, characters, places, and incidents are either the product of the author's imagination or are used fictitiously, and any resemblance to actual persons, living or dead, business establishments, events, or locales is entirely coincidental.

TO MARRY AN IRISH ROGUE

A Jove Book / published by arrangement with
the author

PRINTING HISTORY
Jove edition / April 2000

All rights reserved.
Copyright © 2000 by Lisa Hendrix.
Portions of *The Midnight Court* by Brian Merriman,
English translation by J. Noel Fahey, from *Cuirt an Mheadhon Oidhche—
The Midnight Court* Website, © 1998 by J. Noel Fahey.
Quoted by kind permission of J. Noel Fahey. The material appears at
www.homesteader.com/merriman/welcome.html.
This book may not be reproduced in whole or in part,
by mimeograph or any other means, without permission.
For information address: The Berkley Publishing Group,
a division of Penguin Putnam Inc.,
375 Hudson Street, New York, New York 10014.

The Penguin Putnam Inc. World Wide Web site address is
http://www.penguinputnam.com

ISBN: 0-515-12786-8

A JOVE BOOK®
Jove Books are published by The Berkley Publishing Group,
a division of Penguin Putnam Inc.,
375 Hudson Street, New York, New York 10014.
JOVE and the "J" design
are trademarks belonging to Penguin Putnam Inc.

PRINTED IN THE UNITED STATES OF AMERICA

10 9 8 7 6 5 4 3 2 1

To Sheila,

friend, cheerleader, and Queen of Soy.

Thanks for the love, the support,
and the occasional use of your brain
when mine isn't functioning well.

and

To J. Noei Fahey,

whose delightful, bawdy, online translation of
The Midnight Court
inspired and delighted me.

Go raibh maith agat.

One

The door to the pub blew open on a gust of wind, admitting the smell of country rain and peat smoke along with a damp and disheveled young woman. Her face was pinched and flushed with anger, and as she slammed the door shut, flipped back the hood of her Mackintosh, and started ripping open the buttons, conversation in the pub skittered to a stop.

"Looks to be a storm," said an old woman to no one in particular and everyone in general. "Bad day, is it, Aileen?"

"More like a bad decade," said Aileen, fluffing out a boyish mop of carroty curls. She looked to the woman wiping down the high, age-blackened bar. "A pint, if you please, Mary."

"Something with Tommy, don't you suppose?" A dozen heads nodded in agreement, and a series of murmured conversations, rife with speculation, began around the room while Aileen hung her coat on a hook and crossed to get her stout.

Tara O'Connell sat in a quiet corner of the pub, unnoticed, her reporter's ear taking in everything automatically.

It was Ladies' Night at the Bishop's Nose, the best pub in Kilbooly and the only establishment for miles around to

offer such a modern institution as Ladies' Night. That it did
was thanks to Mary Donnelly nagging her husband about it
for nearly five years, her being a bit of a feminist. Tara had
learned all that and more from the woman who ran the tiny
hotel just up the road, all for simply asking where she could
have a pint after dinner.

But the Bishop's Nose sounded like the sort of place Tara
wanted, and so she had come. Still, she hadn't expected to
find the pub filled almost to bursting with women, with only
a trio of men nursing pint jars and looking put-upon at the
bar.

Aileen squeezed in at the big table that occupied the center of the room, where half a dozen women had shifted their
chairs to make space for her. The sense of anticipation was
palpable. There was a story coming.

Not that they'd hear it too soon. Timing is all in telling a
good story, and Aileen obviously knew that basic rule.

Tara finished her Guinness and signaled Mary Donnelly
for another while Aileen exchanged greetings with the other
ladies and pouted a bit over her glass. Conversation, thick
with west country accents and occasional phrases of Irish
mixed in, drifted from the weather to the new teacher up at
the primary school to the awful price of flour these days.

Finally, someone, probably by way of urging Aileen on,
mentioned a cousin's wedding in Galway City and how
they'd brought in pink roses from the south of France.

"Father Breen's allergic to roses," said Aileen flatly. "But
it's no matter. There'll be no call for pink roses in Kilbooly
any time soon."

A muffled "Aahh," went around the room.

"So, Tommy's still not asked you?"

"Of course he hasn't. The thick-headed bastard." Aileen
blushed and glanced across the table to a dark-haired
woman. "No disrespect meant to you, Peg. You raised a fine
son, except on this one point."

"None taken," said Peg. "I've been hoping he'd finally break down. I want his room for my sewing." She sighed. "I don't know what's wrong with him."

"He's as allergic to marriage as the good father is to roses," said Mary from behind the bar. "That's what's wrong with him."

Laughter rippled around the pub. Even Aileen smiled as she stared down at her beer.

"Well, I asked him," she said.

Tara was listening, and she barely caught Aileen's words. It was several seconds before they registered on the other women at the table. The chuckling faded.

"What was that?" asked Peg.

"I said, I asked him. I'm twenty-nine years old and I'm tired of waiting. I asked Tommy to marry me."

"You bold thing."

"Good girl."

Aileen waved off the congratulations. "A lot of good it did. He said no."

"The eejit," muttered Peg.

Drawn in by the unfolding drama and by empathy born of recent experience, Tara waited with the others while Aileen took a long, lubricating quaff of her stout.

"Oh, he was very nice about it," Aileen said at last. "Apologetic, and all. 'This isn't the right time,' he said. He doesn't make enough money, and neither do I, he said, and we don't want to wind up on the dole. We couldn't have a house of our own for a long while yet—"

"We've the old cottage. You could make do," said Peg.

"And don't I know it?" said Aileen. "It's all excuses anyway, but what it comes to is, he's not ready to marry. So I pushed him. I put my foot down. Marry me, I said, or I'm off to find a better job and a more willing man."

"You wouldn't," said a concerned woman from one of the other tables.

Aileen barely paused. " 'Why do we need to marry at all?' he asks then, smooth as honey. 'Why can't we just go on like we have been?' And all the while, he's kissing on me, trying to distract me, like. And then it slips out. 'The Brian seems to manage fine without getting married,' he says. 'Why can't you just be happy to be with me, like the Brian's women are with him?' "

Aileen's glass hit the oak table with an angry thunk.

"The Brian's women," she repeated with a sneer of disgust. "As though I'm anything like those Dublin girls."

Mutters of condemnation for Tommy, the Brian, and the lax morals of girls from the city rose up around the pub. The men at the bar huddled together more closely, finding safety in numbers.

Tara was barely aware of the uproar, her mind was racing so far ahead. *The Brian.*

The Brian was none other than Brian Patrick Seámus Hanrahan, the golden boy of Kilbooly and heir apparent to the Hanrahan merchant fortune. He was as close to a jet-setting playboy as the village was ever likely to produce. And he was the reason Tara was sitting in a pub in the wilds of County Clare on a rainy Tuesday night.

She'd spent the last month in her producer's office, begging and bartering for a busman's holiday to have time for the story she'd wanted to do for ages, a story on Brian Hanrahan. She'd finally pointed out that she'd been a regular little RTÉ soldier for nearly five years, never taking a single sick day, much less a proper holiday, and she'd stated flat out that she wanted this as her reward. Besides, she'd argued, a piece on the Brian would be just the cure for too many stories on stalled peace talks and squabbles over the Euro. If he really was going to make a run for the *Dáil*, as rumor had it in Dublin, people deserved to know what sort of man he really was.

And Tara was just the one to show them.

She'd finally made her case and gotten her holiday—three weeks—and her assignment, and now here were these lovely women, just handing her the first bits of her story.

That's why she'd come to Kilbooly in the first place, of course; no one knew a man's character better than the people in his home village did. But she'd hardly expected to get so much so quickly. Tara quietly leaned over and pulled a pen and a slim notebook out of the weathered leather bag that contained her life.

Aileen raked her hair out of her eyes. "All I know is, I'm tired of the men of this village thinking that Brian Hanrahan is the be all and end all of masculine behavior."

"Here, now. Don't go running off about the Brian," called one of the men at the bar. "He's a good lad."

Aileen turned around. "And just when are *you* getting married, Rory Boland?"

Rory reddened and sputtered.

The man next to him guffawed and thumped him on the back. "Are you proposing to Rory, too, then, Aileen?"

"No. Daniel, I'm not." She stared pointedly at the fellow's hand, which still rested on Rory's back. "I wouldn't want to come between you lot."

Laughter erupted as the two men jerked apart.

"Go on with you," said Rory and retreated back to his beer, muttering. "Viciousness. That's what Hugh Donnelly's modern institutions have brought us. Pure female viciousness."

As the laughter faded, one of the women nudged Aileen. "You're wicked, girl."

"I'm out of patience with the lot of them, is what I am," said Aileen. "Can any of you say when the last wedding was in this village?"

"Annie and Peter," said Peg. "Nearly four years, now."

"No, it cannot be so long, can it?" asked a black-haired woman. As she recorded the conversation in her private scrawl, Tara wished she knew more names. She'd have to fill them in later.

"Aye, it is. I made Annie's going-away dress," said Peg. "And it was over two years since the last one before that."

"Don't you think that's bloody odd?" demanded Aileen, eyes flashing. "A village this size, and only two weddings in six years?"

"A lot of the boys have left," said Peg. "Gone to university."

"Or up to Dublin for jobs," said another.

"There are plenty who've stayed," countered Aileen. "And I'm not talking about boys, I'm talking about men, old enough to be married. But none of them are, because they're like that lot—" She gestured over her shoulder toward the men at the bar. "—imagining they're Brian Hanrahan without the money. Other than Peter Jury, I can't think of one man from my class at school who is still in Kilbooly and married. Nor from the class ahead of mine. Can you, Crissy?"

Crissy couldn't, nor could any of the other women. Someone produced a pencil and an old envelope and started writing down the names of every unmarried man over the age of thirty that still lived in the village or the surrounding townlands. They began with the three at the bar. There was much scribbling and shouting and contradicting, along with various jokes at the men's expense. Contributing more names—and more jokes—than anyone was Mary Donnelly, who, as the publican's wife, knew more about the men of Kilbooly than any respectable woman had a right to.

All the while, Tara took her notes and silently chuckled and groaned with the women. She could understand their concern. Three and four years between weddings was too long, even in a village the size of Kilbooly. That lovely stone church on the edge of town should be seeing more regular use.

The longer the list of bachelors grew, the more pointed the jokes became, and the more uncomfortable the trio at the bar looked. Finally, they settled up their bill and slipped out the door, grumbling all the while.

"I do believe we've frightened them off," said Aileen cheerily. "Too much talk of marriage. I hope we haven't cost you business, Mary."

"Only for the night. Rory will hardly start going elsewhere when he rooms right upstairs, now, will he?" Mary picked up the three glasses and dunked them into the sink. "And if he's here, so will the other two be, more's the pity. How many on that list, then?"

There was a moment of counting, then the announcement. "Twenty-one."

"That many? Are you certain?"

"I can count, can't I?"

"And tin whistles to sewing needles there are more we're not thinking of," said Mary.

"'Tis no allergy," said the old woman who'd spoken when Aileen had first come in. "'Tis a disease. And your Tommy's not the only man that has it."

"Hanrahan Disease," said Aileen.

"Well, it will be hard to cure them of it, that's certain," said Crissy. "Look at him. Rich. Handsome as the devil, himself. Traveling all over the place. A new woman on his arm every month. It's no wonder the men want to be like him."

"Well, they never will be, so they might as well marry and get it over with," snapped Aileen. She grinned suddenly. "Imagine Tommy driving a Mercedes."

That brought another laugh. Tara wished she knew Tommy, to be in on the joke.

"I wonder if they will all come 'round once Brian finally marries," said Peg.

"*If* he marries."

"Too bad we can't force him into it."

"I suppose we could hold a protest," said Aileen. "Outside the gate at the big house. We could carry placards demanding marital responsibility among the wealthy."

Mary brought a tray with another round.

"He'd just drive around us," said Crissy, passing a glass to Peg. "What we need is one of those hypnotist fellows, like was on Pat Kenny last Saturday." She waggled her fingers in front of her face and put on a deep, mysterious voice. "At the sound of the bell, you will have an uncanny desire to propose to the nearest woman."

"And I suppose you'd arrange to be there, ringing the bell."

"Thank you, no. I already had my go-round with Brian, if you'll recall," said Crissy. "Before he developed that penchant for city girls."

"He always had a penchant for city girls," said the black-haired woman whose name Tara still hadn't learned. "We were just practice. It's hardly fair. First he broke the hearts of half the girls in Kilbooly, and now he gives the men an excuse to break the hearts of the other half. I think we should load him up with liquor, shanghai him, and ship him off to Amsterdam. Let him wake up married to some nasty old Dutch whore. It'd serve him right."

"Viciousness, pure female viciousness," said Aileen, imitating Rory perfectly.

"He deserves it."

"It'd be better than waiting for the men to smarten up on their own."

"True enough." Aileen raked her hair back again. "The whole mess reminds me of the old days my ma used to talk about, the men waiting 'til they were forty or fifty to marry, and the women having to wait along with them, drying up like old bread. I thought we'd gotten over all that."

"Tommy won't take that long," promised Peg. "I'll boot him out the door, first. Him and his laundry, both."

"I'm not sure I'll have him, then, if all he wants from a wife is to have his washing done," said Aileen.

"Mum always says, 'It's a lonesome wash without a man's shirt in it,' " said Crissy. "Anyway, it'd just be a nudge, like. After all, he loves you, doesn't he?"

"He says he does."

"There, you see?" Crissy swiveled to face Tommy's mother. "Why don't you do it, Peg? Toss him out and see if he doesn't get the sudden urge to propose." Crissy's delight with the idea spread in a broad smile that lit her face. "Maybe we ought to have all the bachelors tossed out on their ears. Ask all the mothers and sisters and landladies that keep them fed and clean to bar the door."

"They'd just board somewhere else and send their shirts out." Aileen sighed. "Tommy, too, probably."

"Oh." Crissy's smile faded then slowly came back. "What if they couldn't?"

"What do you mean, if they couldn't? They can. There are plenty of places, right here in Kilbooly."

"But if no one would have them, then what?"

The women looked at Crissy with blank faces.

"Don't you see?" she said. "A boycott."

There was a moment of silence, and then a roar of laughter.

"There's the ticket."

"What a thought."

"The whole lot of the them?"

"We can't."

"Why not?" demanded Aileen. "Crissy may be on to something here. Cut them off. No laundry, no warm food, no housekeeping, no courting. Not so much as a friendly smile. None of it. If they don't want female company enough to marry, then let them have none at all."

"You're talking foolishness," said Peg, but her brow creased as she considered the idea. "How would we get the whole village to go along?"

"We wouldn't need the whole village, now, would we? Just the women. There's not a woman in Kilbooly who wouldn't go along."

"The men won't stand for it. They'll just go over to Glenmore or Kilmihil to get what they want. Or to Ennis."

"We'll slip the word to those women, too. We all know somebody in the villages around. They'll help us. And if they want to drive to Ennis, let them. They'll soon tire of having to go that far for every little thing."

Excitement spread around the room and ruffled the hairs on the back of Tara's neck.

They were going to do it, she realized. In the space of a minute, this boycott had gone from an idea tossed out on a whim to an accepted plan. More paper and pens appeared, and logistics were calculated.

Suddenly Tara wanted to report this story, as well as the one on Brian. The boycott of the bachelors of Kilbooly would make a terrific sidepiece to the Hanrahan story. It would make a terrific story, period. And she already knew the angle she'd take.

Slowly, Tara realized that she'd made a mistake. In her enthusiasm for the story unfolding around her, she'd abandoned her pretense of disinterest and leaned toward the center table. Now Peg Ahearn was staring at her with suspicion, and one by one, the other women turned to join her.

Outsider. Tara could feel the label as though it were a brand on her forehead. She had to erase the mark, and quickly.

She flipped her notebook shut and took a deep breath.

"Ba ghnáth mé ar siúl le ciumhais na habhann, Ar bháinseach úr is an drúcht go trom."

The corners of Peg's eyes crinkled, almost ready for a smile. *"Cúirt an Mheán Oíche."*

The whole room nodded, the half smile spreading from face to face. They all knew Brian Merriman's epic poem—after all, he'd written it not far away, just over in Feakle.

But they'd know it even if he hadn't been a Clare man. The first few lines of *The Midnight Court,* as it was known in English, were memorized in Irish by generations of schoolchildren. It was the tale of a mythic trial, in which a court of women holds a representative bachelor guilty for the crimes of Irish manhood, namely marrying late in life, and thus leaving the women either sexually unsatisfied or saddled with bastard children from illicit liaisons.

"You're right," said Aileen, "That's just what we are: a midnight court."

Tara rose and stepped toward her. "Pardon me for eavesdropping, but I couldn't help myself. It's a hazard of my work."

Aileen gave her that look, the one Tara was used to. "Do I know you?"

"No. I—"

"You're from RTÉ, aren't you?" asked Crissy, naming Ireland's national television network, *Radio Telefís Éireann.* "That reporter from *Ireland This Week.* Tara something."

"Tara Bríd O'Connell." Tara put her hand out, first to Crissy, then to Aileen and Peg. All three women shook it with a vaguely shocked air as the others oohed a bit and allowed to each other how they'd thought there was something familiar about her.

"What brings you to Kilbooly, Miss O'Connell?" Aileen sounded more than a bit wary.

"Tara, please. I'm doing a story on Brian Hanrahan. I'm to have an interview with him." Not quite true—yet—but it would be soon. "I was just having a quiet drink when I heard you talking about your boycott. Here he is, Ireland's most eligible bachelor and you with your troubles . . ." She let them draw their own conclusions. "As I said, I couldn't help myself. My apologies. Now if you'll excuse—"

"Would you care to join us?" asked Crissy.

Without waiting for a reply, the ladies around the table, crowded as they were, shifted and squeezed and somehow produced enough space to slip in yet another of the heavy oak chairs that furnished the pub. Someone passed over Tara's glass, and she was installed as part of the group. That was one nice thing about being on the television every week—people forgot they didn't really know you. This wasn't the first time that familiarity had worked to Tara's advantage.

"Let me get you a fresh jar," said Mary, whisking away the half-full glass.

"I'd better switch off to orange squash," said Tara.

"Squash it is. Anyone else?" Mary took orders and rolled off toward the bar.

Introductions went all around, so many names that even Tara's excellent memory failed her—not that the beer helped. She wasn't the only one feeling the effects either, from the level of voices and gaiety. The fresh drinks came, Tara's squash a brilliant orange against the darker stouts with their creamy heads of foam.

Glasses were raised. *"Sláinte."*

"Sláinte."

"Did I notice you taking notes?" asked Aileen, when the toast had been drunk.

"You did. I'm sorry. I know it's rude, but it helps me get the sense of a place. The people. The rhythm of the village. It's for what we call 'color.' I toss out most of what I write down, but I never know where I'll find that one scrap that will make the story come to life for the people watching."

"You're not going to put the boycott on the news, are you?"

"It would make a good story, wouldn't it?" Tara took a long, contemplative draw of her drink, as though she hadn't already thought of it. "Provided it works, of course."

"It will work," said Crissy.

"Have we decided to go ahead, then?" asked Peg.

"You want to see Tommy and Aileen married before you get too old to coddle the grandbabies, don't you?" asked Crissy.

Peg nodded. "You know I do."

"Then a boycott is the only thing for it."

"It's craziness," said the black-haired woman, who Tara now knew was called Siobhan. "We can't cut two dozen men off from all creature comforts and expect that they won't come after us."

"Why not?" asked Crissy. "If we do it the right way, they won't notice at first. And by the time they do, we'll have them over a barrel."

"And just what is the right way, Miss Expert?" asked Siobhan.

"Do you remember a few weeks back, Louise was telling us how to train a dog? She said you tell them what you want them to do, and give them a treat when they do it. And you ignore everything else."

"That's not it exactly," said Louise, a sloe-eyed but rather plain woman across the table from Tara. "Sometimes you have to give a tug on the leash."

"Right," said Crissy. "Now listen. Each of you that has a man that won't marry should tell him what you want—Aileen, you already did that tonight. Then if he doesn't do it, you ignore him. You don't give him his treat, so to speak. Then the rest of us will tug on the leash a bit by not giving him any aid or comfort either."

The women considered this for a moment.

"You know, that just might work for the men who have

steady girlfriends," said Mary. "But what about the ones that aren't going around with anyone? Like Rory."

"Include them just for general purposes," said Crissy. "Maybe they'll come around, too, if they get desperate enough."

Mary snorted. "All you'd have to do to make Rory desperate is cut him off from his food."

Laughter rippled around the room. Tara grinned, too. She'd noticed Rory's square build. He looked like an eater.

"There's a point," said Siobhan. "What if we all sort of concentrate on what's important to each one of them?"

"You mean that Rory's fond of his food, while Tommy likes his clothes just so, and so on?" asked Peg.

Siobhan nodded. "They might not notice what we're up to as quickly if each one's catching it a different way."

"I don't know." Crissy looked to Aileen. "Do you think?"

Aileen considered. "That might be a good way to start off, at least. So long as we make it uncomfortable enough in the long run."

"That's what it'll take, you know," said Crissy. "Making them uncomfortable. Being unmarried will have to be clearly more miserable than they *think* marriage is." She blinked. "Did I say that right?"

Siobhan patted her shoulder. "I don't know, but we all understood it."

"So, are we on, then?" asked Aileen.

"I am," said Mary. "I took Rory in because my cousin asked me to, but he wasn't to stay six years. Anything that might make him move on, I'm in."

"I'm in for Tommy," said Peg.

One by one the women agreed, and so the decision, already made, was confirmed with another toast. "To the bachelors of Kilbooly. Soon may they marry."

"Which reminds me," said Mary. "Did any of you hear about the rich old bachelor who sat down next to a pretty young thing and offered her a whiskey and soda. She was af-fronted, but she managed to swallow the insult." The jokes were on again. Tara was able to contribute a good share from the newsroom, and it was a good half hour before the women got back to dealing with their own bachelors.

The first item was to figure out what each man thought was important. Seeing as most of the listed bachelors had a girlfriend or a mother present in the pub, that didn't take long. The women were congratulating themselves about how well the boycott would work when Aileen spoke up

"We've been forgetting something. There's one tree we must take down if the rest of the forest is ever going to fall: Brian Hanrahan."

There was a moment's silence, then a round of dejected nods.

"But how will we ever do it?" asked Crissy. "He's not tied to the village like the others are. Whatever we do to them, he'll barely notice. And if he does, he'll just stay in Dublin more. The man has enough money to buy whatever he wants, if you know what I mean."

"No, he doesn't," countered Peg. "We all talk about Brian being rich, but we're forgetting that most of it's not really his money. Not yet. Excepting his salary and a bit from his mother's side, all the money and property still belong to old Ailís. Imagine how it'd hurt him if *she* cut him off."

"And why would she do that?"

Peg smiled with the cockiness of a person who knew a secret. She motioned the others at the table to come closer. Tara leaned in, too, firming up her place as part of the group.

"I go up to the house, you know, to do the mending and take in her dresses and such. I tell you, she gets smaller every time, just wasting away. I think she's going to just keep going until she vanishes, like a puff of smoke on the morning breeze."

"Get on with it, Peg."

Peg gave Crissy a sour look. "We chat while I work. She gets a bit lonely, you know, sitting up there in the big house and Brian gone so much on business. Anyhow, the one thing she says over and over again is how she wants to see Brian married and with children of his own. She's almost despaired of it. I think if we ask her, she just might join us. And then we'll have him."

Tara almost groaned; the story was so perfect. "Are you really going to boycott Brian Hanrahan?"

"We have no choice," said Aileen. "Him and his playboy ways are what give the other men ideas. If Ailís will help . . ."

"Oh, ladies. I want this story." Tara looked toward the whitewashed plaster ceiling, lost in her own private vision. "Imagine it. The introduction, with all of you explaining why you started this, intercut with file shots of the Brian and all the women he's been seen with over the years. Hidden camera shots of him and the other men being turned away from your shops and not understanding why. The frustration building up. The eventual capitulation. The weddings."

"You wouldn't want to show it until there were weddings, of course," said Crissy. "The tale wouldn't be complete without the weddings."

"She's not going to show it at all," said Aileen.

"And why not? Where's the harm in it, if the men never see it until after a few of them are married? You said yourself that Brian is the key. Once he's married, the rest won't have their excuse."

"By now, it's habit. We'll have to keep at it until they've all given in. You even said so, yourself."

"She's right," said Tara. "You don't want to leave off before you win the battle. A man who refuses to marry is hardly worth having about. I sent one of my own packing last year. More than three years he'd been stringing me along, swearing undying love, but wanting his freedom. Well, he has it. And may he choke on it."

"See?" said Crissy. "She understands."

"I do, completely. But that aside, it truly is a fine story." Tara drummed her fingers on the table. "I can hold it back, you know, until after the boycott is over. All I'd have to do is say that I'm not done yet, that things are still unfolding."

"It might be months," said Aileen. "Tommy's a stubborn man."

"I have the patience," said Tara. "If I have to, I can even come back every few weeks. It's not that rare for a story to take us a year or better."

"No matter how long you wait, the men will still want to round us up for the firing squad when they see themselves as laughingstocks on the telly. Not that I'd mind. They've made fools of us for long enough."

"Wouldn't you, really?" asked Siobhan. "You'll be married to one of the laughingstocks. Several of you will."

"And that's the point of it, isn't it?" said Peg. "They'll be *married* to them."

"And I'm sure we can find some way to help them get over it," said Aileen, eyes twinkling.

The other women tittered at the double meaning, and that set off yet another round of jokes, this one slightly bluer due, perhaps, to Mary's free hand at the spigot. The pub grew warmer and warmer from the press of bodies, of which there seemed to be a steadily increasing number. It appeared word was already spreading among the townswomen. Thirsty, Tara took a deep drink from her glass and discovered that somehow her orange squash had transmogrified back into a Guinness. Well, it was wet, anyway. She took another drink and joined in the laughter.

Siobhan was the one who brought the gaiety to a crashing halt. "I'm less worried about the men looking like fools than about us looking like bitches."

All eyes, suspicious once again, turned to Tara.

"I'd never do that to you," she vowed.

"You say that now," said Aileen. "But what's going to happen when you get back to Dublin?"

"I'll let you see the tape first," Tara found herself saying, in violation of all good news standards. A reporter should never let the subject of the report have final say over whether it was shown. Nonetheless, when she saw the doubt in Aileen's eyes, she went on. "I'll edit the story myself, and we'll have a showing before I give it to my director. If you don't like it, you can burn it."

"You'd do that? Really?"

"Really." She held up her hand as though swearing in court. And she meant it, at least in regard to that particular story. She'd still have all that footage for the story on the Brian, though. And perhaps she could hunt up a few other bits of news while she was out this way. "I'll ask for a woman camera operator, too, so she'll be on your side. What do you say?"

The women looked at each other. One by one, heads began to nod, until the question got 'round to Aileen. She hesitated.

Tara pulled out her final argument, the one that always seemed to work in villages off the beaten track.

"The story will make Kilbooly famous, of course. It might bring some tourist trade. People will want to visit the site of the famous Bachelor Boycott."

"We could stand the business," said Mary thoughtfully. "The saints know there's not much other money coming into town."

There was a murmur of agreement.

"Are we on then?"

"Aye."

"Aye."

Assent followed assent around the room, finally coming back to the center table. Crissy looked to Siobhan.

"Oh, all right," Siobhan said. "So long as we get to see it first."

"It's up to you, then, Aileen."

Aileen looked at her friends, closed her eyes a moment, then nodded. "So long as we get to see it."

"It's unanimous, then," said Crissy. "You have your story, Tara."

"And you have my word." Victorious, Tara raised her glass. "To the Midnight Court."

"To the Midnight Court."

It took some fancy talking to convince her producer to send out a camera crew solely on the basis of Tara's enthusiasm for an unnamed story—she wasn't about to tell him about the boycott and risk invoking his sympathies with the male side. However, Tara was nothing if not a talker, and a slightly lubricated one at that, and so despite the fact that it was well past midnight when she made the call, and she woke Oliver from a sound sleep, she managed. The camera operator with surveillance equipment would be in Kilbooly by midmorning. She went to bed a happy woman.

While she slept, the storm blew itself out, so that the next day dawned soft and misty. Tara lay in bed until after eight, a treat for a woman who was regularly up at five, then enjoyed a leisurely breakfast in the hotel dining room.

She was just sweetening a second cup of tea when a boy stuck his head in.

"Ma told me to say there's a gent waiting for you in the front hall, Miss."

"Thank you."

A gent? That didn't sound good at all. Frowning, Tara abandoned her tea and followed him into the hall out to the lobby.

"Look at her," said a familiar voice from behind her.

Tara turned to find camera operator Finn Kelleher slouching in a wingback chair. He bore deep circles under his eyes, and long hanks of brown hair escaped from the queue he always wore.

He looked Tara up and down like an aggrieved older brother. "All relaxed and well-fed, and me up driving all night with nothing but a bag of Taytos and two Coca-Colas. I better not find out you were ossified last night when you rang up the old man."

"I had barely two glasses." Well, three, but they were glasses, not full pints. "No offense meant, but what are you doing here? I asked Oliver to send Maeve this time."

"She went to hospital with food poisoning last evening. Sick as a dog."

"Shit."

"Doing that, too, no doubt."

"I see driving all night doesn't elevate your sense of humor."

"Telephone for you, Miss O'Connell." The manageress held out a receiver. "It's Aileen McEnright."

"Thank you." Tara turned back to Finn. "Go ahead and get yourself some breakfast while I answer this."

She had the call rung through to a house phone in a corner alcove and waited for a pair of tradesmen to clear the lobby before she picked up. "Aileen? Hello."

"I hear your van came," said Aileen.

There wasn't a wire service on the planet that could match the speed of bush telegraph, thought Tara. "I was just saying hello to my cameraman."

"I thought you were going to have a woman out."

"It turns out she's ill. Finn's a good man, though. Once I explain it all to him, he'll be the soul of silence."

"You're certain?"

"I'd risk my life on it. I've worked with Finn for years,

and he's kept every secret he's ever been told. I know for a fact that he got his hands on Salman Rushdie's home phone number last year, but I've never been able to weasel it out of him."

There was long, hissing silence on the line while Tara waited for Aileen's approval. This might be a village-wide boycott, but it really belonged to Aileen and everyone knew it. If she changed her mind about Tara, that was that.

Fortunately, she didn't. "All right, then. Peg called up to the house this morning. Ailís will see us just after lunch."

"Does she know what you're coming about?"

"Peg only said it has something to do with Brian. If she agrees, we'll tell her about you and your cameraman and ask if she'll talk to you."

That was unexpected. "Thank you."

"Don't. I do mean just talk. You'll have to ask for an interview yourself. I don't know you well enough to be making recommendations for someone else to let you film them." Aileen paused. "Ailís is an odd old bird, though. You may get further than I think."

"Whatever happens, thank you, Aileen. You won't be sorry."

"We'll see about that, won't we?"

Tara sighed as the line went dead. Celebrity didn't go far with Aileen, that was certain. Tara rather liked her for that.

It appeared that the kitchen had decided—correctly—that Finn looked like a hearty eater and had created a fried breakfast twice the size of any Tara had seen to that point. Finn was tucking in with amazing efficiency, and he barely paused when Tara joined him.

"So," he said, rinsing down a bite of black pudding with milky tea. "Just what is this mysterious story of yours?"

Tara glanced around. The farm couple that had been discussing the price of a new cow over rashers of bacon had disappeared, leaving the dining room to Tara, Finn, and the manager's son, now clearing tables. When the lad disappeared with a tray into the back room, Tara extracted a promise of confidentiality from her cameraman, then gave him a brief history of the boycott.

"That's why you wanted Maeve, eh?" said Finn when she had finished. "You thought that being a woman, she'd go along with this."

"Yes, as a matter of fact. And now that I'm stuck with you, I expect you to go along, too."

"This wouldn't have anything to do with good old Joseph not coming through with a ring, now, would it?"

The sound of her ex's name hit Tara in the pit of the stomach, and she answered in reflex. "No. Of course not."

"Of course not," echoed Finn dubiously. "Poor sods. Someone should protect them. They don't stand a chance with you egging the ladies on."

"I'm not egging the women on," said Tara, glaring at Finn. "Any more than you'll be 'protecting' the men, not if you want to keep that pigtail of yours."

"Ahhh." He waved off her threat as though it were a gnat. "This is work, woman. You know I never talk out of school when it comes to work. The Prime Directive of news reporting: don't become part of the story. Just you be remembering it, too."

"I will. I want your word again, now that you know what you won't be telling." She stuck out her hand, and Finn took it in his calloused paw.

"My word. What now, Captain?"

"We'll get your room."

A smile relaxed Finn's face. "A couple of hours of sleep sounds heavenly."

"A couple may be all you have time for. The ladies are going up to visit Brian Hanrahan's grandmother after lunch." She explained how Ailís fit into the women's plans. "We may have to go talk with her later."

"The Brian is one of the men to be boycotted?" Finn asked. He hooted with laughter.

"Hush!" Tara glanced over her shoulder to be sure no one had come in.

"Now I'm certain you have a hand in this."

"I swear, I didn't. These women came up with it all by themselves. I just happened to be there."

"Conveniently enough," said Finn. "Oliver may not know what you're up to with this holiday of yours, but he's never heard you rant when we drive past a Hanrahan factory. I have."

"What I'm up to is an honest portrayal of the Brian. *All* sides of him."

Finn tossed his napkin down by his plate and rose so he had to look down at her. "You just keep telling yourself that, Tara Bríd. I'm off to get me nap."

TWO

While Finn slept and Aileen and Peg pled their case before Ailís Hanrahan, Tara wandered through the village getting a feel for it. She always went walkabout when she came to a new place on business, but the driving rain and the late hour had kept her from it the day before. Now she took advantage of the soft weather and strolled to her heart's content.

The mist had lightened further since breakfast, so that vague shadows now showed at her feet and against the walls as she passed. Here and there, patches of color underlined a window or highlighted a roadside where flowers were beginning to lift their blossoms. Over the ever-present perfume of burning peat, she caught the scent of furze and new grass and an occasional whiff of livestock.

For today, she satisfied herself with window-shopping. Kilbooly's small merchants were the usual odd mix of necessity and luxury found in a village: the grocer and the stationer, the flower shop and the mortician, the mechanic/bicycle shop and the Internet service provider.

That last one caught her off guard, although it shouldn't. Ennis, the county town of Clare, and less than twenty minutes away by car, was the official Information Age Town for all of Ireland. Cables were being laid, electronic cash cards distributed, and computers acquired in an effort to put every citizen online.

But Killbooly? Tara shook her head. Technology truly was everywhere, and that would make a story in itself. Filing it away for future reference, she peered in the window and saw a young man hard at work over a keyboard while the Cranberries buried the hatchet in the background. He glanced up with that blank look of someone lost in cyberspace and went back to his computer without even noticing her.

"There's a bachelor who won't be caught unless they cut his power cable," she muttered to herself.

"Meow."

Tara glanced down. A huge orange tabby cat had appeared from nowhere to sit on the stoop staring at her.

"Meow."

"Glad you agree," Tara said. There was something disconcerting about Puss's green eyes—they were a bit too knowing for comfort. She turned and strolled off.

Out toward the edge of town, in front of a tidy, modern looking house, she spotted a sign for "Margaret Ahearn, Seamstress." So this was where Peg lived.

No wonder the woman wanted her son's room for her sewing. The place was hardly bigger than the smallest cottage; she must be doing her work on the kitchen table. If they'd moved out of their old cottage to live in this, Tara wondered, then just how small was the old place? Perhaps that's why Tommy was unwilling to marry Aileen and move into it.

The cat followed her on up the road, hopping through the tall grass that grew along the hedgerows and stone walls. Appreciating the company, she addressed an occasional comment his way and got back the odd meow.

They were nearly at Tara's goal, a tall ash tree that

marked the corner of the primary school play yard, when she heard the putter of a car coming and turned to spot a blue Mini smoking up the road in her direction. She stepped onto the verge and waited for it to pass, and the tabby began rubbing in and out between her ankles.

But the car didn't pass. Instead it squeaked and huffed to a stop, and Aileen rolled down the driver's window.

"I see you've met Jack," shouted Aileen over the tin can rattle of the motor.

Tara raised an eyebrow. "Who?"

"Jack." Aileen pointed at the cat. "He's the village layabout."

"Whose is he?"

"Nan Laurey claims he's hers, but the truth is, Jack's his own cat. Very independent sort. Good mouser, too, when he wants to be."

Peg leaned over and peered up at Tara from the passenger seat. "Ailís wants to see you and your camera fellow, both. Right away."

"Damn. Finn's asleep. I'll have to—"

"We dropped Crissy at the hotel," said Aileen. "She'll have him awake by now. You'll want a lift back."

Peg opened the door and popped out before Tara had a chance to answer. "Come on, then. Ailís likes people to be prompt. Do you mind sitting in the back? My knees don't bend half as well as my elbow."

"The back is fine. Sorry, Jack, you're on your own to get home." Tara clambered in, Aileen turned the car, and they rattled back down the hill.

A quarter hour later, she and a freshly showered Finn headed out of town in the news van.

Bramble Court, the Hanrahan family seat, sprawled over a low rise on the northeast side of Kilbooly. The hill wasn't the highest about, but it was certainly the prettiest, with its woods and its view westward across the village and the countryside. In good weather, Tara was sure, a person on the top floor of the house would be able to make out a scrap of blue sea in the far distance.

The big gray stone house was a grand manor of the Ascendancy, the old Anglo-Irish aristocracy that had ruled and raped the countryside for so many generations. Tara had done her homework and knew that Mick Hanrahan, Brian's grandfather and founder of the dynasty, had bought the abandoned hulk from the English heirs of the old owners sometime during the forties, as soon as he'd put together enough money to indulge in symbolic acts. Restoration and modernization had had to wait for Brian's father and his even greater success in the late sixties. The family hadn't actually moved up the hill until the year Brian had started school, which partly explained why the village still considered him to be one of their own.

The odd thing was not that the family had bought the big house—several newly rich families had done the same in the first decades of the Republic—but that they continued to live so thoroughly in it when a house in Limerick or Galway City or Dublin would have served them far better. Even Brian clearly considered the place his home. He might have a luxury flat in Dublin and standing reservations in fine hotels all over Europe, but Bramble Court was home, and to Bramble Court and Kilbooly he returned whenever time and business allowed.

Tara and Finn pulled up on the wide gravel carriageway before the house and climbed out of the van. Finn took a last draw on his cigarette, dropped it, and ground the butt under his heel.

A butler in a black suit answered the door and greeted them in a voice so raspy and low that it sent shivers down Tara's spine despite his friendly appearance. He took their coats, then ushered them into what he referred to as the conservatory, a room of high windows and hothouse flowers.

Installed in a high-backed chair at one end was a tiny woman with pure white hair and eyes of such an intense blue that they put Tara in mind of peacock tails. A teacart sat beside her, fully loaded.

She motioned her visitors forward.

"I was just having my tea. Sit down, sit down before the water cools. We'll have proper introductions as I pour. You here, miss, where I can get a sense of you." She patted the arm of the settee to her left, then looked at Finn. "And you, sir, next to her."

She was obviously used to being obeyed, and Tara wasn't about to be the exception. She sat where she was told.

Despite her ninety years or more, Mrs. Hanrahan poured the tea with a steady hand and passed the cups around as Tara introduced herself and Finn. Mrs. Hanrahan smiled as Finn accepted the dainty china cup and saucer in his huge mitts. "I should have had a bigger mug for you, Mr. Kelleher, but Lynch insisted this was the proper thing for television people. According to Aileen McEnright, you were supposed to be a woman."

"Sorry to disappoint," said Finn. He gave her his charmer's grin. "I can put on a skirt, if you like."

Tara kicked his ankle, but Mrs. Hanrahan only chuckled. "That would be a sight. Do I detect a bit of County Mayo in your voice?"

"I'm from Swinford," said Finn.

"Ah, I thought so. My father came from Castlebar."

"Right down the road," said Finn in a way that implied that his family probably knew hers even though several generations had passed. "Tara here is a Kerry girl."

"You don't sound it," said Mrs. Hanrahan to Tara.

"My director made me take lessons to soften my accent before he'd let me on camera," said Tara. "He said it was too thick for anyone east of Killarney to understand me."

"You're from the *Gaeltachte*, then?" Mrs. Hanrahan asked in Irish.

"No, Barraduff." Tara slipped easily into the old language as well. "But my mother was from Ventry, and she spoke Irish at home, so we'd all have it."

Ailís nodded and Tara relaxed, and it was as easy as that. It wasn't the first time her Kerry roots had won the confidence of an older person. The *Gaeltachte*, the protected Irish-speaking parts of the country, might be quaint and backward, but they were also magic, the last traces of old Ireland. Any person who had ties to it, or who could speak more than schoolroom Irish, held part of the magic in his or her hands. At the least, it proved one wasn't some Dublin jackeen, out to swindle the country folk out of their land or their dignity.

A whole pot of tea and a platter full of fancy cakes and biscuits disappeared before Mrs. Hanrahan saw fit to turn the talk back toward the business at hand.

"So," she said, setting aside her cup. "You're out to do a story on my grandson. Haven't there been enough?"

"Apparently not," said Tara. "My producer wants another." Finn snorted, and Tara booted him again. "And then I heard about the boycott, and I knew that would make a lovely story, too."

"So what do you want of me?"

"To sit down and talk on camera about Brian's early days, how he came to be the man he is, how you feel about the company's success, and that sort of thing. Then I'd like to have you tell why you're going along with the women and their boycott."

"Who says I am?"

That caught Tara flat-footed, but Finn said, "Why else would you be bothering with us?"

"Entertainment," said Mrs. Hanrahan. "Not enough new people come to the house these days."

"Have you ever done a television interview?" asked Tara.

"I suspect you know that I haven't, if you've done your research properly. I was Mick's wife, then Thomas's mother, and now Brian's gran. No one ever wanted to talk to me."

"Well I do."

"I'm sure you do." Mrs. Hanrahan nodded and took a sip of her tea. "But I'm not certain I want to talk to you, especially about the boycott. It's going to be an embarrassment to the men. Brian doesn't take kindly to embarrassment. He never has."

"I'm not going to pretend people won't find it amusing," Tara said. "It's a funny story, after all, a whole village full of women setting out to get their bachelors to marry. But I can tell it without mocking anyone. And I won't let the story be shown until the boycott is over, whether it works or not. The men should be able to see the humor in it, once they have some distance."

"That's all well and good, but what guarantee do I have you won't change your mind once you're back in Dublin?"

"Only my word, but I'll make you the same promise I made the other women last night." Tara refused to so much as glance toward Finn as she repeated her radical offer of an advance viewing of the final piece, with rights to refuse to have it shown. Things got very quiet from his end of the settee.

Mrs. Hanrahan assessed Tara with narrowed eyes. "You really want to do this story, don't you, young lady?"

"I do. Both stories."

"Aileen says you're staying at the hotel."

"Yes, ma'am."

"I'll ring you there when I make up my mind."

And the interview was over, just like that. Tara and Finn said their good-byes and retrieved their jackets from the butler, who was standing by the front door as though he knew exactly when they'd be on their way out. They emerged into a single, brilliant ray of sunlight that had poked its way through the clouds.

"What the bloody hell was that about?" demanded Finn when they reached the relative privacy of the van. "You can't give every woman in the village the option of killing your story. What if one of them doesn't like the way she looks on camera?"

"It's your job to make certain that doesn't happen, now, isn't it?" Tara yanked open the passenger door. "There wouldn't be a story at all if I didn't give my word they could see it first. These are their men. Their sons and cousins and nephews and *friends*. They may be willing to put them through the flames of hell to force them to marry, but they won't have outsiders making fools of them for the whole world.

"And it will be the whole world, Finn. Every news agency is going to pick this up, from CNN to the BBC to Reuters."

"If it ever gets on the air at all. I can't believe you've stuck your neck out like that just to get the best of Brian Hanrahan."

"The boycott story has nothing to do with my story on the Brian."

"You actually have yourself convinced of that, don't you?" Finn slammed his door shut and stuck the key in the ignition. The engine roared to life and he shoved the transmission into gear. "When Oliver finds out, he'll have that pretty red hair of yours on his belt."

"Then we won't let him find out, will we?"

"Ach."

And with that articulate comment, they thundered off down the street.

Being stood up was an unfamiliar sensation for Brian Hanrahan, but it had happened tonight.

Fiona, his current lady friend, had called just after six, claiming unexpected houseguests had arrived and vowing she'd make it up to him as soon as they left. Unwilling to attend the theater by himself—he'd only agreed to go to the damned play because the lady's cousin was second lead—and frankly looking forward to the making up, Brian had passed off his tickets to his housekeeper and her husband. Right now, sitting in a front row stall at the Abbey Theater was a largish woman in a serviceable but highly unattractive black dress, alongside an equally large gent in a worn blue suit.

At loose ends, Brian put in some time on the Dunloe project, going over engineers' drawings and cost estimates and making reams of comments and notes until it occurred to him that the stereo had launched into the third repeat of the compact disc.

Brian rose and stretched, rolling his shoulders to loosen the kinks, then plodded out to the stereo to change CDs. That done, he headed toward the kitchen for a bite of leftover roast lamb, but the shrill ring of the telephone made him detour back to the study. He picked up on the fourth ring.

"Mr. Hanrahan? Lynch here."

As though he'd ever mistake those dulcet tones. Brian smiled. "Yes, Lynch, What is it?"

"Your grandmother, sir. She's taken to her bed, and she's asked me to ring you and request that you come home."

"Gran's ill?"

"Apparently, sir, although she won't let me call in the doctor."

"Does she have a fever?" demanded Brian, already ticking off in his head what he needed to do to clear out of Dublin. He walked around his desk and pulled his appointment calendar out of his satchel.

"She won't let me near her with a thermometer. You know how she gets, sir."

"I do. Do you really think I need to come? Perhaps it's only indigestion."

"Perhaps, sir, but she's quite adamant about wanting you home straightaway. And if I may say so, sir, I am concerned. She seems to be . . . resigned, if you know what I mean, sir."

"Hmm." That didn't sound good. Brian flipped his calendar open and quickly scanned the pages for the next few days. "All right. I don't see anything in my schedule that can't wait. Tell Gran I'll be there by morning."

"Yes, sir, and thank you. I'm sure this will put Mrs. Hanrahan's mind at ease, knowing you're on your way."

"I hope so, Lynch. If she shows any sign of deteriorating, call for an ambulance and have her taken straight to hospital, whether she wants it or not."

"Yes, sir, I will. And you travel carefully, sir."

"Thank you, Lynch."

He hung up, then lifted the receiver again and punched in his secretary's home number.

Fifteen minutes later, he'd thrown a few items into a bag, poured the remains of a pot of tea into a vacuum bottle, grabbed his laptop, and was out the door.

"Thank you, Lynch," said Mrs. Hanrahan, grinning across the library at her butler. "It sounded like it went well."

"Mr. Hanrahan is on his way, yes," said Lynch.

"What precisely did he say?"

"That I should call for an ambulance if you deteriorate," said Lynch. He brushed a speck of lint off the draperies that hung behind Mick's old desk, then straightened the pleats. "He's quite concerned about you, madam."

"Good," said Ailís. "He should be. I'm ninety-three years old, and I could depart any minute if I was of a mind to."

"I hope not, madam. However, I am concerned about Mr.

Hanrahan's reaction when he discovers that you're in perfect health. And that I knew it."

"He'll be in a roar, of course, but he'll get past it." She reached for her tea, which sat on the table next to her chair. This time it was in a more practical crockery mug instead of the delicate bone china that her guests had used. As she sipped, a secretive smile turned up the corners of her mouth. "However, I'm thinking this might be the time for you to visit that sister of yours in Wicklow. Stay on opposite sides of the island, so to speak."

"Thank you, madam. I shall leave at first light. Will there be anything else before I retire?"

"No, Lynch. I think you've done more than your share this evening. Good night to you."

The butler excused himself and stepped out of the room carrying the tray upon which the tea had come just a few minutes earlier.

Ailís sat in her chair, surrounded by books and thinking about her grandson. He'd be in a roar all right, and not just because of the state of her health.

Well, let him roar. She was going to have great-grandchildren out of this, one way or another. Speaking of which, she'd better ring up that Miss O'Connell and tell her she could begin on her stories.

Three

Mrs. Hanrahan's call came too late to do anything about it Wednesday evening, but the next morning Tara and Finn had their heads together down in the dining room, quietly plotting strategy over fried potatoes with sausage and mushrooms.

"We should do the interview with the old lady first," said Finn. "A good breeze could blow her away at any instant."

"She said we can't come up for a few days. Something about her butler being gone." Tara paused, her fork halfway to her mouth. "And we can't get the whole Court together until Tuesday. Maybe we should start out with footage of the women at their work."

Finn agreed, and so after breakfast they headed up to the Ahearns'.

"I was thinking you might come by," said Peg simply as she swung the door wide.

"Is this a good time?" asked Tara.

"Aye. The men are at work and I have the kettle on. *Fáilte.* Welcome."

They said yes to tea, of course, as good guests always did, and after several cups and the brown bread and butter necessary to hold them down, Finn set up his equipment in Peg's cheery yellow kitchen. Rather, he set up in the parlor just outside the kitchen, there not being enough space for him and his camera and lights. He shot in through the open door, catching some fine footage of the kitchen table spread with blue and white check cloth that Peg was cutting for a dress. Behind it, Peg with her rosy cheeks and slightly mussed hair was a vision of the harried but loving mother.

As Finn adjusted his lights, Tara asked about the dress and the sewing work in general. Peg spoke proudly of being the best seamstress in Kilbooly and claimed she could be the best in the county if she had a decent place to spread out her work.

"We built this house after the children were grown and all gone but one," she explained to Tara, as the camera started rolling. "I told Frank to make it smaller than the cottage, so that none of the boys would be tempted to come home and sponge.

"Oh, doesn't that sound awful?" she said, blushing. "I do love my children, but we had five great hulking boys, and they were terrible slow in leaving home, if you know what I mean. I got so tired of the washing and the cooking and the muddy boots and all. So when there was just Tommy left, we built this place. The second bedroom was to be my sewing room when he left. But he never has, and so here I am, still cutting my cloth on the kitchen table, just as I always have."

"You mentioned the old cottage is vacant. Perhaps you could use it for your sewing," suggested Tara.

"Aye, I've considered it, but we carried the old Stanley down here, now, didn't we?" Peg looked at the big cast-iron, solid fuel stove that hulked in the corner, spreading its steady warmth through the house. "It's a good old stove, but having it here leaves nothing up at the cottage to keep it warm, and we can't afford to heat both places, can we?"

"What about Tommy moving up there?"

"It's the same problem. He'd have to buy a stove, too, and they're so very dear anymore and him trying to save up something for when he and Aileen marry. Of course, they're going to need a stove anyway, assuming they ever actually make it to the church."

Which comment lead easily into the subject of Tommy's reluctance and the boycott. Tara had only to ask a few questions to keep Peg talking for the rest of the morning.

It came out in the course of the interview that Tommy had a habit of taking Aileen for lunch at Deegan's when she worked Thursday surgery at the clinic, so when they finished with Peg, they headed that way. They parked just down the road, and within minutes, they spotted a brawny fellow sauntering up the road in their direction.

"They're here already," Aileen said to Peg, looking out the front window of the surgery toward the RTÉ van parked in front of the bakery next door. "How did you know they were coming?"

"I just spent the best part of the morning talking to them, didn't I? Now do you remember what you're supposed to do?"

"Aye, I remember. Training a dog."

"And try to give them a bit for the camera."

"Are you sure about this, Peg? I mean, having it all on the television . . ."

"I know. I've been thinking about it for two days, wondering if we weren't a bit foolish the other night. But we did promise. And Tommy's such a one for being the center of attention, he may turn out liking it that he's on the telly. You've seen how he is at the pub when there's a good crowd. Besides, I trust Miss O'Connell. She has kind eyes."

"But—"

"It will be fine, dear. Really it will. You'll see."

Aileen bit her bottom lip. "Oh, all right. Look, Peg, I've got to ring off. The patient is coming out." Aileen hung up and took care of Mrs. Laurey and her blood pressure medicine. By the time she sent the old woman on her way, she could see Tommy coming up the road. She very nearly waved to him, but instead she stuffed her hand into her pocket and retreated back into the office.

Well, now, if she was going to give Miss O'Connell and her camera a show, she'd better head him off outside.

She knocked on the door to the doctor's office. "Mrs. Laurey was the last for this morning, Doctor. I'll be off to lunch now, unless you need me."

"That'll be fine," said the doctor, a youngish man who drove in once a week from Ennis. "Back at one."

She nodded and shut the exam room door, grabbed her coat and purse from the cupboard, and flipped over the placard on the front door so it read "Closed."

Tommy was whistling. She could tell that from the shape of his lips and the bounce in his step. Whistling meant he was in a good mood, and his good moods were so endearing that for one instant, she doubted the brilliance of what she was about to do. Then she remembered his comments about Dublin girls and the Brian and squared her shoulders.

It was for Tommy's good. And her own.

She met him out in the road, steeling herself against the smile that was already crinkling the corners of his eyes.

"Aileen. Hello, lovely girl."

"Good day, Tommy."

He leaned over and started to give her a quick peck on the cheek, but she managed to avoid it by dropping her handbag and ducking to pick it up.

"Sorry," she said. As she straightened, she could see Tara in the van, and beyond her, the glint of light off a camera lens. She moved a bit, so they could get a better view of Tommy. He might not have the polish to look well behind the wheel of a fancy car, but he did have a manly profile that she knew would do well on camera. He'd be happier if he looked nice.

"Are you ready for lunch?" he asked.

"I don't have much of an appetite today."

"Ah. Well, we'll go for a walk, instead."

"No." She took a deep breath. "The fact is, Tommy, I don't much feel like seeing you today."

"Oh. Tomorrow, then," he said blithely. "It's Friday. We'll drive over to Ennis, to the cinema."

"No, Tommy," she said. "Not tomorrow night, either."

"You're angry at me, aren't you? You have that look." He put his hands on his hips and set his lips in a thin, prissy line that she supposed was meant to look like her.

Well, that corked it.

"No, I'm not mad," she said, very sweetly. "I'm just enlightened. I finally figured out that there's not much point in spending time with a man who has no real intention of marrying me."

"But I told you, I—"

"I know what you told me," she said, cutting him off. "I've heard it so many times I have it memorized. The fact is, I asked you to marry me and you said no."

"All I said was, I'm not ready."

"That's right. You're not ready. *Thirteen* years I've been seeing you, Mr. Ahearn, and you're not ready. Well, fine. Don't be ready. But don't expect me to be waiting about for you anymore."

His good mood vanished like a wisp of fog in the sun, and his jaw solidified. "You're going about this wrong, Aileen. I won't be forced."

"I'm not forcing you into anything, Mr. Ahearn. I'm just telling you what *I'm* going to do."

"Aileen . . ."

"Go to lunch, Tommy. Your stomach's rumbling like a

cement truck." She turned smartly and marched off up the street, clutching her bag to her chest.

When she finally had the nerve to glance back, he was stalking away in the opposite direction. She waited until he rounded the bend toward Deegan's, then walked slowly back to the RTÉ van.

"Are you all right?" asked Tara.

"Fine, once he made me angry." As she said it, the anger drained away and her shoulders sagged. "It was hard."

"It may get harder."

"I know. But I've already decided that I'll just keep telling myself it's worth it. 'Patience is the cure for an old illness,' they say. Well, this Hanrahan's Disease is getting pretty old, and it's going to take quite a lot of patience." She nodded to the man with the camera. "Here I am performing for you and your camera and we haven't even met."

"Sorry," said Tara and did quick introductions.

"She says you can keep a secret," said Aileen.

"Especially from my wife," said Finn.

"You're married?"

He nodded. "Ten years."

"So does that make you sympathize with us, or with the men?"

Finn laughed. "A bit of both. But my sympathies have nothing to do with my job. I'm just here to shoot what Tara tells me to."

"Did you shoot me and Tommy?" asked Aileen.

"I did. And just so you won't be surprised later, I should tell you I could hear you, as well." He tapped a monstrosity of electronics that poked out from the front of his camera and looked like it'd been pinched from one of those outer-space movies. "This microphone will pick up a whisper across a rugby field. You and Tommy were as easy to hear as a loud priest in an empty church."

"I had no idea. I shall have to watch what I say, so long as you're about, Mr. Kelleher."

"You needn't worry about me abusing my awesome, god-like powers," Finn said, grinning. "And it's Finn, by the way. Finn the Magnificent, if you insist on being formal."

Aileen blinked, then looked to Tara. "I imagine he's a bit of a pain to work with."

"You're right on that one," said Tara. "So. I was wondering if we could do your interview Saturday morning."

Aileen considered, then nodded. "That'd do as well as any other time, I suppose. Where shall we meet?"

"Your house," said Tara. "I want to show each of you—the women, that is—in your day-to-day lives, but I didn't think the clinic is the place for a camera."

"No. We'd have to tell Doctor, and then the jig would be up." Aileen glanced at her watch. "I'd better be going. I have to scrounge up something to eat before afternoon surgery. I'll see you Saturday."

She started off down the street, away from the nice hot meal she knew was waiting at Deegan's and off to a cold sandwich at home. Suddenly the sight of the peaked roof of Bramble Court off in the distance reminded her.

She turned, but the van had already pulled away, and she wasn't about to chase after it. Ah, well, it made no never mind. Tara would just have to find out for herself that Brian Hanrahan was home.

Tara folded her arms across her chest and stared at Finn as they drove through the village.

"Where to?" asked Finn when they reached the open square that marked the center of town.

"Somewhere for lunch," she said.

"Deegan's? We could get some film of them torturing Tommy."

She shook her head. "Too much risk of being caught. We'll see what we can get of him later."

"Hotel, then?"

She shook her head again.

"Why're you looking at me like that?" he asked.

"You're *not* married, Finn Kelleher."

He laughed. "And I don't intend to be, either. Yet here I am, shackled to a conniving co-worker, in a town full of women hell-bent on marrying off every bachelor in sight."

"And what makes you think they won't find out? What makes you think *I* won't tell them."

"Mutually Assured Destruction. You and I are like the Russians and the Americans—each capable of destroying the other, and so neither willing to take the risk."

"You're not Finn the Magnificent, you're Finn the Incorrigible."

"Perhaps, but don't you appreciate having a stronger threat to hold over my head than chopping off me ponytail?" He waited until the thought sunk in and Tara smiled. "What about lunch?"

"Ugh, no. That breakfast is still sitting on my stomach. Drop me by the grocer and I'll grab a bit of fruit or something and meet you back at the hotel."

Tommy Ahearn walked into the café at five after noon on Thursday, as usual, but without Aileen. Siobhan Deegan nearly dropped the teakettle.

So, the boycott had started. And Mary must be at work, too, because there came Rory Boland in the door right behind Tommy, and Rory never ate anywhere but the pub during the week. Good Lord, there was Daniel Clohessy, too.

Damn. What was she to do with three of them? She couldn't very well refuse to serve them, not with Da in the kitchen and witnesses about.

All she could think was to make them go away on their own. Aye, that was it.

The café was crowded, as it always was at noon, and the three men decided to share a table near the front door. Good. That made them easier to avoid, even when they noticed they hadn't been served and starting trying to get her attention.

But there came a time when she had to pass by to carry a plate to another customer in the front, and as she did, Rory practically stuck his hand in her face.

"We're wasting away here, woman. Haven't you seen me flapping me arms trying to get your attention?"

"Is that what you were doing?" she asked, incredulous. "And here I thought you were trying to teach Dan and Tommy how to fly. I'll be back 'round in a minute, lads. Don't go getting your knickers in a knot."

She took the plate to its owner and then poured tea for three more patrons before she came back to the bachelors. "What would you like?"

"Ham sandwich and chips," said Rory.

"The same," said Tommy.

"Sorry, we just now ran out of ham."

An instant of panic flashed over Rory's face. He did love his food, and his ham most of all. He recovered, though. "Roast beef, then."

She folded her arms. "That, too. Sorry, lads."

"You can't be out of everything."

"Look around. It's jammers in here."

"Well, you brought that fellow stew," said Tommy. "You must have more of that."

People were starting to stare.

"I think we might have another plate or two," Siobhan conceded.

"That'll do fine for me, too," said Rory. "And be quick about it. I've work to be getting back to."

Daniel made it unanimous.

"Lamb stew it is," said Siobhan.

She carried it into the kitchen, where her father was standing over the grill frying up some sole. "What do you need, darlin'?"

"Just some stews, Da. You tend to your fish. I'll do them."

She ladled the wide bowls full and wiped the edges where she slopped a bit.

"I nearly forgot," she said. "Could you check the oven for me? I don't want those scones to burn. "

"Certainly, darlin'."

When her father turned away, she grabbed the salt bowl.

It hurt her pride. It truly did. She and her father had a reputation as good cooks. But this was for Aileen and all the other women Brian and his little admiration society had toyed with. She salted away.

A few minutes later, as she watched the boys downing tea as though it was free beer, she decided it was worth it. All the other patrons were looking at them like they were crazy men, making such a ruckus over perfectly good stew.

Red-faced, Tommy, Daniel, and Rory stood up. Each drew a pair of pound notes out of his pocket and threw it down before they stormed out the door, fussing all the way.

"What the devil is wrong with those lads?" asked a customer.

Siobhan stared at the door with wide-eyed concern. "I really can't imagine, Mrs. Furey. They were having the same thing you did."

They looked at each other and winked. Mrs. Furey had been in the Nose the night before last.

Siobhan slipped the money the men had left into the pocket of her apron, feeling a twinge of guilt that the boys had paid for inedible food, then carried the plates back to the kitchen.

"Is there something wrong with that stew?" her father asked.

"I don't think so." She took a clean spoon from the drawer and tasted a bit from the pot. "No, it's fine. They must have remembered something they had to do. I'll dump this out back."

"It's a bloody waste."

It certainly was, thought Siobhan as she lifted the lid on the bin and scraped two of the plates into the trash. But at least it was a waste in a good cause. She'd drop the money into the poor box on Sunday morning.

Just then she spotted the old orange tomcat that everyone called Jack lolling on a wooden crate beside the rear door to the post office. When he saw her looking his way, he rose and stretched, then stood there, staring at the plates.

Why not? She scraped the salty top layer of stew off the last plate, carried the remains over to the crate, and tipped it out before the cat.

"There you go, boyo. You'll not need a mouse today."

"Meow." He sniffed at her offering in that suspicious way cats have, and his tail went straight up in excitement. He tasted a bit, then settled on his haunches and began eating with all the gusto Tommy and Rory had lacked.

"I'll be sure to pass your compliments to the chef," Siobhan said. As she carried the plates back inside, she shook her head. "There can't have been too much wrong with the stew, Da. The cat liked it."

Brian had let himself in the front door of Bramble Court just before dawn. At that hour, the house was silent as a tomb, a state that had done nothing to ease the concern that had dogged him all the way out the N7 from Dublin. A quick check in on Gran found her propped up on fat down pillows, looking like a favorite but aging china doll in the dim light of a bedside lamp. He stepped into the room far enough to determine she was resting comfortably, then headed off to bed, exhausted but glad he'd come home.

Now, with the sun well past the meridian and his stomach demanding a decent meal, he dressed and went back to her room.

She wasn't there. In fact, it hardly looked as though anything were amiss: the bed was made, the windows thrown wide as usual on a sunny day.

Frowning, Brian headed downstairs to find out what the devil was going on.

"Mr. Brian," said Mrs. McWeeney, his former nanny, now the head housekeeper. "How lovely to see you home."

"Hello, Nan." Brian kissed her on the cheek. "I take it my grandmother is feeling better this morning? Did Lynch carry her down?"

Nan gave him an odd look. "Mr. Lynch isn't here. He left this morning for Wicklow, to visit his sister."

"With Gran ill? I'll have his head."

Her face screwed up a bit tighter. "I don't know what you're talking about, son, but your grandmother is in the garden. Perhaps you'd better speak with her."

Brian opened his mouth and then shut it again when he realized he had nothing pertinent to say. He frowned again. "I believe I will."

He went by way of the dining room, hoping to find a bit of something left over on the way out. He and his stomach were both disappointed.

Gran sat in a wicker chair in the sun, reading. It was a moment before she acknowledged his presence, so Brian had time to look her over closely. To his eye, she didn't look ill at all, but she seldom did. Even when she'd had pneumonia two years ago and the doctors had said she might not make it through the night, she had looked as though she was just a bit tired and a nap would be the cure.

At long last, she slipped a ribbon into the book and laid it on her knee.

"I'm sorry, lad. I wanted to finish that story. At my age a body can't presume she'll be able to do anything later. Come give your old granny a kiss."

He obliged happily. "Hello, Gran." He bent and pressed a kiss to her forehead. Her skin was cool and dry; at least she had no fever.

"How is the company?" she asked.

She always asked him how the company was, just as she'd always asked his father and his grandfather before that, even before it had come into her hands. And from the answers to that simple question, asked for seventy-odd years, she had accumulated nearly as much knowledge as Brian would ever have about Hanrahan Limited, even though she'd only been in the offices she owned three times that he could recall.

And so he told her, summarizing the current state of finances and work in progress, and finishing with, "I was just going over the Dunloe project when Lynch rang last evening. Why is he in Wicklow?"

"His sister lives there."

"That's not what I mean, and you know it. Why would he go off and leave you here, ill, with no one—"

"Oh, hush. We have a house full of servants, and you're here, now, aren't you? I told him to go." Her bony fingers toyed with the satin bookmark. "Besides, I'm not ill."

"But Lynch told me—"

"He told you precisely what I told him to tell you, and then I sent him off so you couldn't shout at the poor man." She looked out across the gardens, her eyes seeing something his could not. "I wanted you home, Brian."

"Damn it, Gran, I cancelled a week's worth of appointments, thinking you might be—" He stumbled to a halt as he realized what he was about to say.

"Dying?" she asked dryly. "And only a week's worth? I thought I was worth more mourning than that."

She was baiting him, and he let her know that he knew it with a wink as he said, "That was only so I could get some riding and fishing in after the wake."

"Pphht." She flapped a hand at him, but grinned.

"So why all the fandango with pretending you were ill?" asked Brian.

"I told you, I wanted you home."

"I come home all the time."

"For a day here and a weekend there. I want a good bit of your time, and I knew you'd tell that secretary of yours to clear out your schedule if you thought I was ill."

Brian's sigh came from a mixture of frustration and relief. She was a cantankerous old thing, was his Gran, but he wouldn't be the one to change her after all these years.

"All right, Gran, I'm your captive audience. However, before you tell me why you want this 'good bit of time,' may I at least have some lunch?"

She smiled and nodded. "I think Cook put aside a sandwich for you. Help me in and we'll talk while you eat."

A few minutes later they were settled at the table in the dining room. Before Brian sat a sandwich, thick with Cook's best roast beef, buttery Kerry cheese, and sliced onions, and next to it a pile of apple salad and some pickled beets.

"I've never seen anything that looked so delicious in my life," he said sincerely, reaching for the pot of horseradish. "Now, what did you call me home for."

"I've been doing a good deal of thinking, sitting here in this big, empty house, and I've come to the conclusion that it's time you marry."

He smiled. So, it was back to this subject again. She brought it up every few months. "Perhaps so, but I'm not ready to get married."

"You're the heir to one of the largest fortunes in Ireland,

and you're thirty-six years old. It's time you stopped galli-vanting around like a buck goat and settled down with a wife and children of your own. I want you to pick out one of those females you seem to enjoy so much and marry her."

He listened with growing amusement until she finished. "I'm afraid I don't enjoy any of 'those females' enough to spend an entire lifetime with her."

"Then find someone new, if you must. I want to see my great-grandchildren before I die. And then there's the com-pany to think of. What if something should happen to you? There'd be no one for me to pass things on to."

"I don't think my sister would appreciate hearing you say that."

"Pphht. Kathleen doesn't care a fig about the company and never has. I'm not even certain where she's at these days."

Brian had trouble keeping track of his anthropologist sis-ter, too, but this time he could report, "I got a letter from her last month. She's doing some sort of research in Burkina Faso."

"Ah, that's right. I don't even know where that is."

"West Africa. They used to call it Upper Volta."

"Ah. Well, it doesn't much matter, now, does it? She's not likely to find a good Irish boy there, and even if she does, I can hardly see her bearing children just to drag them off around the world on her expeditions. You're the one to pro-duce the next generation of Hanrahans, and it's time you got down to it."

"I will, Gran, sooner or later."

"It's later than you think, boyo." She folded her hands on the table and sat staring at him, and there was something about her eyes that made his back stiffen. Finally, she sighed. "This pains me to say, Brian, but if you don't marry soon, I'm going to cut you off."

"What?" Brian dropped his fork and it clattered against the plate.

"I'll cut you off," she repeated. "Unless you get married."

"You can't do that."

"I can, and I will. You may be running the company, Brian, but most of it still belongs to me. Either you'll do as I ask, or I'll start selling off the whole lot a piece at a time and giving the money to the Sisters of Mercy. If all your grandfather's hard work isn't going to pass on to future Hanrahans, then at least I'll see it do some good while I'm still alive."

Stunned, he could only sputter.

"Now, if you can't find a girl in Dublin," she went on, "perhaps you should look 'round the village again. There are lots of fine young women in Kilbooly."

"Aha! You've got someone in mind, I can tell it. This isn't the old days, Gran. You can't make me marry some woman you've picked out."

She looked unperturbed. "You're free as a bird to marry anyone you choose."

"So long as I marry," he growled.

"So long as you marry. You've done a bang-up job running the company since your mother and father died, Brian, so I'll give you some time: I won't start selling off until your birthday."

"My birth— That's only five months away!"

"Nearly six. Your grandfather met and courted and married me in half that time. And you have this whole week with no appointments to adjust to the idea and start sorting through that black book of yours. That leaves you plenty of time to convince the young lady."

"Damn it, Gran." He slammed his hand down on the table so hard that the china danced and rattled. "I'm not some bloody great bull that needs you to tell me when I should mate. For God's sake. You're acting like an old—"

"Watch your tongue, boy," she snapped. "I'm your grand-mother and you'll speak to me with respect." Scolding done, her voice sweetened. "Now, calm yourself. Have some tea. Such temper isn't good for your digestion."

"My digestion be damned." He stood up and threw his napkin down on the table. "If you'll excuse me, Grand-mother. I've suddenly lost my appetite."

His temper carried him through the house, out the front door, and halfway to the village before he realized that last remark had been a lie. He quickly began to regret leaving his sandwich behind.

But the air was clean and the temperature warm, so he walked on down the hill and into town, headed for the Bishop's Nose. Mary Donnelly's roast beef was almost as good as Cook's was.

With his anger fading, he managed to get his mind around what his grandmother had said.

Irritating old woman. The pisser was, she was right. As the only Hanrahan with an interest in the company and the ability to run it, he needed to provide the clan with an heir and a spare. He'd thought of it himself a few times over the past year.

But he just wasn't ready, and there was still plenty of time. He'd have to go back and talk with Gran. There was a reasonable streak below the stubborn one. He'd change her mind.

After he ate.

He was just passing the small supermarket that had re-placed the greengrocer's when a head of hair just the color of his best bay hunter distracted him. The hair rode atop a lovely young woman Brian thought he knew but couldn't quite place, and she was going into the store. Curious, he followed her inside.

She found her way to the fruits and vegetables and started picking through apples. Brian maneuvered to get a better look at her face, but still couldn't put his finger on it. She had to be some village girl, all grown up—and grown up nicely, from the looks of the curves beneath the softly pleated trousers and short jacket.

Damn it, who was she? Brian prided himself on his memory for faces. He was often able to greet a man by name when they'd only met once and years earlier. That he couldn't come up with this lovely creature's name frustrated him no end. When she chose her apple and moved on to the cooler that held the milk, he cut around the end of the canned goods section to get a better view.

"Brian. Good to see you." Mr. Haggerty, the store manager, stopped stocking cans of green beans and put his hand out.

Brian took it and spared a moment to ask after Mrs. Haggerty and the children. It seemed three of the four had the chicken pox just now, and chuckling over the itching and the spots took a few more moments. By the time Brian broke away and made it to the dairy case, his quarry had vanished.

Oh, well. He wasn't going to chase around the store anymore looking for her. Surely they'd bump into each other during the next week. Or he could ask Gran about her—except that it would give Gran ideas, which was exactly what she didn't need more of just now.

He was headed for the door when he spotted the hair at the checkout. Now, there was the ticket. Moving quickly, he grabbed a tin of mints and slipped into line just behind her, cutting off a man with a cola and pack of cigarettes.

The check out girl was Haggerty's oldest daughter, and as she finished with the young woman—without saying her name, blast it—and saw who her next customer was, she burst into a smile.

"I'd heard you were back, Mr. Hanrahan. It's good to see you."

The woman turned and looked up, and he got a good look

at her face. Intelligent green eyes, full, wide mouth, barest sprinkling of freckles over high cheekbones. My God.

Recognition dawned in her face at the same instant it registered in Brian's skull.

It was one of those damned television reporters, that red-headed barracuda from *Ireland This Week*. She didn't belong here. She was out of context. That's why he hadn't been able to recognize her. Damn. As he sought some way out of this predicament, she smiled and stuck her hand out.

"Mr. Hanrahan," she said. "I'm Tara Bríd O'Connell, with RTÉ. I've been hoping to run into you."

Four

Lord, he is handsome in person, Tara reflected as she stood there, staring into Brian Hanrahan's face for the first time. In fact, he was far more handsome than in any tape or photo she'd seen, probably because his features avoided the sort of bland perfection that cameras love. His nose had a bit of a crook and a tiny scar on the bridge, like the remains of a boyhood fistfight. One eyebrow went slightly askew, as though he were chronically doubtful. And his lips were a tad full and feminine for a man's face. Yet it all went together well. *So very well.* She hadn't realized.

But it was the eyes that truly made the man. No camera would ever capture their blue—a slightly turquoise shade that put his grandmother's to shame—any more than a camera could capture the vitality, the sheer sexiness, behind them. A flash of that blue would probably charm the clouds from the sky. No wonder women fell all over themselves from Kilbooly to Paris.

And to think, it was all a front. From what Tara had learned, the Brian used his good looks and easy charm to throw people off guard, then ran right over anyone who got in his way.

Just now, however, charm was clearly the last thing on Brian Hanrahan's mind. The blue had gone positively frigid between lids narrowed with suspicion.

"Run into me for what?" he demanded.

Tara let her hand fall to her side when it became embarrassingly obvious that he wasn't going to shake it, but she kept her smile firmly in place. She could charm, too, when it served her purpose. "For an interview."

"All interviews are arranged through my offices in Dublin." He fished into his trouser pocket for a few coins, threw them on the counter, and stepped past her. "As a reporter, you should already know that, Miss O'Connell."

Tara scooped up her sack and followed him out the door. "Of course I do. But I don't want one of those tinned interviews your PR people arrange."

"I pay them a lot of money to arrange those tinned interviews."

"Really? Well, you should tell them to shift the potted palm to your right once in a while, instead of always having it to the left."

She thought she heard him chuckle, but he never broke stride, and with his longer legs, he was quickly leaving her behind. She had to get his attention.

"They're going to have to do a better job if you expect to sit in the *Dáil*."

He stopped, and now he definitely was laughing. "Where did you hear that one?"

"You know very well the rumor is all over Dublin. However, if it's wrong, I'd be happy to take your statement. My cameraman's at lunch, but I can round him up in half a shake."

"Nice attempt, Miss O'Connell, but that would be an interview. And the answer is still no."

"Why not?"

"Because I am at home. I come here partly to get away from you . . . people." His tone implied "vultures."

She ignored the jab. "That's exactly why I'm here. To most people, you're just a businessman and a playboy, and a bit of a folk hero. Almost a myth. 'The Brian.' But I suspect there's a different side, and I'd like to show it to them." Tara considered crossing her fingers to cancel out the way she was skirting the truth. "And of course, if you *were* thinking about standing for the *Dáil*," she continued, "you'd want to give people a closer look at you, away from business and all those women. Show them the country boy who comes home to visit his old granny."

"*If* I were thinking of it." He folded his arms across his chest, stubbornness in every line of his body.

Tara shrugged. "I'm going to do a story on you, anyway, Mr. Hanrahan. It's going to be a good, solid, accurate story. But it'd be better and more complete with an interview. I'm at the hotel if you change your mind about the potted palms."

She headed up the street toward the hotel, and now she really did cross her fingers, but for luck. She could feel his eyes on her as she walked and tried very hard not to sway her hips. That would just make him think she was trying to get him with sex. Of course, with his reputation, that just might work.

"Well done," he called after her.

She turned and stopped. "Is that a note of sarcasm, Mr. Hanrahan?"

"It's not meant to be. If you ever tire of television news, though, you might consider going into sales. How well can you sit a horse?"

What was he up to? She hedged her answer. "Well enough."

"Do you have suitable clothes with you?"

"I can make do." She'd beg or borrow if she had to.

"Then go riding with me this afternoon, and we'll talk."

"My cameraman is afraid of horses."

"He's not invited." He shook his head. "Don't press your luck, Miss O'Connell. You've only just convinced me that the idea is worth considering. Now you'll have a chance to convince me—alone—whether it's actually worth doing, and whether you're the one to do it. I won't promise you an interview, but we'll at least discuss it while we ride."

Apparently the ride was to be some sort of test. She smiled. She was good at tests. "That's fair enough."

"Three o'clock sharp, then. At my stables."

She nodded and he nodded, and they headed off in their separate directions.

Any sense of impending victory eluded Tara, however. That had been too easy. *Damned cagey bastard.* What did he want?

He had never denied that he planned to stand for the *Dáil*, Tara noticed.

She pulled an apple from her sack, polished it on her sleeve, and took a bite as she contemplated the conundrum that was Brian Hanrahan. A rank taste made her spit the bite on the ground.

She looked. The apple, so perfect and sweet-looking on the outside, had gone rotten at the core.

She wondered if she wasn't looking at the answer to the conundrum.

Even sitting in the Nose with a cup of strong coffee and one of Mary Donnelly's sandwiches, Brian wasn't quite sure why he'd done it.

Tara O'Connell was annoying. She was nosy. She was a reporter, for God's sake, and he loathed reporters. He suspected her promises of a fair and balanced story were just so much blarney.

Yet he had invited her into his stables and his home, and

just when Gran was getting high-handed about marriage and children.

Lunacy, that's what it was.

He'd blame it on a full moon, except it was broad daylight. So it must be that hair of hers.

That or the fact that she was the first reporter to confront him about whether he intended to stand for office. Despite her statement that rumors were flying all over Dublin, she must have her ear pretty close to the ground—he'd only begun to consider it in the past month or two.

Flat denial would never work with Tara O'Connell. She'd just put it in her bloody story and he'd look like an indecisive fool if he announced later. But if he admitted he was considering a move, then decided against, he'd look just as foolish. She might have him against the wall on this one.

On top of that, there was his sense she wasn't strictly interested in his political aspirations. He'd seen her work, and it tended less toward political analysis and more toward championing causes and rabble rousing on behalf of the underclass. She was a bulldog when it came to getting her questions answered, particularly when the answers were embarrassing. More than one career had crumbled in front of the dynamo that was Tara Bríd O'Connell.

So, what, precisely, had put him in her scopes? And why had she been snooping around Kilbooly when he'd been very publicly in Dublin, with no plans to come out to Clare until Lynch's call?

Or had she followed him out from the city and somehow maneuvered him into this meeting?

A few questions asked of Mary Donnelly cleared up that fancy and confirmed what he already suspected: she'd been here two or three days already.

So the plain fact was, he'd followed Tara into the store of his own accord, just as he'd invited her out to ride on his own accord, on a whim born of wanting to see if her hair really was the same shade as his hunter. Idiocy. If there was any harm done, he'd done it to himself. Now he'd have to find a way out of it by himself, as well.

Ah, damn, he hated reporters.

"Watch it!"

The warning saved Rory Boland a finger, just. He yanked his hand out of the way with barely a centimeter to spare as the engine settled onto the block where he'd stupidly rested his hand.

"Jayzus," said Martin, shutting down the hoist.

Rory wiped the sudden sweat off his forehead with his sleeve. "Thanks. I owe you."

"What's wrong with you? You've been a danger to yourself all afternoon."

"I'm bloody starvin', is what's wrong. Me navel is pressin' against me backbone."

"How's that? You have your meals from Mary Donnelly every day, don't you?"

"I'm supposed to." Rory wiped his hands on the grimy green rag that hung from his back pocket. "But this morning she up and told me she won't give me board with my room anymore. I'll have to fend for myself. And then I threw away good money at Deegan's for the saltiest mess of a stew I've ever tasted in me life."

"At *Deegan's*?" asked Martin, incredulous. "I've never had a bite of bad food at Deegan's."

"And neither have I, until today. Nor service so poor from Siobhan." Rory laid out the whole, pathetic story for him.

"So you had no real breakfast and no lunch at all, then?" asked Martin.

"None at all."

"Poor lad." Martin shook his head over the terrible state of affairs. "It's no wonder you can't keep your mind on your work. Here you go. It's time for a break, anyway. Slip out for a bite, why don't you, and get enough to hold you to supper. You'll work better, and we'll both be safer for it."

Rory nodded. "I believe I'll do that."

He took off his overalls, raked his fingers through his hair, and set out for the bakery, the closest food to the repair garage where he worked for Martin Jury.

Being well past noon, the bakery wasn't busy at all, but neither was there much choice left. As Rory stood looking over the nearly empty cases, he felt Crissy Carmody staring at him.

"What is it?" he asked.

"I was just wondering why you're loafing about here in the middle of the afternoon."

"I'm hungry, and why else?" he said, and launched into his woeful story again.

"Oh, my, a great big lad like you with no food all day? It's criminal, that's what it is. Too bad you didn't come by here at lunchtime. We had just taken the pasties out of the oven. You know, the ones with the onions and taties and chopped meat."

Oh, he could practically taste it. Those pasties were his favorite, next to a good plate of ham.

"I'll have one," he said thickly, through the juices already running with the thought of it.

"We sold out," said Crissy.

"Sold out? Then why did you tell me about them, woman? Are you tryin' to torture me?"

"Don't you go jumping all over me," she said, arching her back like a spitting cat. Rory thought he caught a flicker of a smile, but surely not. "All I said was, you should have been here. But you weren't. And now there aren't any more."

"Then give me two of those currant buns." He pointed at the nearest tray on the top shelf.

"Fine," she said. She found a white paper sack and her tongs and reached into the case for the buns. "That'll be one pound even."

"I'll have some butter for them, too," said Rory.

"No butter. We're out." She popped the buns in the sack and folded over the top.

"Surely you can't be out of butter. This is a bakery."

"The delivery didn't come and there's just enough for in the morning," she countered. "I'm not going to ruin tomorrow's baking by giving out the butter today."

"Well, I can't eat them plain."

"Why not?" demanded Crissy.

"They'll be too dry by half."

"Drink some water. It's free for the taking. I imagine Martin even has some in the shop."

"Ah, Crissy, what are you being so mean for?"

"I have work to do in the back, Rory. Do you want the buns or not?"

"I'll have them," he grumbled, digging into his pocket. "Butter or no."

"Fine," she said.

"Fine," he said.

He dropped a pound coin in her open palm, took his sack, and walked out the door.

Behind him, Crissy bit her cheek until he was out of sight, and then her merry laugh rang out over the glass cases like a bell.

This might be even more fun than she thought.

Tara drove up to Bramble Court that afternoon and was pointed toward the stables by a man trimming the hedges out front.

She followed his directions, steering her VW around the north end of the house and down a narrow lane through a grove of ancient oaks that had somehow survived English shipbuilding through the centuries. She'd have been hard-pressed to miss the stables, even without the directions: the long, redbrick building must hold a good twenty stalls, with paddocks and lunging rings and all the other facilities of a serious horse operation nearby.

And there stood Brian Hanrahan in the wide doorway to the barn, in casual riding togs and gently worn brown boots, holding the reins of the most handsome bay hunter Tara had seen in a long while. He was consulting with a second man, who stood bent over, working on the gelding's right rear shoe.

Tara turned off the engine and pushed her door open, and the scent of the stables washed over her, thick with horse and hay and fresh manure. She took a good, deep breath, and felt a corner of her soul relax. As far as she was concerned, the Brian couldn't have picked a better spot to meet.

"Good afternoon, Miss O'Connell," said Brian, "I'll be right with you."

She stood back until they finished with the shoe, and when the second man straightened up, she was surprised to see that it was Tommy Ahearn. Now that was interesting. He moved up one notch in her estimation because of the horses and down one because of his choice of employers.

Brain said something to Tommy that sent him off into the recesses of the stable, and Tara moved forward.

They shook hands this time, a sign of the truce, however tentative, that he'd granted.

"Hello, you beauty," she said to the horse, letting him sniff at her hand. His ears pricked up and he snuffled into her palm and pushed at her shoulder, hunting for treats.

"Sorry, lad. That's just lunch you smell on me." He pushed at her again and blew steam at her cheek, and she laughed as she wiped at the dampness with the back of her hand. "I know. I should have brought you a sugar from the hotel."

"Stop it, you beggar," said Brian, reaching for the cheek-piece on the bridle to tug him away. "He's like a great puppy, always slobbering on people."

"Oh, no, he's brilliant. 'Bold, proud, and hardy.'"

"'Fair breasted, fair of hair, and easy to move,'" he responded, adding the next triad of the ancient litany on the points of a good horse. "You impress me again, Miss O'Connell. Do you know the rest?"

She began circling the gelding as she searched deep in her memory. "Let's see, that's the three points of a man and three of a woman. Ah, I've got it.

"'Of a fox: a fair tail, short ears, with a good trot. Of a hare: a great eye, a dry head, and well running. And of a donkey: a big chin, a flat leg, and a good hoof.'" She ran her hand over the big animal's withers and croup and down his legs as she checked his conformation. "I haven't seen him move yet, but I'd lay ten punt that this fellow has all those points plus a few de Worde never thought of."

Brian nodded, a smile tugging at his lips. "Now, let's see if you actually know one end of the horse from the other, or if this is a clever bluff."

Tara smiled and kept her mouth shut.

Tommy led out another gelding, this one a dapple-gray who stood a half a hand taller than the bay and showed a good deal more fractiousness than Tara liked to deal with in a strange horse. She was relieved when Brian offered her the bay.

Tommy had also brought a helmet, and she took it with a thank you, getting her first close look at Aileen's beau while she was at it. He was a hulking thing, with his square shoulders and his broad, strong hands. For all his brawn, though, he wasn't bad looking, and there was a sweetness in those thickly lashed brown eyes that could make a girl sigh. The horses seemed to trust him, too. That said a lot, in Tara's book. No wonder Aileen had stuck it out for so long.

"His name's Brigadore, miss. Brig for short," he said as she strapped on the helmet. He checked the girth again, then gave her a leg up. "Are your stirrups a bit long?"

"One notch, I think."

Tommy quickly shortened the stirrups, and she checked them again and thanked him.

"All set?" asked Brian from atop the gray, who was dancing sideways across the yard, his ears laid back.

"Perfect. Lead on."

They rode out across the fields that rolled out in back of the stables, letting the horses work out their kinks in a light canter. The bay was a terrific mount from the get-go, anxious to move out but willing to be controlled, and Tara's cheeks soon ached from the grin of delight she wore. Brian had to wrestle the gray a bit, however.

"Is he always such a handful?" Tara asked, after the gray had startled yet again, this time at a bird taking off from a copse.

"He doesn't get ridden enough," Brian said. "He belongs to my sister, Kathleen. She's been out of the country for several years, and I don't get to him like I should. I thought I might as well give him a workout today, though, since you're on Brig."

"This is your horse? Why did you put me up on him?"

"I can trust him. I wasn't sure how good you are," said Brian. He shot a glance her way. "I'm still not, actually."

"Then why don't you find out? Can your Brig handle that gate over there?"

"He can if you can. I won't hear from RTÉ's solicitors if you break your neck, will I?"

"Not likely." She tapped the bay with her heels and turned him loose. "Let's go, boy.

They thundered across the meadow, the heavy hunter's hooves pounding in a rhythm to match Tara's heart. Brian and the gray caught up, and for a moment it turned into a race.

The stone wall loomed ahead. She slowed Brig a bit, letting Brian take a clear lead. He guided them toward the gate, not much over three feet high, and he and the gray took it neatly.

Adrenaline surged through Tara's blood as her mount followed. It had been a long time.

"I'm with you, boy," she murmured as she leaned into position and reached forward to give him his head.

The horse knew his business, so it was simply a matter of following old reflexes and they were over. Brian had pulled up well away and was watching as they landed.

"Looks like it wasn't a bluff," he said. "You could have made the wall itself, with air under you."

"Da would thrash me if I boggled one that low," she said, purposely letting her heavy Kerry brogue slip through.

That one quizzical eyebrow lifted even higher. "And your Da would be?"

"Christopher O'Connell of Barraduff, County Kerry."

"You're one of Kit O'Connell's brats?" Brian leaned back, shaking his head. "Your father is quite possibly the best trainer in the country, and you said you can ride 'well enough.' "

"Ah, but I'm not competition material, and in my family, if you're not fit for the Olympics, you're only just fair. Plus I haven't ridden much since I left for university."

"All right," said Brian. "I'll chalk up your false modesty to high standards rather than a deliberate effort to mislead me."

"I'd hardly waste my effort misleading you about horses. It's too easy to be found out. So, did I pass your test?"

He looked at her, his eyes shifting back and forth between her and the horse, and an odd sensation crawled over her skin.

"Both of them, I think," he said cryptically, and turned his horse down along the hedge. "Brig was trained by your father, you know."

She thumped the bay on the neck. "I should have guessed by the way he handles. If I'd had a mount like him growing up, I might have changed my mind about competing."

"Surely you must have had your own horse."

"You might think so, but I rode whatever was at hand. My father wasn't so well known then, and with seven of us about, money was tight. He only gave us our own horse when we showed we were ready to commit our lives to it, the way he had. I was always running about with a little tape recorder, interviewing my brothers after they won some event or other. Da knew early on the horse trade wasn't for me."

"Was he disappointed?"

"If he was, he never showed it. I wasn't the only O'Connell who didn't catch the fever. My middle brother, Albert, is off in Canada, being a doorman at the Toronto Hilton, and Da is just as proud of him as any of the rest of us. I think he had enough children following his footsteps to keep him happy."

They rode for over an hour, touring the Hanrahan estate, taking a few more easy jumps, and talking about horses, farming, the local hunt, the weather—anything but Brian Hanrahan or television interviews.

In fact, some time passed before Tara remembered what she was actually there for. It was the horses that did that to her. She might not be the horsewoman her father wished she were, but riding had always been her favorite way to spend a fine day. And it was a fine day, not perfect, but fairer than most in the west country, with a few clouds drifting high overhead and the sun warm on her cheeks.

They passed through a gate into an old, overgrown boreen. The narrow lane, hemmed in by fuchsias run wild, was barely wide enough for the two horses abreast, and Brian rode so close that his calf brushed Tara's. The casual contact set her nerves jittering like a silly schoolgirl's. Tara passed it off as simply the reaction of a body that hadn't been around men much in the past few months.

They brushed again, and Brian looked over at her in a way that made her think the contact wasn't purely accidental. A flush of warmth crept over her skin.

This was ridiculous.

"I often wonder how they managed to run wagons up and down these old lanes, they're so narrow," she said, trying to get her mind onto another subject. Any other subject.

Brian just looked at her. "Why have you been loitering about Kilbooly all week?"

So, he'd been poking about. Well, if he wanted to catch her off guard, he'd have to do better than bump her leg a few times, jittery nerves or no.

"Not quite all week," she said lightly. "Just since Tuesday late. And Finn—my cameraman—came Wednesday, in case your informants didn't tell you. Although I must say, I'm flattered that you bothered to ask."

"Don't be," said Brian. "That's a long time to hang about, just hoping I'd turn up, especially since I was in Dublin with no plans to come out. Which, I might add, you would have known if you called my office."

"I had background research to do. Plus we're to do some other stories in the area, to use to fill in when the news is slow."

"I didn't think it was ever slow anymore."

"It isn't often," she said. "But we still try to give people a break from the relentlessness of it. An occasional story about a small village and some fellow who paints pictures or makes his own fiddles always gets a good response from people."

"You'll want to talk to my stableman, then," said Brian. "He does exactly that—makes fiddles."

"Tommy?" she asked in surprise.

"He plays them, as well, and—" Brian stopped, and suspicion came back into his eyes. "How did you know his name?"

"I, um—" *Oops.* "I've seen him about, is all. Kilbooly's not that big. It doesn't take long to find out who everyone is. Tommy goes around with the nurse, Aileen McEnright, doesn't he? And his mother takes in sewing, and her name's Peg or some such. And then there's Rory Boland who lives over the pub and works for Martin Jury at the garage. Crissy is the girl at the bakery." She prattled on, disarming him with the names and bits of gossip she'd picked up in her short stay in Kilbooly.

"All right, all right," he said. "You've made your point. It's a small village."

"And a talkative one," she said.

"Mmm. I take it you've been asking about me, too."

"About you and other things."

"And have people been answering?"

"About you or the other things?" she asked.

His eyes narrowed.

"Some of them have and some of them haven't," she said. "And before you ask, no, I won't tell you who is who, although a few have been on camera, so you may find out one day, if I decide to use the tapes."

"You must know, I don't much care for reporters."

"So I've heard."

"Particularly ones who pry about behind my back."

That comes from having too much to hide, thought Tara. Aloud, she reassured him.

"It's simply good reporting. I can't very well tell the nation who you are and where you came from without talking to the people you grew up with and who know you best. You have a reputation for expecting the best from every employee, Mr. Hanrahan. I have the same standard for myself. I do whatever I have to do to get the full story. I should think you'd appreciate that."

"I do. It's being the target of all your thoroughness that I don't I appreciate. If you—What's that?"

A flash of movement at the far end of the lane caught Tara's eye. She peered down the boreen, but could make out only a few branches waving. "A bird? Or a fox."

Brian stared, then shook his head. "Perhaps. Let's go through here." He led her through a gap in the hedgerow and into a freshly plowed field. "It hasn't been planted yet. We can cut across and head back toward the house."

"Oh. All right."

"You sound disappointed."

"I am a bit," she admitted. "This is a treat. I don't always have time to ride out like this when I'm home, what with all the nieces and nephews to coddle and bounce."

"We'll stay out a little longer, then."

"Always the gentleman, eh, Mr. Hanrahan? Even when you don't like the company."

"I don't like the reporter. The horsewoman's fine. Is there anywhere in particular you'd like to go or shall we just wander some more?"

"Actually, I had been hoping we'd go to the top of that hill," said Tara, pointing to a round crest nearby that bore a pile of stones at its bald peak. In most places, it wouldn't be much of a hill, but in this part of Clare, it was the tallest point for several miles. "I always like poking about in ruins."

"Do you? Let's go, then." He turned the gray toward the hill, and Tara followed.

A thin trail led through the wood that circled the lower part of the hill. The path was steep enough to require some attention, but not so much that Tara couldn't appreciate the

sight of the man in front of her. He really did cut quite a figure on a horse, with his square shoulders and his black hair
gleaming darkly in the sunlight that flickered through the
trees. She might as well enjoy the view. Chances were she'd
never have another chance to join him on a ride. If he didn't
like reporters now, by the time she was done he wouldn't
allow one in the same county.

They broke out of the wood and into the breeze that ruffled over the crest of the hill. Brian soon dismounted.

"It's a bit of a scramble through the rocks from here.
We'll leave the horses."

They tied the reins to some furze bushes and hiked up
through a leg-breaking field of boulders and broken stones.
At the top, the breeze turned into a good stiff wind that
smelled of the sea, not so far distant. Brian climbed up on
the wide base of the ancient tower, then turned to give Tara
a hand. Together they clambered up on the few stones still
standing one on the other.

"Your ruins," he said.

"Look at the size of the stones," she said, staring down at
the rubble spread below. "I'd love to know who troubled to
drag them all up here."

"According to the people who trek out from Trinity every
now and again, the site probably started as a ring fort, but
someone in the Middle Ages turned it into a small keep with
a wall. It must not have been much. There are no records to
be found."

"I don't see any sign of excavations."

"There aren't any. Gran won't let anyone dig. She says to
leave it the way it is. I tend to agree with her."

"They might discover something important."

"Or they might not, but the hill would be ruined anyway.
It's not as if they lack places to tear up."

"True enough," said Tara, wondering at a man who could
ruin a town and worry about a hilltop. Of course it was *his*

hilltop, which undoubtedly made all the difference. He would actually have to live with the mess.

She turned a slow circle, surveying the entire vista. The tower, or at least the bit that was left, stood higher than the house by a good deal. Below them, Kilbooly spread out over the shallow green valley of the Creegh like a pastel starfish in a tide pool, its arms made up of white and pink and tan buildings strung out along the river and the roads that crossed at the center of town. On a low rise at the far side of town sat the school. North and west, well beyond the green hills that rolled into the distance, a wide swath of the Atlantic shone silver in the late afternoon sun, looking closer than the five miles she knew it must be. Far to the south, a white line of fog marked what must be the mouth of the Shannon.

"I think a person could spot a ship sailing into the bay at White Strand from here," said Tara. "No one could slip up on you unawares. Neither Viking nor Englishman."

"Nor reporter," said Brian.

She turned and found herself against his chest, with no place to go because of the height. His hands went to her waist, to steady her, then lingered.

She looked up. "Mr. Hanrahan."

"Brian," he said, and kissed her.

It caught her off guard, and like a fool, she kissed him back, opening her mouth to the insistent probing of his tongue. The elevation must have increased, if that was possible, because suddenly all of her air was gone and she felt giddy and light-headed.

Oh, god, it had been too long since she'd been kissed like that. Maybe forever. She closed her eyes in surrender, and when his hands left her waist and started a slow climb up under the edge of her shirt, she not only didn't protest, she moaned and lifted against him.

He slipped his arms around her and gathered her closer.

His kiss deepened briefly, then he moved away from her mouth and blazed a fiery line down her throat and back up to her earlobe, where he paused to nibble another groan from her.

"Do you think he got that?" he whispered.

"Hmm?" asked Tara, still drugged by the lack of oxygen.

"Your cameraman. Do you think he got a clear shot of us up here?"

Reality yanked her back as if she were on a bungee cord. Tara stiffened and tried to pull away. "What are you talking about?"

"Hold still before you kill us both," ordered Brian, keeping his grip on her so she had to stay against his chest. "And stop trying to play innocent. Your cameraman has been zipping up and down roads all afternoon, trying to get a good shot of us riding. That was him you pretended not to see back on the boreen."

"I don't know what you're talking about. There was no one there."

Brian ignored her. "That's why you wanted to come up here, I assume, to give him a nice, clear shot of me. Well, there he is." He turned her in his arms and pointed, and far below Tara could see what might have been the RTÉ van and a figure with a camera. He took her wrist and lifted her hand high. "Wave."

"Oh, Jayzus, Finn." She spun back to Brian. "I didn't put him up to this. I swear."

"Now why don't I believe you?" He set her loose at last, and jumped down off the wall. "Well, I hope he got his shot, although the effect would have been better if you'd been wired for sound. You're quite a moaner."

Tara clutched at her shirt, her skin burning where his hands had wandered so freely. He'd been checking her for microphones, not making love to her. She felt sick.

"I'm sure your producer will be pleased at how far you'll

go to get a story," said Brian. "I'll be watching for us on *Ireland This Week.*"

"You're a bastard, Hanrahan."

"Only when I need to be, Miss O'Connell. It's time to go back."

He walked off and left her to scramble off the tower as best she could.

Five

Underhanded. Conniving. Devious.

Seething, Brian leapt stone to stone down the hill, each step bringing another adjective to mind.

Phony. Deceitful. . . . Reporter. That's what the litany came down to. She was a reporter. Any bloody thing to get her story. She'd even said so.

Well, this time she'd connived herself right out of it. Any inclination he'd had to grant her the damned interview had vanished when he'd realized what she and her cameraman were up to.

At least he had the satisfaction of knowing that tape would never see the light of day, not if she wanted to keep any credibility at all. Given a decent lens, the camera would almost certainly have caught the way she had kissed him back, the way she had moved into his arms and let him touch her.

Her skin . . . An unexpected surge of desire made Brian lose his footing, and he missed his step and hit the ground between stones with a painful lurch. His high boots saved his ankle, but he tore his trousers and scraped the side of his knee.

"Damn it to hell."

Blood oozing down his leg, he cursed his own stupidity in several languages. The horses whinnied at the anger in his voice.

The racket of Tara scrambling down behind him urged him on in spite of the pain. He reached the horses, waited just long enough to make certain she didn't break her damned neck on the rocks, then, feeling spiteful, swung up onto his own horse. That left Tara to contend with the gray, who was none too happy at the change in riders.

"It looks like Ajax is a better judge of character than either of us," he muttered to Brig.

The gray danced sideways, and Tara had to fight to keep her seat and keep the horse's feet under him on the slope. For a heartbeat as they struggled, he thought they were going to fall, and he kicked himself for his pettiness. Then the O'Connell blood showed itself, and she brought the gray under control. Brian breathed easier and led the way downhill.

They rode in silence all the way back to the stable. Tommy met them outside with a quizzical look at the change of mounts, then shrugged.

"There's a gent to see you. From television, I think." Tommy gestured toward the side of the barn, where the RTÉ van sat beside Tara's car.

Next to it stood a lanky man wearing a pigtail and a look of chagrin. Brian swung down, as did Tara, and they handed their reins to Tommy, who led the horses away. Tara stomped past Brian as her co-conspirator stepped forward.

"I'll have your ass for this, Finn."

"I know. It's yours. Later." The fellow held out a thick, professional-format tape to Brian. "I thought you might like to have this."

Surprised, Brian took it. "Thank you, Mr.—"

"Kelleher. Finn Kelleher." He had the sense not to offer a

friendly hand, and he avoided looking at Tara altogether. "Don't be angry at Tara. She told me you didn't want me along, but I had nothing else to do and I thought I could shoot some nice footage of you two out riding to cut into the story. I got a bit more than I bargained for, though. So there you are.

"Not that we could use it, anyway," he added, a bit of mischief lighting his eyes. "Pretty steamy stuff. At any rate, it was my idea, and you can punch me in the jaw, if it'll help the situation any. It won't hurt half as much as what *she's* going to do to me."

Brian couldn't help but chuckle, even though he felt like a fool. "I can well imagine. I'll just settle for burning the tape, however, and leave you to your fate." He turned to Tara. "You have a loyal friend here, Miss O'Connell."

"He just comes about it from the wrong direction," she said, glaring first at Finn, then at Brian. "I told you I didn't do it."

"So you did. And I apologize. On two counts."

She flushed at his meaning, and once again desire caught him off guard and tightened his belly.

But they weren't on the hill now, and she was all reporter. "I don't want your apology. I want the bloody interview."

The reasonable part of Brian cried "No," but it was drowned out by the part of him that admired her persistence and remembered the taste of her lips and wanted some excuse to see her again, even just on business. Besides, he owed her something for the abominable way he'd chosen to make his point—a point that wasn't even valid, as it turned out.

"All right, Miss O'Connell. You have your interview."

A smile of relief flickered over her face, but she tamped it down quickly. "When and where?"

"Early Monday morning, here. At the house, I mean."

"Thank you, sir." She put out her hand, all very businesslike, and Brian took it, even though a rebellious voice urged him to seal the devil's bargain with another kiss. God, where was his mind? She was a reporter.

"If you want to do this early, we'll have to come up Sunday to set up lights and microphones. I'll ring ahead confirm times," she said. "Come on, Finn, before we provide Mr. Hanrahan with some reason to change his mind."

Kelleher hustled to the network van and drove off, while Tara got in her car. Instead of driving off, however, she steered toward Brian, rolled down her window, and handed out the borrowed helmet.

"I've been wondering all morning," she said. "If the first test was whether I could ride, what was the second?"

"Frivolous," said Brian, taking the helmet. "I was being foolish."

She looked down at her lap, like a small girl trying to mind her manners when she didn't want to. "Thank you for the afternoon. It really was grand." She hesitated and looked up and past him toward the hill. "Most of it."

"My pleasure."

His voice came out strangely husky, and Tara's eyes widened in awareness. She blushed again and quickly pulled away, her tires throwing bits of gravel at his feet.

"Certifiable, that's what I am," said Brian to himself as he watched the rear of her car disappear up the lane. He unbuckled his own helmet. "I have no idea what I'm doing."

"It's the hair, sir."

Brian started at the voice. Tommy had come out of the barn leading Brig, now unsaddled. "What was that?"

"I said, did you notice her hair, sir? Miss O'Connell's. It's just the color of old Brig's coat in the sun. I tell you, there's something about red hair on a pretty woman. It steals a man's good sense right away from him." As he held forth on the virtues of red hair, he tied the bay to a stanchion and began brushing him out. "Aileen's is quite a bit lighter and

more carroty-like, but it's the same thing. Terribly distracting. Sometimes I look at it and I forget me own name."

From the mouths of stablemen, thought Brian. He handed
both helmets to Tommy and headed up to the house to put a
plaster on his knee and change his trousers.

"All right," said Finn as he climbed into the VW. He and
Tara had both pulled off the road at a turnout just beyond
Hanrahan's gate, and he'd shut off the van and come over to
her car to take his medicine. "By my calculation, you're either figuring out how to get me fired or planning the burning of my pigtail, with me still attached. Just tell me which
it is, and have it done."

"Neither one's bad enough. I'm thinking up something
entirely new." She smacked the door with her fist. "Damn it.
What were you thinking, Finn?"

"We do it all the time. I didn't think he'd spot me."

"I don't mean trying to film us, although that was stupid
enough when you'd been told not to. But whatever pos-
sessed you to give him that tape?"

"I was just trying to patch things up for you. I could see
from clear down on the road that he was angry as a hornet.
Besides, you're one to talk. You're planning to hand over
tapes to his grandmother and every other female in the
parish."

"Not tapes of me kissing the man."

"Ah." Finn folded his arms across his chest and leaned
back against the opposite door. His voice dropped and took
on exaggerated tones of lechery. "And you *were* kissing
him, weren't you, you naughty girl? And liking it, too, or
I'm not Finn the Wise."

"Finn the Maggot, more like. Thanks to you, he's got me
now. He'll hold that tape over my head, sure as anything."

"He said he'd burn it."

"Are you daft as well as thick? That's better than cash in

the bank for him. He'll hang onto it, for certain, and as soon as he doesn't like the way things are going in the interview, he'll trot it right out and start making demands."

"Maybe," Finn allowed. "But if I hadn't given it to him, you wouldn't have the interview at all."

"You don't know that. He might have accepted your apology without having it."

"And he might not."

"Well you could have held it back until you found out, at least." She hugged herself, suddenly chilled. "God, Finn. What if he sends it to Oliver?"

"Then I'll explain my part in it, and you'll figure out a way to convince the old man that you were being put upon by a masher. Although that might have been a wee bit easier to manage if you'd bothered to slap the man when he put his hand up your shirt."

"Shut your gob," she snapped, cutting him off before he could say anything else rude. Or true. "And get out of my car."

"If it's any consolation, he looked as though he was enjoying it every bit as much as you were."

"Jayzus. You have no idea when to stop, do you? Out. Now." She reached across him and popped the door open, then gave him a shove.

"Ah, come on, Tara, I was just codding you a bit."

"Out." She barely let him get clear before she stomped the gas and roared away from him and his earnest protestations.

Oh, lord, what a mortifying mess. Why on earth hadn't she smacked Brian silly as soon as he grabbed her? Was she that susceptible to a decent kiss?

No, not merely decent. Damned fine. And that, when he was just doing it for the camera. How well could Brian Hanrahan kiss if he were serious about it? She had a sense it

would be awfully easy to find out, and just the thought of
doing so made her toes curl inside her boots.

Enough. She'd made a *hames* of this already without
putting the seduction of Brian Hanrahan on her list of mis-
takes. What she needed was to be figuring out ways to put
the whole morning behind her and regain control of the situation.

What she needed was perspective, and she knew just how
to get it.

Back at the hotel, she ordered a cup of tea brought to her
room and opened the closet to pull out the black laptop case
she'd carried upstairs that first rainy night in Kilbooly.

Settling into the chintz-covered wing chair next to the
window, she plugged in and booted up, then waited impatiently, fingernails tapping the case next to the cursor pad,
until the screen came up. She clicked through hierarchies
until she found the folder marked Trullock, opened it, and
started paging through the documents and photographs
she'd scanned in. They revealed a story she knew well.

Not so long ago, Trullock had been a quiet little village,
the sort of place where the neighbors all knew one another
and came together over births and deaths and weddings and
all the other joys and sorrows of life. It had never been a
wealthy area, despite the little cattle market in the square,
but the people had long enjoyed a reputation as being
friendly and accommodating. The village itself had been the
lovely sort of place that appeared on postcards and in pho-
tographic books, representing the beauty of rural Ireland.

No more.

In the last seven years, that village had disappeared. Pop-
ulation had more than quadrupled. Banks of shoddy row
houses rose like cancers between lovely old cottages that
had stood for generations. An ugly, noisy traffic circle had
replaced the square where cattle had come to market for
centuries. A large chrome-and-concrete supermarket and a

matching do-it-yourself store had driven out the grocer, the butcher, the hardware, and a dozen other small merchants. Fast-food burgers and chicken had invaded the domain of pub grub and local cafes. Crime was up, traffic was up, and noise was up, while common courtesy was down; people seemed to believe that there wasn't much return in being pleasant to people they didn't even know.

And the whole mess was Brian Hanrahan's fault.

Instead of keeping his damnable factories and warehouses in cities big enough to absorb them without noticing, he had rolled into poor little Trullock, built his packaging plant, and rolled back out again, leaving the village to cope with the workers, the traffic, and the general upheaval.

And Trullock wasn't the only town to have suffered at the Brian's hands. In the past few years, a dozen villages had gone down the same road, all in the cause of soft drink factories, chemical storage facilities, pharmaceutical warehouses, or distribution centers.

Now he'd decided to build in little Dunloe. She'd been able to watch the whole process unfold.

With its narrow economic base, the village was exactly the sort of place Hanrahan Ltd. loved. Once the village had been targeted, the Brian and his minions had marched in with promises of jobs and prosperity, along with glowing architectural renderings of what the village would look like in ten years. When objections arose, they'd waved a load of money before the county and town councils. There would be new roads, they purred. New schools, new facilities.

Of course, all this magical prosperity would only appear if the council approved the project as presented, no changes. When it came to his precious project, all that fabled Hanrahan charm vanished and the Brian turned into a hard-nosed bastard. He was very clear on one thing: it was his way or no way.

Tara even suspected that some of the waving money

might be bribes—it was disturbing how quickly much of the early protest had gone silent, although she hadn't been able to prove anything. But bribes or not, councils from Wexford to Donegal had all proved as willing to roll over as the Dublin girls Brian preferred. Not once since he'd taken over the chairmanship of the Hanrahan combine had any council failed to approve a new facility.

And not once had the village come out looking anything at all like those fancy artist's renderings. Oh, the targets of the Brian's industry were financially prosperous, and they looked fine at first. But by the time a few years passed, they were ugly and stripped of everything that made them fit to live in. All those new people that rushed in to work for Hanrahan had jobs and houses, but not one had a place to call home.

Brian Hanrahan used up villages like other men used up handkerchiefs. Left to continue, he'd do more to destroy Ireland's spirit than the British had managed in all those hundreds of years.

So Tara was going to stop him at Dunloe.

She was going to expose the true Brian Hanrahan to the country, ruin his chances at a seat in the *Dáil*, and demand that some brakes be put on him and the sort of unfettered growth he represented. No one had ever seriously challenged him, but she would, and she'd follow through because unlike the male reporters he usually dealt with, she didn't secretly admire his luck with the ladies. And she wasn't going to fall for his phony charm.

Not again, anyway.

She settled back and began rereading the transcript of the interview she'd done with the new curate of Dunloe. By the time Finn worked up the courage to knock on her door to ask if she wanted supper, she was back on her mark and ready to go.

The Brian had better beware.

• • •

Unfortunately, she had other fish to fry as well. After her walkabout the day before, Tara had e-mailed Oliver to ask if he'd like an update from Ennis on the Information Age Town story. He'd answered with a curt, "OF COURSE," all in capitals, as usual, as though he were constantly yelling. No one had bothered to break him of the habit, possibly because he *was* constantly yelling and it seemed natural.

At any rate, he wanted the story, so the next morning armed with names and addresses he had supplied, Tara phoned ahead for some interviews. Fortunately, no one could see her right away, and she had to schedule things for the next week.

With a whole day ahead of them and no clear filming opportunities in Kilbooly, Tara strong-armed Finn into driving to New Moyle, the nearest of the Brian's company towns.

They parked just outside the gate of a Hanrahan storage facility, this one for agricultural chemicals. From here, all that was visible were the warehouse building, banks of stainless steel tanks, and several large silos—tidy enough, considering the nasty stuff stored inside.

For pure toxicity, however, a person would be hard-pressed to beat what sat outside the gates. Tacky commercial culture had been allowed to thrive unchecked and had mushroomed into a thick, tawdry crescent around the plant. No less than five fast-food restaurants sat cheek by jowl with an equal number of bars—not good old-fashioned pubs, but neon-laden disco joints, one with an underdressed young woman hanging about the door, staring pointedly at Finn. In the near distance, several banks of yellow row houses had taken root like so many weeds. Every building appeared to be the shoddiest construction permitted under the law.

"What a god-awful mess," said Tara. "I want footage of this."

"There are only so many ways to shoot a hamburger stand."

"Just do it," she said. "You're always telling people what a fine cameraman you are. Prove it. Capture the crassness of twentieth-century commercialism in a form I can edit down to eight seconds."

He looked at her, then nodded, accepting the challenge. "Just let me analyze a bit."

He analyzed and calculated, then climbed out of the van and walked around to the panel door to retrieve the camera.

"Prepare to be dazzled by crassness."

"I frequently am with you about," she said.

"Ah. Cross your legs, boys. She's aiming low today."

While he filmed, Tara crossed the road and struck up a conversation with the guard at the gate. He was a reticent sort, and Tara was just getting him warmed up when a dark blue Mercedes Benz pulled up.

Tara's stomach slid to her toes as the window powered down, but she dredged up a smile.

"Mr. Hanrahan."

"Miss O'Connell. By any chance are you following me? Again?"

Six

Brian was not a happy man, at least not the rational part of him. He stared at his nemesis through the open window of the car, waiting for her to explain her way out of this one.

"I was about to ask you the same question," she said. "We've been here for over half an hour already, so it's not likely we were following you."

Brian looked to the guard, raising one eyebrow in question.

"Oh, yes, sir. I saw them pull up some time ago. It's been at least a half hour."

Brian grunted. "Once again, a witness saves you, Miss O'Connell. Speaking of which, where *is* your loyal cameraman?"

"Right over there," she indicated a general direction with a tip of the head. Brian looked across the road and straight into the lens of the camera. Kelleher raised his hand and waved, much as Brian had from the hill.

"You're not getting this tape, by the by," said Tara, "And I should inform you that he's using a microphone that can pick up everything you say."

"Thank you for the fair warning. Since you're not shadowing me, may I ask what you are doing here?"

"Getting some background shots. Asking a few questions. The usual things a reporter does when preparing for an interview."

"Fine. However, I must ask you not to talk to my employees without clearance from their supervisors." *Which would never be granted, once the memorandum went out this afternoon,* Brian vowed silently.

"I was just referring her to the plant manager, Mr. Hanrahan," said the guard quickly.

"That won't be necessary now," said Tara. "I'm sure Mr. Hanrahan will arrange a tour, now that he's here."

"You are, are you?" asked Brian. *Presumptuous creature.* He was about to send her packing when the conversation he'd had the previous afternoon with his PR consultant came back to him.

Two words the man had said seemed to apply: Spin Control. Of course, controlling spin would be much simpler if he knew from which direction Miss O'Connell was serving the ball. Another hour or so observing her in close proximity might not be a bad idea. Plus he could have a bit of fun with her.

"It just happens you're right," said Brian. He checked the name on the security man's badge. "Mr. Quinlan, I would like you to get Miss O'Connell and her cameraman some visitors' badges, then phone the Administrator's office to let him know we're coming in."

"Yes, sir. Right away."

"Pull your van into the car park, Miss O'Connell, and we'll get you your tour."

Fifteen minutes later, the three of them shook hands with the plant administrator and started out. Tara was now carrying one of those handheld microphones familiar from most on-scene news reports.

Brian proceeded to deliver the most numbingly dry tour he could manage, explaining each control panel and safety valve in excruciating detail, until Tara's eyes glazed over and her cameraman openly yawned.

"This facility's average score on inspections is 9.89 out of 10." It was hard not to laugh at the outright boredom on their faces. That should disabuse them of any idea that there was something interesting going on in the plant. "Now, let's head outside and you can have a look at those tanks."

"Lovely," said Tara, rolling her eyes at Finn.

The fresh air perked them up a bit, and Brian soon caught Kelleher pointing the camera toward the top of one of the steel tanks as Tara nodded thoughtfully. Brian stepped in behind the cameraman and peered upward.

"What's so fascinating?" he asked.

"Nothing, really," said Tara as Kelleher slowly circled the tank, filming all the while. "Finn thinks he's an artist, and he liked the way that tank reflects the area around the plant. I told him to go ahead and film it. I figured one of us might as well be amused." She looked up at Brian and smiled pleasantly. "You know, you really can be very boring when you want to be."

"Were you bored?" he asked, all innocence. "And here I thought I was giving you the sort of detailed inside information you reporters crave."

"Very amusing. But I'm on to you."

Kelleher finished his perambulation of the tank and returned.

"So, what would you find more interesting than the plant systems?" asked Brian as he led them back through the rows of tanks and into the main building.

"Human factors," she said. "I'm more interested in talking to your workers."

Ah-ha. She *was* on one of her crusades. But what sort? Hanrahan wasn't having any union trouble. Their safety record was excellent, and their environmental record was the best in the industry. What did she want?

"Like that fellow," she said, indicating a man on a cat-walk who was dipping a long sensor rod down into a tank. "What's he doing?"

"He's measuring the—"

"Not your version," she interrupted. "I'd like to ask *him*."

"He'll only repeat a lot of what I've already told you."

"Then I'll ask about where he lives. How he likes working for you. All sorts of things."

He started to repeat his request not to disrupt the men during work hours, but it occurred to him that if she couldn't talk to them now, she'd only track them down after work, probably at one of those hellholes across the road. It was always easier to get a fellow to complain about his job when he had a few pints in him.

"Go ahead. You," he called to the worker. "Come down here when you're through, please."

Tara blinked. "I get to speak with him?"

"Certainly. Why not?"

She didn't answer, which spoke volumes in Brian's mind.

The workman finished up and came down to ground level. "Yes, sir, Mr. Hanrahan? Do you need something?"

"Only your time." Brian asked the man's name, then introduced Mr. Scully to Tara and told him to answer her questions insofar as he felt comfortable.

"Oh, there's a help," she said. "He's hardly going to feel comfortable with you lurking about, now, is he?"

"I won't be lurking about. I drove over here to speak with my administrator, not to play nanny to you and Mr. Kelleher. I'll leave you to your interview."

"You will?"

"Yes."

She glanced to the cameraman, as though she didn't believe it and wanted him to confirm what she'd heard. Kelleher shrugged.

"Well. Thank you," she said. "May I talk to anyone else after I'm done with Mr. Scully, here?"

Her enthusiasm set off more alarm bells, but Brian was in much too deeply now. "I'll speak to the floor supervisor. He'll see you have free access to anyone you like, within the bounds of safety and efficiency, of course. If you need me, I'll be upstairs."

"Thank you," she said again.

He hied off toward the office before he could lose his nerve.

The security station lay along his path, and as he passed, the image on the center video monitor caught his eye. By some good fortune, Tara had positioned herself right in the line of sight of one of the many security cameras.

Brian stood outside the plate glass window, watching her and Mr. Scully laughing in black and white, and then the man's face growing more serious as he began to speak. Brian had seen Tara use that little trick in some of her more notorious interviews: relax her subject with her easy wit, then move in with the serious questions. It had proved to be an effective tactic more than once.

So, just what was she asking? The sound pickup on the security camera could possibly tell him.

Brian's hand was already on the doorknob when he stopped himself. No, he wasn't going to do it. Whatever he might think of Tara O'Connell—and he wasn't certain precisely what that was yet—young Mr. Scully was his employee and deserved a measure of trust.

Ah, but it was tempting.

Brian jammed his hands into his pockets like a boy trying to stop himself from pilfering candy in a store, and went on about his business.

•   •   •

The interviews with the workers were very nearly as boring as the tour with Brian, and Finn pointed that fact out to Tara more than once on the way home.

"There's not a decent thirty seconds in the whole lot," he grumbled.

"Will you just stop," she said. "I had to try, didn't I?"

"I still don't understand what you thought you'd—"

A loud pop interrupted his whining, and the van careened across the road. Tara shrieked as they aimed straight for an oncoming car.

Finn cranked the steering hard over. The van obeyed, then went too far. The wheels caught on the soft dirt at the edge of the road and yanked the van off and into the grassy ditch. They lurched to a stop at a steep angle, with the left side hard up against a hedgerow.

"Shit. Are you all right?" asked Finn, unbuckling his safety belt.

She nodded. "I think so. I've always wondered what a blowout felt like."

"And now you know. Sit tight while I check to see how bad it is."

He checked over his shoulder to see that the camera and equipment were all right, then heaved the door open and crawled out. While he surveyed damage, Tara unbuckled her own seatbelt and gingerly tried moving the arm she'd landed on. It was sore, but not unreasonably so, and she soon managed to climb uphill over Finn's seat and escape, unladylike as the venture was in a short skirt.

A car was backing up the road to them. When it stopped, Tara recognized it as the vehicle they'd almost hit, even though the driver's face had relaxed a bit since the glimpse she'd caught of him barreling at her kneecaps.

"You two all right there?" he called. "Do I need to ring for an ambulance? "

"We're fine, " Tara said. "I'm so sorry. Are you all right?"

"Me knickers are a bit damp," he said, chuckling, "but the rest of me's fine."

Finn went over to second the apology and shake the man's hand. They chatted a moment, then Finn sent him on his way. When he came back to Tara, he reported, "He said that he knows the man at the towing service in that village we just passed through. He'll send him along."

"Can't you just drive it out and we'll change the tire?"

"I don't think so. The ground's pretty boggy. The wheels are in up to the hub."

"One of these farmers has a tractor. I can hear it. We'll have him pull us free."

"I don't think we should," Finn said, shaking his head. "I'm not sure but that the axle's broken, too. We're better off waiting for the truck and someone who knows what they're doing."

"Lovely."

So wait they did. And in country style, it was a bloody long wait. Everyone in a dozen villages around probably knew about the crack-up within five minutes of the accident *and* had opinions on how to get the poor television people out of their predicament—except for the one man who could actually do something about it.

The van was tilted too much to one side to be comfortable to sit in, so after placing the mandatory call to the Irish Motorist Bureau to report the accident, they dug out some tarps from the back and laid them next to the hedgerow. With their coats added, it made a comfortable little nest, and they settled in for the duration.

"I bet he's off fishing," Tara speculated at two o'clock, when yet another attempt at reaching the towing service on her mobile phone had failed. "I should try to raise someone else."

"And then they'll both come and we'll have someone

angry at us," said Finn. He optimistically waved on yet another car that had slowed. "Be patient. He'll be here."

By three-thirty, even Finn was frowning, and Tara had her head in her canvas bag, digging for stray mints to keep them from starvation.

"We could have walked nearly back to Kilbooly by this time," she groused from the depths. "Now will you let me ring someone else?"

"All right. No, wait. There's a car stopping." Finn clambered to his feet.

Tara pulled her head out of her bag, only to want to stick it back in.

Of course. It had to be him.

Tara scrambled to her feet. Bits of leaf and grass stuck all over her skirt and pullover, and she brushed at them quickly.

"Is everyone all right?" asked the Brian.

"We're fine, thank you, Mr. Hanrahan," said Tara. "However, we're having a bit of a problem getting a tow out."

"We were about to call someone else," said Finn.

"I don't think that will be necessary," said Brian.

Tara followed his glance to see a bright yellow tow van headed up the road, trailing a dirty gray plume of smoke.

"About bloody time," she said.

Finn went to meet the driver, who got out and started his own assessment of the situation. He shook his head several times as he went, and Tara's spirits sank.

"It looks like this may take a bit," Brian said, echoing her thoughts. "Let me give you a lift back to Kilbooly while Mr. Kelleher deals with it."

"That's very kind, but I—"

"I think you should go with him, Tara," said Finn, who had come up with the tow driver. "It's late, and it's starting to cool off. There's no need for you to catch a chill. And you don't want to hang about a garage, anyway."

"But what if you have to leave the van?"

"He won't, miss," said the driver. "There's nothing broken I can't fix by tonight."

"And if it turns out there's more wrong, I can find a room for the night. It'll all be on RTÉ's tab anyway. Go on."

She hesitated. All three men stared at her.

"I won't bite," promised Brian.

"Oh, all right," she said, capitulating to logic. "Thank you. Let me get my gear."

Brian waited by his Mercedes while she retrieved a couple of items from the van and collected her coat and bag, then he held the door for her. A moment later they were cruising down the road.

"Thank you," she repeated. "I seem to be saying that a lot today."

"How long were you sitting there?"

"Three, no, three and a half hours."

He shook his head, chuckling. "I wish I had come along sooner. I could have had a tow and a mechanic out from the plant."

"Well, it makes no difference now." Tara toyed with the strap on her bag, feeling awkward and guilty. Here she'd spent most of the morning trying to dig up some dirt on the man, only to have him come along to act the gentleman and rescue her.

They drove in silence for a while, until they came to Gort. Tara spotted a petrol station with a forecourt shop.

"Could you stop, please?"

"Certainly." He slowed and turned in.

Tara made a dash for the loo, then stopped on her way out for a packet of cheese biscuits and two bottles of bitter lemon. When she slid back into the car, Brian frowned.

"I brought one for you, too," said Tara, handing Brian the second bottle. "I hope you don't mind me eating in your car. I'm famished and dry as dust. We were going to have a late lunch in Ennis, but we never made it."

"No, of course I don't mind. I'm sorry. I should have thought to ask. We could have stopped at a decent restaurant. There are several in town."

"Oh, don't worry. This will tide me over until we get back to Kilbooly. The Bishop's Nose serves a fine roast beef sandwich, I hear."

"They do at that." Brian opened his bottle and took a healthy swig, then set it in the cup holder in the console. He swung out onto the main road through the village. "Do you like shellfish, Miss O'Connell?"

"I adore them. Oysters especially."

"Good." He suddenly whipped the car onto a narrow road that backtracked through town.

"Kilbooly's the other way."

"You're not going to be eating at the Nose tonight."

"What are you . . . ?"

He spun the wheel again, taking them onto yet another road, this one with a sign pointing toward the N18 and Galway City.

"North?" she said, a smile slowly spreading as understanding dawned. "Moran's or Paddy Burke's?"

"Moran's. Have you been there?"

"Not in ages. It's my favorite oyster bar in the world." She looked down at her skirt, still showing bits of grass and leaves. "You can't take me to Moran's."

"You need food, and Moran's is closer than the Nose."

"But I look like a vagrant."

He glanced over, and his gaze lingered before it flickered back to the road. "Pretend we've been picnicking at Coole."

"But I—"

"Hush. Think of it. Warm up your taste buds with oysters or perhaps the garlic mussels, then on to some smoked salmon. Or crab with brown bread. Or those prawns of theirs, swimming in cream sauce."

Tara's stomach gurgled so loudly, she was sure he could

hear it. "You win. You're a cruel, cruel man, Brian Hanrahan, taking advantage of a poor starving girl this way."

He grinned. "Ah. So you can say Brian. I was beginning to think it was against your religion. I did ask you to yesterday, after all."

Her cheeks went hot at the recollection, which she'd been trying to avoid all day. She glared at him, but he kept his eyes on the road.

"I didn't think you were serious," she said. "Given the circumstances."

"You might be surprised what I'm serious about, circumstances or not," said Brian. "But for right now, we'll limit it to you having a decent meal."

He slowed the car, then swung north onto the N18, toward Kilcolgan and Moran's Oyster Cottage on the Weir.

Tara sat back and accepted her fate. *Perhaps the crab.*

"Hang on a minute," said Crissy as Aileen walked into the bakery Friday after work. "Just let me finish with Mrs. Fallon, here."

"Are there a dozen of the apple crumb cakes?" asked Mrs. Fallon. "Nellie called to say she's coming from Dublin with her brood tomorrow. My usual six won't even get us through tea."

Crissy checked the shelf. "It looks like we can do it."

Mrs. Fallon nodded, and while Crissy put the crumb cakes into the bag—adding the obligatory thirteenth—Aileen inquired after the grandchildren. A few moments later, Crissy followed a grateful Mrs. F. to the door.

"'Bye, now. Enjoy those grandbabies of yours." She threw the bolt behind her and turned to Aileen. "I'm glad this day's over and done. I've never seen such a rush as we had for lunch."

Aileen scanned the cases. "Looks like you're almost sold out."

"I didn't realize the boycott would be such a boon. Men are coming in that I haven't seen in months."

"That's good. Your mother and father will be pleased when they see how well you and Owen have done while they're on holiday."

"It's worked out well, you know, him coming over from Ennis early to bake, and me staying to close up," said Crissy. "But it's a good thing he's married, isn't it, or I'd have to give my own brother fits. What would you like?"

"I've been gabbing instead of deciding. Let me cogitate a bit more."

"I've a better idea. Come for tea, why don't you? It will just take me a few minutes to close up, and I'd love to have an entire conversation that didn't end with me stuffing something in a sack."

"That sounds lovely," said Aileen. She was feeling at loose ends. Her Friday nights had been Tommy's for years.

"Shall we have orange cream cakes or butter cookies?"

"The cakes, I think."

Crissy fetched a paper box from behind the counter and put several cakes in it. "How are things in—where are you Fridays?"

"Lisseycasey. It was the usual bunions and earaches and gallstones. Sometimes I think I should go to work at the hospital in Ennis. It would be a good deal more interesting."

"But the bedpans," said Crissy, wrinkling her nose. "And I doubt your car would survive all that driving."

"With the better wage, I'd be able to afford a new one. Or newer, at the least. And I could get on full time. It would be nice to have the money."

While they discussed the pros and cons of driving to Ennis every day, Crissy busied herself cleaning the counters, doing the final bit of washing up, and putting up the day's leftover goods. There was one pasty remaining, golden and shiny under its egg wash.

"That reminds me. Rory didn't come in today. I wonder where he ate."

"Deegan's, I'm sure."

"I doubt that. Didn't Siobhan tell you what she did to him and Tommy and Daniel Clohessy?" Crissy told the tale of the salted stew, embellishing until tears of laughter ran down Aileen's cheeks.

"And then she scraped off the salt and fed the stew to the Jack, the cat," Crissy finished.

"Oh, lord. The poor lads. And they actually paid for it, you say?"

"They did. At least we know they aren't stingy along with everything else."

"I already knew that. It's one fault Tommy does not have."

Crissy eyed the plump pasty. "Would you like this for your supper?"

"No, thanks. I ate lamb pie for lunch. You should have it."

"I eat so many of the things, I'm starting to look like a pasty. I hate to throw it out, though." She contemplated for a moment. "I know."

She picked up the cold pasty and carried it over to the back door, where she bumped the screen open with her hip. "Here, kitty, kitty. Come on, Jacko. Where are you, you lazy slug."

A flash of orange around Crissy's feet signaled the cat's appearance.

"It's your lucky day, cat." Crissy broke open the pasty and laid it on the ground. "Have a go."

"I've a feeling Jack is one of the few bachelors who is going to enjoy the boycott," said Aileen

Crissy finished locking up, and they walked down the road to the cottage where Crissy lived with her parents. A kettle was soon steaming on the stove.

They had just sat down with their tea and cakes when Siobhan stuck her head in the back door.

"I suspected you'd be here," she said to Aileen as she came in. "I was thinking that the three of us should go over to the flicks in Ennis."

"Tommy was going to take me there tonight," said Aileen, feeling a bit misty all of a sudden.

"Oh." Siobhan pursed her lips. "Sorry. That was a poor effort at distracting you, wasn't it?"

"But well meant, and thank you," said Aileen. She propped her chin on her hands, moping. "Except for when I was in nurse's training, this will be the first weekend I haven't seen Tommy since we were sixteen."

"Ah, that's hard," said Crissy, reaching over to give her shoulder a squeeze. "Anyway, if Tommy might go to the movies on his own, we shouldn't go. We wouldn't want to run into him. He'd think you were following him."

"He won't be in Ennis," said Siobhan. "Martin said they're having a session at the Nose, after all. Since Tommy can be there."

Aileen sighed again. One of the things she loved best was sitting in a pub somewhere, listening to Tommy play fiddle with the Jury brothers and whoever else showed up.

"Poor thing," said Crissy. "You miss him already, don't you?"

Aileen nodded. "And the worst of it is, they've got a job up at Ballyvaughan tomorrow."

"Martin told me," said Siobhan. "That's a good gig."

"Tommy's so proud he's about to burst, and he's written a new song for them to do. He dedicated it to me, and I haven't even heard it yet." Tears threatened, but Aileen sniffled and brushed them aside. "This is silly. It's a couple of evenings, is all, and if the boycott works like it's supposed to, the next time he plays in Ballyvaughan we can check into the hotel and spend the night properly, as husband and wife."

"And if it doesn't," said Siobhan, eyes twinkling, "you can do it anyway and get a reputation."

"If it doesn't, I won't need to check into a hotel to get a reputation. Getting arrested for public drunkenness will do it just fine. Do you have this week's *Champion*, Crissy? Let's see what pictures are playing."

"Every corporation has its own culture," Tara said, cracking a crab claw. "And that culture is a reflection of the man or woman at the top. I thought your employees might give our viewers a different insight into the real Brian Hanrahan, just by talking about their work and their own lives."

It being a Friday evening and a fine one at that. Willie Moran's thatched cottage was busy, but by arriving so early, Brian and Tara had gotten a prime spot outside in the garden. Their table overlooked the weir and the dozen swans sailing around like Egyptian barges.

Thus far, however, Brian hadn't paid much attention to the swans, or to the sunset that unfolded over the water in shades of gold and pink and pewter. Watching Tara eat had proven much more interesting.

As hungry as she must be, she didn't simply devour her food the way one might expect. She savored it. She toyed with each bite, almost playing with it, and when she'd gotten thoroughly acquainted, she consumed it, her eyes rolling back just a bit in pleasure. His own plate of mussels, as redolent as they were with garlic and Pernod, had gone bland beside the apparent succulence of Tara's half-dozen oysters, lightly steamed and with a simple sprinkling of parsley and a squeeze of lemon. And now that she was demolishing a plate of crab claws with such obvious relish, he wished he hadn't settled for the rich velvet of the smoked wild salmon. It couldn't possibly compare.

She fished the meat out of the claw with a slim fork, dipped it in melted butter, and let it drip in abstract patterns across the empty claw before she slipped it into her mouth with such sensual delight that Brian almost groaned. He had to force his mind back to the topic at hand. *What was it? Oh, yes.*

"Even given that you're right about corporate culture— which I'm not sure you are—what makes you think the 'real' Brian Hanrahan isn't the man who took you through the factory this morning?"

"Because I don't believe anyone's actually that boring."

He grinned. "And if you find out you're wrong?"

"Then that will be my story," she said. She propped her elbows on the checked tablecloth and leaned toward him. "I'll tell the whole world what a dull boy you are, then show today's tape as evidence."

"You'll lose your entire audience, " he said, resisting the impulse to wipe a tiny pearl of butter off her lower lip. "They'll all turn to football."

"Well, you could hardly blame them. 'Bi-directional flow control fail safes.' Bah."

They glanced at each other, then burst out laughing.

"All right. I was deliberately tedious," he admitted. "I have an aversion to being caught unawares, and you've done it twice in two days." She'd done it more often than that— every time she moved, if he wanted to be honest—but he wasn't about to admit such juvenile nonsense aloud.

"Well, I hope you got it all out of your system, because I expect something better on Monday."

"All I can promise is that I will at least try to be more interesting."

"That shouldn't be too difficult," she said, dabbing at her lip with her napkin. "But I'll help. I'll ask some good questions."

When reporters said good questions, they usually meant

tough ones—the kind that exposed or trapped the person they were aimed at. Brian cut a piece of salmon and ate it thoughtfully. With his body reacting to Tara's presence the way it did, he'd almost lost track of the fact that she was poking around for some reason he still hadn't discovered. He needed to stay on his toes.

Yet when she picked up another claw, his reaction was just as visceral. It had been far easier to remember she was a reporter when she'd had that damned microphone jammed in his face this morning.

They finished their dinner about the same time as the last light disappeared from the sky. The swans had long since vanished into the reeds up the weir, their places taken by wisps of fog that wafted in on the night air and came ashore, swirling about them damply.

"It's getting chill, sir. Would you and the lady like to move inside for your sweets?" suggested the waiter as he cleared their plates.

Brian looked to Tara. "Apple tart or the cheesecake?"

She shook her head. "I think I'm full, if you can believe it. We should head back. I want to make certain Finn got the van fixed."

Brian paid the bill and they strolled out to the car, taking a few moments to cross the road and watch the moon on the waves. A tiny breeze riffled the water and stirred Tara's hair, deepest bronze in the dim light from the cottage and the moon. She lifted a hand to push a wayward strand out of her face.

"Oh, lord." She raked at her hair. "Why didn't you tell me I still had leaves?"

"I didn't think you did."

"I can feel one." She poked and tugged at her hair some more. "It's tangled. I can't get it."

"Allow me."

As soon as his fingers touched her hair, he realized he'd

been looking for an excuse to do this for two entire days. He tried hard to focus on untwisting the fine strands from the broken scrap of leaf, but his actions released a faint perfume from her hair and the scent triggered a dozen fresh fantasies.

"Tara?"

She looked up, a bit warily.

"The way I kissed you yesterday," he said, the words coming awkwardly through the press of desire. "I'm sorry."

"You thought you were justified."

"It was unforgivable. Anger is not a valid reason to kiss a woman."

"No," she said.

"I can think of things that are valid reasons, though." He drew a strand of hair through his fingers. "And I find myself faced with several of them right now."

Her eyes closed, and for an instant he thought she was going to move into his arms, but instead she drew a deep breath.

"I'm a reporter, Brian. I'm doing a story on you."

Her quiet words were as effective as a slap. Brian let the strand of hair slide through his fingers and stepped away, where he could extricate himself from his fantasies.

"Of course. It was foolish of me to forget. Or to imagine you would." He retrieved his key chain from his pocket, pointed it in the general direction of the car, and pressed the button. The car chirped and the headlights flared to life. "Let's go back, shall we?"

Stupid, stupid, stupid.

Again.

Tara sat next to Brian, watching the darkened shapes of the countryside roll past the car window and kicking herself.

She shouldn't have let him take her to dinner. Shouldn't have enjoyed herself so much. Shouldn't have let down her guard.

Shouldn't have remembered to be good quite so quickly.

No, that last was her body talking, not her brain, and fortunately reason had managed to drown out that particular noisy voice at the crucial instant.

It was a good thing, too, knowing how she reacted once he did kiss her, forgetting everything else.

All she needed was to ruin her career by getting involved with the subject of a story, and to do it by succumbing to a pass from a man with the Brian's reputation for womanizing would be just too pathetic. The man was a notorious playboy, for heaven's sake. He was probably simply out to compromise her professionally or to effect the final story, but even if he wasn't, there was certainly nothing more than sex on his mind. She had more respect for herself than to become the Brian's sex toy of the month.

But oh, lord, had she wanted that kiss.

And that just proved how stupid hormones could be.

She rode back to Kilbooly in near silence, exchanging just enough conversation with Brian to remain polite. Between sentences, she reminded herself yet again why she objected to the man on grounds from business to personal and congratulated herself on narrowly avoiding disaster.

At long last they pulled up in front of the hotel. Nervous at the prospect of Brian asking for a goodnight kiss—or worse, simply taking one—she popped the door open and jumped out before he had a chance to shut down the motor.

"It really was a lovely dinner," she said. "I'll, um, speak to you Sunday, as I said, about arranging the lights and all."

She sounded anxious and chattery, even to her own ears, and in the shadows of the car, Brian's blue eyes glinted with amusement. "I doubt it will be as long as Monday before we see each other. As you pointed out to me once, it's a small village."

"Oh. Of course. Well, then I'll see you about. Good night, and thank you again."

"Goodnight, Tara." His low voice caressed her, as erotic as a touch.

She escaped up the hotel steps quickly as the car purred away toward Bramble Court.

She had to hit the little bell on the counter to bring Mrs. Fitzpatrick, the manageress, out to her desk.

"My key, please."

"Of course." She reached for the row of boxes behind the desk and pulled the key out.

"Did Mr. Kelleher come in yet?"

"From your little smashup, you mean? Oh, yes. He was back and had a late supper and he's down at the Bishop's Nose just now. They're having a bit of a *seisun* tonight. The Jury brothers and Tommy Ahearn and some other folk, too, I would imagine. Mr. Kelleher said to tell you to come down if you weren't worn out from your adventure with the Brian."

So, thanks to Finn, the whole village already knew about her going off with Brian. Well, she couldn't let on that anything had happened—not that it had. She'd better head down to the pub and go on as though nothing were amiss.

In the meanwhile, she might as well counteract rumor with a touch of truth.

"It was hardly an adventure. We just decided to have dinner at Moran's, since we were already up that way." Tara smiled and handed the key back. "I won't need this if I'm off to the Nose."

"We'll leave the outside door unlocked for you. If it's after midnight, just throw the bolt and get your own keys, if you would."

Tara could feel the beat of the *bodhrán* as soon as she went out the door. The motor of Brian's car must have drowned out the drum before. As she got closer to the pub, a rollicking rip of fiddle music sailed out the open door and made her smile. Tommy was good.

And so were the Jury brothers, she discovered as she joined Finn at a table. The pub was crowded and filled with smoke and noise and good spirits.

And men.

There were precisely five women in the entire pub, counting Tara and Mary Donnelly, and, unless Tara was mistaken, she was the only one not married. Not having been in the Nose enough, she couldn't know for sure, but she suspected that a session usually brought out more women.

As a whole, the men didn't seem to notice. Feet were pounding, hands clapping, voices shouting encouragement to Tommy's exuberant solos. But as Tara sipped at a Guinness, she studied the crowd, and here and there sat men who didn't look at all happy.

She leaned over to Finn. "Too bad we can't get some of those faces on film."

"Who says we're not?" asked Finn quietly. He patted a sad old leather bag that was sitting on the table. Tara looked closely and spotted a tiny hole in one end.

She raised an eyebrow. "Is that what I think it is?"

"It is."

A hidden camera. Tara beamed. "You're brilliant."

"One of us has to be, when the other is gallivanting around the countryside. I was beginning to wonder if you two had checked into a hotel someplace for a wild night of passion."

"Hush," said Tara, even as the idea produced a flutter of warmth over her skin. "We just went for dinner up at Moran's."

"Oysters?" Mischief lit Finn's eyes. "Now that doesn't suggest anything at all."

"Oh, shut up, you lout."

He laughed. "Fine. Then I won't tell you I already made arrangements with the band to film them tomorrow over in Ballyvaughan."

"Good boy. But we'll have to ring the pub for permission to bring the camera in."

"There's no need for that," said Finn. "I have connections. I dated a girl from Ballyvaughan a few years back. We drove out from Dublin every chance we had. They know me well at both Monk's and O'Brien's."

Tara shook her head. "You know, Finn, for a lout, you're a wonder."

He raised a glass. "That's why I'm Finn the Magnificent."

She lifted hers and touched it to his. "To Finn the Conceited. Long may he aggravate me."

Seven

"Tell me about Tommy," said Tara.

It was Saturday morning, and Finn had set up in the parlor of the tiny cottage Aileen shared with her mother. Mrs. McEnright had already stepped out to visit a neighbor to make Aileen less nervous, but Tara was still having trouble with her.

Aileen glanced at the camera, which sat on a tripod in the corner. "That thing is on, is it?"

"It is," said Finn. He raised his head and winked at Aileen. "Pretend it's just me with one giant eyeball."

"That should be easy enough. You both have long, skinny legs."

"I modeled for the original design, don't you know."

She laughed and relaxed back on the flowered armchair, and Tara was finally able to get her started.

"I've known Tommy since we were in nappies. Well, since I was, anyway. He's two years older, you know. He was my big brother all through school." Her eyes got far away. "Taunted me something fierce about my hair, and I used to make fun of his fiddle playing. And then when I was older, things changed. We were at a dance—not together, just both there with our friends—and Crissy dared me to get him to kiss me. It wasn't very hard to do, I realize now. And that was that. We've been seeing each other since."

"Do you go out often?"

"Every weekend." Aileen described their usual outings: films in Ennis, sessions at the area pubs, picnics, dances, and going on *cuaird*, the country term for visiting friends. They were the typical sorts of dates in a village—except that when Aileen spoke of Tommy's part in the *seisuns*, pride radiated from her face.

"There was a session last night at the Bishop's Nose and you didn't go," said Tara. "Why?"

"You know. The boycott."

Tara smiled. "*I* know, but nobody else does."

Aileen glanced up at the camera. "Oh, sorry. Well, the other night I was in such a fury, I didn't know what to do with myself. So I went down to the Nose. Ladies' Night, it was, and there were a lot of sympathetic ears about . . ."

Aileen didn't need much leading, once she got warmed up. As Tara had noticed at the pub, she was a natural storyteller, and she presented the unfolding tale of the boycott, from the Court's concern about the situation in Kilbooly to Brian Hanrahan's part it in all, with just the right mix of irritation, good humor, and determination.

Tara glanced over to Finn, who nodded. This was going to edit up nicely. When the whole story finally showed on television, the men would surely understand and forgive.

Aileen reached the end of her story. "And so here I sit, and hoping and praying that this works."

"I have one last question," Tara said. "This boycott clearly is hard on you. Your eyes got misty when you talked about telling Tommy you won't see him, and about missing the session last night at the Nose. Why are you so determined to go through with it?"

Aileen chewed her lip a moment, then lifted her chin.

"Because for all the trouble the man is, I love him. I want to be married to him, and to have his children, and to grow old with him. I've done everything I know to make that happen. This boycott is my last, best hope. It's either stick with it until he realizes he'd better come through, or I've got to give up entirely and move on."

She looked up at Tara, her eyes pleading. "I don't want to move on. I want to be Tommy's wife and spend my life making him happy. I hope when he sees this, he'll know that I didn't do it to hurt him or embarrass him. I just ran out of ideas."

She folded her hands on her lap and quietly looked down. Tara signaled Finn to stop, then handed Aileen a tissue from the box she'd brought along for just such a need.

"You did a lovely job," said Tara.

"Are we done already, then?" she asked, blotting at the tip of her nose.

"We are. See? It wasn't so bad."

"No." She stuffed the tissue into the pocket of her cardigan and stood up. "Would you care for some tea?"

"Please," said Tara. "I always get so thirsty after an interview, even when I'm not the one talking."

While Aileen was in the kitchen, Tara joined Finn in the corner, where he was reviewing the tape on the camera monitor, checking for technical flaws.

"It looks good." He slowed the speed to normal just as Aileen looked into the camera.

"I love him," the image repeated. "I want to be married to him, and to have his children, and to grow old with him."

"Do I sound that pitiful all the way through?" asked Aileen, coming into the room with a plate of scones. Finn hit the stop button.

"You sound like you love the man, is all," said Tara around a lump that had formed in her throat. "Tommy's a fool."

"Of course you'd think so. You're a woman." Aileen looked to Finn. "But what about you? What do you think?"

"I think," said Finn. He rubbed his hands together and shot a quick glance at Tara. "I think I'd marry you myself if polygamy were legal in Ireland."

"Go on." Aileen flapped a hand at him. "What a lot of blather. Will either of you be wanting milk in your tea?"

"For a man who cancelled all his appointments to sit with his dying granny, you weren't around much yesterday."

Brian looked at his grandmother over the top of his *Irish Times* and grinned. "For a dying granny, that's a hearty breakfast you're eating."

"Was the plant such a mess, then, that it took you all day and into the evening?"

"There were a few things that wanted my attention," he said.

"Only at the plant?"

Chuckling, Brian folded his paper and laid it aside. "What is it you want to know, Gran?"

"I want to know, did you spend any time sorting through that little black book of yours?"

"That's the second time you've mentioned my little black book," he teased. "Have you been watching old American movies on the television again?"

"Answer my question, please."

"No. I didn't go through my book. I already told you, there's no one in it whom I care to marry."

"Then where were you last night?"

He started to suggest she mind her own business, but she'd only get angry. "I had dinner at Moran's, if you must know."

"All alone?" she asked.

"Of course not. There was a whole restaurant full of people."

"Brian Patrick Séamus Hanrahan."

"You've got my name right, at the least."

She stiffened and glared at him. "You're getting flippant for a man who's about to lose a hundred million pounds."

"You can't be serious about that, Gran. Selling everything Grandfather and Dad and I built up, just to make a point."

"I am serious. None of it's any use, anyway, if there's no one to have it in future." She poured herself another cup from the teapot and started sugaring it. "If I were you, I'd be cutting the list back, not lengthening it."

"Who said I was?"

"No one had to say it. You've got that look about you that you get when you have a new woman on the string."

"Well you're wrong. There's no one 'on the string.'"

His grandmother's eyes narrowed. "I don't quite believe you."

"Fine," he said with a sigh. "Then you snoop around and find out for yourself, if you haven't already. You clearly need a project anyway." He downed the last of his tea, stood up, picked up the *Times*, and walked around the table to give his grandmother a kiss on the cheek. "And while you're snooping, I'm off to read my paper somewhere that I won't be disturbed."

The library was just the place for a man beset by female trouble, full of wood and leather and enough books to keep Kilbooly reading for a decade.

Brian locked the door, then spread his paper out on his grandfather's desk and settled into the old leather chair, with its padding still bearing the outline of the man who had founded the Hanrahan fortune.

But the *Times* couldn't hold his attention, and the female trouble slipped right through the keyhole to hammer delicate fists upon the desk and demand to be heard.

No one new on the string, he'd told his grandmother, and

it was the truth, thank God and Tara O'Connell. What had he been thinking last night, trying to seduce the woman?

Even as he asked himself the question, his body supplied the answer: it was lust, pure and simple.

Well, he could deal with that. But what a disaster it would have been if she hadn't had the fortitude, or ethics, or whatever it was, to turn him down flat.

Or had it been flat?

He'd been hearing her answer in his head half the night and all morning, "I'm a reporter, Brian. I'm doing a story on you." Simple enough words, but had there been a wistfulness to them?

"You're an ass," he said aloud. He had no business getting involved with Tara O'Connell.

He glanced down at the newspaper and realized he hadn't read a word of it. He clearly needed a better distraction.

His satchel sat in the corner where he'd left it the evening before when he'd come in. He fetched it and started to get the Dunloe file, but his hand fell on his address book instead.

He pulled it out.

Gran was right. He should at least take one quick look to see if there wasn't someone he'd forgotten. Someone who could move easily between Dublin and London and Paris and yet be at home in Kilbooly. Someone who'd make a tolerable wife.

And maybe he'd ring up Fiona while he was at it.

So. He didn't want to admit he'd been out with Tara O'Connell. Interesting.

It had taken Ailís precisely one telephone call and two minutes to find out what her grandson had been up to—foolish boy, thinking that telling her to snoop would actually keep her from doing it.

She sat back in her favorite rocker and contemplated exactly what this meant.

Brian had never been one to hide his many girlfriends, either from family or the press. Not that he deliberately paraded them about, but if asked, he'd always answered without qualm. He liked the ladies, and he wasn't concerned if people knew it.

But not today. Not when it came to Miss O'Connell. And that, in itself, told the tale.

Brian and Tara Bríd O'Connell.

The names certainly went together: Brian for Brian Boru, first High King of Ireland, and Tara for the hill where his capital city once sat.

A slow smile spread across Ailís's face as she rocked. It was good to know her first instincts were proving right.

She'd recognized the possibilities in Tara the minute the girl had walked into the conservatory: the direct manner, the good humor, the willingness to risk everything for what she wanted—all traits Brian would appreciate. That they were wrapped up in such a charmingly female package had almost guaranteed he'd at least take a look.

But it had gone beyond a look, that was clear. Just how far beyond was the question. Perhaps it was time to see what she could do to nudge these two along.

She'd always wanted to get a touch of red hair into the family.

Tommy Ahearn strolled into the kitchen carrying his favorite plaid shirt, the dark red one he always wore when he had a paying gig. His mother, as usual, sat bent over her sewing machine, feeding yards of material through the presser foot

"That's a god-awful shade of pink," he said, stooping to press a quick peck to her cheek. "What's it for?"

"Nan Laurey's new parlor draperies," said Peg. "It does

look a bit like stomach medicine, doesn't it? But it's not so bad in the room. We had it strung up all over, and it was really quite nice."

"You could hardly prove it by me." He pulled open the refrigerator door and stood looking for a moment, then pulled out a bottle of milk. He fetched a glass from the cupboard. "I need my shirt washed."

"Throw it in the laundry. I'll get to it next week."

"Eh? But . . . I . . ." stuttered Tommy, at a loss. "But I need it tonight, and it stinks from last night at the Nose."

"Maybe you should have thought of that before you wore it." She finished the seam and lifted the foot to turn the fabric. "I promised these for next week, and I'm going to need every minute of the time. The cloth is so heavy, I keep breaking needles."

"But I thought you'd just toss it in the machine for me."

"Sorry, darlin', I can't spare the time. If you want it washed, you'll have to do it yourself."

"I don't know how."

"You're a clever lad," she said, reaching up to pat his back in a motherly way. "You'll manage."

"Can't you show me, this once?"

"I have shown you."

"But I wasn't paying careful attention."

"I can't help that, can I? I guess you'll have to wait until I'm finished."

"But we have our gig in Ballyvaughan tonight. And that Miss O'Connell is going to film us for the television. I've got to have my lucky shirt."

"Then you had better get busy, hadn't you? The instructions are on the lid, and the soap is on the shelf. You'll manage."

"I suppose I'll have to, won't I?" he grumbled.

"Make certain you give yourself enough time for ironing,

too, because that shirt always comes out of the clothes dryer all in a ball."

"Ironing?" He stared at her. She must be loony. "I've never done that."

"And don't I know it," muttered Peg. She smiled up at him. "Maybe you can talk Aileen into it."

"I don't think so," said Tommy, kicking at the table leg. He hadn't told his mother about Aileen yet. He hadn't told anybody. "You're certain you won't have time?"

"I'm certain," said Peg.

"All right, then. I'll get it done somehow."

"So you will." Peg stepped on the pedal, and the machine whine drowned out whatever she muttered after.

"Fine thing when a man's own mother won't wash his shirt." He grumbled all the way to the service porch, where the washer and dryer sat. He tossed the shirt in and started reading the instructions printed on the bottom side of the lid.

They might have been in Greek, for all the sense they made. The box of laundry soap offered a bit more help, and he measured out the advised amount of powder and poured it in on top of the shirt. For good measure, and since he'd heard the washer make awful noises when it went out of kilter, he tossed in the rest of his shirts to balance things. That'd make his mother happy. A few buttons pushed and dials twisted, and the washer began to fill.

Feeling a touch of pride at this accomplishment, Tommy spent a half hour running through songs for the night's gig, then went back to the washer. When he pulled it open, an ocean of pink greeted him.

He pulled out a shirt. It took him a moment to recognize it as his best white shirt, the one he wore to church every Sunday morning. It was just the shade of Nan Laurey's new curtains.

"Ah, damn it all. Ma!"

Eight

Finn's connections in Ballyvaughan proved a tad more tentative than he'd led Tara to believe.

In point of fact, they were more on the order of anti-connections, related somehow to the painting of a pig's ass on the front door a few years back. Only Tara's powers of persuasion and a promise that the pub would be mentioned by name at least twice in the finished story got them in the door.

"I feel like I spend me life in corners," grumbled Finn as he carried gear to the far reaches of the pub.

"And well you should. 'Oh, you don't need to call, Tara.'" She mocked his voice. "'I have connections. They know me well in Ballyvaughan.' Well, apparently they do. And they don't like you at all."

"I can't help it if that night's a blank, now, can I? That was the night Joanna told me she was planning to marry that Brit."

"Fine excuse that is. The only reason the owner let us in at all is that you've taken the pledge since then."

"I have?" asked Finn.

"You have," said Tara. "I convinced him that you left

your Abstinence pin on your other coat. It's tea-total for you tonight, my friend."

"Ah, damn." Finn opened a bag of cables, then brightened. "But then it would be anyway, wouldn't it? I'm driving."

Satisfied that Tara hadn't sacrificed any privileges he wouldn't give up on his own, Finn merrily began setting up lights and microphones.

By the time Tommy, Martin, and Peter drifted in an hour later, the pub was filling up nicely. Encouraged by the size of the early crowd, the boys set up quickly, tuned their instruments, and launched right into "The Devil in the Kitchen." The evening was off.

Somewhere in the middle of the second set, the crowd increased by a large, raucous delegation from Kilbooly, led by Rory Boland and Daniel Clohessy, who commandeered the tables closest to the band and settled in to cheer their lads on. The band showed their appreciation by playing even better.

As music heated up, so did the pub. The owner blocked the door open for air, but the noise only pulled more people in and made it hotter yet. Finally the boys wound up the set with a blazing reel and announced over the applause that they'd be back in fifteen minutes.

"They're a hit," said Finn, coming out from behind the camera.

Tara nodded. "Get some good shots of that lot from Kilbooly."

"They're not that interesting."

"Yes, they are," said Tara. "Unless I'm mistaken, that's our bachelor contingent, almost to the man."

Finn looked them over. "Not a woman among them. I think you're right."

"And the sad part is, I don't think they've even noticed they're on their own."

"They'll notice now," said Finn. He jerked his head toward the back of the room. "The Court's come to visit."

It was the Court, all right, or at least Siobhan and Crissy, followed by several of the other unmarried women Tara recognized from that first night at the Nose. They spotted Tara and made a beeline for the corner. Finn quickly cleared the table where he'd piled his gear, and the ladies rounded up stools.

After a round of introductions, Tara knelt down between Siobhan and Crissy. "Why are you here? Have you called off the boycott?"

"Lord, no," said Crissy. "This isn't a male-female affair. Those lads are from Kilbooly. It's our duty to support our own even if some of them are complete cods. The Jurys are all right, you know. They're married. We'll cheer for them."

"Besides, we couldn't just let them all come over alone," explained Siobhan. "They'd only drink and talk football and imagine they were having a grand time. But with us about, sooner or later they'll realize we're over here on this side of the room, while they're over there, patting each other on the back. And then they'll start to wonder why."

Tara could see some logic to it, but still felt obliged to point out, "But Aileen's not here."

"Of course not," said Crissy, sounding like a patient mother. "Tommy would just think she was here for him specially, and that would do us no good at all."

"Poor sods don't have a chance against you women," muttered Finn.

Siobhan laughed. "You must be Finn. Aileen warned us you had mixed sympathies."

"Finn the Magnificent, at your service."

"Did she tell you about the big head, too?" asked Tara.

"I do believe she mentioned something about that. But what I want to know is—" Siobhan looked past Tara, her eyes widening. "Would you look at that."

Tara glanced over her shoulder, then froze.

Brian stood there, framed in the open doorway, wearing a leather jacket and jeans and looking like an advertisement for all things good and masculine in Eire. The real surprise, however, was the lady on his arm.

Ailís Hanrahan peered around the room until her eyes lit on Tara and the table full of Kilbooly women. She lifted a hand in greeting and started in their direction. Brian hesitated an instant, his gaze locking with Tara's just long enough to send little fairy feet skittering up and down her spine, then stepped ahead, clearing a path for his grandmother.

"There goes the fun of it," muttered Siobhan under her breath. "Everybody keep a lid on while the Brian's about." She shot a particular look at Finn.

"I've already taken me vows of silence," said Finn, raising a hand as for an oath.

"Well, Brian," said Ailís as they came up. "It looks like you and I weren't the only ones with the thought of supporting young Thomas and his friends."

"I told you we wouldn't be. I think they're about to start the next set. We should find a table."

"Do you mind if we join you, ladies?" asked Ailís, not bothering to look around.

"Of course not."

The women shifted around and cleared a space. Crissy bullied a man at the neighboring table into giving up a proper chair in exchange for a stool, which she pulled out of thin air, and they soon had Mrs. Hanrahan comfortably settled.

"I'm afraid there's not enough room for you, Brian," said Siobhan, barely containing her pleasure over that fact. "You'll have to fend for yourself. Maybe the men over there can fit you in."

"Don't be so subtle," said Finn. "He might not realize you want to talk about him."

Siobhan shot Finn daggers, but Brian only chuckled. "Talk away. I'll go get our drinks. What would you like, Gran?"

"Tea, thank you. And take your time."

"Yes, ma'am." He winked at her, then at Tara, before he wove off through the knots of people.

"There," said Ailís, satisfied. "We have a few minutes, anyway. I swear, that boy's been in the oddest temper all day."

"Probably something he ate last night," said Finn.

Tara pretended to snip off an invisible pigtail with scissors.

"I think I'll get a shot or two from a different angle," said Finn, hurriedly pulling the camera off the tripod and plugging in the battery pack. He vanished into the crowd.

"What did I interrupt?" asked Ailís.

"I was just asking Tara about last night," said Siobhan, grinning. "Word has it she went off with Brian and didn't get in until late."

"It wasn't that late," said Tara, trying hard to control the color that had been creeping up her neck since Brian had walked in. "Not that I had much choice in it. He insisted on going to Moran's." She told the tale, borrowing a page from Brian's own book to make it as dull as possible.

Most of the women seemed disappointed that there wasn't more to the story, but Tara had the sense she wasn't fooling Ailís at all. The old woman watched her with those bright blue eyes and a sort of a half smile on her face, nodding at just the points when Tara left something out, as though she knew.

When she finished, Ailís said, "You'll have to forgive Brian for dragging you off like that. He's always had a streak of the pirate in him."

"Is that what you call it?" asked Siobhan dryly.

The band had come back, and much to Tara's relief, they

slipped right into a slow, sweet air that brought the pub to a hush and precluded any further speculation on what she might or might not have done with Brian.

Unfortunately, the music also marked the return of Brian from the bar, carrying two mugs of tea. He set one before his grandmother and kept the other as he stepped in beside Tara.

"Do you mind if I share your bit of wall?"

Tara couldn't think of an excuse to say no. "Go ahead. I've no claim on it."

She pretended not to mind, but it was bloody nerve-wracking, standing there with him, wondering what he was going to try next, hoping one second that he did try something and the next second that he didn't. And then there was the way Siobhan and the rest of them kept glancing over their shoulders, as though they expected to catch the two of them in the act, right there in front of God and everyone.

Martin broke a string on his guitar and the band had to stop for a moment while he changed it out.

"They're very good," Tara said conversationally, just because their corner seemed like the only place that people weren't talking.

"I'm glad to see you here," said Brian. "I wasn't sure you'd remember what I said about Tommy and his music, after the way I behaved up at the ruins. I was concerned that I had cost Tommy his moment of fame."

She didn't want to be reminded of the ruins. "He deserves more than a moment. With any luck, the story will bring him some attention from the right people. He should be making records."

"We see a lot of good fiddlers in Clare."

"Not this good and with this much original music. I don't know why no one has noticed the band before this. Have you kept Tommy locked away in the barn or something?"

"I suppose I did. We kept him busy, that's certain. He asked to cut back to just over half time about a year ago. I think that's when he got so good." He set his empty cup on a ledge. "I'll admit, I hate the idea of losing him altogether. But when I listen to him play, I realize that he's even better with the fiddle than he is with the horses. The world will be a better place with him doing what he's meant to do."

That piqued her interest. "You sound like you envy him."

"I do," said Brian. "Talent like his is a rare thing."

"Some people say you have a great deal of talent in certain areas."

"Some people, but not you, eh?"

"I didn't say that."

"Well, whatever talent I have doesn't do much good if I can't bring it and my dreams into accord. That's where Tommy has my envy. And that's why I wish him the greatest success."

The idea that the Brian had unachieved dreams gave Tara pause. She wanted to ask him more, but the ability to keep up any sort of philosophical discussion vanished as the crowd pounded to the rhythm of Peter's drum. She made mental note of the question, though. She could ask it in the interview Monday. That might make for some interesting television.

She was thinking of the interview, Tara noted with a touch of pride and a certain amount of relief. She *could* keep a professional distance and deal with the man. She didn't have to respond like a teenager in heat.

Then Finn came back and took up enough space for two men, forcing Tara to crowd closer to Brian, and the whole idea of professional distance vanished in a whiff of leather and spice and temptation.

Finn got the camera back onto the tripod then checked the viewfinder. "You're in the shot, Tara. You'll have to step back."

"Hang on." She shifted around. "There's no room."

"Yes, there is," said Brian. He put his hands on her waist and pulled her back against his chest. "Right here."

The pub is too hot for this, thought Tara as she tried to hold perfectly still. It really wouldn't do to squirm around and make a scene, although the wild side of her begged to do it and find out whether any parts of his body were even harder and more manly than his chest. Some professional. She gritted her teeth.

"If you don't breathe, you'll faint," Brian whispered in her ear.

"I am breathing," she muttered.

"I don't think so," he said. He slid his hands up onto her rib cage, staying well within safe territory but nonetheless making her nipples harden with the threat. "Let me feel a nice deep one."

"Stop it." She pushed on his hands.

"Shhh." He breathed against her hair. "You don't want the whole table turning around, do you?" He kissed the side of her neck, and Tara shuddered, then drew in a huge breath.

"There. See?" He moved his hands down, but slipped his arms around her instead.

"Turn loose of me."

"I can't. You'd get in the shot." He settled back against the plaster wall, pulling her just a shade off balance so she had no choice but to lean into his arms. "And why would I want to, anyway?"

Thank God, Tommy picked that moment to demonstrate what he could do when he really got warmed up. The music was so dazzling that no one paid any attention to what was going on in the corner. Even Finn seemed unaware, his eye glued to the viewfinder and one foot tapping silently to the tunes.

So there they stayed, cuddled together for all the world like a pair of lovers. Slowly, the tension drained out of Tara's body.

"That's better," breathed Brian. He brushed her hair aside and dropped another kiss on her neck.

And that was when his grandmother decided to turn around.

Tara sprang forward.

"Damn. You ruined my shot," said Finn.

"It doesn't matter. The set's almost over. I've a few more questions for Tommy during the next break."

"Whatever you say," muttered Finn. "I'm only the cameraman."

Behind her, she heard Brian sigh.

Questions for Tommy. Questions for the publican. Questions for the bachelors. Questions for every living soul in the bar, so long as they weren't anywhere near Brian.

Ailís watched and shook her head with amusement. If ever there was a young woman afraid of fire, Tara Bríd O'Connell was she. And Brian was having all too much fun striking matches and throwing them at her feet, messing about just enough to aggravate her without setting her on fire.

Time to stir things up a bit.

She kicked her handbag well under the table, then waited patiently until she saw Tara disappear toward the W.C.

"I must have left my bag in the car," she said, calling Brian out of his corner. "Would you get it for me?"

"I thought I saw you with it after we came in."

"Well I don't have it now, and I haven't been any place to leave it."

"I think—" began Crissy.

Ailís kicked her beneath the table. "Run along, Brian. It's time for my pill."

"Yes, ma'am. I'll be right back."

Ailís barely let him reach the door before she caught Finn Kelleher's attention and motioned him over. As he made his way through the tables, she snaked her handbag back out from under the table with her toe and reached into it.

"I knew you had it," muttered Crissy, rubbing her shin.

"Of course I did," said Ailís. "Now hush and learn."

"I might find that easier if my leg didn't hurt so."

Finn reached the table. "Can I do something for you, ma'am?"

"You smoke, don't you, Mr. Kelleher?"

"I do."

"I thought I recognized the look of a man in need of a cigarette."

"You have that right. I'm trying to cut back and it's a bitch. Begging your pardon."

"Far be it from me to encourage a man in his vices, but are you certain it's not time you had a break?" She laid a ten-pound note on the table and slid it toward Finn. "I hear there's a good spot out back where no one will find you too quickly."

"I'm desperate enough that I won't even ask why you want me gone." The tenner disappeared into Finn's shirt pocket. "Keep an eye on this." He set the camera in the middle of the table, gave her a wink, and sauntered off.

"What the devil are you up to?" demanded Siobhan.

"Patience, girl. Patience."

Tara soon returned. She peered about through the haze, then gave up and came over to the table. "Where did Finn go?"

Everyone looked to Ailís expectantly.

"He said something about having a smoke and a bit of a walk," she said.

"Damn. He would pick now to go off." She turned and looked at the front door.

"I think I saw him turn toward the dock as he went out," said Ailís helpfully. "If you hurry, I'm sure you can catch him."

"Thanks." Tara grabbed her jacket and barreled off toward the dark rectangle of the open door.

Ailís laid a finger by the corner of her mouth. "Oh, my, I'm afraid I got confused. That's the way Brian went, not Mr. Kelleher."

"You must be off your bleedin' nut," said Siobhan.

"I cannot imagine that your mother knows you speak to your elders that way."

"But you—" Siobhan bit her tongue. "Sorry, Ailís. But what do you think you're doing, throwing those two together that way?"

"I'm not throwing them together, dear. I'm providing an opportunity for them to throw themselves together."

"I'm so glad you explained the difference." Siobhan tossed off the last of her stout in one unladylike gulp. "You realize, don't you, that the whole point of the boycott is to avoid that sort of opportunity?"

"Is it?" said Ailís. She looked up at the ceiling and considered. "Now that's odd. I thought in Brian's case, the point was to get him married."

"Ah." A ripple of approval and amusement ran around the table.

Siobhan slapped one hand to her forehead. "Just stand me in the corner and hand me a pointy hat."

"You're no dunce, darling," said Ailís gently, patting her on the shoulder. "You're just seventy years too young to keep up with me. Now, let me stand you ladies a round while we wait to find out if you're going to have to give me a lift home."

Away from the bustle of the pub, the night was quiet and dark as pitch. A few lamps in houses glowed dimly behind draperies, and far up the road, the interior light of a car made a bright yellow patch in the night. Tara could hear several people moving about, but could make out no detail at all.

"Finn Kelleher!" she called. She'd never spot him out here.

The car light winked out as a door slammed. Somewhere, a man's voice, made indistinct by distance, muttered what could have been a curse.

"Finn?"

She waited a moment for her eyes to adjust to the watery light the moon cast through the high clouds, then pressed forward, following the occasional glint of chrome on the cars which lined both sides of the road. A largish shadow appeared on the far side of the road, moving her direction.

Tara strained to catch a clear glimpse of the form. "Finn. If that's you, get your skinny ass over here."

"I'm not Finn. But if I were, I'd be running the other direction about now."

Tara groaned. "Brian. I certainly bump into you a lot. Have you seen Finn?"

"I can't even see you," he said. "Stand still."

The shadow moved forward and slowly resolved itself into Brian, though his features remained only dark patches against a slightly lighter face.

"I seem to have lost him," said Tara.

"He was inside, the last I saw," said Brian.

"Apparently the demon weed started working its wiles, and he came out to satisfy the urge." She peered around. "There's a glow. Maybe that's him. Finn!"

The only answer was the splash of waves against the shore.

She sighed. "I'd better hunt around a bit more."

"I'll help."

"I can manage," said Tara quickly.

"I'm sure you can. But I'll help anyway. You shouldn't be stumbling around alone in the dark. You could break a leg."

"And it'll be ever so much better if we both stumble around and break legs. I'm sorry," she said, immediately contrite. "That sounded snippy. The help would be appreciated."

They continued in the same direction Tara had been traveling.

"What are you doing out here?"

"Grandmother left her bag in the car."

Tara frowned. Hadn't she seen a bag in Ailís's lap just now?

"Ouch. Watch that rock." Brian took her hand to steady her.

He didn't let go.

And in the dark, wandering over unknown ground, Tara didn't mind. He had a horseman's hands, strong and full of calm command. She felt much safer holding on to him.

They walked on quite a ways, watching for movement or the glow of cigarettes and calling out occasionally. There was no sign of Finn.

"Are you certain he came this way?" asked Brian.

"Your grandmother said he did."

Just as she'd said she'd left her purse. Tara wondered if Ailís had concocted this meeting on her own, or if Brian had put her up to it.

Either way, she decided she'd better circumvent whatever plans had been made on her behalf. "He's not out here. I probably walked right past him already. We should go back."

"Not yet." Brian tugged her closer, so she had to tilt her head back to see his face. "I'm enjoying the night and the company."

Oh, lord, he smelled even better out here away from the smoky pub, with the scent of the ocean washing over them. And she knew how his arms would feel around her, a recollection that brought a blush to her cheeks there in the darkness. A deep wanting filled her soul, making no sense at all.

"Brian, we can't." It took all her concentration to make

the argument aloud. "We've been over this already. Neither of us even—"

—*likes the other*, she meant to say, but his mouth slanted down over hers and cut her off, and she didn't have the will to push him away.

His kiss was gentler than it had been on the hill, more sweet coaxing than rough passion, but it had the same effect, cutting off all her air and making her cling to him for support. She sighed, and their tongues tangled.

They stood there in the darkness for a long time, just kissing until she ached for him to touch her. He seemed to sense her readiness, slipping his hand beneath her jacket and slowly up until he cupped her breasts. Her breathing grew ragged.

She should stop him. She really should.

His thumbs flicked over her nipples, sending sparks across her nerves that disrupted the last train of rational thought.

She lost track of everything, then: where they were, why she shouldn't be with him, what was going to happen next. He slowly undid a button, then another, until her shirt gaped and let the chill night air wash over her. Abandoning her mouth, Brian kissed his way down her neck and toward her bosom. She pressed against him with a soft moan of need.

A light on a nearby stoop glared to life and a door opened.

"Gad, more kids," said a harsh voice.

"Oh, Jayzus," said Tara, scrambling to cover herself. Brian pulled her close, protecting her from prying eyes.

"Get out of here before I call the Guard."

"I'm sorry, sir," said Brian. "We got a bit carried away."

"Tell me something else I didn't know." The man dropped a liquor bottle into the waste bin and banged the lid shut. "If you're going to boff the girl, son, at least take her inside somewhere."

"Yes, sir. Good idea."

The door slammed, but the light stayed on. Curled against Brian's chest, Tara quickly buttoned up and tugged her jacket around her.

"I've never been so mortified in my life."

"I'm sorry, Tara." He wrapped his arms around her and kissed the top of her head. "I'm not sure what came over me. The man did have a good idea, though, taking you somewhere and making love to you. I would very much enjoy that."

It would be so easy to say yes. To go with him to the nearest hotel and spend the night beside him, beneath him, astride him.

Her insides melted.

"No, Brian." The words were pure reflex, an after-reaction to the embarrassment, but once out, they gave her strength. "No. I'm not going anywhere with you."

"Why not?"

Why not? "For one, we barely even know each other."

"We'll work on that."

She pulled her jacket even tighter. "And for another, I have no desire to become one in the long list of Hanrahan takeovers. Now I'm going back, and I'd appreciate it if you would stay out here for a few minutes, so the whole pub doesn't have to know we were behaving like randy monkeys in the middle of the road."

His eyes narrowed like he was angry, but he just nodded. "Fine."

Thus unencumbered, she groped her way back to the pub, where she marched straight up to Finn. "Where the devil were you?"

"Just having a smoke."

"You might have told me before you disappeared into the night. Get packed up. We're finished here." She pulled a power cord out of the wall and started wrapping it.

"Hold on," said Finn. "You're tangling it. You never do it right."

"Then do it yourself," snapped Tara. She dropped the cord on the floor and plunked down at the table. "And don't dilly-dally." She very much wanted to be gone before Brian came back.

"Whatever's the matter, dear?" asked Ailís. "Did something happen outside?"

Tara looked into that sweet old lady's face and realized Ailís couldn't possibly have done anything as diabolical as send her outside to bump into Brian. That was pure Brian. She didn't have the heart to tell her that her grandson was a dog, so she smiled.

"I just stumbled over one too many rocks out hunting for Finn the Lost. It's been a long day. I just want to get home—back to Kilbooly, I mean. I just need a good night's sleep."

More like a good night in bed. Ailís could hardly keep the smile off her face as she exchanged knowing looks with Siobhan and Crissy.

Rocks be damned. Tara's lips wore the smudged, tender look of a woman who'd been well kissed. And Ailís wasn't going to be the one to tell her, but she'd missed a button.

So, they'd found a better corner somewhere.

There hadn't been time for more than a bit of petting, but Ailís was encouraged. With temperatures rising so quickly, the least spark should produce the necessary conflagration.

A frustrated-looking Brian rolled in a few minutes later and went straight to the bar. Tara made a good show of ignoring him, but she was so clearly aware of his presence, and him of hers, that there might as well have been a golden wire connecting the two of them.

The others noticed, too, particularly Siobhan, who had to look at her lap from time to time, to keep Tara from seeing her grin.

It took Finn a good half hour to pack up his gear, and the whole time, Brian and Tara exchanged bolts of electricity across the room while Ailís and the others worked to keep up a steady thread of conversation and avoid laughing out loud.

Finally, Tara and Finn made their good-byes, loaded up with cases and bags, and headed off. Brian stared after them, entirely absorbed.

"Well," said Ailís when they got out the door. "I do hope Miss O'Connell feels better soon."

"She'll be fine soon enough," said Siobhan, laughter bubbling over. "I'm pretty sure Brian has the cure for what ails her, right in his pocket."

They all roared.

Nine

There was nothing quite like sitting in church on Sunday morning after a particularly unfortunate Saturday night, a situation made worse when the party who had contributed to the unfortunate nature of it happened to be sitting directly in your line of sight.

Add to the mix an avuncular, white-haired priest who made a point of greeting you as you came in, and it made for an amazingly uncomfortable start to the week.

Tara sat in the whitewashed interior of St. Senan's, wishing that her mother and a series of teaching nuns hadn't done such a thorough job of indoctrinating her on the importance of attending Mass at least once a week. Then she might have skipped this morning, being in an unfamiliar town.

But no, here she sat, unconfessed and unshriven, praying not for forgiveness but for a rock to crawl under.

And the service hadn't even begun yet.

At least she'd arrived late enough to avoid the exquisite torture of having Brian take a seat next to her; he'd already been in a pew next to his grandmother and thus restrained. Tara had started toward an empty row near the back, planning to sit far off to the side where she could remain unnoticed and perhaps concentrate on the service. Instead, Aileen had grabbed her and dragged her up to where she was sitting with her mother, just two rows in back of Brian and only slightly to the right, where his square shoulders and shiny black hair made a sort of half frame for the altar. He couldn't watch her, but she couldn't keep her eyes off him.

Tara closed her eyes and was trying to get her wayward thoughts under control when she heard a titter of laughter behind her. Another giggle followed, then a snicker and a snort and an outright guffaw.

So, someone had spread the word about the unbuttoned button—she had discovered that charming error back at the hotel and was certain that it had been noticed in Bally-vaughan—and she was now to be the butt of village humor. She stiffened her back and kept her eyes firmly closed.

Beside her, Aileen turned and began to shake with mirth. She elbowed Tara. "Look."

Tara looked. All she saw was Tommy, sliding into a pew near the back of the church with a sheepish grin on his face. As he sat down, his jacket flapped back and a beam of light hit his shirtfront and surrounded him with a pale pink glow. For an instant Tara thought the color came from stained glass, then she realized that St. Senan's had no stained glass, just tall clear panes that let in plenty of light.

"It's pink," said a little boy in awe. "Tommy's got a lady's pink shirt on."

The amusement that had been percolating through the church erupted into open laughter. Anyone who hadn't no-ticed yet, turned to see this amazing sight. Tommy's face went red, which perversely made the pink more noticeable.

"Peg told me she made him do his own wash," whispered Aileen. "He mixed everything together."

"Mmm," said Tara. Sympathetic to poor Tommy but un-able to stop the laughter, she clamped her hands over her mouth and quickly faced front, only to meet Brian's smiling eyes.

Tara's laughter faded as a feeling of vulnerability overwhelmed her. She could be naked as a jaybird, the way he was looking at her, and what was worse, parts of her started tingling that had no business tingling, not in church. The nuns had been right: she *was* going to burn in hell.

Fortunately, the bell rang a final peal and Father Breen took his position in front of the altar. The laughter subsided, and Brian turned to face the front.

The priest made the sign of the Cross. "In the name of the Father, the Son, and the Holy Spirit. The Lord be with you."

"And also with you."

Tara surrendered to the familiar rhythm of the Mass: to the murmur of call and response, to the prayers and the hymns and the reading of the Gospel. For a time the ritual worked just as it was supposed to, pushing all thoughts of the mundane world aside.

But as soon as the last Amen faded and Brian rose, filling her field of vision, she tumbled back to earth, the service forgotten.

She avoided his eyes and stuck close to Aileen as they made their way out of the church.

"I'm very glad you stopped in to join us," said Father Breen, shaking her hand. "I hope you enjoyed the service."

"Very much so," said Tara. She struggled to remember enough of his sermon to comment on, and couldn't. "It reminded me of Mass at home with Father McWilliams."

Father McWilliams had been fresh out of seminary and so tongue-tied that she suspected the old joke about the taffy pull at St. Peter's had been written about him, but she'd liked him and it was the sentiment that counted. Father Breen took it as the compliment she intended.

"Where's that cameraman of yours?"

"I'm afraid Finn likes to do his communing with God

from the middle of a river with a rod and reel. He's out fishing."

An understanding smile creased Father Breen's face. "I can hardly hold it against him when he's likely to wander across a few of my own missing flock while he's praying. If there's anything I can do, please let me know. And of course the confessional is open any time you need it."

Just what had he heard?

Guilt was a terrible thing, Tara decided, and escaped the priest before Brian and his grandmother worked their way to the door.

Rory Boland stood on the steps of St. Senan's, contemplating not the sermon, but his next meal. Breakfast had consisted of a day-old scone and a cup of milk liberated from the pub refrigerator. He was starving.

By all rights, he could eat at the pub, paying just like any other customer. But the indignity of Mary cutting off his board still rankled. And that salty mess at Deegan's had put him right off of going back there any time soon.

So, what was he to do for food on a Sunday, when the bakery was closed?

"Would you care to join us for lunch?"

Rory's ears perked up at the invitation. He turned, a ready "Yes" on his lips.

But Aileen was asking that reporter woman, Miss O'Connell, not him.

And not Tommy, either, oddly enough.

Tommy always ate Sunday lunch at the McEnrights', and had for as long as Rory had been in Kilbooly. Aileen's quiet, "Would you come to lunch, Tommy?" was as much a part of Sunday as Father Breen's blessing. Tommy must really be in the doghouse.

Speaking of which . . . Rory ambled over to where

Daniel Clohessy and Martin had Tommy backed up against a hedgerow and on the defensive.

"How was I to know a shirt that old would bleed all over everything?" demanded Tommy. "You'd think all the dye that was going to come out, would have by now."

"At least the color's good on you," said Martin, snorting.

"The only blessing is, Ma said maybe I could bleach it. But I didn't have time to figure that out and iron *and* get over to Ballyvaughan."

"Washing and ironing? Aren't we the domestic one."

"Get on. Ma's busy with her sewing, is all. I had to shift for myself."

Daniel nudged him. "Come on, now. Admit it, you ran out of clean shirts and decided to borrow one of your ma's."

"Naw," said Tommy. "If you want to know, I got it from Rory's closet."

"Hey." Rory flushed. "Don't start slaggin' me. I only just walked up."

Martin hooted and clapped Rory on the shoulder. "Besides, we know that's not true, because Rory just piles his clothes in the corner. Look, Bernadette and I have got to get over to Peter's. I think Annie's got a roast on."

Rory's stomach rumbled.

"Annie's a good cook," he said, hoping Martin would remember his current situation and invite him along, but he just hurried away.

Rory tried Daniel next. "I'm headed off over to Ennis for a decent meal. Do you want to come?"

"Thank you, no. I'm taking a sandwich out to the old cottage. The roof wants some work and this is the only time I have." He extended a hand to Tommy. "Congratulations again on last night. See you about." He took his leave.

"He's always up at that old cottage of his grandfather's," said Tommy when Daniel had gotten out of earshot. "Every Sunday afternoon and during the week, too, when he can.

And yet nothing ever seems to get fixed. The place looks like a healthy shove would take it right over."

"Perhaps he just likes to hang about. He may as well, with Louise driving over to Limerick every week to visit her cousin in the home."

"Maybe," said Tommy. "But I have this feeling he's doing something up there he doesn't want the rest of us to know about."

"Like what?"

"I don't know. Writing a book, maybe. Or painting pictures."

"Or maybe he's teaching himself the ballet," said Rory. He shook his head over his own humor. "He most likely just goes up there to have a bit of a nap where his mother can't bother him."

"You're probably right. That woman can talk the ears off a donkey. Say, if you're looking for someone to go to Ennis with you, I'm at loose ends. Aileen's in a pucker over something or other, and I decided to let her cool down a bit before I go around there again."

That wasn't the way Rory understood the situation, but he let Tommy have his version of the story. "What about your ma? Isn't she cooking Sunday dinner?"

"If you consider frozen meat pies to be cooking, she is. I'd rather make the drive to Ennis."

"All right, then." Rory pulled his car keys out of his pocket and tossed them in the air to catch them. "Only go change out of that shirt first. I don't want anyone thinking we're dating, you sweet thing."

Siobhan stood outside the church, watching Brian stare after the escaping Tara.

There was a spark between those two, all right. In all the years of watching Brian work his way through village girls, then college girls, and now his Dublin doxies, Siobhan had never seen him quite so stuck on someone. He literally could not keep his eyes off Tara.

He was falling in love for the first time, right in front of them all. Once Ailís had pointed it out, nothing could have been clearer. She and Crissy and the others had discussed the budding romance all the way home, trying to figure out if there was some way to help it along.

Right now, however, she had another mission.

She looked around until she spotted the woman she wanted, then marched quickly down the rows of parked cars. She nodded at Nan Laurey and Mrs. Grafton as she passed.

She reached the end of the row just as Louise got in her car.

"Good morning, Siobhan."

"Louise. I need to talk to you. Right away."

Louise glanced at her watch. "Just for a minute. I have to get down to Limerick to see Cousin Agatha. She counts on me being there just after lunch. She says it makes her week."

"Good. Then she'll be happy to have a whole afternoon with you this time."

Bright red spots appeared on Louise's cheeks. "She always gets a whole afternoon."

"You and I both know that's not true." Siobhan stepped close and dropped her voice. "I've seen you, Louise. You drive back early almost every Sunday and meet Daniel up at his grandfather's cottage."

"I don't."

"You do," said Siobhan. She spotted a couple of kids headed their way and grabbed Louise by the sleeve to pull her farther out of the way. "You sneak in the back road and when you think no one's watching, you park your car in that hollow spot under the hedge. And then you and Daniel go inside and do the nasty."

"What? Have you been watching us?"

"Of course not. I'd been out fishing one day and I happened to walk back by way of the old path. I was just passing by when you two came out. You had that look about you, and Daniel's shirt was off. It was pretty clear what you'd been up to. And I saw where you had hidden the car by the hedgerow, there. I've noticed it there a few times since. Your visits to Limerick are a bit shorter than your parents think they are, aren't they?"

Louise covered her burning cheeks. "Who else knows?"

"No one. At least no one who has ever said anything I've heard. Look, darling, I don't care what you and Daniel do and it's not my business anyway, that's why I've never said a word. But now it's different. You can't be going up there with the boycott on."

"I know." Louise grimaced. "But he says he needs it."

"They all say that, you dope."

"But he gets all tense, he says. Short-tempered."

"Good," said Siobhan. "That will tell him he needs to be with you. And then you can tell him that he will be, as soon as he marries you. He can do without until then. It won't kill him."

"But it may kill me," said Louise wistfully. "Do you have any idea how good it is?"

"I've heard," said Siobhan, embarrassed that the conversation had taken this turn. She really didn't want to discuss her sex life, or lack of it, with Louise. They weren't that close. "That doesn't matter. You were at the Court. You agreed to the boycott. No going to the cottage."

"Oh, all right."

"I'm serious, Louise. I'm going to check. If I suspect you're up there giving Danny-boy a ride, I'm going to suggest that a big group of your friends troop up to give you a surprise party."

"I said I wouldn't," Louise snapped, then looked ashamed. "I would have, though. It really is grand."

"That means it'll be even grander when you're married and not committing a mortal sin." She gave Louise a hug. "Now, go have a nice long visit with Cousin Agatha, and on the way back, you can plan your wedding."

There were two Taras, Brian decided as he rode Brig down along the river after lunch.

One was the reporter, after some unknown story. That Tara wore cynicism as a badge of honor, poked around the village like a detective, and videotaped people in private. He knew for a fact that she'd interviewed Aileen McEnright and Peg Ahearn, though only God and those women knew what she had asked. He also suspected she was hanging about with Siobhan and Crissy because she'd found out they each had a history with him and thought they could tell her—*what?*

The reporter-Tara made him uneasy. She knew altogether too much about the workings of Kilbooly for someone who'd been here only a week; the village women, usually reticent with outsiders, seemed to have taken her to their bosoms much too quickly. Even more disturbing was the mysterious connection she had with his grandmother.

When had those two met and become so chummy?

What was she after?

Tara the reporter occupied his thoughts when he was conscious and away from her, but it was the second one, Tara the woman, who captured his dreams and whose presence excited him beyond reason.

He closed his eyes as the mere thought of her triggered the rush of desire that had grown so familiar over the past days.

The second Tara smelled of soap and spring rain, kissed him back even when he didn't deserve it, and couldn't face him in church. Confusion and longing warmed her eyes, and under her clothes she hid bits of lace and warm skin that beckoned his hands and lips to explore. She tempted simply by existing.

There was no logic at all to the way he reacted to that Tara. The moment he got near her, his concerns about the first one, the reporter, faded to oblivion along with everything else, leaving only raw wanting. He hadn't dealt with that level of pure horniness in years, not since he'd gotten out of Kilbooly and discovered the easy way city women fell into his arms, enamored of his looks or, especially, of his money.

Perhaps Tara was using sex in the same way—as a lure, as bait to ensnare him. Brian's jaw tightened at the thought. She might want a story instead of a bank account, but she was as determined as any fortune hunter. He had long ago discovered that very little was beyond a determined woman. That's why it had been so easy to believe the worst that day when he'd spotted Kelleher and his camera.

He reached the bend in the river that marked the edge of Hanrahan property and sat there for a few minutes, thinking and letting Brig nibble at the tips of the willows.

The accusations he'd spit at Tara up there at the ruins had been sitting at the back of his brain ever since. In some ways, they made perfect sense—why else would she protest that they shouldn't get involved and then move into his arms so willingly, if not to put him off guard while she poked around in his life?

But another part of him recognized that she might suffer from the same ambivalence that plagued him. She could simply be attracted to him, the way he was attracted to her in spite of himself.

For the thousandth time, his thoughts ran back to last night, to the taste of her lips and the passion in her response. He had indeed gotten carried away. Another few minutes and he'd have been pulling her toward his car, ready to have her in the backseat. He knew instinctively that, in that instant, she would have let him.

But as delicious as that fantasy was, he'd actually taken the most delight out of standing there against the wall with Tara in his arms, listening to the boys play. The chance to enjoy such a simple pleasure seldom came his way anymore.

Brian shook himself out of his reverie and checked his watch. It was after three, and Tara and Kelleher would be at the house in an hour or so to begin setting up their equipment for the next day's interview. He turned Brig around and headed home.

The two Taras rode with him, aggravating and seductive by turns, and by the time he reached the stable, he was in tighter knots than before. Yet it occurred to him that, as volatile as the evening might prove to be, he was actually looking forward to spending the time with them.

He dismounted and handed the reins to the boy who worked the stables on weekends, then strolled up to the house, whistling.

Professional, Tara reminded herself as the front door of Bramble Court swung open. The fact that she needed such a reminder was an embarrassment in itself, but in view of the dampness of her palms and the way her heart was pounding, it was probably necessary.

The gravel-voiced butler apparently hadn't returned from the trip Mrs. Hanrahan had mentioned. A younger man greeted them at the door and led them to the library, where Brian sat behind a large, age-worn mahogany desk. He rose to greet them.

"Where would you like to do this?" he asked Tara.

"Someplace you're comfortable," she said. "Where do you spend the most time?" She regretted the question the instant it left her mouth.

"During the day, I'm often right here," he said. The look in his eyes asked if she'd like to know about his nights.

Cheeks heating, Tara looked over the room quickly. "What do you think, Finn?"

Finn paced around the room, checking different angles.

"Those draperies will swallow you alive. But maybe here." He indicated one wall of bookshelves with several sets of matched volumes interspersed with subdued, expensive-looking bric-a-brac. He dragged a couple of chairs over into position and stepped back to check it again. "Let's see what this looks like with some light on it."

"Now we haul gear," Tara explained as she backed toward the door. "You have a few minutes if you need to do anything."

"I don't," said Brian. "I'll help you."

"That's not necessary," she said quickly, but he was already past her and down the hall. She followed, noting that he had blue jeans on again. Very nicely fitting blue jeans that made her want to slip her hands into the back pockets. *Get a grip, girl.* This was a power-mad, development-crazed capitalist whom she intended to expose to the nation. She'd been coaching herself on those facts all afternoon. "We can handle it, honestly."

"I know," he said, holding the front door for her. As she passed, the faintest aroma of leather and horse wafted off him. He'd been out on Brig again, she bet.

Finn handed her a big canvas bag and looped a cable over her shoulder, then loaded Brian down, as well.

"I didn't realize reporting was so glamorous," said Brian as they bumped their way back to the library.

"We tolerate all sorts of things for the right to be underpaid," she said.

It took several trips to carry everything inside. They had just started breaking open bags when the door opened.

"Telephone for you, Mr. Hanrahan," rumbled a low voice. "Your secretary."

Brian glanced up, a surprised tilt to one eyebrow. "Lynch. You're back."

"Yes, sir. I arrived only a few moments ago. Will you take your call here or elsewhere?"

Brian glanced from Lynch to Tara and back again. "Put it through to the solarium. If you'll excuse me." As he walked past Lynch, he murmured, "We'll chat about Wicklow later."

"Yes, sir."

Both men's voices sounded carefully neutral, but Tara caught an undercurrent of tension. She waited until they were gone.

"Am I imagining things, or does it sound like Mr. Lynch went off to Wicklow without permission?"

Finn nodded. "That was my take on it. See if there are any electrical outlets besides this one."

"It doesn't look like it." She made a quick circuit of the room, then flapped the draperies up out of the way. "Only the one."

The door swung open again. Feeling like a child caught snooping, she quickly brushed the draperies back into place and hurried to the nearest equipment case. "We'll be ready in a few minutes."

Brian shook his head. "Never mind. I'm afraid we won't be doing the interview tomorrow after all. That was my secretary. We've had a small . . . incident at one of our soft drink factories. I'm sorry. We'll have to reschedule."

Tara eyed him with doubt. "Why doesn't that surprise me?"

"I swear, I didn't have someone blow a valve and spill ten thousand gallons of cola syrup into the water supply just to get out of this interview."

"Pop in the water spigots," mused Finn. "I imagine the kiddies are happy."

"But the mayor is not, and neither are the county council members. I have to head out to Crook Mill first thing in the morning on a mission of appeasement."

"Ah, Brian. You said you'd be here," said his grandmother, coming up behind him. "You promised me *and* the young lady."

"It can't be helped." His eyes never left Tara. "You will still be here when I get back?"

"I'm not going anywhere until I get my interview."

"It's hardly fair to leave her here in Kilbooly with nothing to do," said Ailís.

"Actually, I—"

"You ought to take her with you," said Ailís. "Let her see how you handle a real problem. It's better than you just sitting there answering questions anyway."

"That's really not—" Tara began.

"That's not a bad idea," said Brian. "But I happen to know that she specifically wants a sit-down interview."

"I do not."

"She already tried sneaking up on me at New Moyle. I was boring."

"Deliberately," said Tara to Mrs. Hanrahan.

"And despite her protestation to the contrary," continued Brian, "I think she also wants a palm tree in the shot."

"Now, you know that's not true."

"Oh? Come here." Brian's lips seemed to be twitching. *What was he up to?*

Frowning, Tara crossed the room. "What is it?"

"Stay right here facing the door and don't move." He went back across the room. "All right. Turn around and tell me what you see."

Tara turned. Brian sat in the chair she'd just abandoned, and behind him, just to the left— "Oh, Lord, Finn. Why didn't you tell me we've got a potted palm in the corner?"

Finn looked. "I think it's a fig."

"Whatever it is, it's just sitting there making a fool out of me." She pressed her hands to her cheeks to cover the blush and, against her better judgment, made the decision. She hadn't seen Crook Mill yet, anyway. She met Brian's sparkling eyes. "Do you promise not to tell me about any unnecessary valves or switches?"

Brian laughed. "I promise."

"Then start packing up, Finnian. We're going on the road tomorrow."

Ten

He really was quite good, Tara thought, watching Brian soothe the ruffled feathers of the people of Crook Mill.

The mayor, the resident sergeant of the *Gardaí*, someone from the national government, three members of the county council, and several concerned residents had all turned out to berate him about the spill. After a brief meeting with his plant administrator and engineers in private, Brian had listened to the locals with respect, walked the committee around the plant to explain the cleanup and repairs, and answered questions—some of them several times over when people either didn't understand or didn't pay attention.

Eventually, the belligerence of one corpulent citizen began to wear, even on Tara's sympathetic nerves. Brian, however, kept up his calm, firm reassurances and for good measure threw in a tour of the bottling line with its gleaming floors and clattering machines. Before it was over, the whole lot of them were standing out in the drizzle, shaking hands and congratulating each other over how well the village and Hanrahan had handled the matter.

It was a virtuoso performance.

And that's all it was, Tara reminded herself, a performance, for her and the camera: Brian had managed to convince the others to let Finn film.

After the last citizen had pumped Brian's hand and climbed into his car, Brian led his employees off to one side, where he gave them brief instructions and dismissed them. They headed off, already consulting amongst themselves, and Brian returned to Tara's side.

"Bored yet?"

"Not nearly, but I am hungry. Take a break, Finn." She glanced around as Finn checked the rain cover over the camera. The mess outside the gates wasn't quite as grim as New Moyle and Trullock, but it was bad enough. "Is there a decent place for lunch around here?"

Brian's eyes raked the businesses across the way. "Not nearby. There's a little hotel in the village with a good dining room, but there's not much in the way of parking near it. We'll take my car and leave the van here."

"I'll stow the camera," said Finn.

"Bring it along," said Brian, opening the car door for Tara. "She may decide to spring a question on me."

"You're being very cooperative for a man who didn't want to do the interview at all a few days ago."

"I'm simply bowing to the inevitable. You're not going to give up."

"True enough," said Tara as he slid into the driver's seat beside her.

"Then I may as well make it pleasant for both of us."

"Very well said. However, it's my experience that such changes of heart usually come with conditions."

He started the car and turned left out the plant gate. "Those are the words of a cynic."

"They're the words of a reporter who has seen enough to know," she countered. "What do you want?"

"Do I have to want something?"

"It would be nice if you didn't. But do you?"

"I may, now that you've put the idea in my head. Ask me again later."

They left behind the clutter around the plant and rounded a bend in the road to enter the village proper. Though on the tattered side, Crook Mill had a substantial feel to it, due mostly to the two-story brick buildings that lined the main road, relics of the days when there had actually been a grist-mill on the river. The buildings bore the signs of years of neglect, but here and there, efforts were being made. White planters full of pansies and daffodils stood before every shop front, even those with dark and dusty windows. Unfortunately, though, the empty shops included those that would have once been the heart of the village: the druggist, the butcher, the hardware, and the greengrocer.

There were very few people about for a village this size, a fact that disturbed Tara. At midday like this, there should have been men and women scurrying between the bank and the post office and the shops, getting their errands done while the rain was light. Instead, they were apparently all out at the big new stores on the edge of town. It was Trullock all over again.

"Here we are." Brian indicated a small, brightly painted hotel as they drove past. As few people as were visible, parking was, indeed, in short supply. They parked up a few doors and walked back, Brian leading the way along the edge of the narrow road.

"Mr. Hanrahan." As they entered, the woman came out from behind the desk to shake his hand like a long lost friend. "How lovely to see you back again so soon, although I'm sorry it's because of that mess at your plant. And who are these good people you've brought along?"

"Television reporters." Brian introduced Tara and Finn. "We're here for lunch, but Miss O'Connell here may decide to ask me some questions while we're at it. Do we have your permission to film in the dining room?"

"Of course, of course."

"Thank you so much. I hope you have those delicious egg mayonnaise sandwiches today."

"I'll see that Hattie makes some up, just for you. Now, come, let's get you settled. I'll put you in the side room, so no one will disturb you. You'll want to drink something other than tea, I'm afraid. The water's still a bit off."

"I'm sorry we created such an inconvenience for you."

"It's not so very bad. I sent the husband off to buy bottled water for the necessary items. We can't be poaching eggs in Coca-Cola, can we, now? And the guests need it, of course."

"You be sure to send the bill to the plant. We'll pay for any of your extra expenses."

Was this part of the performance? Tara wondered as she followed along. As part of her early research, she'd spoken by telephone to a man from Crook Mill who had sworn Brian was the most despised man in town, his motives suspected by everyone. This woman didn't appear to despise him—although that might simply be a false face worn for the sake of his continued patronage.

In the dining room, Finn took a seat next to the wall, where he could set the camera out of the way. That left Tara next to Brian. She slid into the chair he held for her with great trepidation.

He behaved himself, though, probably thanks to Finn's presence. They ordered their lunch—bowls of rich potato soup, a platter of sandwiches, and some fruit salad—and she tucked in with a hearty appetite.

Brian had been right about the egg mayonnaise. Hattie, whoever she was, had added something that made it out of the ordinary. A blob oozed out the side of the sandwich onto Tara's finger, and she sucked it off to see if she could identify the secret ingredient—a touch of curry, perhaps some chutney?

When she glanced up, Brian was staring at her like she was a bug under glass.

She flushed. "Sorry. It's just so good, I didn't want to waste it."

"I understand completely," he said, but his eyes held hers, glinting in an odd way that set her nerves jangling like a defective telephone.

She searched for something to break the hold, and found it in work. Back to the subject. "Crook Mill looks like it was a pretty village, once."

"Some of it still is," said Brian. "Would you like to walk around with me when we're done?"

"Certainly," she said. Then she hedged, "Provided Finn can come along."

His smile faded a bit. "Part of the anti-palm-tree effort, eh? All right."

They finished, and Brian signaled for the bill. Tara reached for her bag, but he waved her off. "This is mine."

"So was the tab at Moran's. They can't all be yours."

"Why not?"

"It's not fair."

"Oh, the injustice of it. Have me arrested." He paid the bill.

When they emerged from the hotel, they discovered that the rain had quit for the time being, and sunbeams were peeking through wide cracks in the clouds. As Finn pinned tiny microphones to their lapels and patched them into the camera, Tara took a deep breath, enjoying the rain-washed air.

"The few minutes just after the rain stops are my favorite," she said to Brian.

"Mine, too. Although there is something to be said for a cloudless summer day at the mouth of the Shannon. Have you ever been sailing?"

"Once. I got sick as a dog."

"There are cures for that," he said, and proceeded to tout several as he led her off. He apparently loved to sail and wanted everyone else to love it as much as he did.

There might not be hordes of people out and about, but of those who did pass, most greeted Brian by name. He returned their greeting, stopping to talk to several. To Tara's surprise, it was all very friendly, not at all the reaction she expected people to have to the man who had ruined their village.

But come to think of it, although the committee out at the plant had started out antagonistic enough, that had mostly faded once Brian had turned on the charm—other than that one pugnacious man. Odd.

"You seem to be well known about town," said Tara.

"I got acquainted with Crook Mill when we were deciding whether to bring the plant in."

Tara bit back a grin. He had just handed her the opening she wanted. She would have to go slowly, though. Seeing as they were already strolling around, it would be altogether too easy for him to simply walk off if he didn't like the questions.

"How do you make a decision like that? Where to put a plant or warehouse, I mean."

"It's a long process, but what it comes down to is, I needed a site for a factory, and Crook Mill needed jobs. We came to an agreement."

One that gave Hanrahan Ltd. every advantage, Tara suspected. It certainly had in other villages.

They walked a little farther, until the brick and plaster of the old village gave way to the newer concrete block buildings that led to the plant.

Brian stopped and stared at the do-it-yourself store for a moment, with the cars and people moving purposefully around it, then frowned. "Let's start back."

"Is something wrong?" asked Tara as they headed back

the way they'd come. She glanced at Finn, who nodded. He was filming away.

Brian gestured over his shoulder toward the conglomeration of new buildings. "That mess. It's damned ugly."

"It's progress," said Tara.

"Nonetheless, I still hate to see them lose the center of the village to it."

"That matters to you?" asked Tara, surprised.

"Of course it matters. I don't come out to these villages to ruin them."

"But you do ruin them," she blurted, then realized her mistake. "I mean, when you bring in a big facility like yours, it's bound to change things for the worse."

"Why for the worse? Why can't it be for the better?"

His question threw her. She looked closely at him, and for the first time noticed tight, haggard lines around his eyes.

"Why *do* you bring your factories out here?" she asked softly.

"I told you. The villages need jobs. They need money coming in. They need reasons for the young people to stay instead of moving off to the cities. If we built someplace like Dublin, we'd be just adding to the problem."

"Some of biggest Hanrahan facilities are in Limerick and Dublin and Galway City," she said

"The older ones, yes. We were like every other company in Ireland, building bigger and bigger all the time, concentrating on the cities. But then it occurred to us that the country would keep hemorrhaging its young people until somebody built in a way to give them work and keep them home and off the dole. So that's what we do. Or try to."

His words left Tara stunned. "So, you're telling me you're trying to save these villages? Crook Mill. Trullock. Dunloe?"

"That sounds a little grand, doesn't it?" he said, grimacing. He checked his watch. "I'm sorry, but we'll have to continue this later. I have other business at the plant, and I'm afraid it's not something I can let you film. Personnel matters. Here's the car. I'll drop you at your van."

As they drove back to the plant, Tara struggled to collect her spinning thoughts. When she'd asked why he came to the villages, she'd expected talk of infrastructure, demographics of workforce, geography, and—most especially—economic incentives. She knew for a fact that Hanrahan Ltd. had picked up tax breaks, land-use waivers, and all sort of other perquisites in exchange for building in some of the villages.

But Brian made it sound like other forces had driven him. She was having trouble getting her mind around that notion.

Brian left them at the factory gate, with a second promise that they'd finish the interview another time. As he entered the building, Finn whistled low.

"There goes *that* theory of capitalist predation on the poor masses."

She stared at the door where Brian had vanished. "I'm not so sure. It's very easy to claim social conscience without having to back it up."

"Doesn't match the story we've been writing in our head, though, does it?"

"Shut up, Finn."

She climbed into the van and slammed the door. He took care of the camera, then climbed into the driver's seat.

"Where next, Captain?"

"Back home."

"Dublin?"

"Kilbooly, you nit. I've got some analyzing to do."

"Ah, good. I can get some fishing in."

"Don't you get tired of catching them and letting them go?"

"Never. But I asked around and found out that they'll fry

them up for me at Deegan's Café for a pound each. Tonight the river will be aquiver at the sight of Finn the Magnificent."

"You mean Finn the Dorsal, don't you?"

"Crissy!"

"Hold on."

Now what? Crissy wondered. Owen was getting so short-tempered, what with coming in early to do the baking for the shop and then going off to his late shift at the hotel in Ennis. She'd offered to do both the baking and the counter work for a day or two, just to let him catch up on his sleep, but he insisted that this was his present to Mum and Dad.

So they had a trip to Greece, and she had a cranky brother to deal with.

She finished the pink icing rose she was making and took it off the nail to harden, then wiped her hands and went to the doorway. "Why is it so dark in here?"

"That's what I was trying to tell you," said Owen. "The big work light just blew out. Where does Dad keep the new bulbs? I checked the storeroom and there weren't any."

"Then we must be out. I'll have to get a new one at the hardware when they open."

"That leaves me in the dark."

"Can't you manage? You should be almost done for the day."

He grumbled a bit, but allowed as he could, indeed, manage. Crissy went back to her roses. Little Emma Gaynor was having a birthday, and her mother wanted the fanciest decorated cake the bakery could manage. Crissy was going all out. She liked Emma.

Between handling customers and lacing together ten perfect pink roses with ribbons and bows, she didn't have time to run to the hardware until after hours. She raced through closing, grabbed the old bulb, which Owen had taken down, then slipped out and ran off to the store.

She was standing in front of the rack, trying to match her bulb to what was there, when she heard a cheery hello.

"Rory?" she asked, turning. He had a big box under one arm and a confused look on his ruddy face. "How are you?"

"Fine. Fine. What brings you in?"

She held up her blackened light bulb.

"Ah," he said. He glanced at the bulb and the rack, then picked one out. "This one, I think."

She checked. It was a match. "Thank you. That saved me some time. You didn't come in to help me, though."

"I'm, um, looking for a pot of some sort. To use with this." He held up his box.

She read the label. "A portable burner?"

"So I can heat up some tinned stew or some such in my room. I can't afford a restaurant three times a day and I'm already tired of cold meat sandwiches. Do you know where the pots and pans are?"

Crissy hesitated. Helping him out would be violating the boycott. But he had helped her without being asked, and she wasn't going to be rude.

"Over here." She led him toward the kitchen things.

He stared at the choices, his mouth working over the problem. "How big do you think I need?"

"Just to heat tinned food?"

"Maybe to fry up some potatoes and ham."

"This set isn't too dear." She picked up a box. "That gives you two pots and a skillet, and there's even some tools inside. That should do you."

"That's fine, then. Load me down."

She stacked the set of pans on top of the burner box and started away.

"Now all I need is dishes," muttered Rory.

She wound up finding a plate and bowl for him, as well

as a fork and a spoon and a cup for tea and a kitchen knife with a tiny cutting board so he wouldn't ruin Mary's dresser trying to slice up potatoes. And then she had to carry the lot of it to the clerk because it was too much for him to balance on top of his burner.

"You're a darling," said Rory as he pulled his money out of his pocket and laid out bills on the counter. "That would have taken me forever. Now I have time to get myself a bit of something to cook tonight, just to try it out."

"You let me know how it goes," said Crissy.

Behind the counter, Louise, the owner's daughter, bagged up the smaller items without comment and handed them to Rory. He gathered together his purchases and headed out the door with his awkward load.

"Good night, Crissy. And thank you again."

"Good night, Rory." The bell jingled as the door shut behind him.

"You were giving aid and comfort," Louise scolded. "We can't do that."

"I was helping Mary. All she needs is for Rory-boy to start cooking in that room without the proper gear."

"He doesn't need to be cooking in there at all."

"You and I know that, but he's going to anyway, isn't he? And there's no use him messing the room up while he's about it."

"I suppose. But you've probably made the boycott longer." Louise did not look at all happy.

"I know," said Crissy. "But I couldn't very well stand there and tell him to bugger off when he had just helped me, now could I?"

"No," said Louise grudgingly. "I don't suppose you could."

"And I'll not help him with anything else," said Crissy. "Now, ring me up, please. My feet hurt, I want to get home."

A few minutes later, she was standing on a chair, putting

in the bulb so that she didn't have to listen to Owen complain the next morning. A few minutes after that, she let herself in at home.

She made shift with a cheese sandwich and a plate of raw veggies for supper. She'd thought cooking for herself would be fun—she could try new foods that her father wouldn't let in the house, and there would hardly be any dishes to wash up. But the novelty had worn off in the first few nights and it turned out that eating her own cooking all by herself was about as boring as food got. Still, she promised herself she'd do up a big pot of stew in a day or two, to eat off of the rest of the week. And she'd have Aileen and Siobhan over for dinner. That would be fun.

She switched the telly on and settled in with her feet up to watch the evening news. The reader had just begun a story on the new tax proposal when Aileen burst in the back door.

"I need your phone. The Nose is on fire."

Eleven

"Stop the lights!" said Crissy

"Really. I saw the smoke as I came down the road." While Aileen dialed 999 and reported the fire, Crissy slipped on her shoes, grabbed her jacket and scarf, and ran out the door and down the road in the rain.

Smoke was indeed pouring out of the upper floor of the Bishop's Nose, but when Crissy saw the source, she stopped dead.

"Ah, Rory," she said, and started to giggle.

For there he was, hanging out the window, his eyes streaming tears. In one hand he held a newspaper, flapping it for all he was worth. In the other, at arm's length, he held his brand new skillet while it billowed clouds of heavy gray smoke. Below, in the middle of the road, stood Mary Donnelly, screaming up at him like a fishwife, threatening various forms of bodily harm.

Aileen rushed up, stopped, took in the scene, and began to laugh just as the fire horn sounded. "Lord. I suppose I shouldn't have made that call."

Volunteer firefighters from all over the village turned out within seconds, as did Tara O'Connell, carrying the television camera. Martin Jury took one look at the situation, then fetched a fire extinguisher from the back of his car and walked into the pub, while the rest of the men stayed outside, hooting at Rory.

"There's Tommy," said Aileen as the pumper truck roared up. He climbed out to join in the merriment. Crissy heard her sigh.

Martin poked his head out beside Rory, blasted the skillet with the fire extinguisher and disappeared back inside, all without saying a word.

"Oh, Jayzus," cried Crissy, tears streaming down her face. "I'm going to pee me drawers." She stumbled to the nearest shop and leaned against the wall, crossing her legs and laughing all the harder as flakes of extinguisher chemicals floated down like snow over Mary's head.

Tommy noticed the camera, stopped laughing, and got officious. "What are we all doing here? The fire's out, now, isn't it? Clear the road. Move on, move on."

No one paid attention.

Even with the constant drizzle and the Guard who arrived in a flurry from Glenmore, the scene took an hour to clear. Everyone had to make the necessary jokes, after all, and tell the latecomers what had happened. Then there was convincing Rory to come out, getting the pumper backed down the narrow roadway, and brushing the white and purple fluff out of Mary's hair. Crissy and Aileen stayed for the whole show, sitting on a nearby stoop and shouting advice between gales of laughter.

Eventually, things settled down some, and a sheep-faced Rory made his way over to where Mary and Hugh waited for him with grim countenances. The remaining crowd quickly dispersed. No one wanted to be around when Rory had to face the music.

"That was better than the flick the other night," said Crissy as they walked up the road. "Come in for tea?"

"Thanks." Aileen followed her into the house and took off her jacket. They were both soaked, and Crissy found two towels and handed one to her friend.

"I wouldn't want to be Rory right now," said Aileen as she dried off.

"I feel bad for him," said Crissy. Another giggle burst from her lips.

"I can tell," said Aileen. "You feel awful."

"I do, really. It's half my fault for not telling him to put away the silly burner when I saw him with it."

"You saw him buy the thing?"

"I did. And Louise sold it to him." She explained about the store and the pots as she ran the water for tea. "I should have stayed out of it."

Aileen shook her head, her coppery curls waving damply. "On the contrary, Crissy, darling, I think you helped move things along a little." She snickered. "Lit a fire under him, so to speak."

They both laughed again, and Crissy picked up her towel and Aileen's and carried them to the laundry basket in the hall.

"I've been wondering," said Aileen as Crissy came back into the kitchen. "Who is it we expect Rory to marry? I haven't seen him around with anyone since he and Sheila McMahon broke off last year."

"Neither have I," said Crissy. She pulled the box of tea off the shelf. "I suppose someone will turn up."

"Well, I pity the poor girl, whoever she turns out to be."

Brian drove toward Kilbooly, thoughts streaming through his mind like the center line on the rain-damp road.

And every thought of Tara.

She *was* on a crusade. His instincts had been right, but as it happened, he hadn't even needed them. She'd told him, outright: "I'm doing a story on the real Brian Hanrahan."

That would be *her* version of the real Brian, of course—undoubtedly the one who rolled into village after village and destroyed them with untrammeled growth. For that's how she saw it. She'd dropped clues all during their walk:

"That matters to you?"

"But you do ruin them."

"It's bound to change things for the worse."

"So, you're telling me you're trying to save these villages? Crook Mill. Trullock. Dunloe?"

The recollection of her words came to him in a singsong beat, like the rhythm of the wipers across the windscreen. The mention of Dunloe had been the capper, finally making it clear to him.

The new packaging facility at Dunloe was hardly more than plans on his desk, approvals barely secured, and already she had the village labeled as the next Trullock.

She probably had the story half written, too, and was just looking for the words and pictures to fill it out.

He'd dealt with enough of her kind to know how it went. Reporters were all the same: they came at a story with their minds made up; they asked questions designed to get the answers they wanted; and they only gathered facts that confirmed what they thought they already knew.

Tara was no different. She'd been so convinced that he must enjoy the results of his ventures into rural Ireland that his revelation to the contrary had left her honestly shocked. Christ, who *would* like that mess?

The outskirts of Limerick loomed ahead. Brian slowed to pass through the city, forcing his concentration back to the road and the heavier traffic that continued through to Shannon.

The open road past the airport allowed his thoughts to drift again, back to Tara. She was probably back in Kilbooly right now, trying to figure out how to edit that tape to make him say what she wanted the world to hear.

And he'd handed it to her. He should have been on his toes.

He would have been, too, if she hadn't sucked that damned sandwich filling off her finger and made his imagination go straight to his crotch.

It was a hell of a thing, wanting a woman so badly that he couldn't keep his mind on what else she was up to. It was also a stupid and dangerous thing for a man in his position, with a crusading reporter on his trail. She could ruin everything he'd worked for, all these years. He had to get his edge back, before his body led him down the merry path to media suicide.

What he had to do was to get the woman out of his system, get over this obsession he had with her.

And there was only one way he knew of to do that.

Experience told him he had a short attention span where women were involved. No matter how enchanting they might be, once they'd shared his bed, the spell wore off. It was why he had so many women in and out of his life, why marriage seemed so unappealing.

It might not make him a sparkling example of manhood, but it certainly provided the possibility of an easy solution to his problem. Bed Tara, and she'd become less enthralling. Then at least he'd be able to think straight.

It was time to give in to the inevitable, to let nature take its full course. It was time to seduce Tara Bríd O'Connell.

He pressed down on the accelerator, suddenly anxious to get back to Kilbooly.

A brisk knock on the door pulled Tara away from the video deck she had carried upstairs and hooked to the hotel television. She hit the off switch and quickly tossed her jacket over the machine.

"Who is it?"

"Finn."

She opened the door. "You stink of fish."

"Good," he said, walking past her. "That means I did it right."

"Where is it?" she asked, looking around for a creel.

"*Them*, if you please. Two of them are right here," he said, patting his belly. "The rest are in Deegan's fridge, waiting for the right moment. I hear I missed a bit of excitement at the Bishop's Nose. Too bad we didn't get film."

"Who says we didn't?"

She hooked a finger under the jacket and dragged it away.

"Hiding that from the enemy?" asked Finn.

"I was afraid you were Rory." *Or Brian.* She cued up the tape and hit play. "Look what I did while you were terrorizing the trout."

"Don't tell me you used me camera."

"It's not yours, it's the network's."

"You're not legal to play with it. The union says you reporters are incompetent."

"It's a good thing they're wrong."

"I'm not sure about that," said Finn, peering at the screen. "It's awfully dark."

"Give it a minute. I had to figure out how to work the thing."

"It's jiggling."

"I was laughing. Just watch, will you?"

The tape lightened up, and Finn stopped criticizing and started laughing, too.

"All right," he said, wiping his eyes as the tape went to static. "You're competent. Which is more than I can say for that poor sod."

They ran it through twice more, once to laugh again, and once because Finn couldn't resist telling her where she'd messed up.

"I'd better get out of here before people start thinking you and I are carrying on behind my nonexistent wife's back," he said when he finished dissecting her camera skills. "Shall I carry the deck back down to the van for you?"

"I'll do it later. I want to go over the tapes from Crook Mill."

"Still resisting the obvious, are we?"

"I haven't even had a chance to think about it, yet," she said defensively. "Rory's little blaze got in the way."

"So I take it we won't be traipsing off to Dunloe or Trullock."

"Not yet, at any rate."

"Good. It's a lovely little river they have here. Nice, plump brown trout."

"I'm the one supposedly on holiday, Fishkiller, not you. You'll be filming bachelors, and tomorrow is Ladies' Night again."

"Then I really had better go," he said, grinning. "I want to be on me toes if I'm going before the Court. *Oíche mhaith duit.* Good night."

"*Gurab amhlaidh duit.* The same to you."

Tara closed the door behind him, then cracked the window to let out the smell of fish and wet wool. The tapes of Brian lay on the dresser nearby, labeled neatly in Finn's hand. She found the last one, the one of the walk through Crook Mill, fed it into the machine, and sat on the end of the bed, ready to find the holes in Brian's story.

The problem, she decided an hour later, was that there were no holes in his story, at least none she could prove outright. She went back through her files, looking for something she'd forgotten, but found nothing except a few glaring holes of her own.

She had come at this with her opinions firmly in place. Not without justification—she'd talked to twenty people by actual count, in seven of the twelve Hanrahan villages. Not one had been happy about what had happened to their village. But had she asked the right questions? Worse, had she found only the people who would give her the story she wanted?

Damn him. In five years at RTÉ, she'd never doubted her skills as a reporter as much as she did right now. At this point, the best she could hope was that a few phone calls the next day would clarify everything. She turned the video deck off and went to wash her face.

Breasts. Lips. Lace. A trail of warm butter across smooth skin. The scent of a woman slick with sex.

Brian woke up in the dark, his bed empty, desire heavy on his body.

"Damn it all."

He raised his head. The clock read four-thirty A.M. He'd been fighting this battle all night, going to sleep only to dream of Tara and wake with an erection. This made the third time. His groin ached.

He flopped back on the bed and considered the possibility of flying solo, but rejected it as ultimately unsatisfying. No. He'd made his decision.

That was half the problem. He'd decided, and now his body was anxious to rush ahead of the game.

There was no use trying to go back to sleep again. He tossed back the covers, walked over to the window, and threw it open. The cold air rushed over his naked body, providing temporary relief.

It had stopped raining since the last time he'd stood here a couple of hours ago. The night was starting to lighten, and the first birds chittered in the woods. Through the trees, he could see the distant glow of the single bare light over the stable door. In the distance, he heard the river spilling over the tiny weir at the edge of the property.

That was it.

He tugged on a pair of jeans and a pullover, found his

boots and slipped out into the silent hall. Minutes later he was astride Brig, racing bareback toward the river.

"Your tea, madam. And the *Times.*"

"Good morning, Lynch." Ailís took the newspaper and laid it beside her plate. She didn't actually read the paper anymore, the news being so grim, but bringing it was part of Lynch's morning routine and she hated to let the man down. "Have you seen my grandson yet this morning?"

He laid a second copy of the *Times* by Brian's plate. "He was not in his room when I knocked. Shall I locate him for you?"

"Thank you, no. I'll wait for him to turn up." She dropped two sugars in her tea. "By the by, did he give you very much trouble about making that call for me?"

"Hardly any, Gran," said Brian, coming in the door. "I realized it wasn't his fault that you're such a conniving old bird."

"Mind your tongue, boyo," she said, grinning. She tilted her head so he could kiss her cheek before he slid into his seat.

They ate breakfast in the conservatory by Ailís's choice—it was warmer there of a morning than in the dining room. More importantly, spending a few minutes surrounded by the hothouse plants inside and the green beauty outside made even the gloomiest day begin on a cheery note.

Lynch returned with the first course of breakfast: orange juice, porridge, and the green Galia melon Brian liked to have brought in from Spain. As he served, Brian sorted out the business pages of his paper, folded them for reading, and became immediately engrossed.

Ailís looked over her grandson with growing curiosity. He was making a great show of normality, but she'd heard him up in the middle of the night, and he looked less tidy than usual. He never came downstairs with his hair damp.

"Why is your hair so wet?" she asked bluntly.

"I was up early to go riding," he said, his usually direct gaze flickering away. "I rubbed along under some branches."

Yet his clothes were dry except for a few drip marks across his thighs. His hair shouldn't be any wetter than that. So he was lying, and that's why he couldn't face her straight on. Very interesting, that was. Perhaps he'd gone off for a little rendezvous in the woods.

She ate a few more spoonsful of porridge and pushed the bowl away. "How was your day with Miss O'Connell?"

"Half day," he said. "I sent her back early. I had other business I didn't want her filming."

"Brian," she said, unable to contain her disappointment. "You're not cooperating with the poor woman at all. She's been here a week and you haven't so much as sat down with her. Well, we're just going to have to invite her up for lunch."

He folded the paper and set it aside. "I ate lunch with her yesterday. Just what is your interest in whether I sit down with Tara O'Connell or not?"

"She's a nice young woman trying to do a story on you. It won't hurt to let her ask a few questions, will it?"

Lynch came in just then to clear the porridge bowls and serve plates of potato pancakes and sausages. Brian waited until he left.

"You didn't answer me," he pointed out. "What's your interest? I got the distinct impression Saturday night that you and Tara knew each other."

"She came up to the house while you were gone," said Ailís. "We talked a few minutes."

"Good Lord, Gran. On camera?"

"Of course not. She came to ask if I would, though. I said I might."

"Gran!"

"Somebody in the family has to talk to the press. You certainly avoid it as much as possible. Besides, I have a good feeling about this girl."

"Which goes to show how little feelings can be trusted," said Brian. "Let me tell you about Miss O'Connell."

He did so. Ailís listened with a growing sense of concern. "Did she actually say she's trying to make you out to be some sort of scoundrel?"

"Not in so many words."

"Then you may have misread her."

"If I did, I'll discover it soon enough. Meanwhile, I don't want you talking to her, Gran, most especially not for the cameras. I'll deal with her in my own way."

His gaze flickered away again, this time to some internal vision. When he came back, he winked at her.

"I need to clean up. And don't worry about Tara, Gran. She's going to get plenty of my time."

Twelve

"Key, please."

"Of course, Miss O'Connell. Here you go." Mrs. Fitzpatrick reached into the boxes behind the desk and came back with the brass key and several slips of yellow paper. "You have some messages, too."

"I was on my mobile phone all morning. No one could get through."

"I wondered. You haven't had very many calls before now. My, that Mr. Oliver you work for has a brusque way about him."

"That's the nice way of putting it," said Tara staring down at the top message: *Ring me. Oliver.*

"Quite a contrast to Brian," the woman went on. "He's always so polite and considerate. Yet not too nicey-nice, if you know what I mean. He always has a joke to tell me."

"Brian?" Tara riffled through the rest of the notes. Three more from Oliver, but the fourth was, indeed, from Brian. *I always finish what I start*, followed by a telephone number and his signature. The voice she heard in her head was as different from Oliver's as the message itself. "Brian's funny enough, but I don't believe I've ever heard him tell an actual joke."

"How odd. But then he knows I write them down and post them to my brother in Boston. At any rate, when he came by, he was quite disappointed that you weren't in, but he still had his joke. I'd tell you, but I'd blush clear to my toes." She leaned forward as though telling a secret. "They're not always nice, but they're funny. Such a delight, he is. And so handsome."

"He is that. Thank you." Tara hurried upstairs before she had to hear anything else about the perfection of Brian Hanrahan. *Handsome is as handsome does.*

She plugged her cell phone into its cradle, then punched Oliver's direct number into the hotel phone. He picked up on the second ring.

"It's me, boss."

"When am I going to get some tape?" That was Oliver: no preamble at all.

"I'm fine, thank you. Didn't Finn send the piece on Ennis?"

"It ran on the evening news last night. You should watch your own network occasionally."

"I am on holiday, you know."

"Kelleher's not. I want something usable to justify keeping him out there among the bogtrotters."

"That's what I like about you, Oliver. Your deep sensitivity to others."

"Tape," he repeated. "How's your story on Hanrahan coming?"

"We're working on it. We spent half a day with Brian yesterday, and I've got a message from him in my pocket right now, looking to finish the interview. His grandmother said she'll talk to me, and I've got some footage of him from down in Crook Mill. He let us go along."

"The spill at the bottling plant? Why didn't I get that? The evening news could have used that, as well."

"It's not of the spill. It's after, when he was talking to the officials. What I have will work better in my story than as a stand alone."

"Nnn," growled Oliver. "What about your mystery story?"

"I told you, that one's going to take a while. We have tons of tape—we've been shooting already today, in fact—but it's an evolving situation, and if I let so much as a whisper out before the right instant, we'll lose the whole thing. You'll just have to be patient"

"So what you're telling me is that you've taken a week of Kelleher's time, used up 'tons' of tape, and have all of one story that I can put on the air in the foreseeable future. And I'm supposed to stay patient?"

"That about summarizes things," said Tara. "However, we did discover that the Brian's stable man is quite the fiddle player." She told him about Tommy and the gig in Ballyvaughan.

"Oh, now there's a story worth two weeks of Kelleher's salary."

Tara grimaced at the sarcasm in her boss's voice. "I've got two big stories going here, Oliver, worth every bit of the time and money. I promise you'll love them, but you've got to trust my judgment."

Papers rattled noisily across the intervening miles. "If I didn't, you wouldn't have Finn in the first place. I've got to have something, Tara. Anything. Or I'll have to pull him back in. Maeve's still out ill."

"My God. Is she still in hospital?"

"She went home Sunday, but the doctor told her to lay off until she's one hundred percent. That puts me in a jam-up. I'm paying camera operators for extra hours and you've got a man out there turning out one two-minute story per week."

This was not good. "We'll send you something, I promise."

"By Friday. Or he comes in."

"I understand." She tried to interject a positive note. "At least you're not paying me."

"And I hope I'm not getting my money's worth. Friday."

"Yes, sir. Give Maeve my—"

The line went dead.

"—best." Tara hung up. Lovely. Just lovely. Her story was unraveling around her ears and now they were going to have to waste their time tracking down some local color to appease Oliver and the accountants. What she really wanted to do was get out to the villages and follow up on the calls she'd made.

They'd been enlightening. Annoying, but enlightening, especially the discussion with the secretary to the mayor of Dunloe. When Tara had mentioned she'd talked to a few people who weren't happy with the Hanrahan project, the woman had laughed.

"Let me guess. That would be Liam Delaney, Skipper Ruane, and Father Eustace."

"How did you know?"

"Long experience, at least with Skipper and Liam. They're what you might call professional opposition—to anything and everything we try to do in the village. I hope you didn't take them seriously."

Unfortunately, Tara had. Very seriously, largely because Father Eustace had once been a parish priest in Trullock.

She had more work to do. She didn't want to shoot color pieces.

She tore up the messages from Oliver and tossed them. That left the one from Brian.

He must have written it out himself. The note was in a different script than the others, bold and impatient, like his hands had been on her skin. In an instant she was lost in the recollection. She wished . . .

She grabbed a hairbrush and raked it through her hair impatiently. This—whatever it was—was pointless. She was not going to get involved with Brian Hanrahan. She dropped the brush into the top drawer of the dresser, crammed the message into her jacket pocket, and went to meet Finn for lunch.

He was just going into Deegan's as she walked down the street, and he waited for her and held the door.

"Tara." Siobhan greeted them with a friendly smile and led them toward a table. "Hello, Cameraman. Come for your little fishies, have you?"

"Little? Little!" Finn drew himself up in a show of indignation. "Fine thing. First I find myself forced to share my catch with a woman who makes fun of my fishing, and now you impugn the size of the very same catch. Fine thing."

"There are bigger in the river," said Siobhan with a smug grin as they sat down. "And I've caught a few myself. This morning, in fact."

"Have you, now?" asked Finn, looking at her with sudden interest. "Where?"

"I wouldn't be much of a fisherwoman if I told you that, now, would I? How would you like Dad to cook these fingerlings of yours?"

"Just fry them up and put them on a plate with some boiled praties," said Finn. "Nice and simple."

"Same for me," said Tara. "But throw something green on the plates, too. The man never eats a vegetable unless he's reminded."

"My brother's the same." Siobhan disappeared into the kitchen; Finn watched her all the way.

"Pretty woman, isn't she?" asked Tara.

"Mmm-hmm." Finn nodded.

"And funny," said Tara.

"Very."

"And she fishes, to boot."

"She does."

"Nearly perfect for you," noted Tara. She smiled sweetly. "Too bad you're married. Now let's figure out what we're going to do this afternoon. Oliver's screaming for film."

"You should see the mess in his room," said Mary that evening as she polished the bar in the Bishop's Nose. "There's a smoky patch on the ceiling, and the wall has a scorch mark as big as my head." She held up her hands to show a circle actually larger than her head by half. "It's a blessing nothing caught fire but his bloody ham."

"Be glad he was hanging out the window when Martin set off the fire extinguisher," said Siobhan. "If he'd used it in the room, you'd be cleaning up that powder for weeks."

"And don't I know it? It was hard enough to get it out of me hair."

"Poor Rory, though," said Crissy. "Have you thrown him out?"

"I'm inclined to, as much to help the cause along as to be rid of him, but Hugh says no. And to be honest, it is the first time he's given us a lick of real trouble." Mary took a final swipe at the counter with her rag. "But I swear, if he so much as opens a can of beans up there again, he'll be sleeping on the workbench at the garage."

General agreement spread around the room. The Nose was filling up early, the village women aware by some unknown method that Tara and Finn planned to film the Court. Along with seats for Aileen and Peg, the women had saved a place at the center table for Tara, but for the time being she was helping Finn get his lights just so.

A man came in and looked around. "What's up?"

"Can't you read?" demanded Mary, coming out from behind the bar. "It says 'Ladies Only,' right out front."

He pulled the door open, looked at the sign, and let the door shut again. "You always let us in here on Ladies' Night."

"Not tonight I don't. The RTÉ wants to film just the women."

"So let them film. I'll have me pint in the corner. Won't make a sound."

"Unless you want to put a skirt on, Bobby Teague, you'll pack that skinny arse of yours out of here."

"Why does that fellow get to stay?" He nodded toward Finn.

"Because I like his pigtail," said Mary. "When you learn to use the camera as well as he does, you can stay, too. In the meantime, you'll have to go over to Slattery's for the evening."

"That's like sending me to purgatory," he said.

"Nonsense. The other men are there. You'll be fine, and you can come back to Heaven tomorrow." She flapped her apron at the luckless fellow. "Now, get on."

He left to a chorus of catcalls, letting in Peg and Aileen as he went out. They hung up their coats and joined the group at the center table. Finn stepped in behind the camera and silently started filming.

Mary brought the first round, and everyone settled up as Aileen revisited the story of Rory's fire, adding new details that brought fresh laughter.

To Tara's relief, the time she'd spent interviewing Peg and Aileen paid for itself. They were used to the camera now, and under their experienced lead, the center table fell right into the pattern of banter and jokes and gossip and cheerful complaints she'd observed the week before, accommodating Finn's presence like old pros. The outlying tables were more reticent to start, constantly glancing sideways toward her and Finn and the camera, but they soon relaxed as well.

After a time, the conversation turned naturally enough to the bachelors and the boycott. Tara hadn't had to do a thing. She leaned toward Finn. "See? Fie on you and your Prime Directive."

Siobhan nudged Aileen. "Call the Court into session."

"I don't have a gavel."

"Here." Siobhan took off her shoe and handed it to her.

Aileen whacked the table three times with the heel and intoned:

A mhná na dúile dúbhadh le háilíos;
Ceapaigí fír-nimh tinte is tairní,
Caithigí smaointe is intleacht mhná leis,
Cuirigí bhur gcomhairle i gcomhar le chéile,
Is tugaimse cumhachta an fórsa dhéanamh.

Which means, if I have it right,

You women of dashed and disappointed lust;
Use female ingenuity to plan the details
Of a hell of fire and a rack of nails
Put your heads together and stay the course
I'll give you the power to put it in force.

She set the shoe aside, blushing a bit when her friends clapped.

"I don't really know it," she admitted, holding up her left hand to show the crib sheet cupped there. "And I couldn't even find me schoolbook. I had to get it off the Internet. So, we all know that Rory's in knots. And Tommy's starting to look like the ragman."

"When he's not Pretty in Pink," added Peg.

"Oh, my," said Aileen, chuckling. "Those two haven't had a good week at all, have they?"

"But at least they've kept their clothes on," said Siobhan.

"Which is more than I can say for a certain fellow we all know."

"What are you talking about?" everyone demanded. Everyone but Louise, who, Tara noticed, turned deep red and shrank into her chair.

"I was out fishing this morning," said Siobhan. Louise perked up. "Down by the weir. And who should I see skinny-dipping but the Brian, himself."

"G'on," said Crissy amid a titter of laughter.

"So that's what he was up to," said a voice from the door.

"Ailís." A chorus of greetings went up. Mary hurried around the end of the bar and across the pub to help the old woman to the empty place at the center table.

"Sorry I'm late, ladies. I had to wait until Brian left the house. A Black Bush, please, Mary."

"Now, Ailís," began Aileen. "Doctor says you shouldn't."

"And I haven't, but I'm ninety-three, and tonight I want a Black Bush."

"Coming right up," said Mary.

Ailís turned to Siobhan. "You say my grandson was swimming in the raw."

"Saw him with my very own eyes," said Siobhan. "In great detail."

"Ooh," said Crissy, blushing.

"Lucky girl," said Mary from the bar as she poured the whiskey. "There once was a day I'd have paid good money to see a fine specimen like him in the nip."

"Only if you were there before he went in. That river is bloody cold, yet. He came out looking a bit like me baby cousin."

The titters swelled into unladylike hoots, Ailís laughing as hard as anyone did. Amidst a flush of unexplained warmth, it occurred to Tara that the old woman might not realize they were filming. She couldn't imagine that she'd want the dimensions of her grandson's masculinity discussed on national television. She'd have to make certain this bit got erased before anyone in the newsroom had a chance to duplicate it. In fact, she'd edit every scrap of tape personally and wipe any sections that would embarrass the men or the women if they leaked out.

"What would ever possess him to dive into cold water like that?" asked Crissy over the laughter.

"Think about it," said Siobhan under her breath.

Crissy looked blank for a moment, and then her eyes grew round as billiard balls.

"You don't mean?" She stared straight at Tara.

Siobhan jabbed her in the side with an elbow, but it was too late. The laughter died, and every eye in the room went to Tara, who silently prayed for the building to collapse around her ears as she slowly turned the brilliant red of a rooster's comb.

Tommy stood outside the Bishop's Nose, glaring at the sign on the door.

Ladies Only.

"Fine thing, locking a man out of his own pub," Tommy muttered to himself. "What's the world coming to?"

He pulled the door open just a crack and was met by a gust of perfumed air carrying the sound of female laughter. He frowned and silently pushed the door shut. Didn't smell right at all. Hugh would have to air the place out tomorrow.

Tommy didn't really want to deal with all those women anyway. He stood there, hands on his hips, debating what to do. Ladies Night or no, he wanted to find Rory Boland to ask about a noise his car was making. He could go back up to Slattery's and wait, for Rory was bound to turn up sooner or later. But he might be sitting right upstairs.

"Rory," he called up toward the window. "Rory Boland."

No answer. He'd just have to go up and check. He'd use the back door, that was the ticket.

He walked around the pub, past the RTÉ van and Ailís Hanrahan's car, with Lynch dozing behind the wheel. Aileen's blue Mini was back there, too, and hanging from the mirror was the old brass St. Christopher's medal he'd given her when she started her job. St. Kit might not be an official saint anymore, but with her spending so much time driving village to village for the doctors, he wanted all possible angels on her side.

He stopped, a tight spot in his chest. He had stayed away from Aileen for nearly a week now, waiting for her to give some sign that her attitude was softening, but he'd seen none. Even last night at the fire, she'd sat there with Crissy, her hair and face sparkling with drops of rain so that she looked like a dew-spangled fairy, laughing and joking with everyone but him.

But if she thought that was going to drive him over the edge into matrimony, she had another thing coming. He'd not be pressured into something he wasn't ready for. He had his pride. He'd ask her to marry him when he was good and ready.

In the meantime, he needed to find Rory.

As he'd suspected, the back door of the pub stood wide open. He slipped past Nan Laurey's yellow cat, Jack, who was lurking around the garbage bin, and eased the screen door open

Once inside, he crept across the pub kitchen on tiptoe so Mary wouldn't hear—not that she could, over the laughter. He peeked around the corner. Apparently the television was filming, because he could see that O'Connell woman and her cameraman. They were set up with their backs to him.

Good. He could slip across to the back stairs unnoticed. He stood there, waiting for an opportune moment.

The laughter died and there was a long silence. Then Ailís's voice, thin and reedy, echoed down the hall. "Now leave the poor girl alone. We don't even know for certain that she's the source of his . . . discomfort."

Laughter exploded again, then slowly trailed off as someone pounded on the table.

"Order," called Aileen. "We've got more to do than talk about the Brian. Where's the list?"

"I have it," said Crissy.

"I want a report on every man-jack on it. We have to see how we're doing."

"Let's see. There's Tommy. We know about him. And Rory, of course."

The sound of his own name made Tommy prick up his ears. *Know what about him?* He tilted his head trying to hear more clearly.

"Next is Daniel Clohessy. Louise?"

"Well, he's, um . . . That is, I . . ."

"She's told him not to come around at all," interjected Siobhan quickly. "And he's starting to get cranky about it, isn't that right, Louise? Really, you've got to get over being so tongue-tied. Next."

"Michael Mahoney."

"I resigned the drama society," said a voice that sounded like Michael's girlfriend, Bridget. Michael was a schoolteacher and the driving force in the village drama society. Hell, he lived and breathed the drama society.

"All the women are going to quit, one at a time. If he doesn't come around soon, he'll have to call off the spring production."

Tommy gaped. That last was his mother. What was she talking about, quitting the drama society? She loved her plays. And canceling the play would just about kill Michael.

"I've got to get more peanuts," said Mary. "Don't let me miss anything."

She kept the nuts in the kitchen.

Any thought of hearing anything more flew out the door just ahead of Tommy.

"Who's there?" called Mary behind him.

He rocketed around the corner before she could get to the door and flattened against the wall.

"Who's there?" she demanded again. "Oh, Jack. You silly damn cat. Here, have a bit of cheese and get out of my kitchen."

Good cat. Tommy gave his heart a minute to catch up with the rest of him.

What the devil was going on with these women? It sounded like a conspiracy of some sort—though what they would be conspiring about, he had no idea. He needed to get his mind around it, and there was nothing better for that than a stiff drink and a few sympathetic ears.

He straightened, brushed his jacket, adjusted his cap, and headed out the road, back toward Slattery's.

He'd no sooner walked in than he spotted Rory sitting right there at the far end of the bar. He took a spot beside him and ordered a shot of whiskey. "You and I need to talk."

Tommy poured out his story, but Rory only broke into a laugh. "If you're going to tell tall tales, you've got to make them better than that."

"It's not tale. I heard them with me own ears," said Tommy.

"Martin. Come hear this." Rory motioned Martin over. A moment later, he was laughing, too. He leaned over and sniffed at Tommy.

"How many whiskeys have you had?"

"Just this one. I had one jar of stout before I walked down there, and you know that's the truth, for I was sitting at the table with you," said Tommy. "I'm saying I heard them. I was in the kitchen, and I could hear every conniving word."

"They're women," said Martin. "They talk about us, the same as we talk about them."

"Ah, this wasn't the same at all. There's a sour smell about this. They're plotting something."

"Against you and Rory? Now there's a waste of a good conspiracy."

"Not just Rory and me. Dan Clohessy and Mike Mahoney, too. And who knows who else."

"The story's growing," noted Martin to Rory. "He'll soon be telling us the women are conspiring against every man in Kilbooly. Going to turn us into Irish zombies."

"Oh, ye of little faith," said Tommy. "You make fun of me now, but just you wait. Those women are up to something. You'll see. And then it'll be too late to stop them."

Disgusted, Tommy tossed back the last of his drink and walked out. He was halfway home before he remembered about the noise in the car.

Brian sat in a corner of Slattery's nursing a pint. He would have preferred a whiskey, but the choices arrayed in front of Bull Slattery's bar mirror were less than stellar. For God's sake, the man didn't even stock Powers. No wonder the Nose had four times the custom on a normal night.

But tonight wasn't a normal night. Tonight, Tara was filming at the Nose. He'd learned that at the same time he'd discovered that the men were banned for the evening.

The question that plagued him was, what was she filming? In his most press-paranoid of moments, he couldn't conjure up any story about him that would require the testimony of a pub full of women. Not women she could assemble in Kilbooly, at any rate.

As he was turning this latest mystery over in his mind, Tommy Ahearn blustered in, ordered a whiskey and started bending the ear of Rory Boland. Rory laughed and called over Martin, who also listened and laughed. Tommy's face grew red, and his voice increased in volume.

". . . just you wait. Those women are up to something.

You'll see. And then it'll be too late to stop them." He pushed his way through the crowd to the front door and disappeared.

Now what was that about? Tommy was normally a very even-keeled sort, which was part of what made him so useful around the horses. Brian gave Rory and Martin a few minutes to finish making their jokes about him, then picked up his glass and ambled over to the bar.

"Brian."

"Martin. Rory."

"How's the car running?"

"Fine. Fine." They spent a few minutes going through the ritual of small talk and sharing news, then Brian said, "Tommy looked a bit agitated."

"Flootered, is what he is," said Rory. "Next thing, he'll be seeing pink elephants march up the street."

"He wandered in the back door of the Nose looking for Rory and overheard the women talking about us," said Martin. "Apparently his ears got burnt and now he thinks they're plotting against him." He took a long, thoughtful draw on his beer, and shook his head sympathetically. "The poor lad's been acting odd ever since Aileen broke off with him."

"She broke off with him?" asked Brian, surprised. *How had he missed that one?* "When did that happen?"

"Last week. Just up and told him to blow off. He's been so down at the mouth that Saturday he wouldn't even let us play the new tune he wrote. It's called 'Aileen's Real.' R-E-A-L, like true blue. Except she's not anymore, not for him."

"Poor fellow," said Brian. "No wonder he's off his mark."

"That could do it," agreed Martin.

They chatted a few minutes more, until Martin finished his pint and announced he had to get home. Brian grabbed the excuse to leave with him, before he wasted a whole evening arguing football statistics with Rory. They said good-bye just out the door, Martin turning right to head up toward his house, and Brian keeping straight, to his car.

The route home took him past the Bishop's Nose, and he was glad it did, for as he passed, he noticed Gran's sedan parked on one side, with loyal Lynch occupying the driver's seat.

He slammed on the brake.

His grandmother, who he'd specifically asked not to speak for the camera, was in the Nose. Tara was filming in the Nose.

"Those women are up to something. You'll see," repeated Tommy in his ear.

Damned right they were. And he was going to find out what.

Thirteen

"*It seems the* archbishop was on his way to town," said Ailís, the round of jokes having come to her. She leaned forward on her elbows, her one Black Bush still before her and a mischievous quirk to the corners of her mouth. "Now to have such a high mucky-muck visit was as rare as summer snow, and Bernie, the local reporter, was desperate to get himself a story out of it. He picked his spot carefully, making sure he was at the front of the pack of newspapermen who gathered at the station. When the archbishop's train stopped and the door opened, our Bernie was the first to shout his question, 'Will you be visiting the red-light district?'

"His Excellency was taken aback, naturally enough, and blurted out, 'Is there a red-light district in this town?'

"Bernie had his headline. The next morning the paper read: ARCHIBISHOP'S FIRST WORDS: IS THERE A RED-LIGHT DISTRICT IN THIS TOWN?'"

It was an old joke, but Tara laughed along with the rest. Oliver was going to love this. Not only did she have nearly two hours of tremendous footage on the Court from which to pick and choose for her story, but it had finally dawned on her that Ladies' Night, itself, was some of the local color she needed. Oliver's demands always had such a focusing effect to them. She'd had Finn keep the camera running when conversation had turned back to the more everyday sort of pub crack, including the inevitable run of dirty jokes.

"Last call," said Mary.

"Dear me, have I stayed that late?" said Ailís. She pushed to her feet. "It's been a pleasure, ladies, but this old woman is tired. Good night to you all. Miss O'Connell. Mr. Kelleher."

"Good night."

Peg and Aileen said their goodnights as well and helped her out.

The departure of the three women marked the unofficial end to the evening, and most of the crowd drifted out just behind them, gathering coats and tying scarves and telling the last few jokes. Within minutes, only Siobhan and Crissy remained. The two of them grabbed trays and helped Mary clear the tables while Tara and Finn broke down the equipment.

"How was it?" asked Siobhan as she wiped down a table next to Finn. "Did you get what you wanted?"

"I got it," he said. "Whether it's what Tara wanted or not is a different matter."

"It was," said Tara, collapsing a reflector, something she could always manage to do to Finn's satisfaction. "You all were wonderful. I couldn't have asked for a better shoot—although most of those jokes will never be allowed on the air."

"Wouldn't want the men to see them anyway," said Siobhan. "It would violate their image of us, knowing we don't faint dead away at the sound of a dirty joke. Then they'd have to think up some other excuse to go off by themselves."

"Is that why we do that?" asked Finn. "To tell dirty jokes?"

"If it's not, then don't disabuse me, please. I don't think I want to know what it is you really do."

Finn laughed and snapped shut the mike case, then swung the camera up on his shoulder and grabbed the case. "I'll be back."

Tara broke down the reflector stand and stowed it while surreptitiously watching Siobhan staring after Finn. *Surely not.*

"Look at the time," said Crissy. "And me with an early day tomorrow. There's some sort of award luncheon at Kilmihil and they've asked for a special cake." She moved to leave. "Come along, Siobhan."

"I'm not at all sleepy," said Siobhan. "Mary, you go on home instead, and I'll lock up for you."

"Oh, that would be lovely," Mary said. "I'm hardly ever home before midnight."

"Then you should go," said Crissy. She lifted Mary's coat off the hook. "That's sweet of you, Siobhan."

"Very sweet," said Mary. "Perhaps I'll hire you two to clear tables every night."

"You don't have that much money," said Siobhan. "I get enough of clearing tables at the café."

Good nights were said, and Finn returned just as the two women left. He held the door for them.

"Hang on," said Tara. She grabbed the light kit, an awkward canvas duffel stuffed with lights and stands and reflectors. It was nearly four feet long and weighed a ton, and she grunted as she lifted it.

"Leave that for me," said Finn.

"I can manage. Just hold the door."

"All right. You'll need these." Finn handed her the keys as she bumped and clattered past.

Outside, Mary and Crissy were dark shadows disappearing up the road. Tara watched them a moment, then glanced around for the van.

Now why hadn't Finn pulled around front? Grousing, she hauled the heavy bag around the side of the pub to the van. She tried to unlock the door with one hand, but the lock was sticky and she had to set the bag down and fiddle a bit. Finally the door popped and she slid it back then reached for the bag.

"May I help? "

Tara squeaked, jumped, and flattened against the door of the van in a defensive pose.

"I'm sorry," said Brian, stepping back a foot or two. "I didn't mean to startle you. I assumed you had seen me. I was standing right over there." He gestured toward a car—his car, she could see now—which stood a few yards beyond the van, looking black in a blacker shadow.

"I've just spent four hours under television lights," she said. "My eyes haven't adjusted yet."

"Of course." He smiled. "I *am* sorry."

"So, are you so desperate for a pint that you've taken to loitering around the back of pubs?"

"It's not a pint I'm after. I've been trying to reach you all day."

"We were all around the village," she said, trying very hard to ignore the wishful flutter that passed through her belly. "Filming."

"I left a message at the hotel."

"I haven't picked up my messages yet," she lied. She didn't want to explain why she hadn't called since noon. She wasn't certain she knew.

He stepped closer and snatched a yellow slip of paper out of her pocket. "Strange. Must have jumped in as you passed the desk." He held it up in the light. "Yes. This is from me."

"I meant to say I haven't *read* them yet."

"Oh. Well, allow me. It says, I always finish what I start."

The low tease in his voice made her suddenly unsure that he'd meant the interview at all. He'd started so many things. If he finished every one . . .

"I've, um, got to put this in," she said, trying to get her mind to veer away from that subject. She reached for the bag.

He bent, and his hand closed over hers on the grip. It put him right next to her, thigh by warm, hard thigh, as together they boosted the bag into the van.

"Thank you."

His hand stayed over hers. "How did your filming go tonight?"

"Fine," she said, then cleared her throat to get rid of the peculiar catch in it. "Fine. Everyone was in prime form."

"Just what was it you were filming?" He curled his fingers into hers and tugged her hand free so that he was holding it.

"Ladies' Night. It's not what you expect of an old-fashioned pub like the Nose."

"Mary had to work hard to convince Hugh to do it," said Brian. "I'm surprised he let her lock the men out altogether, though."

"I asked her to," she said, taking the blame. After all, she'd leave Kilbooly when this was over. "I wanted to ask what life is like for a woman in a village these days, whether anything has really changed over the last few years, that sort of thing. The women wouldn't speak as freely with men about."

"Gran would give you an earful, men or not."

"Actually, she was quite sedate. She hardly spoke at all, except she did tell a joke about a reporter." *There was something else about that joke.* Tara couldn't get hold of it, what with the way Brian's fingers were stroking the palm of her hand and sending tremors up her arm. It made it terribly hard to concentrate.

"I'm sorry." He lifted her hand to brush a kiss across her knuckles. "Gran's like that." Another kiss. "She seems to have a joke for every person or occasion." Another, which lingered so that his breath warmed her fingers.

"She's, um, old enough that she's probably saved up a few."

"Here's the last of it," said Finn.

Embarrassed, Tara tried to pull free. Brian tightened his grip just enough to hang on.

Oblivious to the tug of war, Finn dropped the bag of cords into the van. "Good to see you again, Mr. Hanrahan."

Tara jerked her hand free. Brian gave her a wink, then turned to shake Finn's hand. "Kelleher."

Behind him, Siobhan's quick eyes raked over the situation. "Come on, Cameraman. Walk me home."

"I should load up, first."

"I'm sure Brian and Tara can manage. Can't you, Bri?"

"Certainly," said Brian. "You go on. I'll see that Tara and the van get back to the hotel."

"But I—" began Finn.

"I'll tell you the secrets of the river." Siobhan caught him by the elbow and dragged him off. "Maybe tomorrow you can catch a real fish. Now the first thing you want to do is head down past the bridge . . ."

They headed off up the road into the blackness of the night, Siobhan chattering all the way. Tara took advantage of the distraction to scramble up into the van and start tugging on the light kit.

"I said I would help with that," said Brian.

"It just sticks a bit on the carpet. I can get it." She wiggled and pushed the bag into its Finn-assigned position, safely wedged into a space in the foam cushioning that lined the van. "Could you shove that other bag back here?"

Brian passed in the lumpy bag of cords. She slid it into position and turned to crawl out, only to find Brian blocking her way. He wore a look of mischief and her pulse climbed by several beats per minute.

"You know," she said quickly, "it was probably good that Finn and Siobhan came out when they did."

She started to one side. He moved and blocked her. "Good for whom?"

"Brian. We—"

"I know," he said. "We barely know each other, and there are a thousand reasons why we shouldn't, but the fact is, I do always finish what I start." He captured her hand. "So where were we? Ah, yes." He tugged Tara's hand back to his lips.

"I really need to get to—" She stopped herself before she said bed, then lost her train of thought as Brian kissed his way across her knuckles once again. He reached the last one and changed strategies, focusing his attentions on her index finger. The moist, meandering line he traced caused muscles to tighten and release all the way up her arm and down her back.

She stared, absorbed. "Brian."

"Hmm?" He drew the tip of her finger into his mouth and sucked gently. Tara gasped.

He met her eyes and held them as he drew her finger deeper in to his mouth, then let it slide out and back in, in a slow, erotic signal to the part of Tara that didn't want to think anymore. Warmth flooded her skin and coalesced somewhere in the center of her as raw desire.

Brian moved toward her, coming up into the van on his knees without ever losing eye contact. Tara felt like a hare caught in headlamps, knowing danger was approaching, but unable to move. Closer. Closer.

He shifted, and suddenly his mouth was on hers, his tongue performing the same suggestive dance, and any chance Tara had of recovering her reasoning skills rolled off into the night. With a groan of surrender, she wrapped her arms around Brian's neck.

Finn stood outside Siobhan's door, his hands in his pockets, listening intently to her explanation of the dietary preferences of River Creegh's brown trout.

She truly was a fisherwoman, as addicted to the rod and reel as he was. And pretty, too, as Tara had pointed out. If he were in the market for female companionship, she'd be high on the list.

But he wasn't. Not for one of these woman, at least, with their single-minded focus on trapping a man—and Siobhan Deegan least of all. She was one of the worst, from what he'd seen. One of those bachelors must be hers, though Finn hadn't yet figured out which poor sod it was.

"Well," he said when he'd milked her for as much fishing lore as he could in one go. "It's getting late."

"Thanks for walking me home," she said.

"Thank you for sharing your secrets." He backed off a few steps. "I'll be off."

"You won't go back to the van, will you? They're probably shucking down by now. I wonder if they're actually going to do it in the van."

"I have no idea what you're talking about," said Finn.

"You know. Those two."

Finn shrugged.

"Are you that thick?" demanded Siobhan.

"Tara had better hope so. If I weren't, I might have to mention it to the boss."

"For having a ride in the van?"

"For having a ride with the Brian. She's doing a story on him. Boffing him would be a conflict of interest, wouldn't you say, whether they happened to be in the news van or not?"

Siobhan's lovely red mouth flapped open and shut, and

she blinked. "News van? What on earth are you talking about, Finn Kelleher? Last I saw, Tara was headed for the hotel. Alone."

Finn winked. "That's a girl. I'll see you around."

"Maybe on the river. I go out at least a couple of times a week. Early."

Finn kept backing up. She wanted to go fishing with him. Maybe she didn't have her heart set on one of the bachelors after all. Maybe she was interested in him. There was a sobering thought, even for a man who hadn't had so much as a beer all evening. Good thing he had that fictional wife of his to protect him from the wiles of such women. Thank God for Finn the Married.

He headed back to the hotel, wondering if the van would be there when he arrived.

It wasn't.

Brian and Tara knelt there, kissing, touching, and exploring as they shed coats and jackets. Somewhere in the distance a motor rumbled closer, and for the briefest moment Tara clung to the thought that they would have to stop. They couldn't continue this, not in the van, not with the light on and the door standing wide open and people about.

That thought—fear?—vanished when Brian released her long enough to reach over and drag the van door shut with a determined thud.

The darkness was immediate and complete and welcome; the sound of the door locking amounted to permission. She reached for Brian in the blackness and found him inches away, as heated and full of urgency as she was.

They had to do it all by touch now, for not even a glimmer of moonlight reached back so far into the van. They kissed, and their hands danced over each other, acquainting themselves with curves and planes and soft hips and hard shoulders.

And breasts, oh God, breasts.

Her fingers dug into his shoulders and her breath grew uneven in the darkness. Smiling against her mouth, Brian found her nipples and tugged them to soft points beneath her clothes. He lifted her hands to his collar, then reached for hers.

She worked as fast as he did, tugging open his shirt at the same instant he reached her last button. Her breath caught in her throat as he bent his head to kiss along the top of her bra. He slipped one strap off her shoulder and tugged the lace aside.

"Ahh." His exclamation was less a sound than a sensation of warmth across her breast as he flicked his tongue over her nipple. She shuddered, and he did it again, this time slower and with more deliberate intent. The juxtaposition of roughness and moisture and moving air generated waves of pleasure that rippled through Tara. She laced her fingers into his hair and pulled him closer, then cried out as his mouth moved over her. The scent of him, woodsy cologne mixed with smoke from the pub, swirled around her, intoxicating.

He lingered there, suckling her into insensibility and taking obvious pleasure in his accomplishment. He found the front closure on her bra and eased it open, exposing her other breast for equal treatment, and proceeded to draw groan after shuddering groan from her. Her knees refused to support her, and she began to sway.

Brian instantly abandoned her breasts to pull her into his arms, and they melded skin to skin for a delicious moment, her sensitized nipples pressing into the crisp hair of his chest, before he tipped her back into the narrow space in the center of the van. Their discarded coats made a soft nest amid the equipment, and she wriggled into it as he moved over her. He pushed her skirt high with a knee so he could settle between her thighs. His hands cupped either side of her head, to hold her immobile while he peppered kisses over her face, over eyes and cheeks and the corners of her mouth.

"I want you, Tara." His voice was a husky whisper at her ear, strained and full of need. "You do things to me, drive me mad. I have to have you. Now."

Now or never. A ghost of a no formed in the last remaining sane corner of her mind, but before it could solidify, he bucked softly against her. She felt him, hard beneath the fabric that separated them, and the prospect of having him inside her wiped out every other thought.

Speech was out of the question, so in answer, she kicked off her shoes and hooked her heels behind his legs.

"Ahh, Tara."

The tremor that shook him was her personal victory, proof she could affect him the same way he affected her. She gathered him closer, and he kissed her, his tongue probing briefly in that familiar, primitive rhythm before he began a path downward. He found the pulse racing at the base of her throat, lingered over her breasts just long enough to draw another moan from her, then traveled lower still, to her belly just above her waistband. She touched what she could reach of him as he moved down—back, shoulders, then only his hair, and finally nothing at all as he raised up to strip off the last of her clothes. Skirt, tights, underwear: they all vanished into the darkness, along with any sense of decency as he caressed and explored with mouth and hands.

Somewhere above her, he moved, shedding his own clothes. She wished she could see him but at the same time savored the darkness. In the dark it didn't matter that she was lying there before him naked, her legs apart, her body liquid with need.

Oh, God, she needed him. He was taking too long.

"Brian?"

She jumped as his hands closed around her ankles.

"You're ready for me, aren't you," he murmured. "I can't

see you, but I know it from the sound of you." He ran his hands up her legs and back down. "And the feel of you." He pressed outward, making her more open, and shifted between her knees. His hands stroked upward again, this time all the way up, until he found the soft thatch of hair at her crotch. He brushed his fingers through it and inhaled deeply. "And the scent of you."

She jumped again as he slipped one finger down and into her, then swirled her moisture up and over her most sensitive spot.

"Brian."

"Shh," he soothed, and shifted again so that his soft exhalation touched the same place.

She was ready for his mouth, so ready that the actuality of it shocked her almost back to coherence. She shouldn't. She shouldn't, but his tongue swirled and her hips lifted to him of their own accord, and she slipped back into the place occupied only by the two of them. The universe narrowed to the pitch-black interior of the van, where everything was sound and scent and touch, and the sum total of reality was Brian's mouth on her. He devoured her, pushing her closer to the edge. Her muscles tensed. *So close.*

Then he was over her once more, pressing her legs apart, opening her. Something hot and silky and hard touched her and she knew he was as ready as she was. She wrapped herself around him and pulled him in with a guttural cry of satisfaction at their mutual possession, followed by a moan of frustration as she slipped away from the edge.

So close. Full with him, she squirmed, trying to guide him back to that sweet spot.

"Show me, Tara. Show me how to make you come." He moved with her, letting her set the pace and the motion, and after a moment they found it together. "That's it," he breathed. "Feel it. Give in to it."

Murmuring words of encouragement and sex between

kisses, he raised his torso just a fraction and slipped his hand between their sweat-damp bodies to find her nipple. His fingers played over the tip. "Come, love."

The tension that had been slowly coiling in her belly for days released in a sudden burst that shook her and made her arch beneath him. He stayed with her, deepening the pressure but continuing the steady rhythm, forcing her to experience every convulsion of body and soul.

Only when she began to recover herself did he shift, adopting a motion suited to his own pleasure. He pushed into her with more urgency, striving toward the goal she'd already achieved. She wanted him there, with her, and she skimmed her hands over his driving body, coaxing him on. Her voice returned, allowing her to entice him with the same words he'd used on her, and as she whispered them, she raked her nails up his sides.

With a cry of possession, he drove deep into her. Spasms racked his body until it felt like he would come apart in her hands. She gathered him in, wrapping her arms and legs around him, trying to hold him together and keep him there with her, in her.

Slowly he relaxed, settling onto her but holding himself up just enough not to crush her.

"Beautiful Tara. So sweet. So warm." His voice sounded drugged. "I knew you'd be like this." He kissed her, then rocked side to side, easing deeper even as the last pulses of his orgasm shook them both.

They lay there kissing, bodies linked, sweat cooling on their skin, as reality slowly reasserted itself. Despite the carpet and the tangle of coats beneath Tara, the floor of the van was bloody cold. Rain started, echoing on the roof like gunfire. Tara began to shiver.

"You're freezing." Brian rolled off her and moved away, and she heard him groping around the floor.

She sat up and, conscious of the rush of warmth between

her thighs, found the box of tissues Finn kept under the driver's seat and quickly dried herself.

"Here's somebody's shirt," said Brian. "Put it on."

She waved her hand around until she met the shirt he held out.

"It's yours," she said as she slipped it on.

"Here are your tights."

"I need my knickers first."

"Sorry, these are mine." He rustled around, presumably getting them on, then patted the floor again. "Your shirt. My trousers. Aha. A bra. Must be yours."

"Are you sure?" she asked as he passed it to her.

"I went without tonight," he said with a laugh. "I'll keep hunting."

She removed his shirt and handed it to him, then got into her bra and her own shirt, taking care with the buttons.

I can't seem to find them," said Brian. "We may have to turn on the light."

"No! Jayzus, it'd be like a stage, and me wearing no pants."

"Now there's an image to stir a man's soul," he said. His fingers curled around her wrist and he pulled her into his arms. "Or parts lower."

He was hard again, ready for another go. Everything went soft inside her. Her body felt suddenly unfamiliar, as though she'd been gone from it for a time and a stranger had occupied it.

"Oh, God, Brian. What just happened here?"

He stroked her hair and kissed her. "What we both wanted. Come home with me, and I'll show you again how much you wanted it. How much I wanted you." He brushed a hand up under the tail of her shirt.

"Don't." She pulled away from him. "Jayzus, what was I thinking? In the news van, for God's sake."

She felt her way forward and fumbled around for the

torch Finn always kept in the driver's side door pocket. Once she had it, it took her only seconds to find her underwear and her skirt. She snapped off the light and got dressed in silence, staying as far away as she could from where Brian did the same.

Keys jingled as he sorted through the coats.

"Here." He pressed her jacket into her hands.

"If you're dressed, you'd better go before anyone comes along," she said.

"It's the middle of the night. This isn't Dublin. Everyone went home at closing."

She found the door handle and pulled it down. The door popped and the dome light glared to life. The sight of Brian, disheveled and looking bemused, made her chest squeeze tight. "Just go. Please."

He searched her face. "Tara."

"I'm all right," she said. "Really. But I won't be if anyone sees us. Please, Brian."

He nodded and put his own coat on and climbed out past her, stopping to give her one last disturbing look as he flipped his collar up against the rain. Then he turned and walked away. A moment later, his car started and rumbled away.

Tara hauled the sliding door shut and crawled into the driver's seat to start the van. She put the heater on and was sitting there, waiting for the warmth, when the enormity of what she'd just done hit her.

God. She must be insane. Not only had she put her job at risk, but they'd used no protection at all. He could have something. She could be pregnant right now. The image of a little Brian with black hair and sapphire blue eyes formed itself in her mind, simultaneously stirring longing and fear.

She counted back, quickly calculating dates, and sighed. She should be safe in that regard, at least. Maybe.

She rested her forehead against the steering wheel.

He'd been right. She'd wanted him. Truth be told, she still wanted him, despite the possible repercussions. That alone told her how mad the whole thing was.

She drove the short distance to the hotel and parked, then carefully checked every shirt button before she went in. As it turned out, she needn't have bothered. The lobby was dark except for a single lamp in the corner. Tara locked the front door behind her, retrieved her key from the box, and slipped upstairs as quietly as she could.

A shower was the only thing that made any sense at all. She turned on the tap as hot as she could stand, stripped down, and stepped in.

The steaming water washed away the last of the cobwebs along with the remaining traces of Brian, and she was able to get some sort of perspective. She'd been vulnerable, she decided. She'd been without a man in her life for months and Brian just happened to be there and more than willing. With her prejudices against him being taken down brick by brick, she hadn't had anything left with which to resist him.

Her reporter's mind argued both sides. Perhaps those bricks shouldn't be removed so quickly. What if she had focused on a few ambiguous statements about Brian just to convince herself that he wasn't so bad after all? What if she wanted to believe he was good, just to give herself permission to do what she wanted to do anyway? Or what if she instinctively realized he was a good man at heart and was responding to that on a physical level?

What if she was in falling love with him?

No.

Impossible. She could not be falling in love with a millionaire playboy that she'd met less than a week ago, especially not this one. This was sex, and that was all it was. Just sex. She knew too much about Brian and the way he did business to fall in love with him.

But did she really?

Ailís's joke came back to her, and she realized that was what she couldn't get hold of earlier: old Bernie got his answer according to the question he asked.

That hadn't been a joke, it had been a message—whether by Ailís's intent or not, she wasn't sure. Objectivity was one of the most fundamental lessons of journalism, and one of the hardest to learn. A reporter could fool herself into thinking she was getting a true picture when she was really seeing only half of it, according to the people she talked to and the questions she asked.

The truth she'd been resisting for the past twenty-four hours suddenly stared her in the face: She had no idea who Brian Hanrahan really was because, like Bernie, she'd asked only the questions that would get the story she had set out to get.

But she didn't have to keep doing that. She was a good reporter. She knew the right way to go about getting the whole story. She just had to do it, like she should have done in the first place.

And when she'd done her job correctly, she'd know the truth about Brian, and maybe, just maybe, she could figure out how she actually felt about him.

She shut off the water and quickly toweled down, then put on her nightgown and robe, raked a quick comb through her hair, and walked down the hall to Finn's door.

She had to knock three times, but he finally grumbled, "I'm coming. I'm coming."

He was pulling on a ratty T-shirt when he opened the door. "What's up?"

"I want to be ready to go by six."

He peered over his shoulder, squinting. "It's almost two now."

"I know."

"Where are we going?"

"I'm not sure."

"Lovely. Just lovely," he said. "I always enjoy getting up early to go nowhere."

"Oh, we're going somewhere, all right," she said. "I just have to figure out where. And what I'm going to do when we get there."

Fourteen

Brian stood at his window, staring out at the sky and contemplating another early morning dip in the river.

Seducing Tara hadn't worked out precisely the way he'd
intended. Instead of lessening his desire, it had only sharp-
ened it by letting him experience what it was like with her.

Where fantasy had been his nemesis before, now memory dogged him. Lying in the dark of his room, it had
flooded back: the smell of her skin; the nubby hardness of
her nipples against his chest; the sound of her cries; the flutter of her belly beneath his palm as he discovered the clean,
womanly taste of her. He could even relish the silky tickle
of her hair in his hands when he cradled her head to give her
a simple kiss.

It was all there, burned into sense-memory like a brand.
With sight eliminated, his other senses had focused on Tara
to an extraordinary degree. He hadn't realized how much the
absolute darkness of the van would intensify the experience,
how much it would unhinge him. After the first few minutes,
any consideration of place and time had vaporized in the
heat of his desire to have her right then, right there. It hadn't

been until much, much later that the heat of those memories had reminded him that he'd used no protection.

He blamed himself. He never should have let things unfold there in the van.

He hadn't intended anything more than a kiss or two, a few moments of petting toward the end of getting her to come home with him. He should have known better, though, after Ballyvaughan. Now, not only had he not regained control of himself, he had actually created the potential for several new problems.

Damn it. He slapped the frame of the window and turned away.

He'd never reacted this way to a woman. Always before the aftermath to sex had been release. Relief. Even the first time with a given woman, he always felt the act itself was complete. There was no completion here, just more wanting, just more need for Tara.

What was she doing to him?

It didn't matter. Having made this first step, his course was set. If once with Tara wasn't enough to give him back his sense of self-control, then maybe twice would be. Or three times, or a dozen. Eventually, he would find that completion with her and he'd have his self back and all would be well.

Then he recalled the way she'd ordered him out of the van last night, embarrassed and so clearly upset with him— not that he could blame her. What an idiot he'd been.

He'd have to track her down later today, reassure her that he was both healthy and financially responsible if need be, and see what he could do about rekindling some of that sweet passion she fought so hard to deny. This time they'd do it right, in a private place, in a proper bed with some light, where they both could enjoy it even more, if that were humanly possible. But just in case, when he went calling, he'd also make damned sure the condoms were in his pocket instead of home in his bureau drawer.

The phone on the garage wall rang at midmorning, and Rory slid out from under a car to listen to Martin's end of the conversation.

"Mmm," said Martin sagely. "He'll be right up to see what he can do." He rang off and turned to Rory. "The bakery van won't start. Crissy asked if you could walk up there and see if you can fix it for her."

"Not a problem. I wanted out from under here anyway."

Rory peeled off his overalls, scrubbed the worst of the grime from his hands, and combed his hair. He noticed a smudge of oil across his cheek and soaped up a cloth to wash it off.

"Are you fixing her car or going courting?" asked Martin.

"There's no reason for me to go off looking like a grease rag, now, is there?"

"Ehh," grunted Martin, and went back to the transmission he was overhauling. "She's at the house, by the by."

Crissy was pacing back and forth by the side of the van when he got there.

"Thanks for coming so quickly," she said.

"Thanks for rescuing me from the underside of a Ford. Let me have a look." He opened the bonnet and poked around. "Turn it over."

She got in and turned the key. The motor cranked and whined, but never caught.

He fiddled with the distributor cap.

"Try again," he called, and she did, to the same result.

"I think you've got a bad distributor." He pulled the cap off and inspected it. "Yes, there's a break in the wire, here. You may want new spark plugs while you're at it. It's about time, I think."

She got out and came to stare. "Can you fix it?"

"Of course I can," he said, somewhat offended that she would ask such a question. "It won't take me twenty minutes, once I have the parts."

"When can you get them?"

"As soon as Martin or I goes in to Ennis." He thought. "This afternoon?"

"That won't do me any good. I've got a cake to go to Kilmihil."

"Today?"

"No," she said. "I always let them sit in the van for a week or two to age before I take them anywhere."

"Snippy, aren't we?" said Rory, grinning.

She flushed. "Sorry. I'm starting to get a bit panicky. It's got to be there for a special award luncheon. Maybe Peg would let me use her car. Owen's isn't big enough."

"I'll take you."

"But I—" She stopped and considered. "Could you? It would be a huge help. Meet me at the bakery?"

"Five minutes," he said.

He headed back to the garage where he kept his pride and joy, a big old wood-sided estate car from the States—a woody, according to a cousin who had emigrated to California. It was way older than he was, the steering wheel was on the wrong side, and the annual engine tax ate up far too much of his wage for good sense, but he loved that car. He scrubbed his hands one more time, checked his hair again—much to Martin's amusement—and drove over to the bakery, where Crissy stood by the door, fretting.

Rory opened the rear door and put the seat down flat while Owen carried the cake out. It was a huge thing, in one of those boxes with the cellophane window on top, so he got a peak at the luscious creation inside. They settled it carefully into the center of the car and packed some towels and empty boxes around it to keep it from sliding, then he and Crissy headed off.

They rode in silence for a while, Crissy mostly staring at her hands in her lap while he drove.

That was fine with him. He enjoyed watching a woman when she didn't notice. Crissy was a pretty thing, with her blonde hair and green eyes. Round where a woman should be round. And a good cook, too. But when did she get so shy?

"This really is very kind," she said at last.

"It's no trouble. I wouldn't want you to lose business. What sort of cake is that?"

"A chocolate-cherry torte. Owen baked the cake part, but I put it all together."

"It's pretty," he said. "All those curly bits of chocolate on top."

"It did come out well, didn't it?"

"I've never seen one of yours that didn't. That's why they come to you from Kilmihil instead of going into Kilrush."

Crissy colored at the compliment. "You're sweet. But the real reason is that the vice-president of the committee is my mother's cousin."

"Well they're still getting a good cake," he insisted. "I admire anyone who can cook."

"I can see why," she said, choking back a laugh.

"Go ahead. Take your amusement at my expense," he teased. He'd resigned himself to the jokes as soon as he'd seen the pumper truck coming. Once a man did something as foolish as setting his supper on fire, there was no way to avoid the ribbing in a village the size of Kilbooly. He'd still be hearing the story when he was old and gray. "You were certainly enjoying yourself the other night."

Giggles leaked out around the hand she clamped over her mouth. "I'm sorry, but the sight of you hanging out that window was too funny. And it wasn't just you. There was Mary shouting, and Tommy strutting around like he thought he was actually doing something, and then Martin popping out like the weasel in the nursery rhyme and blasting that fire extinguisher over Mary's head . . ."

The more she talked, the more she laughed, and the more she laughed, the more Rory could see the scene from her viewpoint. He was soon chuckling along with her.

They reached the outskirts of Kilmihil, and Rory followed Crissy's directions to the hall where the luncheon was being held. Other cars were already parking on the gravel pad around the building.

"Oh, lord. I was supposed to be here before people came." She jumped out of the car as soon as he stopped. He set the hand brake and met her at the rear of the car.

"I'll carry it in for you," he offered.

"Be careful," she said unnecessarily.

He raised an eyebrow. "Do I strike you as a man to ruin a perfectly good cake?"

Ten minutes later, the cake sat in the center of a white table, every chocolate curl in place, and he and Crissy were on their way back to Kilbooly. The ride was pleasant, as was the conversation, and the miles went quickly. Before he half knew it, he was letting her out at the bakery.

"Tell Martin to come tow the van down to the shop," she said. "I hate to spend the money with Dad out of town, but we've got to have it."

"We don't need to bring it in," said Rory. "I can do it there at the house tonight."

"Will Martin mind?"

Rory shrugged. "I'll do it on me own time. For a price of course."

"How much?"

"Dinner."

Crissy looked taken aback. Her lips worked as though

she were trying to say several things at once and wasn't certain which should come out first.

"All right," she said finally. "I can hardly turn down a bargain like that. It just so happens I have a big pot of stew from yesterday. If I share with you, maybe I won't have to eat off it all week. But you mustn't come into the house until after dark, and you mustn't tell anyone. I don't want to get a reputation just because you're starving."

Her obvious reluctance didn't thrill him, and neither did her conditions, but at this point, for a plate of home-cooked stew, Rory was pretty sure he would have sworn celibacy. "I won't tell a soul."

Brian gave Tara a few hours to wake up and get her day started before he rang down to the hotel. Apparently he gave her too long.

According to Mrs. Fitzpatrick, Tara and Kelleher had left just after dawn, carrying overnight bags. They hadn't checked out, she added, just gone off for a night or two and asked her to hold their rooms. And no, they hadn't mentioned where they were going.

The relief Brian felt at hearing that Tara wasn't gone permanently warred with his suspicions about where she *had* gone. He should have rung her earlier, or even gone down there to wake her up. He could have talked to her, settled a few things, perhaps gotten some idea of where she was off to and whether this sudden trip had anything to do with the story on him.

Frustrated in his efforts, however, he turned to work, handling his e-mail, sending a few faxes, and generally annoying his secretary, who insisted that everything was running along smoothly despite his absence.

"Oh, there was one thing this morning," she finally admitted when he pestered her a bit. "When I rang Trullock for the daily production figures, the girl mentioned that she'd seen an RTÉ van parked in front of the plant. I immediately spoke to the administrator, but he had nothing to add. Apparently they hadn't contacted him at all, so perhaps they were in the village for another story."

"Perhaps," said Brian, his mind already racing ahead. "Thank you, Sylvie. I'll speak with you later."

He hung up, then picked up the phone again and dialed Trullock.

"Yes, sir. I was just about to ring you," said his man in Trullock when Brian asked about the van. "Since I spoke with your secretary this morning, there's been quite a buzz developing in the village. Apparently that reporter spent a good deal of the morning asking questions all around town."

"Is this a red-haired woman, with a tall fellow on the camera?"

"I didn't see them myself, of course, but my bookkeeper says she recognized the reporter. It was apparently that young woman from *Ireland This Week*. Tara Brid O'Connell."

Brian's fingers tightened around the receiver. "What sort of questions did she ask?"

"I'm told they were mostly regarding the plant and how it changed the village. And apparently there were some questions about you, sir. Unfortunately, by the time I heard about it and went to see if I could do something, they had already moved on. I had just come back to the office when you rang."

"And they never spoke to you?"

"No, sir. Not so much as a courtesy call. And I hate to tell you, but one of the places they went is up to St. Brigid's church."

Damn it. Father Eustace's old stomping grounds. He'd left the place infected with much of his bitterness when he'd transferred to Dunloe—and Brian still wasn't certain that he hadn't asked for that transfer just to aggravate him, despite the priest's insistence that it was purely the hand of God.

"Is there anything you'd like me to do?" the director asked. "Shall I go to the people they spoke with and see if I can find out what they were fishing for?"

"No. I have a pretty good idea already. However, please let me know if they come back."

Brian rang off.

Tara in Trullock. Apparently she was still out to make it look like he haphazardly destroyed villages just for sport. Nothing had changed—not that a romp in a parked car *would* change things for a woman willing to use sex to distract her quarry.

By damn, if that had been her purpose, it had certainly worked. Here he'd sat, thinking about her, planning how he'd apologize for not protecting her, wanting her again, while she'd been out digging for as much dirt as she could manage to find.

But was she really digging for dirt, or was she doing her job? A part of him wanted to believe that Tara would be the one reporter who would strive for a balanced story, unaffected by either previous prejudice or current passion. Anger warred with an emotion Brian couldn't name.

But at least anger focused the mind when nothing else had.

He placed another call to his secretary.

"I want you to telephone all the village facilities," he said. "Put out the word that if they hear of an RTÉ van anywhere nearby, I'm to know immediately."

They worked out a few details and hung up. Brian nodded in satisfaction.

One way or the other, he was going to know what Tara was up to.

Fifteen

Crissy peeked out the window, chewing on a fingernail. This was a mistake.

Rory was out there, messing about with the car. Good to his word, he had waited until dark to come over, but Crissy hadn't allowed for the fact that he'd have to hang a great bloody work light from the fence so he could see. He was more obvious than if he'd come by day.

She dropped the curtain back into place.

The stew was hot, she had a loaf of brown bread nearly ready to come out of the oven, and she'd remembered to bring home two lovely raspberry tarts that had been left over at the end of the day. She just wished Rory would finish up and come in to eat before any of the neighbor women happened to glance out their windows. It was probably already too late.

She paced across the parlor and back, then stopped to check her hair in the mirror that hung by the front door. Her blue flowered dress made her look like a deacon's wife, she decided: substantial. She smoothed at the bodice, trying to flatten it and herself down to a more fashionable profile. She was still tugging at it when Rory knocked.

Finally.

She yanked the door open and motioned him in, then pushed it shut and latched it as soon as he was clear.

"All complete," he said. "I started it up twice. You should be fine."

"Thank you," she said. She stood there, uncomfortable, trying to think what to say, until she noticed her purse on the hall table. "How much do I owe you?"

"Nothing. I told you dinner would be the only charge."

"That's for your labor. What about the parts?"

"They hardly cost anything at all," he said. "Is that bread I smell baking?"

She nodded.

"That should cover parts, then. Why didn't you just bring some from the shop?"

"It takes me no time at all to mix up. And since I'm feeding you day-old stew, I thought at least the bread should be fresh."

"You needn't have worried yourself—stew's better the second day anyway. But I won't turn away the bread." He held up his hands, black with grease. "Where can I wash up?"

"Through there." She directed him down the short hall.

The bell for the bread rang and she hurried to the kitchen and opened the oven door. Fragrant steam roiled around her as she thumped the bread to see if it was done. The hollow sound made her smile, and she reached for a towel to protect her hand. By the time Rory came out, scrubbed half raw, bless him, she had the stew on the table, with the bread on its board next to it.

The look of ecstasy on his face as she lifted the lid off the stew almost made her laugh aloud. *Poor boy.* It was all he could do to wait for her to serve up. His fingers kept drifting toward his spoon, touching the end before he'd realize it and snatch his hand back again.

Enjoying herself, Crissy took her time, making certain his bowl contained a perfect proportion of meat to onions and potatoes, with just enough gravy to keep them company. Then there was hers to do, just as carefully, and the bread to slice, and grace, which she dragged out twice as long as usual. By the time she was done, Rory was chewing on his bottom lip like it was a slab of roast beef. If she tried to take his dish away now, she suspected she'd lose an arm.

Still, he sat there, hands curled by his plate, trying to be polite. *Poor boy.*

"Go on, now. Eat," she said, taking pity. "What are you waiting for—an engraved invitation?"

He nearly snatched up his spoon.

"Oh," he said, as the first bite touched his tongue. He chewed and swallowed. "It's the stuff of angels." That was the last she heard until he finished the bowl.

It was a pleasure to watch him tuck in with such appreciation. Stew was such a commonplace thing that no one—at least no one in her family—ever seemed to notice how well she did it. That was the problem with living in a household of cooks—she and Siobhan had talked about it often. Certainly the woman who married Rory Boland would never have that problem.

By the time she dished out a second bowl for him, she thought he might be able to carry on a conversation.

"I don't know anything about motors," she said. "What does a distributor do?"

"It takes the current from the battery and puts it to all the spark plugs in the proper order, so they spark and make the engine fire. There's a little part inside that spins around." He described a circle with one finger on his opposite hand, making contact with his thumb and fingers in sequence. "Like so."

"What I don't understand is what made it go bad so suddenly. It was fine yesterday."

"There was probably a fine little crack in the main wire for some time." He wiped his mouth with his napkin. "Something happened to make it wider—it could have been anything—and there you were with your cake and no current to your plugs. It's a common enough thing."

"Oh. Are you certain Martin doesn't mind you doing the repair off the clock?"

"It didn't bother him at all. May I have another slice of that delicious bread?"

They spent the entire evening at the table, moving from eating, to talking, to playing a round of cards so they had an excuse to keep talking. She brought out the tarts late, having forgotten them in the midst of conversation, and to make up for the tardiness, she poured a puddle of thick cream into the center of each. Afterward, when Rory finally had the satisfied look of a well-fed cat about him, she put on the tea. They moved to the parlor and talked some more while the water heated and the tea brewed, and they talked still more over the tea.

Finally, she had nothing else to keep him, even by pretense, and she had to tell him it was time to go. He got up to leave without protest, said his thank-yous, and opened the door.

He really was a very nice man, she thought, and then he leaned over and kissed her.

It was one of those kisses where they touched only at the lips, as sweet and brief as it was surprising. Crissy never even had a chance to close her eyes before it was over.

He gave her an odd look then, like he'd just figured out something that had been confusing him for a long time. One corner of his mouth lifted in a shy sort of smile. "Good night, Crissy."

"Good night, Rory."

She watched him walk down the street. He was a very

nice man, indeed, and she'd known it for months, even if Siobhan and Aileen didn't recognize it.

Now she just needed to figure out a way to yank on the leash a bit—preferably something that didn't involve wrecking another distributor.

Tara squinted against the lights of the oncoming vehicles. She could hardly believe it was still Wednesday and that they'd left the hotel in Kilbooly only that morning. She felt like she'd been awake a week.

"Do you have anything for a headache?"

"In the emergency kit under your seat," said Finn.

She leaned over and fished blindly beneath the seat until her hand fell on a flat plastic box. She dragged it out, popped it open, and sorted through the contents until she found a small bottle of Anadin. She held it up in the glare of the next passing car. "Jayzus, Finn, they're two years past date."

"Sorry. They're all I have."

She opened the bottle and swallowed two tablets dry. "Uck. Nasty."

"I couldn't do that if you paid me," said Finn sympathetically. "It's been a rugged day for you, hasn't it?"

"Bloody awful," said Tara, thinking back over the past sixteen hours. "I don't know which is worse, figuring out the truth in all this or deciding how I feel about it."

"You're in a tough situation," Finn agreed. They passed a sign, and he read, "Twenty-one kilometers to Crook Mill. I'm still not clear on why we're back or what you expect to find out."

"Neither am I. But I know it's the right place to be just now."

"And what are we going to do at this time of night?"

"After we find a room? Track down the men who really understand what's going on in this village, of course."

He pounded out a reggae rhythm on the steering wheel.

"In other words, you made me get up at five o'clock in the morning, drive halfway across Ireland and back, and work a double shift while I was at it, all to finish it off by spending another evening not drinking in a pub."

"It sounds awful when you put it that way."

"It is awful," he said. "I hope you feel guilty as a nun in the backseat with a priest."

"Not nearly that bad," she said. "But I promise to make it up anyway, once we're back home."

"In Kilbooly?"

"No, in Dublin, you nit. Next left, I think."

Tommy left the stable a half an hour early on Thursday. He spent part of his extra time out in the rain stealing a bouquet from Mrs. Hanrahan's side garden, being sure to get the big yellow tulips that Aileen loved. Then he took a minute to stop by the house and get the least pink of his shirts. He hadn't had time to iron yet, and neither had his mother, but at least the shirt was clean and dry and wouldn't smell of horse.

By noon, when Aileen flipped the sign in the clinic window from OPEN to CLOSED and headed off for lunch, he was standing in a doorway down the road.

He followed her. She headed toward Deegan's, and he smiled. She was keeping their date this week. She'd gotten over this marriage nonsense. He waited until she took a table and had her menu, then walked straight in, took off his hat, and sat down across from her.

"I'm so glad you're here, love," he said, holding out the flowers.

"Tommy." A smile lit her face, then faded quickly. "What are you doing here?"

"Having lunch with you, like always. I'm just glad you decided to forgive me. This week has been hell on earth."

"Has it?"

"Of course. But it's over now, and you're here and all is right again."

She looked from his face to the bundle in his hands. "You brought flowers."

"The prettiest I could find," he said. "Though not nearly as pretty as you." He pressed them forward again, and when she didn't take them, reached across and laid them right in front of her. "Oh, Aileen, I've missed you so."

"I'm glad," she said. She picked up her napkin without touching the flowers. "How much have you missed me?"

"So much that I couldn't even play the new song the other night at Ballyvaughan. I'm saving it for when you can be there."

She looked down at her lap and blinked hard, and Tommy knew he had her. She'd been waiting for that song. In all the years they'd been together, it was the first one he'd ever dedicated to her. It was because he was finally good enough, he'd told her, to write a song that deserved to have her name on it.

Siobhan came over just then. "Are you . . . two . . . ready to order?"

"We are," said Tommy.

"We are *not*," said Aileen. "I'm waiting for Peg and Mother to join me. Mr. Ahearn here just stopped in to say hello. Don't forget your flowers when you leave, Tommy."

"Those are yours, and you know it. I came to make up."

"I don't want flowers, and as for making up, there are only—" She counted out something on her fingers. "—four words I want to hear out of your mouth. Until you can say them, there'll be no making up."

"Now wait a minute." Tommy was uncomfortably aware of two dozen pairs of eyes turned his direction, but he wasn't about to back down in public. "You can't just turn me away like this. Not after all the years we've been together."

"I can and I will," said Aileen. "And all the years we've

spent are precisely why. I'm not wasting any more time waiting for you. Now go, before you embarrass yourself any more."

He smacked the flat of his hand on the table. "Embarrassment be damned. This has something to do with that reporter, doesn't it? Ever since she came to town, you women have been up to something. I know you were plotting down at the Nose the other night. That's why you locked us out."

"God, are you still on that, man?" called Martin from across the room. "Give it up."

"Kiss off, Jury," shouted Tommy back. "There's something going on, I tell you. Look at her. She can't even look me in the eye."

"Maybe she doesn't want to, because you're being such an ass," said Siobhan, putting a hand on his shoulder. "It's time for you to go, Tommy. Out."

Siobhan's father came to stand in the kitchen door, a heavy meat cleaver in one hand.

"Do you need help, darlin'?" he called cheerily.

"It's fine, Da. Tommy's just saying good-bye." When Tommy glared at her, she only shook her head like he was a naughty child. "Go on. And I want you to stay out of here until you can behave like a grown man. Do you understand?"

"Aileen?" he wheedled. "I love you, and I know you love me. Just tell me why you're doing this to me."

She reached out and almost touched his hand, but didn't. "You already know the answer to that. Now go on."

He scooped his hat off the seat next to him, popped it on his head, and mustered the ragtag ends of his dignity to walk out the door with his chin high. His mother and Mrs. McEnright were just outside the door, and he brushed past them without a word.

"Tommy?" his mother said, a worried lift to her voice.

He grunted and touched the brim of his hat and kept

walking. Behind him, he could hear Mrs. McEnright say, just as plaintively, "Aileen?"

She wasn't going to do this to him. *They* weren't going to do it to him. No conspiracy of women was going to make him marry Aileen one second before he was ready.

A gust of wind slapped him in the face with cold rain and made him realize what a spectacle he'd just made of both himself and the woman he loved. In Deegan's, of all places. At lunch. And in front of her friends and his. Everyone in the village would know by suppertime. Half of them would agree with Siobhan that he was an ass, and the other half would argue that he was just a besotted fool. There was a very good chance he was both.

As he stood there in the rain, finally feeling the embarrassment that should have stopped him five minutes earlier, he decided that he probably needn't worry about when he'd be ready to marry Aileen anymore. She'd never have him now.

He wiped the dampness off his cheeks, then pulled his coat tight across his chest and walked toward home. Damned bloody rain. It never stopped.

Crissy looked up from the potato rolls she was boxing up for Mrs. Liddy and smiled.

"Rory." She remembered the boycott and wiped the smile off her face just as Mrs. Liddy frowned.

"Crissy." He took his cap off, something he'd never done before when coming into the store. "I thought today I'd try to get here in time for the pasties."

"You only just made it. I have one left. Let me finish with Mrs. Liddy here, and I'll get it for you."

She popped the last roll into the box, closed the lid, and rang up the sale. Mrs. Liddy handed over her three pounds, gave Crissy a warning look, and left with a good-day to Rory.

"I'll get your pasty," said Crissy.

Rory fidgeted a bit with his hat while she bagged the pasty and rang it up.

"One and forty," said Crissy.

"I'll have one of those apricot squares, too," he said.

She got it and added it to the bill. "Two and ten. Anything else before I total up?"

"Just one thing." He rolled his hat and stuffed it into his back pocket, then leaned forward over the counter so his face wasn't a foot from hers. Thank goodness no one else was in the shop. "I was wondering if you'd go for a drive with me tonight, over to Kilrush. I have some business, and then we could have a walk around town or something. Maybe have tea in that little shop on the main road."

"Oh, Rory. I can't."

His face fell.

"It's choir practice tonight," she explained. "I can't miss that. I have a solo coming up."

He cheered up a bit. "What about tomorrow, then?"

"I'm supposed to go to Aileen's for supper," she said. "But we could have sweets at my house after. Owen said he's going to do napoleons in the morning. I'll set aside a couple to carry home."

"That sounds wonderful," he said. "What time?"

"I can make certain I'm home by nine," she said—it should be quite dark by nine.

"Perfect."

"Perfect. That'll be two and ten."

Brian sat in the library, staring at the Michelin map of Ireland that he had spread out over his grandfather's desk.

As calls had come in over the past twenty-four hours, he'd been marking the map with heavy red circles where Tara and her sideman had been spotted. She was visiting the villages where he had plants or distribution centers.

However, she wasn't taking them in chronological order as he'd first suspected, nor was she working strictly north to south. She seemed to be popping up all over the place, passing over a village in Connemara and skipping another east of Cavan. He highlighted those two in yellow, then did the same to all the rest of the villages for good measure.

He put his marking pens down and reached for his cup of tea. There was a pattern here. He almost had it.

There was a discreet knock at the door.

"Come."

Lynch opened the door just wide enough to announce, "Telephone, sir. Mr. Bertrand in Caracurra."

"Thank you, Lynch."

Brian reached for the telephone and simultaneously circled the name of the village.

"Bertrand, I would like you to—"

Suddenly the pattern fell into place, and a ripple of excitement ran across his shoulders. He had it. She was zigzagging back and forth on a line that ran more or less straight from Trullock to—

"Hold a moment, Bertrand." He covered the mouthpiece of the phone and bellowed, "Lynch."

The door opened immediately. "Sir?"

"Have my car brought around. And pack an overnight kit for me."

"Yes, sir. Shall I tell your grandmother where you'll be going?"

Brian considered for a moment. "Say I'll be visiting a friend."

"Dunloe just ahead," said Finn. "I hope this is the last of them."

"It is." Tara rubbed the back of her neck. "I was just calculating. So far, we've talked to fifty-three people in seven villages, all in two days. I think we may have set a new record."

"We will with this one, that's certain." Finn sighed. "I suppose we're going to the pub again."

"Only to have a beer and some supper. I can't bear asking any more questions tonight."

"Bless you, my child."

They covered the remaining miles in exhausted silence, and soon pulled up in front of the tiny hotel.

"I saw a pub a few doors down," said Tara. "If you want to go ahead, I'll see to your room."

Finn's eyebrows turned down. "I think I'm too tired. You've run me to the ground, girl."

"Poor Finn." She reached across the van to rub his shoulder. She knew it had to ache from the camera. "I'll ask the desk to send a tray up to your room. And I'll even come in and rub liniment on your shoulder."

"The recommendation to have you beatified will be in the post to Rome tomorrow." He patted her hand. "You get our keys. I'll lock up the van and bring the bags."

"I'll want my computer, too, please," she said and jumped out.

A young man stood behind the desk, sorting through cards and listening to Garth Brooks complain that he was much too young to feel this damn old. *Amen.* As she walked in, he glanced up and reached to shut the radio off. "May I help you, miss?"

"Two rooms, with baths if you have them."

"We do," he said. He turned the guest register the right way around and held out a pen. "Would you sign in, please?"

She scrawled her name on one line and Finn's on the next, along with the RTÉ address. She could tell she was tired: her handwriting was almost legible.

The man read her signature upside down. "And how will you be paying, Miss O'Connell."

"A credit card. Hold on." She set her bag on the counter and started ratting through it, searching for her wallet and the company card. Finn came in.

"While you do that . . ." The hotel man picked up the telephone and dialed a number. "Sorry to disturb you, sir, but that envelope you wanted was delivered. My pleasure, sir. Thank you."

Tara gave him the card and he took the imprint and handed it back, along with two keys. She held them out to Finn. "Even or odd."

"Odd, of course, to go with me personality."

She swapped the key to number three for her overnight case and her laptop, and they turned toward the stairs.

Her heart stopped, then started again at a gallop.

"Brian."

There he stood three steps up from the bottom, his hand on the brass railing and his face a neutral mask in which his eyes glittered like shards of broken glass. He didn't say a word, but she understood immediately that he was balancing a razor's edge between anger and some other emotion that was equally unnerving.

"Damn," she breathed. He knew.

Sixteen

She was caught, and she knew it.

Brian stared down at Tara from the stairway, his emotions roiling like the center of a storm. He'd been running a seven-hour internal debate about whether to strangle the woman when he caught up to her or do his damnedest to make her forget she was a reporter at all, with a third, slightly more rational corner of his brain suggesting a wait-and-see posture.

Well, he'd waited, and he'd seen, and now the guilt engraved all over her face was rapidly shifting the balance toward strangulation.

"Well," said Finn, backing up. "Isn't this amazing. I feel a sudden burst of energy. I think I'll head for that pub after all."

"No," said Tara. "I mean, it looks like we may be . . . finishing that interview?"

Apparently she had decided to try to brazen it out. Brian had to admire her for the attempt, but he shook his head.

"Oh," she said.

"You're on your own, Captain. This expendable is beaming off the planet before the phasers start firing." Finn set his bag and his key on the counter. "Would you mind keeping these for me? I'll be back later." He glanced at Brian and Tara and continued backing toward the front door. "Much later."

With her cameraman on the run, Tara turned a malevolent glare on the desk clerk. "An envelope, am I?"

He blushed furiously. "Sorry, miss. He gave me fifty pounds to let him know when you came in."

"Fifty pounds? Well, good. You won't be needing a tip from me, then." She looked to Brian. "If you're that highly invested, I don't suppose you'd let this wait until morning."

Brian shook his head.

"I didn't really think you would." She took a breath to brace herself. "Let's get it over, then." She shifted her bags in her hands and put a foot on the bottom step.

Brian stood aside, motioning Tara past him. "After you."

She took the stairs with stiff back, erect head, and measured step, as though she were a particularly brave prisoner climbing to the gallows. As they reached her room, she stopped, set down her bags, and stuck the key in the lock.

"I'll be along in a minute," she said—not a request for permission, but a statement of fact.

"I'll be waiting." He went on to his door, at the far end of the hall. Behind him, her door opened and closed firmly.

It was a very small hotel, with tiny rooms that contained large beds. Her room would be mostly bed, in fact, a detail that waved about in the back of his mind like a bright red flag. Fortunately, he had a slightly larger room, a "suite" by Dunloe standards, in which the bed was in its own alcove separated by a curtain. He let himself into his room and firmly pulled the curtain shut, thus closing off the alcove and hiding the bed.

Still, he wondered if he'd made a wise choice in deciding to talk to her here in the hotel. Tonight of all nights he needed to keep sex out of the equation. He needed his wits about him, to finally find out what she was up to and decide

what to do about it. For another thing, anger was too close
to the surface. If he found out his suspicions were correct,
they might both be better off out in public, where he'd have
no choice but to walk away.

Venues in Dunloe were limited, however, and before he
could come up with any reasonable alternative, she
knocked. He opened the door. She had brushed her hair, and
her face was freshly scrubbed and determined.

She also had her computer case over her shoulder.

"It's got all my notes," she said, when she noticed him
frowning at it. "I may want to show you some of them."

Her explanation made his stomach go sour. It meant she
knew—or thought she knew—why he'd come to Dunloe,
and that pointed toward guilt. She was making it bloody
hard to keep an open mind.

As she set up the computer on the desk that occupied one
wall of the "parlor," Brian stared blindly at the cheap print
of "The Potato Pickers" that hung on the wall over the armchair, trying to gather his thoughts.

When he turned, Tara was standing next to the desk, casually flipping through a notepad he'd left lying on the table.
His hackles rose immediately.

"Is that in-born?" he asked. "Or do they train you to
snoop at university when you say you want to be a reporter?"

She jerked her hand away, a wash of pink coloring her
cheeks. "Sorry. It's a bit of both, I think. I was always the
first to find out when one of my brothers or sisters had done
something they shouldn't."

"And what did you do with that information?"

She looked down, recalling, and smiled. "Blackmailed
them, of course, like a proper little sister."

"Is that what you intend to do to me?"

Her smile faded. "My God, Brian, is that what you
think?"

"It's one of many possibilities I've considered," he said. "I've dealt with enough of your kind—"

"*My* kind?"

"Crusading reporters. You all shout about being fair and objective, but I have yet to see objectivity in action. And *you* are no different than the rest."

"I resent that."

"Not nearly as much as I resent being the butt of your story."

"You don't even know what my story is."

" 'Brian Hanrahan, Destroyer of Villages'?" he guessed.

She winced as though he'd slapped her and sagged into the desk chair.

"I knew it." He paced back and forth, talking half to himself. "I knew it the minute you asked me for an interview out in front of the grocer. I just wasn't sure what you were really after. I should never have talked to you."

"If you hadn't, I'd have done the story anyway."

"Without ever talking to me? Without ever asking me a single question about why I'm doing what I'm doing?"

"That's right," she snapped. "I could have treated you just like you're treating *me* right now. But at least I had a basis for what I believed about you. I had talked to people— a lot of people—and person for person, they didn't like what you'd done to their villages."

"And just what did I do?" demanded Brian, barely hanging on to his temper. "I built factories and brought them jobs. That's all. What happened after—all that mess outside the gates—was not my doing. I don't like it any more than you do."

"Well, that wasn't the story I heard." She stared him down as he loomed over her. "I was told that you bulldozed your way in, demanded wide privileges for your company, and said you wouldn't build unless you got your way, then told the villages to deal with the mess as best they could."

"That sounds like Father Eustace talking," he said, nodding when two bright circles of red appeared in her cheeks. "I thought so. For God's sake, Tara, couldn't you get yourself a better source than that old crackpot?"

"He's a priest," she said in her defense. "And besides, I spoke to nearly two dozen others before I ever came to Kilbooly. Every one of them held you responsible for destroying their way of life."

"You of all people should know that the old village way of life is on its way out anyway, whether we bring our facilities in or not." He paced across the room and back again. "Do you realize that ten years ago fully sixty percent of the adult men in Trullock were on the dole? That's not a way of life, it's ongoing degradation of the human spirit. Now the rate is something like eight percent, and still going down. Some of us may not like the way the village looks, but at least the people who live there can hold their heads up while they walk through it."

"You can't take credit for all of that," she said. "The whole country is in the middle of a boom."

"I know. But I also know that what I'm doing is helping to spread that boom around, so it's not just confined to the cities." He stopped in front of her, raking his fingers through his hair. "If you do this story, you could bring the Dunloe project to a crashing halt."

"I know. And to be honest that's what I had planned, but—"

"Damn you!" he exploded. He dug his fingers into his palms to keep from wrapping them around her throat. "I wish I'd never laid eyes on you."

"*Had* planned," she repeated sharply. "Past tense. Jayzus, Brian, what do you think I've been doing the last two days?"

"Searching for the final nails to drive in."

"No, damn it. I've been trying to find out if I'd gone

wrong, and where—although right now, I'm not sure why I bothered."

"Why should I believe you?"

"You shouldn't," she snapped. "But I met an old man in the pub in Crook Mill last night. He's lived there all his life, and he told me that your plant's ugly as sin and so are all those new buildings around it. He wants his village back the way it was, jobs or no."

"Confirmed your opinions, did he?" asked Brian, struggling to control himself.

"He did. But he also happened to mention that you bought a piece of land near the old mill and gave it to the village to be used for a car park. When I asked around, I found out that they had put a new clinic on the parcel, instead, thinking that's what they needed. But traffic to the clinic makes the parking in town even worse, so people prefer to shop at the super and the do-it-yourself when they come in from the farms. It's easier to park and they don't have to carry their parcels all over creation. And now that the big stores are there, of course, they pull in even more people from the surrounding villages, so it gets worse yet."

"You did hear me the other day," he said, slightly stunned. "I didn't think you had."

"Well, I did. I didn't want to, at first, but I did. And that's why I went back."

"There's more to the story than Crook Mill's parking."

"I know." She sighed and brushed a strand of hair away from her mouth. "You have no reason to believe it, but most of the time I really am a good reporter."

"What happened this time?" he asked dryly.

"I got sucked in by Father Eustace. And by my own prejudices against playboy millionaires," she added, getting back a bit of her own before she glanced up at him with a sparkle in her eyes. "I finally understand what you're up to in Dunloe."

Did she, or was she trying to put one over on him?

"Tell me what you have," he challenged. "I'll tell you whether you're right or not."

"I'll do one better." She swiveled around and hit the power button on her laptop, then stood up. "It's just asleep. It won't take long. Sit down so you can see."

He obliged. A moment later, the machine finished coming up, and she reached over him to run her finger over the cursor pad, clicking through files. "There we are."

While Brian scanned through the file, Tara fidgeted behind him. The screen bore notes on the villages, arranged in alphabetical order. She had entered interview notes, information on each plant and warehouse, and details on the proposals presented to the various village and county councils and commissions, including the full particulars of concessions he had requested and received.

"All very thorough," he said. "What did it tell you?"

"Nothing at all, until I did this." She reached past him again to bring up another file. Her arm brushed his shoulder, sending a shock down his spine, which he quickly suppressed. "Here is the same information in chronological order. That's what I was missing. I knew you had gotten pushier and pushier as you went along, and I thought it was pure Hanrahan cockiness. But it isn't, is it?"

"You tell me."

"All right, I will. It's not. All that bullying the councils about land use and roads and how you want this exclusion and that waiver—that's not for you." Tara sank to her knees beside the chair and looked up at him with huge green eyes full of apology. "Whenever one village finds a way to muck up, you tie up the next one so they can't do the same thing. It's your way of trying to protect the villages from themselves. You're working very hard to keep them all from winding up like Trullock."

Brian's anger drained away as though she'd pulled the stopper in a sink.

"Why on earth haven't you told anybody?" she asked quietly. "If people knew . . ."

"The councils know."

"But no one else seems to, and that makes it very easy to assume that you're rolling over the councils. Even Father Eustace might come around if he understood that you're not being a heavy-handed bastard just for the fun of it."

Brian shook his head. "You might think so, but I've tried to sit down with him more than once. He simply won't hear me."

"It's probably hard for him. He did witness firsthand what happened in Trullock."

"That's part of it. But the real problem is that the man can't bear any kind of change at all." Brian reached for her hand and pulled it to his mouth to brush a kiss over her knuckles. "If the Blessed Virgin herself came down on top of his church, he'd complain about the glow."

Tara chuckled, and he realized how much he'd missed that sound and her smile. With the anger and suspicion gone, he found himself dealing with the emotions that lay underneath. One he recognized: desire, now fully exposed and even more insistent than before. But alongside desire was that sweeter feeling he had noticed earlier, and which was so unfamiliar that he couldn't find a name for it.

He shifted around so he could hold her hand between both of his.

"I was an ass," she said.

"So was I." He turned her hand over in his and studied the lines of her palm, tracing them with a fingertip. "We both had our reasons, poor as they were."

"I didn't do my job well at all. Can you forgive me?"

"I don't know," he said. "It depends on whether what you told me when you first came to Kilbooly was true."

Her brows knitted in confusion, but she couldn't seem to pull her gaze away from what he was doing to her hand. He raised it to his mouth again, so he could look her in the eyes.

"You said you were looking for the real Brian Hanrahan."

"Oh," she said as he gently bit the fleshy pad at the base of her thumb. She wobbled and shifted her free hand to his knee to balance. Heat ran from her fingertips up his leg.

"Do you think you found him?"

"Oh, I hope so," she breathed as he nibbled his way up her wrist to her cuff. It was held by a single brown button, which he unfastened without removing his lips from her skin. "And I hope he has some condoms this time."

Her words curled around his groin like a warm hand. He bit down a little harder, until she gasped, and then pulled her to her feet as he rose. He leaned forward so that his mouth touched her ear. "He does."

He led her through the curtain into the semi-darkness of the alcove without saying another word, stopping to turn on the light.

Not just a single light, either. Tara stood there watching as Brian pushed the curtain aside and turned on every lamp in the room. By the time he finished his circuit, the room blazed with so much light it was almost painful.

He made one final stop, at the chair where his overnight bag sat. He riffled through it briefly, then, with a completely serious expression, turned and dumped the contents of a box onto the bedside table. A dozen blue foil packets glinted at Tara.

She bit back a giggle that was half nerves. "Going to use all of those tonight, are you?"

"I'm going to do my best." He unfastened his watch and laid it next to the condoms, then turned to her. "I expect the same from you, Miss O'Connell."

"That's a lot of condoms, especially considering you were ready to kill me a few minutes ago."

"I'm quickly learning to be a realist when it comes to you."

When he kissed her, it was like a breeze blowing across a slow burning fire. The heat of it lifted her against him in a rising flame, and their tongues tangled like sparks within the sound of a moan so low that Tara wasn't sure if it came from her or Brian.

It didn't matter. All that mattered was the feel of his hands tugging at her other cuff, the softness of his hair through her fingers, and the knowledge that tonight there would be light.

Light.

She pulled away from him and drew her fingers over his face and down the firm line of his jaw, retracing angles she had previously only followed in the dark. The corner of Brian's mouth quirked up in a smile and he abandoned her cuff to smudge a thumb over her mouth.

"You look well kissed," he said, then slipped his thumb between her lips.

She sucked it the way he had done to her finger, drawing it deeper into her mouth and circling the tip with her tongue. His eyelids flickered and his gaze went slightly unfocused, and she knew what he was thinking of and promised herself that when she got around to fulfilling that fantasy, she'd try to figure out some way to watch his eyes.

But for now there were more urgent matters, like the heat building in her blood and his mouth descending on hers again. He dragged his thumb away, drawing a damp line down her throat to her top button, which he slowly unfastened while he kissed her. A second button and a third followed before he left off the kiss to check his handiwork. His eyes glowed as he slipped his fingers into the gap and tugged her shirt out from her skin so he could see.

It would be like that tonight for both of them, she knew, wanting to see everything, because of the darkness the last time. The first time. The center of her clutched and released as she thought of having him inside her again. She wanted him now. "Brian."

"Soon, *a chroí*. My heart."

The breath caught in Tara's chest as he undid more buttons and trailed his fingers back up to the front fastening of her bra. He hesitated there, the back of his fingers resting between her breasts. She closed her eyes, waiting.

He released the hook. She felt the cool wash of air over her skin and heard the sharp intake of his breath, and then she opened her eyes to see the look of fascination on his face.

She followed his gaze down as he cupped her breasts. It was like watching his hands on someone else, except for the incredible sensations that purled through her body in time with the slow circle of his thumbs over her nipples.

"Tara."

She looked up and met his eyes just as he tugged gently. She winced at the intensity of it, and a whimper of pleasure escaped her. Brian chuckled softly.

"I could watch your face all night long," he said. "Except there's so much else I need to see."

He unbuttoned the last few buttons of her shirt and pushed it off her shoulders along with her bra. She shook it clear and kicked off her shoes as he reached for her belt.

He quickly stripped away her trousers and socks, until she stood before him only in her knickers. His gaze burned over her skin, following the featherlight touch of his fingers tracing random patterns across belly and breasts and down over the lace to slip between her legs.

He sat down on the edge of the bed, pulling her along to stand between his knees. Hooking one finger under the elastic, he tugged it aside to expose her to his sight and to the erotic explorations of his fingers. She began to tremble.

"You really are a redhead," he whispered, and bent low to place a kiss on her belly as he slipped his fingers inside her. Her knees buckled, and he caught her with a hand at the small of her back and chuckled again. "Don't give out on me yet, love. I've only just started."

"Nnn," she said incoherently as he proved his point, bringing her right to the edge. "Oh, god, Brian. Brian?"

"Not yet, sweet." He left her hanging there as he pushed her knickers off her hips and slid them down her legs in one smooth stroke. She had to put her hands on his head to balance as she stepped out of them.

He looked up at her, his eyes narrow and intense, his mouth inches from her breasts. She curled her fingers into his hair.

"It's hardly fair," she said. "Here I stand, naked as a baby, and you still have all your clothes on."

He grabbed her wrists and pulled her hands around behind her back, so that her breasts jutted out even more. Catching her wrists in one hand to pin her, he grinned up at her.

"Tough."

With careful deliberation, he wet one nipple with the flat of his tongue, then breathed over it. Evaporation cooled her skin, and her nipple puckered in response. He grinned and did the same to her other breast, then wet them both again and used his fingertips to mimic the feel of his mouth on her before he finally gave her the real thing.

She watched the whole operation, not moving, not able to move, simply wallowing in the lush sensations that accompanied his every action. By the time he had his fill and stood up to kiss her again, she was so tender the barest whisper across her breasts made her moan in delicious agony.

He raised his arms so his shirt cuffs were toward her. "How about some help with these buttons?"

She got to turn the tables on him, then, slowly unbuttoning and unfastening and stripping away his defenses the way he had done to her. In the effort to exact revenge, she found out what it was that had made him take so long. He was beautiful, and discovering the shades of his skin, the copper of his nipples hidden in a scattering of black curly hair, and the ripple of the muscles down his belly, made her desire even sharper. She watched his face as she did things to him, learning by the flutter of his lashes or the tension in his jaw how much power there was in a kiss or in the stroke of a tongue or fingertip over sensitive skin.

The more she explored and teased, the more her own need built, so that by the time she reached for his belt, her fingers were so anxious and clumsy that he had to help her. Together, they peeled away his trousers and in a few seconds she could see precisely how much he wanted her. Looking him straight in the eye, she curled her hand around him.

With a growl, he pulled her hand away. "If you do that, we're not going to get very far this time."

"But I—"

He kissed her, and he kept kissing her until she couldn't remember what she intended to say and simply gave up and wrapped her arms around him. Then he took her down onto the bed and kissed her more while he brought her up to the edge once again, and yet more while he reached over to get one of the foil packets.

There was the sound of a tear, a moment of abandonment as he put the condom on, then in one motion he was between her legs and pressing her knees apart to make a place for himself. But instead of moving into her, he rested there, looking at her, until Tara thought she was going to go up in flames from the heat in his eyes. Her fingers curled into the bedcovers.

"If you don't do something soon, I'm going to die," she whispered.

"We can't have that, now, can we?" He knelt back, then put his hands on the inside of her knees and spread her legs wider. "How's that? Ah, you're blushing. Right here." He touched her.

"Jayzus, Brian, you're driving me mad."

"It's only fair," he said. "You've been doing it to me for a week. Every minute, waking or asleep, Tara, all I can think of is having you like this, ready for me. I want you." He traced a finger through her moisture. "But what do you want, beautiful Tara? Tell me."

"You."

He shook his head and circled his thumb against her, drawing a moan from her throat. "Too vague. Exactly what do you want?"

"You inside of me."

He shifted over her, so that his hands gripped her head and held it for his deepest kiss, and his hardness lay against her, heavy and warm. "Are you certain, Tara? There'll be no going back. Not this time."

"Tóg mé," she urged in Irish, wrapping her legs and arms around him. "Take me."

He did, in one long press that wrenched groans from both of them. They began to move together, slow, circling strokes that quickly carried her back to that point where she lost all awareness of anything but Brian. She closed her eyes to concentrate, and somewhere in the room two voices murmured words of desire that melted into incoherent urgings as they pushed toward what they both wanted.

At the last instant, just as she balanced between earth and sky, he whispered for her to open her eyes. It was a battle, so ingrained was it to retreat into herself for that last bit of the climb, but she obeyed his gentle wish. He was right there, his expression so full of love and desire that something inside her broke.

And then she was over, arching, crying out for him, and she could see him following her, and their eyes bound them together for the long, sweet fall.

Seventeen

It was nearly closing time, and Tommy was drunk. He'd put a lot of effort into getting that way, starting with a glass of whiskey at home shortly after the debacle at Deegan's, and continuing with a visit to the Nose for a pint after another of his mother's "I'm too busy to cook" bloody frozen dinners.

He'd hurried himself through the crying in his beer stage by switching back to whiskey for a round or two early on, but now he had himself a good, solid numbness that was well past tears and it was time to go home.

He couldn't leave the last of his pint, though, and he sat on his stool at the bar, along with all the other men still in their jackets and caps, as though they'd never intended to stay in the first place.

"One quick jar, Hugh."

Tommy swiveled his head carefully so as not to slosh his brain at all and took a look at the man that had taken the empty spot beside him. "Daniel. You're coming in late."

"I've been up at the cottage working."

"Oh," said Tommy. "You know, the fellows and I were talking, wondering what it is you do up there."

"Work, I told you."

"Work at what?"

"The cottage. Keeping it up."

"Well it doesn't look like it, for all the time you spend at it. The place is only standing because the bugs are holding hands." He took another sip of his beer. "We thought maybe you were taking up the arts and didn't want us to know about it 'cause we'd think you were a pouf."

Hugh Donnelly set Daniel's stout in front of him. "Here you go, son. Drink up."

Daniel ignored him. " 'We were,' eh? And who would 'we' be?"

It occurred to Tommy that Daniel looked a bit white around the mouth, but he couldn't figure out why. "Me and some of the lads."

"Well, now, we can hardly have a more knowledgeable authority than yourself, can we?"

Tommy straightened, a jolt of anger burning off part of the numbness. "And what's that supposed to mean?"

Daniel took a long draw on his stout then pushed his glass back from the edge. "It means that I'm not too worried about the opinion of a man who wears pink shirts and plays the violin."

"Now, lads," said Hugh.

"Fiddle, you wanker," said Tommy, coming up off his stool.

Daniel hit him.

Tommy touched the corner of his mouth and his fingers came away bloody. He grinned. A fight felt just right. He hadn't known he needed one.

With a roar, he swung at Daniel. His fist connected with a satisfying smack and the next thing he knew, Daniel threw his arms around him and they were tumbling over a table onto the floor, pounding the bejeezus out of each other until someone dumped a bucket of soapy water over their heads.

They came up spluttering, water and sudsy tears streaming down their cheeks. Strong arms hauled them both to their feet.

"Knock it off, you hooligans."

"Ah, let me hit him some more," said Tommy, wiping suds out of his eyes.

Daniel jerked free of the fellows holding him and stepped forward. "Have at it."

"Closing," announced Hugh. "Everybody out."

Martin Jury clapped a hand on Tommy's collar and propelled him toward the door and someone else did the same with Daniel. "If they want to fight, take 'em outside. Come on, lads."

The whole crowd moved out in the street, and Hugh threw the lock behind them. Tommy and Daniel faced off in the middle of the road, fists raised.

A heartbeat passed. Tommy belched and took a good look at Daniel.

"Ah, forget it," he said. "All the fun's gone." So was most of his drunk, sad to say. He put out a hand and Daniel took it. "Good lad."

"Jayzus," said Martin in disgust. "Couple of *omadhauns*."

"Kiss me Swiss," said Tommy. "Are we playing at the session tomorrow night?"

Martin nodded and Tommy headed off. Daniel was right behind him, as they lived only three houses apart.

"You think they're talking about us?" said Tommy after they'd left the others behind.

"I would be if I were them," said Daniel.

"Why'd you hit me?"

"Felt like it. You?"

"Same." They walked on a ways, Tommy contemplating the nature of men's fights. "Did it have anything to do with Louise, by chance?"

Daniel stopped, then took a couple of quick steps to catch up with Tommy. "It might."

"Aileen broke off with me," said Tommy.

"I heard." They walked a bit farther. Daniel cleared his throat. "Louise cut me off, as well."

"Cut you off how? Oh." It took a few seconds longer than usual for thoughts to percolate through the remaining fumes, but Tommy finally got his meaning. "Is that what you've been doing in the cottage? Meeting Louise for a little flash?"

"God, man, announce it to the whole village, why don't you?"

"Sorry."

"I don't expect to hear this coming back at me from someone else, either."

"I'll try, but you should never tell a drunk man a secret," said Tommy with great sincerity.

"You're not that drunk, or you wouldn't hit so hard." Daniel touched his jaw, grinning. "Louise comes back from her cousin early on Sundays. And she slips up there after choir practice, too. Except she didn't tonight and she didn't Sunday, either. And last Thursday, her mother was sick, so she didn't come out. I haven't seen her for over a week, now, and I'm feeling the strain, so to speak."

"I know it well," said Tommy with more than a little envy that Daniel had thought of using the old family cottage. All this time he and Aileen could have been going up to his parents' old place, instead of waiting for the occasional night when her mother was out. His chest tightened at the thought that he might never have a chance to suggest it. "Why are you telling me now, when you've kept it secret for so long?"

"Because I thought you should know why I hit you." Daniel frowned and scratched his head. "And because I'm beginning to think you're right about the women."

• • •

Tara lay against Brian's side, twirling her fingers through the hair on his chest. Spent but not tired, they were talking, and inevitably, the talk turned to the villages.

"At least people in Crook Mill seem to understand," she said. "I heard the term 'well intentioned' more than once. And of course the women love you to death. One old lady even called you 'that darling boy.'"

"Well, they may be happy about the state of things, but I'm not. I imagine this ideal village in my head, Tara. It has my buildings and the jobs, but none of the ugly development that's dogged me so far. Its soul is intact. I won't be satisfied until we can achieve that."

"That's the dream you were talking about that first day when we were riding," she said softly. "That's why you envy Tommy."

He nodded and put his hand over hers. "Another of my secrets."

Hand stilled, she nuzzled his shoulder and pressed a kiss to his chest. "Does your ideal village look like Kilbooly, by any chance?"

"It would, if I ever find the way to make it happen." He stared at the ceiling. "When my father first thought of going into the villages—"

"Your father?"

"It was his idea to bring something to Kilbooly, but it was too far off the beaten track to make it work. He looked around and settled on Trullock just before the accident, and I finished the project as a tribute to him. Then I saw how well it worked for our end and decided to try it again and see if I could get the village's part of it right. And then I did again. And again. And I'm still trying. Eventually, I'll get it, and only then will I take the company into Kilbooly. That's another reason I don't want the story out yet—I don't want my neighbors let down if it takes me a while to figure it out. Why are we talking about this?"

"Because you needed a rest, you said."

"Did I?" He lay there staring up for another moment, then grinned. He extended the arm that was under Tara's head, grabbed a foil packet from the table, and dangled it over her. "Do you know how to put on one of these things?"

"I think so."

"Well let's find out. Rest period over."

By dawn, they still hadn't slept. All the lamps had long since been put out, but a soft golden glow seemed to light the room from within. On the bed table, several open blue packets bore witness to Brian's best efforts, but even now, though his eyes were closed and his face relaxed, his hands drifted over her restlessly. It was as though he couldn't get enough of her, and she loved it. She'd never felt so desired in her life.

Brian rolled slightly to the side and pulled her up for a kiss. "You may have finally worn me out, woman."

"Me?"

"It must have been you. You're the only other person in the room and I certainly didn't do it to myself." He kissed her again, a long, slow kiss that pressed her down into the pillow, and after a time she felt a gentle stirring against her thigh. She slipped her hand beneath the sheets.

"See there," she said as he groaned. "You're not done in after all."

"You're a terror," he said, laughing and raising a knee to block her.

She let him win the battle and snuggled back into his arms, pulling the covers up around her neck. He kissed her again and continued to toy with her body through the sheet, and as she drifted with the sensations, a yawn finally caught up with her and spread to him.

"I'm going to have to get some sleep before I drive," said Brian.

"Which means I'd better move along to my own room," she said. "You'll never get any rest with me here. And besides, Finn will be knocking on my door soon."

"So, back to the real world. What next, Miss Reporter, now that you've discovered all my secrets?"

She sighed. "I don't know. I'm in a very tough spot here, Brian. You say you don't want what you're doing spread around, and I can understand why. But I'm a reporter. I get paid to do the news, and this is news. And a good story."

"Just hold it back for the time being," he said. "If things turn out in Dunloe—"

"It'll be years before we know that. I can't possibly sit on it that long. There are already going to be people after me to turn the story over for someone else to finish it."

"Someone else? Why?"

"One of your favorite concepts: objectivity." She looked down to where he had his hand curled possessively over her breast, slowly rolling her nipple between thumb and forefinger. "Mine's a bit compromised, wouldn't you say?"

"But you've done your best work in the last few days."

"I know. But how is it going to look to my director when he finds out? And *you* can't have it both ways, either," she pointed out. "You can't lace into me for not being objective and then turn right around and expect me to do the story when you want, the way you want, just because I happen to be—"

She abruptly pulled away and got up to retrieve her drawers, which had somehow ended up over the steam register. "Never mind."

Brian came up out of the bed like a hound after a hare, pursuing her across the tiny room. "Because you happen to be what?"

"Never mind, I said. Nothing."

He cut in front of her so she had to look at him. She tried

to turn away again, but he caught her by the shoulders. "Tara?"

She squeezed her eyes shut. "You're going to make me say it, aren't you? You're going to just keep at me until I admit it, and then you'll do what you men always do when the woman is the first one to say she's in love. You'll get all panicky and weird on me."

Brian went very still, until Tara fancied she could hear her own blood rushing through her body in the silence—not the pounding of her pulse, but the actual noise of the corpuscles tumbling along through her veins.

"What?" he asked finally.

"See?" she said, peeking out through one open eye. "You're doing it already. I should have given you something you could get your hormones around. I should have just told you that all I can think about twenty-four hours a day is lying beneath you, touching you, wanting you."

He filled his lungs and slowly blew out the air. "I thought I was the only one."

"Then you're not panicking?"

"That's not the word I would use right now, no." He glanced down.

"Oh, good," she said, a soft smile curving her lips. "Because before I go take my shower, I was sort of hoping maybe I could be compromised a little more."

He wrapped his arms around her in a bear hug and laughed miserably. "I'd love to, Tara, but I truly don't believe I have the energy."

"It's all right," she said. She slid her hand between their bodies. "I understand. I'll just have to compromise you this time."

Finn didn't knock on her door until after nine, a sure sign either that he knew what had happened and was being discreet, or that he'd discovered Dunloe had some sort of a stream with fish. The lack of accompanying aroma and the way he avoided the topic of Brian entirely told her which it was.

But at least his late arrival gave Tara time to bathe and get a little color onto her cheeks. While she'd been in the bath, it had occurred to Tara that handing over a complete story would go further with Oliver and possibly get Brian the fair treatment he deserved, so when Finn arrived she had a plan. Together they pretended nothing at all was amiss, had a hearty breakfast, and went off to see the mayor, to get the last few pieces to the Hanrahan story.

She had interviewed the mayor by telephone early on in her research, of course, but she'd been looking for specific information that matched what the infamous Father Eustace had told her. Now, with the right questions, a version closer to Brian's emerged. She did a complete interview with the mayor and two council members, visited the pub at lunchtime, and wound up with exactly the right ending to her story. Well, *someone's* story. Maybe when she showed it all to Oliver, he'd see . . .

She soon realized how optimistic that was.

A muffled electronic ring issued from her canvas bag just after two, when they were well on their way back to Kilbooly. Tara stared at the bag.

"If you didn't want to talk to him, you should have left it off," said Finn.

"It's never too late." She dug around, found the phone and flipped it open, ready to hit the Power button.

"O'Connell. Are you there?" Oliver sounded like a tiny, harmless little thing with the phone at arm's length. "Is there something wrong with this bloody thing?"

She caved in. "No, Boss. I'm here. Sorry."

"It's Friday."

"Is it?"

"Don't make me ask, O'Connell."

"Didn't you get those tapes Finn sent in?"

"That was three days ago. You'll have to do better than that."

"I know Oliver, and we've been working our tails off, but—"

Tara held the telephone away from her ear as Oliver unloaded a string of his favorite expletives.

"Ouch," said Finn.

"He's a handful today."

"I'm a handful every day," said Oliver when she came back to the phone. "I want tape, O'Connell."

"You'll have it. Next week."

"You're damned right I will. Finn will bring it back with him. I want him in the studio Monday first thing with everything you have."

"Oliver you can't. The stories aren't nearly complete. We haven't even finished the interview with Brian Hanrahan yet."

"What? Bloody hell!"

Tara held the phone away again while he ranted about her having Finn for over a week and getting nothing worthwhile at all.

"But I have," she insisted when he wound down a bit. "I uncovered some new information on Brian—"

"There's a unique way of putting it," muttered Finn, too low to be heard on the other end.

"What kind of new information?" demanded Oliver.

What would hold him until she could get back to explain? Tara improvised quickly. "He has some very interesting plans for his home village."

"Like what?"

"I can't tell you over this phone," she protested. "It's very sensitive and anyone might be listening."

"Damn it, Tara, you can't leave me hung out with no information on either of your so-called big stories. I've got mucky-mucks breathing down my neck to get Finn back in here."

"Then plead confidential sources. I promise you, this story on Brian, combined with my other story about the go-ings on in Kilbooly, will give you segments enough to keep you and every mucky-muck at the network happy for a week at least. We'll talk about the particulars when my holiday's over."

"I need tape, not talk."

"You'll have it, but there are a few, um, issues that came up, that's all. I will need Finn just a little longer."

"You bloody well can't have—"

"Oliver? Oliver? Are you still there?" She dragged the mouthpiece back and forth across her jacket a few times to create some "static," then hit the Power button.

"He's going to kill me," she said. "He's going to strangle me with his own two pudgy little hands."

Finn nodded sagely. "And well he should."

The great thing about sessions as compared to gigs was that you could walk out in the middle of a session because there was always some other musician hanging about to take your spot. Tonight, it was a fellow from over Cranny way who played a fine mandolin. Once Tommy was certain the visi-tor was a good fit with the others, he was out the door and up to Aileen's to apologize and see if he couldn't find out what was going on.

He had been wavering on the subject of the women. Skepticism from the other men—Martin, in particular, be-cause he was always so levelheaded and practical—had nearly convinced him that his imagination had run away with him. Then Daniel had come along. Finding out that someone believed him was worth the split lip and the swollen jaw, plus it had reinforced his spine. He was going to find out what was going on, or at least find proof that there was, indeed, some sort of conspiracy that he could show to the other men. To Rory Boland, especially.

Unfortunately, when he got to the McEnright cottage, he discovered that Siobhan and Crissy were over for the evening. He had no desire to deal with those two, and he particularly wanted to avoid Siobhan for a few more days after the ass he'd made of himself at the café. But he didn't want to head back to the Nose, either, not until he at least tried to set things right with Aileen.

He poked around outside the front window a bit, hoping he could hear what they were talking about, but their voices jumbled together with the music Aileen had been playing. All he could really tell was that the three of them were laughing a lot. Probably about him.

He loitered in the area for a while, strolling up and down the road, in hopes that Crissy and Siobhan would leave, but the merriment in the house only increased. After a time, the rain grew heavy enough to be annoying and it came down to either finding a dry spot or packing it in. He looked around quickly as the rain picked up even more. His gaze settled on Aileen's little Mini, parked in the street. She wouldn't mind, not once he talked to her.

He got into the car, quietly pulled the door shut, and settled in to wait.

Remainder of your holiday cancelled. Return to Dublin immediately with all footage. Oliver.

Tara stared at the message, written in Mrs. Fitzpatrick's tidy hand.

"There's a similar one for Mr. Kelleher," volunteered Mrs. Fitzpatrick with a sympathetic lift to her voice.

"He headed straight down to the Nose," said Tara. "We heard music as we drove by."

"There's a *seisun* most Fridays. Didn't I hand you a note from Brian?" She shuffled a few papers on her desk then turned and looked in the box. "Here it is, way in the back. He called not five minutes before you walked in. It's a shame you missed him."

"Mmm." Tara took the message, folded it and slipped it into her pocket like a candy to be savored later. "It looks like we won't be staying past the weekend."

"What a shame. But surely you'll be coming back for visits; you've made so many friends here. Some very good ones, I think."

Tara smiled at the gentle snooping. "That I have, and yes, I do intend to come back. But duty calls. I'll let you know when we'll be leaving. But for now, I've got to get some sleep. I'm so tired, my eyes are crossing."

She trudged upstairs, the fingers of one hand curled around the slip of paper in her pocket. The room was too warm when she opened the door. She cracked the window despite the rain, kicked off her shoes, and sat down in the middle of the bed to read her note.

"Business requires me to come home by way of Dublin. See you tomorrow and we'll work out some sort of compromise. Brian."

She laughed even as flames did a pagan dance through her belly. How either of them could even think about sex after last night was a mystery, but obviously they could. Thank goodness she hadn't read this in front of Mrs. Fitzpatrick—she would have blushed so hard that the woman wouldn't have had to pry about Brian.

Tara left the note on her pillow while she changed into pajamas and took off her eye makeup. As she was brushing her teeth, she wandered out and flipped on *Ireland This Week*.

She listened with half an ear as she finished her teeth and moved on to her face scrub and her toner. She was halfway through her moisturizer when she heard her own voice and a familiar fiddle.

She dashed out. It was the piece about Tommy and his gig in Ballyvaughan, which she'd edited and sent in earlier in the week. Damn it. Oliver should have let her know the story was to air tonight, so she could have let Tommy and the rest of the town know about it. This was an event, and Tommy deserved to be the center of attention.

She sat down on the end of the bed, slowly rubbing in the lotion as she watched. It was hardly what she'd call an important story, in the scheme of things, but she and Finn had done a good job on it, and it showed off Tommy's music well. The pub's name appeared twice, as promised. She gave herself a pat on the back.

Until the program's host came back on.

"That was Tara Bríd O'Connell reporting from Ballyvaughan," said Jean. "Next week, Tara will begin a series of special reports about some very interesting goings on in the little village of Kilbooly, County Clare—home of Ireland's most eligible bachelor, millionaire businessman Brian Hanrahan. And now we move on to our weekly look at . . ."

Tara stared at the screen, stunned. Interesting goings on in Kilbooly? The women would think that meant the boycott. Brian would think it meant him and his plans for the village. All of them would think she'd betrayed them.

"Oh, Jayzus. Oliver. What have you done to me?"

Eighteen

Brian returned to his flat exhausted. The five hours of sleep
he'd gotten in Dunloe had seemed adequate at the time, but
now, two meetings and a business dinner later, all he could
think of was bed and Tara. It was probably fortunate that the
two objects of his desire were several counties apart. He
needed the sleep.

Not that distance reduced Tara's powers of seduction a
whit. All it took was the most casual thought of her to send
a rush of heat through his blood—even, as he had learned
that afternoon, during a discussion of accounting revisions.
It certainly made for tedious meetings, what with him constantly asking for things to be repeated.

The need to talk to her was suddenly as sharp as the need
to be with her. He looked up the number for the hotel in Kilbooly and rang her. She wasn't in yet, according to Mrs.
Fitzpatrick—hadn't returned at all that day. After a moment's thought about how he could disrupt her sleep as thoroughly as she would probably disrupt his, he left a message.

Frustrated, he took a few minutes to check his voice mail,
then headed straight for the shower, stripping off as he
passed through his bedroom and taking the few seconds to

hang his trousers and jacket and toss everything else in the laundry. A two minute shower and a quick pass with a toothbrush, and he was ready for bed.

Except, as he quickly discovered, nine o'clock was too early for him to fall asleep. Or perhaps he was too tired. Either way, after thrashing around for the best part of an hour, he gave up, pulled on a robe, and went out to the front room to watch a few minutes of television until his brain went numb.

"—reporting from Ballyvaughan. Next week, Tara will begin a series of special reports about some very interesting goings-on in the little village of Kilbooly, County Clare, home of Ireland's most eligible bachelor, millionaire businessman Brian Hanrahan. And now we move on . . ."

He sat there staring at the screen, not hearing a word of what came after.

"It's a good story," she had said. "I'm a reporter."

She had never agreed to hold it back. She had simply distracted him with talk of love, and with sex that still exerted power over his mind as well as his body.

She didn't love him. She had used him.

In other words, she'd done exactly what he had expected her to do—anything for a story. Too bad he hadn't heeded his own warning.

His telephone rang.

He sat there staring at it, knowing it must be her with a string of excuses or perhaps a little phone sex to distract him yet again. And if by some chance it wasn't her, there was no way on earth he could carry on a civil conversation right now. He let the voice mail pick up, as he did the next five calls that came in on its heels, and when it became obvious she was going to keep trying, he got dressed, picked up his overnight kit, and walked out the door to go check in at a nearby hotel.

As he turned the key behind himself, he could hear the telephone begin ringing yet again.

"Come on, Brian. Answer. Please."

Tears of frustration scalding her eyes, Tara slammed down the phone before the electronic voice came on again.

He'd seen Oliver's damned teaser. He wasn't going to answer. He might never take a call from her again.

She started to dial once more, then stopped. If five messages weren't enough, six or fifty wouldn't help. She'd have to find a way to get through to him later.

She had other, equally vital concerns. Brian wasn't the only one who was angry with her just now. She had to convince the women of Kilbooly that she hadn't done this, that she truly was on their side. She also needed to find a way to protect them from Oliver—if he saw those tapes, he wouldn't be able to resist putting the story on, happy ending or no. Too bad she couldn't get rid of all those tapes without getting herself fired or arrested.

Maybe she could.

She pulled on her jeans and a pullover, grabbed her jacket and bag, and headed downstairs. She had to stop herself on the top step and calm down. If she wanted to get away with the outlandish plan that was congealing in her brain, she had to look perfectly calm and innocent.

A couple of deep breaths eased the tightness in her chest. She plastered on a smile and bounced down the stairs.

"Why Miss O'Connell. I thought you were headed for bed."

"I was *in* bed," Tara said. "But I'm too tired to sleep. And since I was awake anyway, I thought I couldn't let that fine music at the Nose go to waste. Maybe Tommy will play me a lullaby."

Mrs. Fitzpatrick laughed. "I'm not sure he'd dare play anything so sweet out in public. He's still catching it from his friends over that pink shirt, you know. In fact, he and Daniel Clohessy had a real mix-up last night over it."

"Did they?"

"Oh, yes," said Mrs. Fitzpatrick, and proceeded to tell her all about it. Tara nodded and smiled and actually laughed at the story, all the while itching to get out the door

"Well," said Mrs. Fitzpatrick at last. "You wanted some music, not one of my stories. Go on your way, and I'll leave the door unlocked like always."

"Thank you so much. I really am going to miss this place when we go."

"Well, you're not gone yet, are you? You enjoy yourself at the pub, and I'll see you in the morning."

Tara said good night and went out the front door. Instead of heading for the Nose, however, she ducked around to the side of the hotel where they'd left the van.

It was locked, of course—Finn was religious about locking up all those thousands of dollars in cameras and gear. She checked every door just in case. She didn't really want to break in if she didn't have to, but when she discovered that Finn the Efficient had stayed true to form, she quickly convinced herself that the end justified the means.

First things first, however. She pulled her VW up next to the van and left the engine idling, lights off, then hunted around for a box, turning up one outside the kitchen door. It smelled of rancid bacon fat, but she couldn't be finicky just now.

And then she pulled out her secret weapon.

Not all of the camera operators Tara worked with were as organized as Finn was. Maeve, in particular, had a tendency to leave things lying around—things like keys, in places like the van floor. More than once they'd returned after a shoot and had to ring for help to get into their own vehicle. In the interest of saving time, Tara had approached one of her less savory informants and convinced the gentleman to teach her how to unlock a locked car. The tool he had provided her with, a flat strip of steel he referred to as a slim jim, was part of the reason she carried such a big bag and suffered the occasionally painful shoulder that went with it.

Her skill had already proven useful more than once, however, and tonight it was invaluable. Tara had the door unlocked in a matter of seconds. The dome light flared as she crawled in, but she shut it off. Working as quietly as possible in the dark, she located every tape in the van, used or not, and loaded it into her bacon box. Within two minutes, the tapes were in the back of her car. She stood for a moment, a sense of responsibility dictating that she relock the van, a sense of self-preservation arguing that real vandals would do no such thing.

Self-preservation won on the rationality that nothing was actually likely to be stolen in Kilbooly—and if it was, Oliver had only himself to blame for forcing her to such extreme measures.

She got in the car and prepared to head off. The question was, to where?

In the flurry of getting her hands on the tapes, she hadn't considered what to do with them. She couldn't very well keep them in her car—they'd be found in a matter of minutes and then she'd be in trouble for certain. An arrest record didn't look very well on an employment application—and she'd be filling out a lot of those before this was over.

It occurred to her to take them where they would do the most good.

She headed up the road.

The McEnright cottage blazed with light as Tara pulled up behind Aileen's blue Mini. She checked up and down the road to be certain no one was watching, then quickly got out, retrieved her box, and carried it to the back door. Inside, Siobhan's voice railed.

Tara winced, but knocked anyway and stood her ground

as Aileen swung the door open and stood there glaring at her.

"I didn't think you'd be back," said Aileen.

"You did see it, then. I swear, that was all my producer's doing. I was as shocked as you were—are."

"Shocked?" demanded Siobhan over Aileen's shoulder. "Bloody well furious, is more like it."

"I know."

"You promised us," said Aileen.

"And I have every intention of keeping that promise, which is why I've brought you these."

"Now what would we be wanting with rashers?" asked Siobhan.

Tara choked on a laugh. "Would you just let me in for a minute, before someone sees me. I don't especially want to go to prison."

Aileen and Siobhan gave each other doubtful looks, then stood aside. Tara carried her box to the kitchen table.

"So what is it?" demanded Siobhan. "And how is it going to keep your promise?"

Tara flipped open the box and pulled out two tapes, handing one to each of the women.

"Tapes?" said Aileen.

"Inside this box is every tape we shot for the past two weeks, except the few that have gone to Dublin. If you're willing, I'd like you to keep them. Hide them, I mean. I can't have anybody knowing that I left them here."

"You're giving them to us?"

"Until I can shake some sense into Oliver, I am."

"So you really didn't tell anyone."

"I really didn't. And I won't, and neither will Finn. Finish out your boycott. By then I'll either have Oliver well in hand or I'll have a new job and I can finish up the story the way we discussed—with some weddings."

Aileen smiled a bit sadly. "Right now that doesn't look very likely for Tommy and me."

"You've only just started. It will work. Be patient." Tara took the tapes back from Aileen and Siobhan and returned them to the box, then reached into her bag for the slim jim. "I think I'll mislay this, too. Do you have some packaging tape? I want to seal it all up."

Aileen got a roll of brown paper tape out of a drawer and handed it to Tara. "We won't watch them, if that's what you're concerned about."

"You couldn't," said Tara as she tore off a length of tape. "You don't have the right machine. But this way, if someone stumbles onto the box, you can claim you had no idea what was in it."

"You mean we might be arrested?" asked Aileen.

"I hope not. But just in case . . ."

"There you go," said Siobhan, nudging Aileen. "You can ruin your reputation that way. Now don't get all fussy on the woman. She's doing her best. The least we can do is help her."

"I wasn't going to say no," said Aileen. "I just wanted to have an idea what to expect."

Tara finished sealing the box, then dug back into her bag for a pair of business cards and a pen. She scribbled her home phone number on each and handed one to each woman.

"If anything happens—anything at all—let me know. But otherwise, as far as anyone is concerned, you never saw me tonight. And when you hear that the van was broken into and all our tapes were stolen, please do your best to look appropriately surprised."

"It's appalling," said Siobhan earnestly. "That such a thing should happen in our peaceful village. Whoever did it should be tracked down and pilloried."

"You'll do," said Tara. "But if anyone is about to be pilloried, you call me. I don't want some other poor soul to suffer because I didn't handle my job well. That includes you, of course. If you get caught with the tapes, just send the *Gardaí* after me."

"If we do, we'll warn you they're coming."

"Good. Then I can find someone to water my plants while I'm in jail." She gave Aileen and Siobhan a hug. "Now I have to get out of here before Finn decides to go back to his room."

"Take care of yourself," said Aileen.

Tara nodded and dashed out to her car. A minute later she pulled back into the same spot beside the hotel, locked the car, and headed down to the Bishop's Nose for a bit of music.

As she stepped into the crowded, noisy pub, she checked her watch. Twelve minutes from start to finish. With luck, no one would notice the missing time.

He'd never make a good private investigator, that was certain, thought Tommy as he hunkered down in the Mini, waiting for the sound of Tara O'Connell's car to fade to silence. If his experience eavesdropping in Mary's kitchen hadn't proved it, tonight surely would.

He hated it, just sitting in a car and waiting. It was the most nerve-wracking thing he'd ever done, and worse when someone passed by. He'd almost been caught three times already tonight: once when Crissy had come out, just after he'd gotten there; once when Miss O'Connell arrived; and again when she left, because like an idiot he had sat up, never imagining she'd stay such a short time. If he stayed any longer, he would surely be spotted, either by Mrs. McEnright coming home, or, more likely, by Siobhan leaving. She was as quick-eyed as she was quick-tongued.

Getting caught mooning about outside Aileen's door would be the death of any reputation he had left. Added to the fight and the shirt and every other mistake or misadventure anyone could remember clear back to his childhood, it would just about guarantee a lifetime of ribbing. He'd have to leave Kilbooly—possibly emigrate to America—just to find some peace.

Tommy opened the door and slipped out of Aileen's car as quietly as he'd slipped in. He had every intention of getting back down to the Nose and was already thinking up excuses for his absence when he heard Aileen laugh.

Oh, lord, he missed that laugh.

The sound of it drew him toward the kitchen window. After a careful look around, he dared a peek through the glass. Aileen and Siobhan were standing at the table, discussing where to put the box Miss O'Connell had carried in. Siobhan suggested burying it in the backyard, and they giggled like schoolgirls. Aileen was as pink as a new rose with excitement.

Tommy's fingers curled around the handle of his fiddle case. She was as pretty now as she had been at sixteen, maybe more so, with her curves filled out and her face more womanly. Only when had she grown into such a termagant on the subject of marriage?

The answer to that particular question, along with the grander question of what the women were up to, would have to wait until he figured out a better way to find out than eavesdropping and playing spy.

With a last, longing look at Aileen, Tommy headed down the road.

By the time he got back to the Nose, Tara O'Connell was already installed next to her cameraman, looking as though she'd been there all evening.

He thought nothing at all of it until the next morning, when he heard about the missing tapes.

•   •   •

Tea and sweets with Rory was as pleasant as any time Crissy had ever spent with a man, and by the time they moved into the parlor for one last cup, she was in a dither.

Would he kiss her again or not? She wanted him to, very much, and she suspected he knew she wanted him to. However, not wanting to seem too anxious, she sent him ahead and took a minute to collect herself before she poured the tea and carried it out.

"Here we are," she said, handing him his cup. "Two sugars and a bit of milk, just the way you like."

"You already have it down." He looked up through those thick lashes of his and patted the sofa next to him.

Heart fluttering, she sat down beside him, and was gratified when he slipped his arm around her shoulder.

They sat that way for a long time, sipping at their tea and chatting a bit. Rory gave his version of the fight between Daniel and Tommy, as relayed by Martin since Rory hadn't been in the Nose at the time. Without giving away anything, Crissy compared it to the version going around among the women, who had a different take on it, altogether. Together they laughed at the foolishness of the two men.

"It's getting late," she had to say, finally.

"I know," he said. "Those little cakes really were delicious. What did you say they were called again?"

"Napoleons. Like the Frenchman. Have you never had one before?"

"Not that I remember," he said.

"That surprises me," said Crissy, "I thought you must have tried every sweet in the bakery."

"Not every one, no." His voice sounded husky, and she looked up to see a glow in his eyes that set butterflies swirling in her chest. "I've missed at least one."

With a gentle tug, he pulled her into his arms. It was like being wrapped in a big warm blanket. She loved the right feeling of it.

And then he kissed her—not a peck like the other night, but a true, deep kiss that went on and on. He was good, too, using his tongue to tease and probe until she was half dizzy with it before he left off to sprinkle kisses all over her face: cheeks, eyes, temples, and back to her mouth for another sweet, long kiss. It was too much; she took his lower lip between her teeth.

He groaned and hauled her up onto his lap, and that was even better, because now they could trade kisses on an equal basis, each learning what the other liked best.

"Ah, Crissy," he said as she kissed her way down his neck. "Right there in front of me, all these years. How did I miss seeing you?"

He found a sensitive spot at the base of her jaw, and she shuddered. "The same way I missed you for so long," she whispered. "But we found each other now."

"Mmm," he groaned. He burned a fiery path of kisses down to her collar, nuzzling it aside to nip her shoulder. "You're so sweet, so warm." His hands, which had been still at her waist, began lazy explorations of their own over hips, arms, back, and belly, moving closer to his goal.

He approached her breast tentatively, then more boldly, finding the peak of her nipple beneath her dress. A calm deep spot inside her began to spin slowly, pulling all the incredible sensations into its center. She moaned softly, and he reached for her buttons. "Ah, Crissy. I have to touch you."

"No," she said. "Rory, don't."

"But you're so beautiful. I want to see you. To touch your skin. To kiss you there."

Something flared in her at the thought of it. She wanted it so much, wanted to know what his mouth would feel like on her. And not just on her breasts. She'd heard other women talk, had read books. He could kiss her down there, where she ached right now for him. She was certain Rory would do it, if she just let him.

"No," she repeated.

"But Crissy."

"No, I said. You can't just come in here and start pawing at me. I'm not that sort. There's only one man who is ever going to get me out of my clothes, and he's going to be married to me."

A slightly wicked look passed over Rory's face. "There's ways to do it with your clothes all on."

The low throbbing between her legs increased. "And I suppose you're some sort of expert in the field."

"Well, no." Red crept up from his collar. "But I've thought about it a lot."

"Well, so have I. And if you want the truth, I've even thought about it with you."

"You have?" he croaked, then cleared his throat. "Well, then, we could—"

"No, we can't. Not unless you want to deal with my brother."

"Owen?"

"No, Michael. *Father* Michael. You've never met him because he was away at seminary and then was assigned to a church in the north, but he takes after Mother's side, like I do. He's at least half a head taller than you. And he boxes."

"Oh."

"But that's not the real reason I won't do it, Rory. The real reason is me. I've seen too many girls sleep with a man and get nothing but heartache and babies in return. I don't intend to give myself to any man jack that comes along. I'm saving myself for the one who really loves me."

"But *I* love you," he blurted.

She stopped dead and leaned away to get a better look at him, to see if he was serious. He was.

"You do?" she asked.

He looked as startled as she was. He chewed his lip a minute, then shot her a grin. "I believe I do."

"And I love you too, you big oaf." Crissy wrapped her arms around his neck and gave him the most passionate kiss she could muster, using up every trick she'd absorbed from school days on. She only quit when his hands started wandering too much again.

"Now stop it." She batted his hands away from her buttons. "I told you, that's for the man who loves me enough to marry me."

"God, woman. We've only just figured this out and already you're wanting me to marry you."

"That's right," she said. "Just like we've only just figured it out, and already you expect me to spread my legs for you." She stood up and smoothed her mussed clothes, then wiped her mouth with the back of her hand. "I don't think so, Rory Boland. You'd better go."

He started to argue, then clamped his mouth shut and stood up. "All right. I'll go."

She scooped his hat off the hall table and handed it to him as she pulled the door open. "Good night, then."

"Good night." He put one foot on the stoop, then turned around, grabbed her, kissed her quite thoroughly, and set her down.

"I'll be back," he said, and turned sharply to saunter off down the road.

Crissy watched him clear past McMurtry's, then slowly pushed the door shut. "Yes. I believe you will."

The phone in the hotel rang, and Brian answered it before he was aware enough to stop himself.

"I thought so," said a familiar voice.

"Gran?" Abruptly awake, he swung his legs over the edge of the bed and sat upright. "What's wrong?"

"The very question I should be asking you, except I think I already have the answer. Saw the news last night, did you?"

It all flooded back. He said bitterly, "I did."

"I thought so. You always did run off someplace when someone hurt you."

"That was when I was a child. And no one has hurt me."

"Brian, Brian." She tisked.

"How did you find me?" he asked to get her off this particular track.

"When I couldn't get you at the flat, I gave up. But then I woke up a few minutes ago, and for some reason, I knew just where you were. How are you taking this?"

"As you'll recall, I expected it."

"Perhaps at first, but things changed somewhere along the line, didn't they? You started trusting her."

Only with my heart. "If I did, it was clearly a mistake." He laughed with the irony of it. "The corker is, she actually proved me wrong. She went back and redid her story and figured out what I'm really trying to do with the villages."

"Did she, now?" Gran's voice cheered a bit. "Well, then, I don't understand why you're so put out."

"She got me to tell her about the plans for Kilbooly. That's what her story is going to be about."

"Maybe it's time that came out."

"No," he said flatly. "It may be years before we're ready. It's not fair to raise everybody's hopes and then leave them dangling that long. And what if I never can get it right? Just this morning, I asked Tara not to do the story."

"And what did she say?"

"She didn't. And I let her . . . distract me instead of pursuing the subject."

"Ahh," said a voice too wise by half. Brian blushed at having his grandmother know that much about his relationship with Tara, something he hadn't done since his youth. "Brian, you should know, the story they were talking about on television—it may not be about you."

"And upon what do you base this remarkable conclusion?"

"Bah," said his grandmother. "You're talking like Trinity College. Whenever you start doing that with me, I know you're not listening with an open mind."

That drew a laugh from Brian despite his foul mood. "All right, Gran. So why do you think it's not a story about me?"

"Because I happen to know that she's doing another story about interesting goings-on in Kilbooly."

"About Tommy and his music. I know."

"Don't be silly. They showed that one last night."

"Oh. I must have come in just afterward. So if Tara's other story isn't on Tommy, what is it?"

"I can't tell you."

"Damn it. Why are you, of all people, keeping secrets on behalf of Tara O'Connell?"

"It's not my place to be telling other people's tales."

"That's never stopped you before."

"This isn't ordinary gossip, Brian. Among other things, it affects her livelihood—which is something you need to keep in mind, by the by. She's only doing her job."

Brian snorted. "She's doing it on me."

"Don't be crude, boyo. And she is not."

"Then tell me what the other story is, Gran."

"No, I told you. I can't. But I will tell you this: you should talk to the woman yourself."

"It won't do any good," said Brian.

"Perhaps not. But if you don't and you find out you're wrong, you're going to feel like an ass."

"That's a risk I'll have to run, then. I'm in no mood to spar with Tara this morning."

She made a noise of disgust. "I warn you: stubborn pride will lose her."

"Not if I never had her. Good-bye, Gran. I'll see you in a few days."

"Ah, Brian." She sighed. "I love you, boyo. Take care."

"You, too, Gran."

He dropped the receiver back on the cradle and looked at the clock.

It was four-fifteen: too early to be up, and too late to go back to sleep.

He scrubbed at his head with both hands, trying to clear away the cobwebs.

Running away, Gran had called it, and she was right.

She had a way of making a man take a look at himself even if he didn't want to. As a child, he'd hidden in the stable hayloft; now he took a suite in an expensive hotel, but it was all one in the same.

And he even knew what he was running from, because she'd tricked him into naming that aloud as well.

Not if I never had her.

That's what it came down to. Deep in his heart of hearts, he was afraid that the woman in his arms had not been real, that the words had not been real. That he'd never had Tara at all.

Damn it. He wanted to believe in Tara. He wanted to have her. He wanted to love her. But she was making it so damnably difficult.

It might be easier if he had some real information to cling to. What other story could there possibly be in Kilbooly that was worth so much secrecy? Even Tommy . . .

Tommy.

Adrenaline poured into Brian's blood.

A conspiracy among the women, Tommy had said. And it had something to do with Tara.

He picked up the telephone and dialed the front desk.

"This is Brian Hanrahan in Suite 417. I'm checking out right away. Please have my bill ready in five minutes."

Nineteen

"I'm certain I locked it," protested Finn.

"I know you did," said Tara, curling her arm through Finn's. "You always do."

Together, they watched as the Guard assigned to investigate their call walked around the van, then opened the sliding door to take a thorough look inside.

Nothing else had gone missing, thank God. Tara would cross herself, if there weren't so many of the honest people of Kilbooly watching. They'd gathered at Finn's first roar of discovery and called in the *Gardaí* before Tara had had a chance to convince Finn it wasn't necessary.

"It doesn't appear that anything significant is missing," said the Guard, who looked to Tara to be barely out of school and thus highly inexperienced—thank heaven for small favors. "Just some tapes, you say?"

"Just some tapes?" asked Tara, highly offended. "Excuse me, but that's two weeks' worth of work for the two of us. Both of my major stories are gone. And that is significant."

The men in the small crowd muttered their agreement, but most of the women seemed altogether happy about the tapes being gone. More of them must have been watching the program than she suspected. Well, that was good for Tommy, at least.

"Of course, miss. I'm sorry," said the Guard. "It's just that with so many thousands of pounds' worth of equipment here, it's striking that they didn't disturb any of it. Perhaps it was just kids, thinking they could get their hands on some free tapes."

"If it was, the little buggers will be in for a shock," said Finn. "Those are professional format tapes. They'll find they can't put them in a regular video player."

"They'll probably dump them," suggested Tara.

"Don't you worry, I'll be poking through the waste bins in the area as a matter of course. However, the first thing is for me to talk to the other guests in the hotel and people who live nearby to see if they heard or saw anything last night." He looked to the crowd. "Did any of you people see anything?"

"No, sir," came the answer, almost like a response during Mass.

"I didn't think so. We know it happened late." He leaned over to peer at the passenger side door. "Now there's something interesting. The dust is disturbed here, right along the window. It almost looks like someone jimmied it open."

Finn glanced at Tara, who quickly stepped in to look where the officer was pointing.

"Well, isn't that usually how people break into cars?" she asked.

"In the cities. Out this way, it's usually a brick or a rock through the window, the rare times it happens at all. Is there a locksmith in the village? I'll have him look at this."

"Nobody out here ever locks anything," contributed someone from the crowd, generating a laugh.

"That's probably why their tapes got stolen," added another wag. "Someone took offense at finding a locked door and decided to teach them to be more trusting."

Even Finn laughed at that one, though a bit ruefully.

"They may not be far off," said Tara. "Someone might have seen it as a challenge."

"If so, it was a challenge they were unusually well-equipped to meet," said the Guard.

Finn shot Tara another glance, this one full of significance.

"Is there something you might want to tell me, Mr. Kelleher?"

"Hmm? Oh, I was just wondering how long we'll have to stay. We're supposed to go back to Dublin today."

"We already checked out of the hotel," said Tara.

"Well, let me think. The actual value of the tapes isn't that great. As compared to the value of your work, that is," he added hastily, glancing to Tara. "Unless you insist on it, I don't think I'll bother to call a man out from Ennis to search for fingerprints. Let me take your statements and ask a few questions around the hotel, and you'll be free to go."

The Guard pulled out a notebook and a pen, scrawled a few sentences, and then turned to Tara. "You first, Miss O'Connell. Let's step over out of the way. Would you stay here, sir?"

"All right," said Finn.

Tara followed the Guard to the edge of the car park, where he proceeded to ask a brief but thorough set of questions. She answered them all as truthfully as possible, neglecting only to mention the missing twelve minutes and that she'd stolen the tapes herself. He dismissed her and called Finn over. Twenty minutes later, he had also talked to the Fitzpatricks and the guests with rooms on that side of the hotel, and was satisfied.

"The gentleman in room nine recalls hearing a car idle

for a minute or two sometime after the news, but he didn't bother to have a look out the window. I'm certain that's the best we'll get, unless, as you say, I happen to turn them up in a waste bin. You can go ahead back to Dublin. If I discover anything at all, I'll be sure to let you know. I have your numbers."

"Thank you." Finn and Tara both shook his hand, and he headed up the road, stopping now and again to open a rubbish can.

With nothing left to see, the villagers slowly dispersed. A few came over to say good-bye—all men, as even Aileen and Siobhan walked away without a word, playing the role of aggrieved womanhood to the hilt. Crissy would be at the bakery. Tara ignored the ache beneath her breastbone as she and Finn shook the men's hands and accepted their best wishes, and soon they were alone in the car park.

"Well," said Finn. "What a fine state of affairs."

"It's awful," said Tara. "All that work."

"Mmm." He rolled a pebble back and forth with his toe a couple of times. "You know, when that Guard mentioned a jimmy, I couldn't help but think of that thing you carry in your bag."

"I know," said Tara. "I thought of that myself. It's a good thing I didn't bring it with me this trip. That would have looked bad, wouldn't it?"

"I thought you carried it everywhere."

"Not on holiday. And not when I work with you." Lord. Her next confession was going to take an hour, not even counting the part about Brian.

"Mmm," he said again. "So the fact that your car has moved since we pulled in last evening would be just coincidence?"

Shit. She should have known Finn's eye for detail would pick up every little thing. "What are you talking about?"

"You were about a foot farther left," he said.

"You must be remembering wrong," she said brightly. "Either that, or it was too dark to see properly. I haven't even been in the car in days. Since before we went to Dunloe."

He stared at her, and she could see the cogs turning. He knew, and he knew that she knew he knew.

"You're probably right," he said finally. "I'm remembering it wrong."

Pact.

"Of course I'm right. Why would I want to steal our own tapes?"

"Of course. Silly of me. Damned kids, anyway. Someone should find the gene for troublemaking and cull the carriers at birth."

"Neither of us would ever have made it to adulthood," she pointed out. She opened her car door. "Let's go home, Finnian."

"Aren't you going up to the house to say good-bye to Brian?" he asked.

She stopped half in the car. "First off, he's in Dublin. And second, I pursued him like a hound to get my story and when I finally ran him to the ground, I told him I loved him and seduced him—"

"Ach! I didn't hear that."

She clapped a hand to her mouth. "And I didn't say it. Sorry. Anyway, then Oliver put that spot on last night. If the women think I meant the boycott, what do you suppose Brian thinks?"

"Ouch," said Finn. "Well, you can't just leave it that way."

"He won't take my calls. I tried again three times this morning while I was packing."

"You're a reporter. You know a hundred ways to get around that."

"And then what? It's not like I'd be storming in to shove

a microphone in his face and demand he answer to the people."

"Why not?"

"Ah, go to hell, would you? He's furious, and I don't blame him. I'm pretty furious with myself right now. All I want is to crawl into a cave someplace and hide until I have to come out to face Oliver Monday morning."

"Where are you going to be?"

"I don't know. On holiday," she said sourly. "It may be my last one for a while. Here." She pulled her phone out of her bag and handed it to him. "You take this. I don't want Oliver using it somehow to track me down. If something important comes up, leave a message on my machine at home. I'll check it a couple of times. See you Monday before the firing squad."

She gave Finn a quick hug, got in her car, and drove away from Kilbooly telling herself that she wouldn't cry. Not until she got to where she was going. Wherever that was.

"What do you mean, she's gone?" Brian gripped the edge of the hotel desk until his knuckles cracked.

"I'm sorry, Brian. She and Mr. Kelleher both left about an hour ago, after the Guard was done."

"The *Gardaí* were here? Why?"

"Just one, but oh, it's a shameful thing. Someone here in Kilbooly broke into their van and stole every one of the tapes they worked so hard on. I'm positively mortified for the whole village. Here I thought we were safe from all those criminal influences and gang nonsense and now to find out . . ."

Brian quickly lost track of Mrs. Fitzpatrick's crime and morality lecture as his brain tried to incorporate this new information. All the tapes stolen. The Guard called in. Tara gone. What the devil was going on?

"Do you know where she went?" he asked, interrupting.

"Why, no. I don't. Back to Dublin, I assume. Why, I imagine you two passed on the road just the other side of Ennis."

Brian left her still talking and walked out into the patchy sunshine that was struggling to wrest the day away from yet another bout of rain. An hour ago. That would put her in Dublin by midafternoon. He could either chase her back to the city or stay put and ring her up. Unlike him, Tara would answer her phone to at least yell at him. She wasn't the type to let it ring.

Phone. She had a mobile phone. He retrieved his own phone from the car and found the business card she'd left as she'd slipped out of the hotel room in Dunloe. He punched in her mobile number, then let it ring for a long time. She was driving; it might take a while.

"Hello. Tara's phone. Tara isn't available right now but—"

Brian bit back a curse. "Kelleher. It's Brian Hanrahan."

There was a long, angry silence on the other end before Kelleher spoke.

"I'd say it was about bloody time, man, but it's actually too late."

"Where is she?"

"I don't know."

"Kelleher. I know you're loyal to her, but—"

"I'm tellin' you, I don't know. She just ran off. Said she was going to crawl into a cave somewhere until Monday."

"I hear your tapes were stolen."

"They were. Including the ones of you, if that's what you're worried about."

Brian opened his mouth, but realized any denial would sound hollow. And what difference did it make what Finn Kelleher thought, anyway?

"I was more interested in that other story she was working on," he said instead.

"What other story?"

"The one about the women and what they're doing."

"Are the women doing something?" asked Finn.

"Don't be clever. You spent all Tuesday evening filming them at the Nose."

"Oh, that. Those tapes are gone, too."

"What was on them?"

"There's the key, isn't it? You might just as well ask what was on any of the tapes," said Finn. "Now if you'll excuse me, I've some traffic to deal with." He rang off.

"Bloody ass." Brian flipped his phone shut and jammed it into his pocket.

Dealing with Tara directly had been an afterthought anyway, conceived during those last vacant miles between Ennis and Kilbooly. She probably wouldn't have told him anything anyway. But there was still Tommy.

He headed for the Ahearn house.

"Sorry," said Peg, apologizing for the fabric, which spilled off the kitchen table. "It's a busy time."

"I need to talk to Tommy, if he's home."

"He's in his room." Peg motioned him on through the kitchen. "Working on his fiddles. It's a mess. Tommy!"

A head popped out. "What? Oh. Brian. Come on in."

"Tea will be half a minute," said Peg. "The kettle's still hot."

Brian followed Tommy into his room. The tiny cubicle held a narrow bed, a chair, and a full-sized workbench surrounded by wood shavings.

"When your mother said you were working on your fiddles, I thought she meant you were polishing one or something."

"I do all of it in here, out of the damp. I don't have a proper shop and there was never enough decent weather in a year to finish even one fiddle when I worked outside. So when we moved down here, Da and I put down this vinyl flooring and off I went. It gets a little rank when I'm varnishing, though."

On a shelf lay several fiddles in various states of completion, the woods ranging from pale ivory on the roughed out blocks to deep russet on the one finished instrument. Every curve exhibited all the elegance of a Stradivarius.

"God, they're beautiful, Tom."

"It's not how they look that matters," said Tommy. "It's how they sound." He took a bow off a peg, tightened it, and lifted the russet fiddle off the shelf. He ripped off a phrase and then ran it slower, ending in a sustained note so sweet it made a lump form in Brian's throat. "This one's tolerable."

"Are you making any money off them?"

"I'm just starting to. With any luck, that story Miss O'Connell did will help with this and the band."

"Gran said it was on last night. I'm afraid I missed it."

"So did I," said Tommy, chuckling. "We had a session down at the Nose. But Ma saw it, and she said it did well by us. I already got one call this morning. A man wants us to play in Doolin next month."

"Good for you." He clapped Tommy on the back. "One day I'll have to say 'I knew them when.' I suppose I should start looking for a new stableman to break in."

"Not yet," said Tommy. "It's only one gig."

Peg came in with tea, and it took them a few minutes to pry her loose and get back around to business.

"You didn't come to talk about fiddles," said Tommy.

"No." Brian stared at the milky brown liquid in his cup. "I came to find out just what you actually heard Tuesday night down at the Nose."

Tommy gave him a long, hard look. "You think I'm right, don't you?"

"I know something is going on, and that Tara—Miss O'Connell—is somehow involved. I would like to know what you heard, to see if I can figure it out."

"I have a better idea," said Tommy. He leaned close, his voice dropping to a murmur. "How would you like to see the tapes, themselves?"

"What?"

"Hush. My mother's one of them, you know. Would you?"

"Don't tell me you're the one who broke into the RTÉ van."

"Jayzus, no. What do you think I am, a common thief?"

"Then how . . . ?"

"I know where they are. At least I think I do. We'll have to find a way to get our hands on them, but then we'll know for certain. Are you on?"

Brian stuck out his hand and they shook.

"Then let's get out of here," said Tommy. "We have plans to make, and we need to make them without the enemy sitting in the next room."

Motherly Peg Ahearn, the enemy? Brian laughed aloud. "Come on. I know just the spot."

After another afternoon spent trying to reach Tara, an evening spent not talking to Gran about Tara, and a night spent dreaming of Tara, by the next morning Brian was ready to do whatever needed to be done.

He made excuses to Gran about not attending Mass and sent her on her way with Lynch behind the wheel, then drove into town and parked next to the Nose. If anyone noticed the car, they would assume he intended to have a drink after Mass.

He walked up the road to Deegan's, where Tommy had been lurking in the mist for at least a half an hour.

"They're at Mass," said Tommy.

"Are you certain?"

"I watched them drive past, not three minutes ago," said Tommy. "Aileen and her mother, both."

"Then we're clear."

"As soon as the last of the neighbors leave."

They loitered under the overhang in front of Deegan's empty restaurant until the first church bells rang.

"They must have gone by before you came," said Brian. "Let's get this done."

They strolled casually back toward the Nose to pick up Brian's car, then drove out past McEnrights' house, turned around and cruised slowly back, pulling up two doors down. With a quick glance around, they got out and walked toward the house.

The neighbor's door opened. Tommy froze, his face white.

"Morning, Tommy. Brian. Shouldn't you be over at the church already? I heard the bells."

"Good morning to you, Eamon," said Brian. "Bernice. Is that a new dress?"

"This old thing? I've had it for ages."

"It must be that the color flatters you."

"Or you do," she said. "You lads had better hurry. You don't want to be late for Mass."

"We'll be along shortly," said Brian. "We're just having a small debate and didn't want to carry it into the church."

"Ah. We'll see you there." Eamon and his wife climbed in their car and drove off.

"I'm not going in," said Tommy.

"You are. You're the one who knows his way around the house."

"But I told you, I'm not cut out for this. Look at me. All Eamon did is say hello, and I'm sweating like it's the bloody Sahara."

"You're going in," said Brian firmly. "Now come on."

He took one last glance around, grabbed Tommy by the sleeve, and pulled him around to Aileen's back door. A moment later, they were inside.

Tommy plopped down on a kitchen chair and mopped his face on his sleeve.

"All right," said Brian. "Now, where would this box be?"

"A closet, I suppose," said Tommy. "You take the front hall and her mother's room. I'll check Aileen's room and the pantry."

They split up, Brian rustling through the hall closet as Tommy disappeared through a door.

A layer of ladies' shoes and Wellies covered the bottom of the closet but hid nothing. The hat shelf looked more promising, with a large white box sitting on it. Brian pulled it out far enough to determine it held nothing but gloves and scarves in assorted shades, at which point it occurred to him that he had no idea how many tapes Tara and Finn might have shot in two weeks, or how large a box they would occupy.

He closed the door and pushed open the door to Aileen's bedroom.

Tommy stood in front of the dresser, holding a framed photograph of Aileen and him, taken, if Brian wasn't mistaken, within the last year or two up on the Burren. He kissed his fingertips and touched them to Aileen's face in the picture. His expression pinched with pain.

Brian gave him a moment, then cleared his throat. Tommy looked up, embarrassed. "Sorry. I got misty there for a minute. Did you find something?"

"Not yet. Just how big is this box we're looking for?"

"About yeah by yeah." Tommy indicated a rectangle with his hands. "And about so high. It had some printing on it. I don't recall what."

"Great help you are."

"I was looking through a window," Tommy protested.

"All right. All right. I'll check her mother's room."

"Wait a minute." Tommy cocked his head, listening toward the window. "Jayzus. That's Aileen's car. And it's pulling in."

Twenty

Brian's eyes widened in alarm as the rumble grew louder. He stepped further into Aileen's room and pulled the door shut.

"No. It was open a bit," whispered Tommy holding his hands a few inches apart to show him. Brian quickly cracked the door to match.

"Come on." Tommy pulled open Aileen's closet and stepped in, squeezing past clothes into some dark recess. He held the dresses aside for Brian.

"There's not room for two," said Brian.

A door banged open.

What had appeared to be a closet stuffed to overflowing suddenly looked as spacious as the Taj Mahal. Brian plunged in next to Tommy, and as a woman's heels clicked across the kitchen floor, he stuck a hand back out and quietly tugged the door shut.

"I'll be right there, dear," called Mrs. McEnright. Her voice dropped to a scolding mutter interspersed with the opening and closing of several kitchen cupboards.

The clicking changed to a murmur of feet across carpet, then back to clicking as she stepped into the toilet. The wall just behind Brian's head thumped and shook as she searched the medicine cabinet and shut it.

A few more steps.

"There they are."

Damn. She was in Aileen's bedroom. Brian braced himself to explain to Mrs. McEnright just what he and Tommy were doing in her daughter's closet. Her footsteps moved straight toward them. Another second and life would change forever, never mind standing for the *Dáil*.

She stopped. Something rattled like a bottle of pills. The footsteps moved away, back to the toilet, where this time she ran some water.

"Come on, Mother," called Aileen. "We're already late."

"Just hold on. If you'd put the aspirins back when you used them, we'd be on our way back by now, wouldn't we?" Glass rang against porcelain as she put the cup down.

Toilet, parlor carpet, kitchen floor. Brian traced her route to the back door by sound. *Go on. Leave,* he urged silently.

"Hey! Get out of there," said Aileen. Feet scuffled across the kitchen floor.

"Just leave him," said Mrs. McEnright. "He won't hurt anything and we're late anyway."

The back door slammed, but neither Brian nor Tommy moved a muscle until the Mini's rattle had faded well into the distance.

Hesitantly, Brian reached out and cracked the closet door. Fresh air washed over them, and Brian took his first real breath in five minutes. Overhead, rain pounded on the roof.

They stayed in the closet another minute or two, until it was clear the women weren't coming back, then crept out.

"Jayzus," said Tommy fervently. "Her and her headaches. I swear, I'll never do this again in my entire life."

Brian wiped the sweat off his forehead and flapped the front of his jacket trying to dry his shirt.

"You look like you've been in a steam bath," said Tommy.

"You're no rosebud yourself. Don't you ever take that jacket to the cleaners? It smells like a smoked hog."

"Rashers!" said Tommy. "That's it. That's what was on the box. Black Label Bacon. It must be in there."

He dragged a chair to the closet, climbed up, and started clearing the shelf, passing down hats and old dolls and small boxes to Brian, who dumped them on the bed.

"Aha." He dragged a large white box off the shelf and stepped down from the chair to hand it to Brian. "The missing tapes, if I'm not mistaken. And there you were, casting aspersions on my jacket."

The box did, indeed, smell of stale bacon grease. Brian wrinkled his nose.

"All right," he conceded. "It wasn't you. Now put things back in order while I make certain we have the right box."

He turned to leave and nearly tripped over a large yellow cat. "Damn it. Get out of the way. Where did this thing come from?"

"That's Jack," said Tommy. "He must have gotten in as they were leaving."

Stepping carefully to avoid treading on the cat, which seemed very interested in his burden, Brian carried the box out to the kitchen and set it on the counter. Jack immediately jumped up and climbed on top of the box to rub around on it in ecstasy. Brian got a knife from the drawer and shoved the cat aside; Jack crawled right back. Brian picked him up and dropped him on the floor; Jack jumped back on the box by the time Brian had cut one end.

He glared at the cat. "All right. You win. Let's try this another way."

Brian quickly searched the fridge and found just what he needed: a dish of leftover sausages.

"Here we are. Come on, cat." He dangled a sausage between his fingers.

Jack knew a good thing when he saw it. He abandoned his spot on the box and came over to swirl around Brian's feet once by way of thanks, then rose up on his hind legs, snagged the sausage, and killed it with one quick shake before he started eating.

Brian shut the fridge, grabbed his knife, and made quick work of the box while Jack was still gnawing away.

"What's taking you so long?" asked Tommy as he came into the kitchen.

"Cat wrestling," said Brian. He lifted one of the tapes and read the label. "Dunloe #2, 210400. The twenty-first of April. These are the tapes, all right."

"That looks big," said Tommy.

"It's what they use for television. Did you get everything back into the closet the way it was?"

"She'll never know a thing has been touched. Of course, if we were smart, we'd move the tapes into something else and put the box back up there. She wouldn't notice for ages."

"We don't have time." Brian tossed the tape back in and picked up the box. "Get the door."

No one was visible on the street, but in case someone was watching from a window, Brian carried the box through the rain as though Aileen had personally asked him to come fetch it. Tommy wasn't quite as confident in his manner.

"Smile, man," said Brian. "You look guilty as hell."

"I am guilty as hell," said Tommy, but he managed a grin. "But at least I'm not carrying stolen goods."

A moment later, they sat in the car, the box securely locked in the boot. Brian started the car and flicked on the wipers.

"So, if those things are an odd size, do you have a machine to play them?" asked Tommy.

"Not here. Are you up to a trip to Dublin?"

"You don't even need to ask. Just run by the house so I can grab me toothbrush and leave a note for Ma, and I'm your man."

"This whole building's yours?" asked Tommy as he trailed Brian onto the elevator.

"Not mine, precisely. It belongs to the company."

"I had no idea. I mean, I work for you, and I read about you in the newspapers and the magazines, and we all know you Hanrahans have money, but this part of it is so far away, it's like it belongs to someone else. Around Kilbooly, you're just the Brian. One of the lads."

"Good. That's how I want it."

"It's going to be hard to think of you that way, now that I've seen all this."

"If you don't, I'll have to call you out and punch you in the nose again."

Tommy laughed. "Just remember who won the last time."

"I do every time I look in the mirror. God, that box reeks. It's amazing Jack didn't follow us all the way to Dublin."

The elevator slowed and stopped, and the door opened onto a darkened hallway. Brian led the way past sculptures and expensive paintings to his private entrance, where he punched in the code that unlocked the door. Lights blazed as he hit the panel inside.

"Let's get that box out of here before my whole office smells like a rendering plant."

He found an empty banker's box in his secretary's closet and dumped the tapes into it.

"What's this?" he asked, holding up a flat piece of metal.

"One of those gadgets they use to unlock a car door, I think. I heard that's how they—she—broke into the van."

"Reporters," mumbled Brian to himself. How the devil had Tara learned to use one of those things? He threw it back in with the tapes and hauled the bacon box out to the service hallway for the janitor to find the next morning. When he got back, he ducked into the lavatory to wash the stink off his hands.

"Shall I put them in some kind of order?" called Tommy.

"We don't even know what we're looking for. Let's take them how they come and see what unfolds."

"All right." Tapes clattered as Tommy picked one off the top. "Here's the first one. Where's this fancy machine of yours?"

Towel in hand, Brian came out and hit a switch on the wall. A whole section of cabinets opened up, revealing a complete media center with large screen television and a bank of video decks in various formats.

"Jayzus," said Tommy. "If you had one of those at the house, you could open it to the village for movies once a week and save us all the drive into Ennis."

"That's not a bad idea. Maybe it would get more of you up to visit with Gran." He tossed the towel back into the washroom and took the tape from Tommy to put it into the deck. "I'll get things going, if you want to scrub up."

Tommy emerged from the washroom smelling less like a side of bacon, and they settled into the leather chairs that faced the media wall. Brian raised the remote and the show began.

And it was quite a show.

Unlike the program, where Tara laid out her stories in tidy packages that a person could digest without much thought, the tapes made them work. This was raw footage, rough and unedited, with her slant on the stories left in limbo.

Still, they discovered what the women were up to early on when they stumbled onto a long interview with Peg that made her son splutter in indignation. By the time the screen went blue, Tommy was livid.

"Jayzus. My own mother," he stormed, pacing back and forth across Brian's office. "All that nonsense about being busy was just to make me ruin all my shirts. Well, if she wants me out of the house so much, I'll certainly oblige her. But I'm not marrying Aileen until I'm damned well ready, boycott or no boycott. The idea of them thinking they could get away with it, can you imagine? Them and their bloody Midnight Court."

Brian let him rant a little longer, until he began to wind down.

"Put in another tape and sit down," said Brain. "I have a feeling it gets worse for both of us."

It did. As late afternoon wore into evening, they got to sit through Aileen telling Tommy to blow off, parts of the world's dullest industrial tour— "You're about as exciting as a post," Tommy commented—and interviews with several dozen strangers with varying opinions on Brian's effectiveness in bringing economic prosperity to their corners of rural Ireland.

They kept going well into the wee hours, fast-forwarding through the parts Brian already knew and stopping to raid his well-stocked kitchen when what they did watch got to be too much. Between the two of them, he and Tommy swung through every mood from anger to depression to joy and back down to irritation.

The tapes from the past few days had more of Tara in them, doing stand-ups in which she explained and commented on the story of Hanrahan development in the villages. Slowly, a picture emerged of how she intended to present the story, and it was a flattering one. Perversely, the more glowing her comments became, the more uncomfortable Brian grew. He finally hit the stop button on the remote. Tara's face froze on the screen, her eyes bright and her mouth open slightly, as though she'd just said his name.

"You're doing all that for other villages?" asked Tommy.

Damn. This was just what he'd tried to avoid for so long. "I'm trying."

"Why not for us?"

"We support Kilbooly by keeping our trade local."

"That's not the same, and you know it. Why have you worked so hard for those other villages and not done a thing for your own?"

"You saw those other places. Do you really want Kilbooly to look like that?"

"No," said Tommy, looking down. "But I wouldn't mind seeing some of the jobs."

"When I figure out how to do one without the other, I promise, I'll bring something in. That's what this is all about." He told Tommy about his father's plans, and how none of it had worked the way they intended. All the while Tara's huge face glowed over them.

"So," said Tommy, when he had finished. "You're actually taking care of us, in your own way."

"I am."

Tommy looked him straight in the eye. "Paternalistic bastard, aren't you?"

Brian's jaw dropped.

"It's not your place to decide this all by yourself," said Tommy. "You're not the bloody lord of the manor taking care of the peasants, you know. We can take care of ourselves, and pretty damned well at that. Put in a plant or a warehouse or something—you'll get good, hard workers— and we'll all decide what the village is to grow into. Together. And if we get a great, ugly DIY out of it, we'll either love it or keep our trade at the hardware and drive it out of business. It's called a free market."

Brian blinked, then folded and unfolded his hands and pounded his knuckles together. He looked at Tommy, all flushed from his speechifying, and up at Tara, still with his name on her lips.

"You're right," he concluded. "Both of you are."

Tommy grinned. "Miss O'Connell said the same thing, did she?"

"In a roundabout way. She said I should tell people what I was up to, to get their cooperation. I didn't want to because, well, I didn't want to have this same fight I just lost to you. Have you ever thought of standing for office? You'd make a good mayor or councilman."

"Jayzus, no. All I want to do is make fiddles and play them. Since your lady friend and I are right, what do you intend to do about it?"

"Put Kilbooly on the list right after Dunloe, God help you all." Brian hit the button to make Tara fade, then got up and stretched. "There's one more tape in the box. Do you want to watch it?"

"Why not? It's almost morning anyway. We may as well round out the night. What is this one?"

Brian looked at the label. "It says 'Aileen.'"

Tommy's face set in a hard frown. "I've been wondering when she'd turn up. Put her on. Let's see her version of why she's doing this to me."

They watched in silence, and when it was over, Tommy got up without saying anything and started to put on his jacket. Brian hit the rewind and played Aileen's last words again.

". . . For all the trouble the man is, I love him. I want to be married to him, and to have his children, and to grow old with him. I've done everything I know to make that happen. This boycott is my last, best hope. It's either stick with it until he realizes he'd better come through, or I've got to give up entirely and move on.

"I don't want to move on. I want to be Tommy's wife and spend my life making him happy. I hope when he sees this, he'll know that I didn't do it to hurt him or embarrass him. I just ran out of ideas."

The screen went blue. Tommy carried an empty pop bottle to the trash and dropped it in with a loud crash.

"I may be a paternalistic bastard," said Brian. "But you, Thomas Ahearn, are a fool."

"I won't be forced," Tommy repeated stubbornly.

"You shouldn't have to be," said Brian, disgusted. "You've got a beautiful, intelligent woman so in love with you that she asked you to marry her. And even though you turned her down—God only knows why, when you claim to love her as much as you do—she still cares enough to go through with this preposterous boycott just for a chance to be your wife before she gives up on you entirely. Good lord, I can't believe my not being married is the reason you won't marry Aileen."

"Don't flatter yourself," said Tommy. "It's just an excuse."

"Like my protecting Kilbooly is just an excuse. Like Tara being a reporter is an excuse. We're all asses, and there's no excuse for that." He stomped around the room, collecting all the tapes in the banker's box, then stomped back to his desk to get his jacket. Pulling his car keys from his pocket, he tossed them at Tommy. "Here, take these. Get some rest somewhere—right here if you want—and then get yourself home and tell any of the other men that are using me as some stupid, bloody example in their lives that the excuses are bloody well over."

Tommy gaped. "You're letting me drive the Mercedes back? Alone?"

"I am. And if you're so bloody anxious to live a life based on mine, then you'll drive it straight up to Aileen's door and give her an engagement ring and beg her to forgive you, because that's exactly what I intend to do with Tara." He picked up the box and marched out of the office. "Bloody hell."

• • •

Tara took special care with her clothes and makeup Monday morning, donning a skirted suit and a little extra foundation and blush and a pretty shade of deep rose lipstick. All this effort occurred partly to hide the ravages of a weekend of tears and sleepless nights, and partly because she hoped Oliver might take pity on a poor, helpless female.

Not bloody likely.

He was waiting for her the minute she walked in the door. "My office, O'Connell."

Co-workers shook their heads in commiseration as she hung her Mac on the coatrack and followed him across the newsroom. She could practically hear the gallows creak.

Finn was already in there, looking just as wary as she felt. Tara took the seat next to him. Oliver went behind his desk and loomed, not even bothering to sit down. That was a bad sign.

"Where are my tapes?" asked Oliver in a very calm, very deadly voice. That was a worse sign.

"Didn't you get my message?" asked Finn.

"The one that said they were stolen from the van?"

Finn nodded. "That'd be the one."

"I got it. I don't believe it. Tapes don't get stolen. Cameras get stolen. Lights get stolen. Whole vans even get stolen. Tapes do not get stolen."

"These did," said Tara. "We even called the *Gardaí* in."

"Do you happen to know the penalty for filing a false report with the Guard?"

"No," said Tara.

"Slightly less than what I intend to do to you."

"I thought it was something like that," she said. "Some kids broke into the van, Oliver. Finn and I can't help that."

"I called the Guard this morning. They faxed me the report. It says"—he flipped through some papers lying on his notepad—"that the thief might have used a slim jim to pop the lock. Now the *Gardaí* don't happen to know that you own one, but I do."

"I knew it," said Tara, coming up out of her seat. "Didn't I tell you, Finn? He assumes it's me, just because I happen to own one of those things to save him the expense when Maeve locks us out of the van. That's the thanks I get for trying to be helpful: innuendo and accusation. Well I didn't have it with me, Oliver, so there."

"Where is it?" he asked, unfazed by her show of righteous indignation.

"I don't know. I got back late last night. I didn't look for it."

"There's another point. Where were you gone all weekend? I left a message for you to get back here."

"I was finishing my holiday. I didn't think there was any reason to rush back when I didn't have any story left to get ready."

"And here I thought you were busy hiding stolen tapes from the Guard."

"That's treading the edge of slander," said Finn.

"It's only slanderous if it's not true," countered Oliver. He leaned forward, hands straddling his notepad. His voice boomed. "I want those tapes. I don't care which one of you is hiding them, or why you took them, but you have until noon to have them on my desk. I announced a series of reports on Kilbooly and Brian Hanrahan, and by damn, I will have the tapes to begin work on it. Today."

His shouting was almost a relief, until he added, "Or you are both fired."

"Jayzus, Oliver, you can't do that," said Tara.

"I don't think it would be wise, either," said a voice at the door. "She might bring suit against you. Both of them might."

"Brian." Her heart skittered to a momentary stop.

"Mr. Kelleher was right," he said, winking at her as he

stepped in and closed the door. "Accusing the two of them of filing a false report with the Guard is, indeed, slanderous, because it's not true. You see, I stole the tapes—although I prefer the term borrowed, since I intended to return them all along. There was simply a mix-up in communication. A message lost."

"Brian, don't." Bluffing never worked for long on Oliver. He always wanted to see your hand.

"You've got them?" asked Oliver.

"Right outside," said Brian.

"Get them in here. We've got editing to do."

"Don't," said Tara, jumping up to block the door. "Damn it, Oliver, that's why I—I mean, neither of those stories is anywhere near done, and I told you that on Friday. I don't care if you are the producer, you can't just take over and mess about with people's lives."

"Maybe I wouldn't if I knew what the bloody hell the stories were," bellowed Oliver.

"I can't tell you that," snapped Tara. "You're just going to have to trust me and announce that the series is delayed by a few weeks."

"That's not necessary," said Brian. "Within a few hours, the boycott will be over anyway."

"What boycott?" demanded Oliver.

"You really didn't tell him?" said Brian, grinning.

"Of course not," said Tara. "How did you find out?"

"I told you, I have the tapes."

"But you can't. I gave them—" She stopped herself, but it was too late.

"Aha!" Oliver pounced. "You did take them, O'Connell. I knew it."

Tara sagged against the door and pressed her fingers to her throbbing temples. "All right. I took them. But I only did it to stop you putting them on the air. You wouldn't listen, Oliver. There's information on those tapes that could cause a war between the men and women in Kilbooly. And even if by some miracle it didn't, it would definitely hurt a lot of lovely people of whom I happen to be very fond."

"Fond?" said Brian. "I'm not sure I like the word fond."

"Who said I was talking about you?" she snapped. "Oliver?"

He growled, but the bristles came down a bit. He jerked his head Brian's direction. "He said something about the boycott being over. What boycott?"

Tara chewed her lip, considering.

"You may as well tell him," said Brian. "Tommy watched the tapes with me, and if he's not on his way back to Kilbooly now, he will be soon."

"Aw, Jayzus. Aileen's going to shoot us both." Shaking her head, she sat back down and composed herself. "All right, Oliver. Sit back and let me tell you all about the great bachelor boycott."

Twenty-one

"*It's fantastic,*" *boomed* Oliver when she finished. He pounded on his desk in enthusiasm. "I can see it. An initial feature on the women and how the boycott started, then regular updates as the men fall, one by one."

"Damn it, Oliver, Tara was right to keep it from you," said Finn, shaking his head. "Would you think it through, man? Once you put the story on, the men will know and then the whole game's up."

"Why? What difference does it make if they know? The women can just keep up their boycott."

"If the men know what's going on," explained Tara patiently, "then they'll also know that they can wait things out. This wasn't to be a battle of wills. The women just wanted to show each of the bachelors how much he needed a wife. That's why they made me promise not to tell you—or anyone—until after *they* decided it had gone as far as it could."

She slumped back in her chair, arms folded across her chest. "Oh, why are we discussing it, anyway? Tommy knows, and so will all the rest of the men by closing time tonight. None of the bachelors have 'fallen,' as you put it. There's no story left."

"Don't be too certain about that," said Brian. "I know at least one man who's teetering."

"Who?" demanded Oliver. "Perhaps we can rescue something out of this."

Brian had never taken a seat, instead leaning against the door. Now Tara twisted to look up at his face. "Don't tell me Tommy has seen the light."

"Not yet, although I believe he will. I was actually thinking of another fellow. And of a way for Oliver, here, to have his story on some 'interesting goings-on in Kilbooly.' Provided you're amenable."

"Me? What are you talking about?"

He reached into his jacket pocket and pulled out a small red velvet box which he held up. "This."

"Jayzus," said Tara, her eyes suddenly leaking. She smudged away the moisture on her cheek. "I hope that's not some sort of joke."

"It's not," Brian assured her. "Do you realize how difficult it is to get a jeweler to open at seven o'clock in the morning? They're as bad as bankers. Now, if you two gentlemen will excuse us . . ."

"The Fall of a Playboy. No. The Playboy Takes a Wife," said Oliver, thinking aloud. "This will be the wedding of the decade. I want to shoot the whole thing, starting with the proposal. Finn, get a camera."

"Certainly, Oliver. Right away. But I'll need you to sign it out." Finn cut around the back of the desk and manhandled Oliver up from his seat and out the door.

Brian pushed the door shut and locked it behind them, then came around in front of Tara and got down on one knee.

"You look silly," she said.

"I know. But it's a good position from which to beg forgiveness—ask any priest. And I do need forgiveness. I didn't trust you, and I ran off and hid when my feelings got hurt, instead of talking to you. I'm sorry, Tara."

"You're not the only one that ran away to pout, you know. And you've hardly known me long enough to trust me. I keep telling you, we barely know each other."

"We can solve that over the next fifty years or so." He opened the box, revealing a simple swirl of yellow gold that bore a diamond suitable for a royal wedding. "Tara Bríd O'Connell, will you do me the honor of becoming my wife?"

"I don't know," she said. "You've never actually said you love me."

Brian's expression flickered from disappointment through surprise and relief to chagrin.

"I did leave out that part, didn't I? But you must know I do love you, more than I ever imagined I could love a woman. I want you in my life and in my arms for as long as we both have a breath in our bodies."

"Speaking of other women," she said.

"I wasn't."

"But we need to. You've spent the last few years with dozens of them flitting in and out of your life. Are you going to get bored with me in a few months?"

"Not bloody likely," he said, laughing. "There are too many Taras: the horsewoman, the reporter, the lover, and undoubtedly more I still need to meet. Between the lot of you, I may be exhausted, but never bored."

"You make me sound like that Sybil woman. Seventeen personalities in one body."

"That's not it at all. You're just a complex, exciting, passionate woman that I want to spend a lifetime getting to know."

"It's not going to be easy, Brian. We're two professionals, with busy lives. I'm not going to quit my job, you know—assuming I still have one by the end of the day."

"I didn't expect that you would, any more than I would

give up mine. Neither of us is the sort to rusticate in Kilbooly. We'll work it out, though."

"I suppose we will. I imagine it will take a lot of compromise." She put a soft emphasis on their private code, and heat flared behind his eyes.

He drew her hand to his mouth and kissed it. "I'm counting on it."

She laughed. "You're terribly easy."

"You have no idea. What about it, Tara? Marry me?"

"In a heartbeat," she said.

"Thank you." He slipped the ring on her finger and they sealed the pledge with a kiss, one that threatened to go incendiary when Brian whispered a suggestion for an alternate use for Oliver's desk. She put the skids on that one, but they necked a little longer, until Oliver thumped on the door.

"What are you two doing in there?"

"Setting a date," called Tara.

A cheer went up in the bullpen.

"I told you I wanted film of him proposing," shouted Oliver over the applause.

"Good thing we weren't on the desk," she whispered. "He'd be wanting to film that, as well. He's going to be a pain."

"Our own private paparazzo."

"Maybe if we let him have his way on the wedding, he'll agree to hold back the story on you and the villages."

"Let him show it," said Brian.

"But I—"

"Tommy's already seen it, including the new and improved footage you did last week."

"Oh, my." She winced. "You two were busy."

Brian nodded.

"I'm sorry," she said. She raked her hair back from her face. "I can't believe the way this whole situation got away from me."

"Now perhaps you understand what happens in the villages after we're done building," he said.

She flushed. "I was a judgmental little ass, wasn't I?"

"You were. Whereas I am a paternalistic bastard, as Tommy so eloquently put it. He was not pleased with my one-sided effort to protect Kilbooly from development."

"Oh."

"He says I should stop playing lord of the manor and let the village decide if they're to be mucked up or not." Brian shifted, to give her another kiss, this time on the cheek. "And since you helped get me into this position, one of your first wifely duties will be to assist me in getting out. Your assignment is to help me figure what sort of facility I can put in Kilbooly that will do the least damage."

A slow grin spread across her face. "As a matter of fact I had a thought this weekend—"

The door rattled again.

"What's the date?" Oliver demanded. "I have a program to schedule."

Tara grimaced. "Impatient thing. He's going to want this wedding to happen quickly."

"That is the one area in which I agree with the man," said Brian. "I intend to plunge into the matrimonial waters with you as soon as the license is valid—unless you have your heart set on a big church wedding."

"The only thing I have my heart set on is you. St. Senan's and daisies will do just fine."

"Not roses?"

"Father Breen's allergic to roses." She thought about it a minute. "You know, though, eight days is a bit soon, even for a small wedding. Can you wait a month?"

"Three weeks," he countered. She nodded.

"O'Connell!" bellowed Oliver.

Chuckling, Brian took time for one last, lingering kiss. "St. Senan's and daisies, in three weeks."

"I'll clear my schedule and notify my family. The whole pack will want to come, you know, even Albert from Canada. We'll have to find rooms for all of them." She reached over and flipped the lock on the door. "All right, Oliver. You can come in and start ruining my wedding."

"Why is the Brian sitting out front?" asked Siobhan from the parlor.

"I don't know," said Aileen. She dried her hands on the dish towel, folded it to hang by the sink, and went out to join her friend by the front window.

Sure enough, there sat the Mercedes, with Brian behind the wheel. No. Wait.

"That's not Brian. That's Tommy."

Siobhan squinted. "You're right. I just saw the car and didn't really look closer."

"What do you suppose he's doing in that car?"

"Maybe he stole it," said Siobhan.

Aileen elbowed her in the side. "Don't be daft."

"Then how did he get his hands on it?"

"I don't know. Maybe Brian lent it to him. I hope." As she stood there, Tommy shifted and she got a better view of his big square jaw. Her chest tightened. "What do you think he wants?"

"To talk to you," said Siobhan. "The question is, do you want to talk to him?"

"I don't know." Aileen sighed. "Yes. Of course I do."

"Then I'd better be off. He'll never come in while I'm here, not after that delightful scene at the café." Siobhan let the edge of the curtain fall. "You know, he doesn't look as peculiar in that thing as we thought he would. I guess a Mercedes looks well on anyone." She tossed back the last of the cup of tea she had in her hand and headed for the kitchen to put it in the sink, then grabbed her coat and came back to the front room. "I'll go out this way, so he's sure to see me leave. Ring me later and tell me what he has to say for him-self."

Aileen let Siobhan out, then stood in the front hall count-ing off the minutes until Tommy worked up the courage to get out of the car. She almost gave up, but then she heard the car door slam, and a long while later, a knock at the front door. She couldn't remember the last time he'd come to the front, like a stranger.

She didn't bother to feign surprise when she opened the door. "Tommy."

"Aileen." He had his cap in his hands and a pinched look around his eyes. "Can I come in, or have I put you off me forever?"

"You can come in." She left it at that for the time being.

He stepped just barely over the threshold and stopped.

"You'll have to come farther than that," she said. "I'm not going to stand here in the doorway like you're selling me insurance." She turned and walked toward the parlor. Be-hind her, he stepped in and shut the door.

She took her mother's favorite armchair. He picked the far end of the sofa, a thousand miles away.

He twisted his cap in his hands "The first thing I want to do is apologize for embarrassing you in Deegan's."

"I was mostly embarrassed for you," she said honestly.

"I know. But either way, it wasn't very pleasant for you, and it was my fault. I'm sorry."

"I accept your apology."

He ducked his head in acknowledgment, but said noth-ing. From the way he was wringing the life out of that cap, he must be working up to something. Aileen pinched her eyes shut and said a quick prayer.

"You owe me an apology, too," he said.

"Oh?"

"Oh?" he echoed. "I know about the boycott, Aileen."

"What boycott?" She managed to sound cool even though her stomach twisted like his cap.

"I take it you haven't checked on that box of tapes recently."

"I have no idea what you're—"

He flapped the cap flat and laid it on the sofa beside him. "Top shelf of your closet. Right-hand side, behind the hatbox."

Concern drove her to her feet, and she started for her room.

"They're not there," he said. "Brian and I took them to Dublin."

"Dublin? Thomas Jacob Ahearn! You broke into our house?"

"I walked in like I always do. The door's never locked."

"But you went into my room."

"I've been there, too, as you'll recall," he said. "And even if I hadn't, I don't think what Brian and I did was any worse than what you did."

"Tara asked me to keep them."

"I'm not talking about you having the tapes. I'm talking about what's on them."

"You watched them?" Her cheeks grew hot at the recollection of what she had said in her interview.

"Brian and I did together. We were trying to figure out what you women were up to, and how Miss O'Connell fit into it. Now we know, and most of it isn't very pretty. The idea of you women trying to force us all into marrying. It . . ." He searched for a word. "It's appalling, that's what it is."

"Tell me what else I could do. I had already humiliated myself by asking you and having you say no."

"You could have waited a little longer. We're talking about a whole lifetime, here. Would a few months, or even another year make so much difference?"

"Yes," she said. "It would, because next year you'd find some reason to put it off another year, and another after that, just like you have been all along. Do you remember when we first started going together and you said we'd be married when I turned twenty-one? Well I hate to break it to you, Thomas, but that happened seven years ago. Nearly eight, now. I don't want to be using a cane to walk down the aisle."

"Then how about my arm?"

"Don't be clever, Tommy. I'm not in the mood."

"I'm not being clever." He shifted to the near end of the sofa. "Brian said I was a fool for not marrying you. I think he was probably right. Did you mean all that stuff you said to Miss O'Connell? About loving me, and wanting to have my babies and grow old with me?"

Aileen pressed a hand to her chest, trying to hold back the tears that welled up. "Of course I meant it, Tommy. I've been telling you that all along."

"It was different seeing it on the tape, knowing you said it for the television and all those people that would be watching. It made it sound, I don't know, more serious."

"I was afraid it would make you angry."

"It did, at first," he admitted. "I don't take well to you trying to force me into this before I'm ready. You know that."

"I do."

"But Brian also pointed out that I shouldn't need to be forced when I love you so much and you love me. And when I had time to think about it—and I had a lot of time while I was driving back—I decided he was right. So I stopped by the house and got this before I came over."

He pulled a ring out of his pocket and held it out, and when Aileen saw the two tiny hands holding a heart and a crown, the tears wouldn't stay down any longer.

"It's the *claddagh* you always said you wanted," he said

unnecessarily. "It's only silver, but I promise I'll replace it with gold one day soon, just like Da did for Ma."

"This was your mother's?"

He nodded. "She said she'd be proud for you to have it. I know it's a little scratched and battered, but it got that way from being worn in love." He blinked, fighting tears of his own. "Would you wear it in love again, Aileen? Would you marry me? Or have I been too stubborn and ruined it forever?"

She sniffled and swallowed hard and managed to find her voice. "You haven't ruined it at all. Of course I'll marry you, Tommy. That's what this was all about."

He came off the sofa, then, to kneel at her feet and kiss away the tears that streamed down her cheeks. His lips found hers tentatively, then more urgently, as two weeks' worth of hell burned away for both of them. She slid forward on the chair and wrapped her arms around him.

"Still as sweet as the first time I kissed you," said Tommy. "When's you mother coming home?"

"It doesn't matter," she said. "We're not going to do that anymore until we're married. After twelve years, I want a proper wedding night, or at least as close as we can manage."

Tommy started to protest, then nodded. "All right. I can't give you much, but I can give you that. In fact, by the time our wedding night rolls around, I'm going to have you so worked up that you'll think you're a virgin again. Even if I go mad from the effort."

A thrill of anticipation ran through Aileen and burst from her as a laugh. "Then we'd better not put this off too long. I don't want to marry a madman."

"We'll drive to the Registry tomorrow, first thing."

"Do you think Brian would mind if we took his car? I've never ridden in a Mercedes."

"He said I could drive it, didn't he? Besides, he's still in

Dublin. So, let me take you for a little drive this evening. I think it would be all right."

"That would be lovely," she said. "You know, Tommy, one of the best places to get a woman worked up is in a car."

That afternoon, Tara and Brian filmed a special segment for that week's edition of *Ireland This Week*. The report, complete with a condensed history of Brian's extensive social life—narrated with good humor by Tara—and a tight shot of the engagement ring, was part of a carefully negotiated arrangement that preserved both Tara's job and at least a tiny portion of their privacy while leaving Oliver to salivate over future exclusives.

There had been telephone calls earlier, to Kilbooly and Barraduff, and welcomes into the respective families. Much to Brian's consternation, Ailís Hanrahan could be heard whooping on the other end of the line, apparently dancing a jig with Lynch. At the other extreme, Kit O'Connell expressed his misgivings about Brian based on reputation, but accepted his daughter's word that all was right and gave his blessing. Then, ever the horseman, he asked after Brig.

By the time they got back to Brian's flat from the studio in Donnybrook, the phone was ringing off the hook. After an hour or more of accepting congratulations from friends and business associates and referring requests for interviews to his office, Brian recorded a new message for his voice mail and unplugged every phone in the flat.

"Time for bed," he said, pulling Tara up from the sofa.

"My clock's all fouled up. I'm not sleepy at all."

"Who said anything about sleeping?"

Warmth rippled through Tara's body and she moved into his arms.

They left clothes all the way to the bedroom, a shirt here, a pair of trousers there. By the time they reached the bed, they were dancing belly to belly.

"You have the warmest skin," he murmured.

"It gets warmer."

"Where?" he asked, eyes glowing.

She tugged his hand low. "Right here."

"Mmm. Let's see how much warmer we can make that."

Twenty-two

They drove back to Clare the next day in Tara's VW, catalogs from the best wedding shops in Dublin piled high in the rear seat and rock and roll blaring on the radio. Finn followed behind in the RTÉ van as official wedding videographer—Oliver's idea.

"Someone's going to see you driving this thing and decide that I've already bankrupted you," said Tara.

"It's a good little car. Maybe we can use it to sneak off for our honeymoon. Speaking of which, where would you like to go?"

"Someplace far away from people like me. Oliver's going to drive me insane before this is over. How did you keep from smacking me that first day I turned up in Kilbooly?"

Brian laughed. "I almost didn't. It's going to get worse, you know, especially if I do decide to announce for the *Dáil*."

"You can't do that now," said Tara. "You're a known break-in artist."

"By the time my public relations people get done with that story, I'll sound like some swashbuckling romantic, out to win his lady fair. And since you're the lady fair and I did win you, the public will love it."

"Damn," she said. "You're already thinking like a politician. It's a shame I won't be able to cover your campaign."

"You'll be too busy being the politician's wife to be a thorn in my side."

"They're hardly mutually exclusive," she warned.

"Then I'll have to keep you busy," he said. "And to that end, with all the distractions of the past twenty-four hours—"

"Like sex at the breakfast table?"

Brian cleared his throat. "I think you mean *on*, but yes, like that. With all the distractions, you never got around to telling me your idea for the development of Kilbooly."

"Mmmm? Oh." She had to retrace her thoughts. "Centralized order processing. It's perfect for Kilbooly: high technology, low environmental impact. And do you realize how many people in the village already use computers and are on the Internet? It's amazing. You'll barely have to train them."

Brian fingers tightened around the steering wheel in excitement. "My god, Tara. You're right. We're getting ready to centralize the ordering for the soft-drink division, but I've been looking at sites nearer to Dublin."

"But with Ennis being the Information Age Town—"

"—the infrastructure is in place. All we'll need is the building and the equipment. And we can integrate it into the village so that it doesn't disrupt things. This is brilliant, Tara. God, I should have seen it."

"You probably would have, if you had been in a hotel in Ennis moping all weekend."

"Ennis?"

She shrugged. "I figured no one would bother to look there. Anyway, there was a computer right in the room, and it made me start thinking that it was a shame you hadn't taken advantage of that for Kilbooly."

He reached for her hand and pulled it to his lips. "As I said, brilliant, even in trying times. You're going to make a hell of a wife for me, Tara Bríd. Maybe you're the one who should stand for office."

"Oh, now there's a terrifying thought."

They talked of plans for Kilbooly all the way into Ennis, where they arrived in time for a late lunch. Afterward, they went to the Registry office to fill out the forms and queue up with everyone else. The stares and whispers that went with being well known would have been tolerable, if they hadn't been made doubly worse by the gawky cameraman who followed their every move.

"Gad, Finn, You're turning this into a show."

"I'm only doing my job. Oliver told me if I missed one minute of this, he'd assign me to every nasty story he could turn up. Meatpacking plants. Sewage treatment facilities. Waste incinerators."

Tara looked at Brian. "We could try your technique and bore the man to death."

"Just hand me a gun and let me shoot myself now," said Finn. "I don't think I can bear up for another Hanrahan-style tour."

At long last, they reached the clerk's desk and handed over their paperwork. The young woman started recording and stamping.

"Would you look at this, Nora," she said, calling over a co-worker. "Another one."

Nora came to look at the form, and in turn called Maudeen, and the three of them stood there exclaiming over the remarkableness of it.

"Excuse me," said Brian. "Our license?"

"Oh, of course, sir," said their clerk, turning back to business as the others dispersed. "It's just that it's uncanny. It's been ages since we issued a license to anyone in Kilbooly, and here you are, the third couple today."

"The third!" exclaimed Tara.

"Good lad," said Brian, grinning. "I knew Tommy would come through."

"But who's the third?" asked Tara. She looked to the clerk. "Tommy Ahearn and Aileen McEnright are one couple, but who is the other?"

"Oh, I can't tell you that."

"Of course you can. It's a public record."

"But it's not processed into the system yet. That will take a week to ten days, and then you'll be able to look at the register. It's not official until then, and I'm not allowed to give out the information, except to the *Gardaí*, of course."

"Jayzus," said Tara, rolling her eyes. "Isn't bureaucracy wonderful."

Brian gave her a squeeze. "I know it's against your character, but you'll just have to be patient."

"Patient? *I'm* not the one who proposed after knowing someone for eleven days."

"Do you want me to take it back?" he asked.

"Don't even think of trying."

The clerk finished her stamping and recording and handed them a license. "There you are. Now don't forget, it's not valid until the eighth day, and in the meantime, you must post the banns in any Irish newspaper. Wouldn't it be exciting if all of you from Kilbooly got married at the same time? I swear, there must be something in the water over there."

"It's not the water," said Tara. She leaned close to tell her the secret. "It's the stout at the Bishop's Nose."

"Really?" asked the clerk. Her friends' ears pricked up, as well.

"God's truth," said Tara, crossing her heart.

"Let's go, my sweet," said Brian, tugging her toward the door. Finn followed, and as they left, they could see the three clerks put their heads together.

"You're awful," said Brian, laughing.

"Just a bit giddy," said Tara. "How long do you suppose it will be before they drag their boyfriends into the Nose, in hopes of getting married."

Finn looked at his watch. "About four hours, if they stop for supper first. I just hope they actually have boyfriends. I'd hate to see another batch of women head-hunting in Kilbooly."

"Maybe one of them will put Rory out of his misery," said Tara.

"Not bloody likely," said Finn. "Sooner or later they'll see that tape of the fire, and that will be the end of it. Where next?"

"The house for us, the hotel for you," said Brian. "And then we'll see you later at the pub."

A half an hour later, Tara waved to Finn out the window as Brian wheeled the car onto the road up to Bramble Court. They turned through the gate, gravel crunching beneath the tires, and moments later, pulled to a stop before the house.

Brian switched off the engine and set the hand brake. "We're here."

"Don't I know it." Tara wiped her hands on her skirt.

"What's wrong?" asked Brian,

"I'm nervous."

"Of Gran? I know she can be a terror, but you two are already friendly."

"But it's different now," she said.

"How?"

"She's going to be my grandmother-in-law. It's just different. You wouldn't understand."

"You're right. I wouldn't." Brian shook his head, then got out of the car and came around to her side. He opened the door and held out his hand. "There's only one way to get it over with."

Tara quickly checked her hair in the vanity mirror, took a deep breath, and let him help her out.

Lynch was the model of decorum as they entered. "Good day, sir. Miss O'Connell. Mrs. Hanrahan is waiting for you in the conservatory." He took their coats and started toward the closet.

Tara couldn't resist. "Lynch."

He turned. "Yes, miss?"

"Were you really dancing the jig with her?"

A smile creased the man's face. "Most definitely, miss. And may I say, it will be a pleasure working for you."

"Thank you, Lynch."

The butler bobbed his head and turned back to his duties, but not before he did a quick two-step and a tiny skip-jump.

Brian stared after him. "My god. He's dancing. I've picked a enchantress for bride."

"I think I like the idea of a dancing butler. Come on, let's go before I lose my nerve."

Ailís sat arrayed much like she had been the first day Tara had seen her, surrounded by orchids whose heavy scent filled the air with exotic perfume.

Brian greeted his grandmother with a kiss, and then tugged Tara forward. She felt the need to curtsey, but resisted.

"Mrs. Hanrahan."

"We won't have that anymore. Start calling me Gran, like Brian does. And come give me a kiss." She let Tara give her a granddaughterly peck, then patted her on the cheek. "I knew the first day that you were the one, just as I knew he'd fight it like the dickens."

"Gran!" said Brian.

"Was he too hard on you?" she asked, ignoring Brian's protest.

"I think I was harder on him," admitted Tara. "I really didn't want to like him, you know. When I first came to you,

I was convinced he was a terrible, awful person, and I fully intended to make him look it on television. I'm afraid I misled you."

"That you did."

"I'm sorry. Will you forgive me? Can you?"

"Look at his face," said Ailís, nodding toward her grandson.

Tara obeyed, and saw an expression of deep satisfaction and honest affection in Brian's eyes.

"Do you think I could bear ill will against anyone who could make him look like that?" asked Ailís softly.

Tara's breath caught in her throat at the old woman's kindness. "Thank you, Mrs. . . . Thank you, Gran."

"You two are going to embarrass me to death," said Brian. He stepped in closer to Tara and slipped his arm around her waist. "If you keep that up, I won't take you down to the Nose after dinner for fear of being humiliated in public."

"You love it and you know it," said Tara. "And you couldn't keep me away from the Nose if you tried. I want to know who the third couple are."

"Third couple?" asked Ailís.

They told her the story of what happened at the Registry.

"Well, Tommy and Aileen are your second pair. Peg called me this morning, bubbling over with the news. But I didn't realize there was another. Let's find out who it is. Hand me that telephone."

"It will be more fun to find out at the pub," said Tara. "Come down with us. We can toast the future with Mary's magical brew."

Which comment led to more explanation and more laughter and eventually to dinner and a trek down to the pub afterward. Ailís insisted they take the VW.

"These are such darling little cars," she said wistfully as

they reached the edge of the village. "I wish I could drive one."

"Any time you'd like to try this one, it's all right with me," said Tara from the backseat.

"Ah, that's sweet. But I have no license. I never learned. Mick always drove me anyplace I wanted to go, and now Lynch or Brian does."

"I'll teach you," promised Tara.

"Now wait one minute," began Brian.

But Ailís's face had already lit up with excitement. "I'll hold you to that, girl."

"Gran's too old to drive," said Brian.

"Just down to the stable and back," said Tara, then leaned forward and whispered in Gran's ear, "To begin with."

"I heard that," said Brian, but they had reached the pub and further argument would have to wait.

The Court had once again taken over the Bishop's Nose, and when they opened the door, the buzz of excitement that filled the air erupted into a cheer. Dozens of women swarmed forward to congratulate Brian and hug Tara and Ailís as they made their way to places of honor at the center table.

"A round on the house," shouted Mary. "But we'll hold the toasts until Tommy and Aileen turn up."

"We'll have to hold them longer than that," said Brian. "The Registry Office said there's a third couple, but they wouldn't tell us who they are."

His announcement raised a murmur of speculation around the room, but the chatter came to a halt as Aileen pushed the door open.

"Here we are," she said gaily.

"It's all women," protested Tommy from outside. "I'm not going in there. It's unnatural."

"I finally got a proposal from you," said Aileen. "I intend to show you off to the women who helped me get it."

"Aw."

"Get your backside in here, Tom," hollered Brian over the laughter. "If I can bear it, so can you."

Tommy put on a great show of being embarrassed, but he was clearly enjoying himself, as were Peg and Mrs. McEnright, who followed close behind the couple, shoving them along.

As they made their way toward the center, Tara shot Brian a grateful smile. "You must have told him the right things."

"Only what I figured out for myself," said Brian. He pulled his chair close and put an arm around her shoulder. The other, he slipped around her waist.

"And what was that?"

"That a good woman deserves a good man." He slipped one thumb under the edge of her pullover to trace a surreptitious line over the bare skin of her stomach. His eyes glittered with mischief. "And you, being the best, deserve the best."

She pushed his hand away. "You're as cocky as Finn. Next thing you know, you'll be wanting me to call you Brian the Bold."

He tilted his head to one side, considering. "Now there's an idea."

Mary interrupted any further discussion with another demand for the third couple to come forward.

"What's that about?" asked Aileen.

Tara quickly explained about the license while Mary announced that there would be no toasts until the final couple revealed themselves.

Tommy added, "So speak up before you have half the women in the village angry at you."

Everyone laughed, but no one stepped up.

"Come on," called Tara. "Don't be shy. We're all going to know soon anyway."

More laughter.

"All right," said Aileen. "We'll figure it out by elimination. Who's not here? Daniel and Louise?"

"I'm here," said Louise from the corner. "Alone, sad to say, but with high hopes. Where's Siobhan?"

"Right here," said Siobhan, coming through the door. "What do you need?"

"We were wondering if you were getting married," said Aileen.

"Just because I'm late?" she said, then blushed when everyone laughed at the unintended meaning. "Gad, you lot. I don't even have a boyfriend. Just who would I be marrying?"

She slid in next to Ailís, but not before Tara noticed the quick glance toward Finn.

A quick run through the remaining couples left everyone as mystified as ever.

"Ah, well," said Mary. "I can't very well make you all hang about here with dry throats. I'll stand another round when whoever it is turns up." She started pulling glasses. Siobhan put on an apron and pitched in to serve.

As the drinks were served, the noise level dropped enough for some decent conversation, and Tara turned to Aileen for details.

"We're getting married as soon as the license is valid," said Aileen after she'd told the tale of the proposal. "We'll have to live with Mother for a time, of course, but that won't be forever. Tommy got a call from a talent scout today."

"Tommy! That's wonderful."

"Well, maybe. He wants us to make a demonstration record, just to see if anyone is interested in us. And it's all thanks to you."

"All I did was tell Finn to point his camera at you. It's your talent. I'm so happy for you both." Tara gave him and

Aileen each a hug and a kiss, then turned to Peg. "And you've got your sewing room, at last."

"Not until we get the old cottage fixed up for a workshop," said Tommy.

"Ah, Tommy," groaned Peg.

"I've got to have someplace to work on my fiddles, don't I? There's no place I can do it at Aileen's, and I don't have the money to rent a shop."

"Ah, clear out, Thomas, and give your poor mother some room for her work," said Ailís.

"And just where am I to go?" he demanded.

"You can have one of the tack rooms at the stable," said Brian. "Put in whatever you need in the way of equipment, and we'll call the first year's rent a wedding present. We'll work out something after that."

"It's the only reasonable thing to do," said Tara, as Tommy struggled with his emotions. "Your mother's going to need the room to make all our wedding dresses. We don't want biscuit crumbs in the tulle."

Tommy's jaw worked a bit more, but finally, he nodded. "Thank you, Brian. I'll start on it tomorrow after I'm done with the horses."

Peg got up and came around to give Brian a hug and pinched his cheek. "You always have been a sweet boy."

Tara laughed as her intended blushed.

Siobhan set a pint of stout in front of Brian. "You're not half bad, Bri."

"You're a pip," Tara agreed.

Brian gave her a wink and patted her on the knee. "Brian the Benevolent?"

She punched him in the arm. "Tara the Tired-of-it."

"Does everyone have a glass in front of them?" called Mary a few minutes later.

A chorus of "Ayes" rattled the walls, and glasses were raised high.

"All right, then. As owner of this establishment and thereby Sergeant of Arms of the Court, I hereby raise a toast to the results of our work. To the happy couples: Tara and Brian and Aileen and Tommy. *Sláinte.*"

"Hey, there. Hold on." A gust of fresh air carried the voice through the pub. "You can't leave us out of this celebration."

Silence fell as everyone turned toward the open door. There stood Crissy Carmody and Rory Boland, arm in arm, blushing like a pair of ripe peaches.

"Come on, now," said Rory. "Toast me and my bride-to-be. Crissy agreed to marry me."

Pandemonium broke loose. Aileen and Siobhan raced across the room to alternately hug Crissy and shake her, while everyone else clamored for the story.

Rory waved the crowd silent. "It's not much of a story. I ate her cooking. I kissed her. And I knew, just like that. So when she said I had to marry her if I wanted to get frisky—"

"Rory!" Crissy punched him in the side, and everyone laughed.

"—I went and bought a ring." He held up her hand proudly, showing the flash of a small stone.

Tara leaned over, her lips next to Brian's ear. "Would that have worked with you?"

"Not nearly as quickly as the way you did it," he said.

Crissy and Rory moved through the crowded pub, accepting congratulations and jibes with equal good humor. Eventually, they made their way to the big table, where the women exclaimed over Crissy's ring while Brian and Tommy pumped Rory's arm and gave him fits about his secret love life.

"Let's try that toast again," said Mary. Glasses were lifted once more. "To our happy couples. Tara and Brian, Aileen and Tommy, and Crissy and Rory. May I see each of you old and gray and combing your grandchildren's hair. *Sláinte.*"

"Sláinte."

Mystery solved and toasts made, the evening settled into the moderate roar of a good time being had by all. The doors were finally opened to the men, who streamed in to join the celebration and catch up on the news and thump the three fallen bachelors on the back. Beer flowed as freely as the gossip, courtesy of Brian's deep pocket, and Tara decided she could, indeed, come to enjoy having money enough that she didn't have to worry about when the round would come to her again.

All the while, Finn stayed with his camera, fussing at people who got in his shot and passing jokes back and forth. But through it all, his gaze kept flickering to Siobhan on a regular schedule. It was mutual, Tara noticed, and she was about to mention it to Brian when Mary let out a yowl of displeasure.

"Who let this damned cat in? Someone get him out of here, would you, before I lose my license."

"I'll get him," said Tara, sliding out of her seat. She found Jack rubbing Mary's ankles behind the bar, and scooped him up. "Lord, you weigh a ton, cat."

"He's such a beggar," said Siobhan coming in with a tray of deadmen. "And getting fatter by the day." She gave him a scratch behind the ears, and Jack pushed his head into her palm and started purring like a tractor. "I like you, too, puss. Maybe I'll start hanging out with you. Both my best friends are getting married."

"It's hard, isn't it?" said Tara, commiserating. "I've been in that situation, myself. You're happy for them, but at the same time, you know things are never going to be the same."

Siobhan sighed. "There's some hard truth. Even after I heard about Aileen, I thought Crissy and I would still be running around like heathens. But now, there she is with Rory-boy, and here am I, alone. And the one man I might be interested in isn't even from Kilbooly. And he's married."

Tara followed her gaze to exactly where she knew it was going.

Finn stood behind the camera, laughing and looking altogether too free and easy, while Siobhan stood over here miserable. Well, Tara knew just how to solve that.

"No, he's not," she said.

"I beg your pardon?" said Siobhan.

"I said, no, he's not. Finn's not married. He told everyone he was because he thought it would make all of you more comfortable about him filming you, what with the boycott and all. But he's as unattached as they come. And I happen to know he wants to go fishing with you while he's here. He's just shy." She crossed her fingers. *Gun-shy, maybe.*

Siobhan chewed her lip. "You're certain? About the fishing, I mean."

"Absolutely. He'll love it."

"Another round over here," called Martin. He had his arms around Crissy and Rory. "We have some serious catching up to do."

"Hold your water," said Siobhan. "We're running low on glasses. I'll have to wash up." With another glance at Finn, she turned and started filling the sink.

"Time for you to go, Jack." Tara carried the cat through the kitchen to the back door and let him out with a warning not to count on seeing Siobhan too much after all. She returned to the bar to see Finn watching Siobhan, who was up to her elbows in suds. He noticed Tara watching and quickly bent over the camera.

"She's going to reel you in like one of your fish," Tara muttered to herself, and when Finn couldn't help himself and glanced over to Siobhan once again, she chuckled.

"Go on, now." Mary nudged her with a dimpled elbow as she passed with a tray of whiskey glasses and two bottles. "Your man is looking for you."

Your man. As unfashionable as the sentiment might be

these days, Tara liked the sound of it. She made her way toward the table. Sure enough, Brian was on his feet, searching the room. He spotted her and extended his hand toward her.

She slipped past Peter and Annie to rejoin Brian.

"I love you," he said. "Come on. Help me make a toast."

He pulled a chair around and stepped up on the seat, then helped her up beside him, wrapping his arm securely around her waist. Sticking a thumb and finger into his mouth, he whistled.

"Another toast," he called. "Hand us our drinks, Tommy."

Tommy passed their glasses, and they waited for the ruckus to subside enough to be heard.

"Because of Aileen, here, and Mary, and all the rest of you, I have found something I didn't fully realize I was missing." Brian looked to Tara, and his eyes glowed so brightly that a lump formed in her chest and all the women in the pub sighed with a collective, "Ahhh." The men shuffled and cleared their throats.

"And so I propose a toast," Brian went on, his eyes never leaving Tara's, "to the women who made it possible." He lifted his glass. "To the Midnight Court."

"To the Court," echoed Tommy and Rory, followed by a chorus of mixed voices.

Tara touched her glass to Brian's with a tiny, crystalline sound that repeated a hundred times around the pub.

"Long may its justice hold sway in Kilbooly."

"I'll second that," said Brian. And he kissed her.

It Takes a Village
To Make a Village

Kilbooly is a figment of my imagination, but I could never have brought it to life by myself.

First and foremost, another thank-you to J. Noel Fahey. I read an English translation of *Cúirt an Mheán Oíche* (*The Midnight Court*) years ago, but when I conceived this book, I was unable to locate one by any method—a sad state of affairs for one of the great works of the Irish language. Then I got online and stumbled onto Mr. Fahey's wonderful Website (www.homesteader.com/merriman/welcome.html). Now any of us can zip over there at anytime and read all 1000+ lines of this lively poem, either in Irish or in Mr. Fahey's original English translation. It's worth doing, believe me.

To Gail Fortune, for seeing the possibilities in a herd of bachelors.

To Sheila Rabe and Angie Butterworth, for convincing me I could do this book in the time I had, for kick-starting me when I was stuck, and for cheering me when I finished.

To David, for eleven years of love and support and daily reminders of what romance is really all about.

To my mother, for giving me the gift of time and folded laundry while I got a running start.

To all those people who keep Irish and Irish-themed Websites up and running so when I needed a detail at midnight, all I had to do was hit a button or two.

To Sean Ahearn, wherever you are, for introducing me to *The Midnight Court* and ultimately making this book possible.

And to all the readers, writers, editors, booksellers, and librarians who love and promote the romance genre and keep the dream alive.

You're all invited to write me at:

Lisa Hendrix
c/o Berkley Publicity Department
Penguin Putnam Inc.
375 Hudson Street
New York, NY 10014

You can also contact me through my Website, where you'll find an e-mail link, along with news, good Irish pub crack, and previews of future books:

www.lisahendrix.com

From the award-winning author of the *Samaria Trilogy* comes a classic **Romeo and Juliet** romance set on a world far from our own...

SHARON SHINN
HEART OF GOLD

On a planet divided between rich and poor, strong and weak, intellect and feeling, only one thing could bring together a scientist born to privilege and a rebel whose family has endured generations of persecution...

"Ms. Shinn knows full well the power of appealing characterization and uses it most skillfully to reflect her ingeniously piquant imagination."–*Romantic Times*

"Rousing...Ms. Shinn takes a traditional romance and wraps it in fantasy."–*The Magazine of Fantasy and Science Fiction*

A new hardcover available now
__0-441-00691-4/$14.95